Golden Voyager

Simon Finch was born in Rio de Janeiro thirty-two years ago where his father served in the Diplomatic Corps, and was educated abroad before attending university in England for studies in Classical History. Now making his home in Manila, he is currently writing the sequel to *Golden Voyager* between his travels to lecture on Slavery and Ancient Customs.

Simon Finch

Golden Voyager

Pan Books London and Sydney

First published in Great Britain 1978 by Souvenir Press Ltd
This edition published 1978 by Pan Books Ltd,
Cavaye Place, London SW10 9PG
2nd printing 1979

ISBN 0 330 25590 8
Printed and bound in Great Britain by
Richard Clay (The Chaucer Press) Ltd, Bungay, Suffolk

Contents

THE ROMAN EMPIRE—FIRST CENTURY

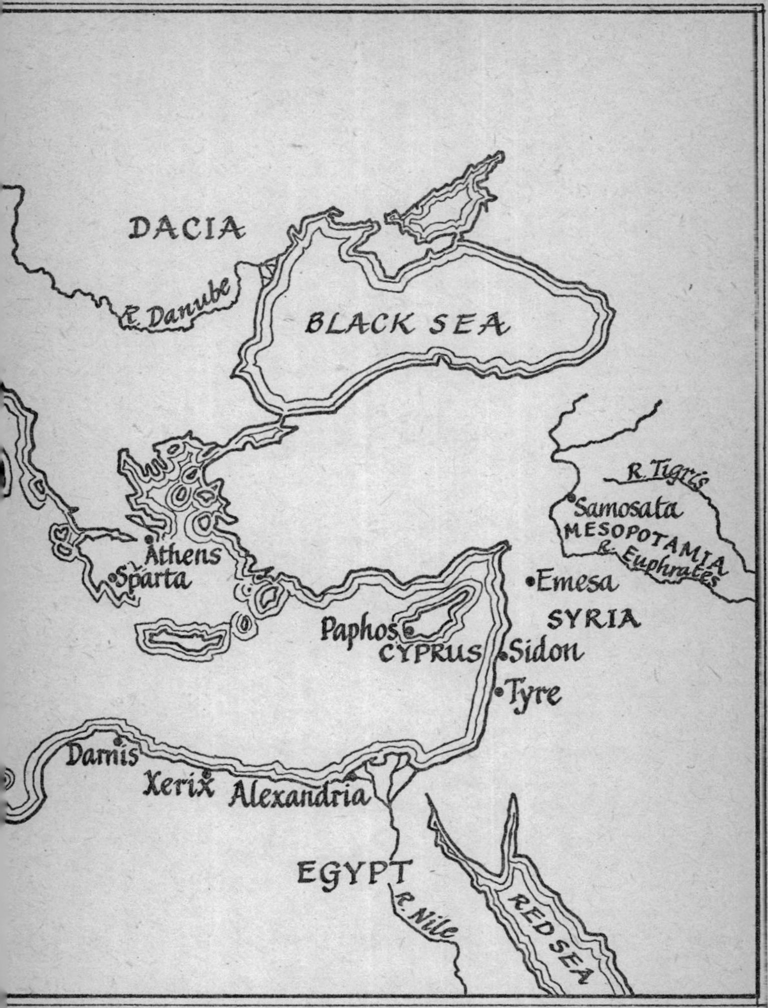
DACIA
R. Danube
BLACK SEA
R. Tigris
Samosata
MESOPOTAMIA
R. Euphrates
Athens
Sparta
Emesa
SYRIA
Paphos
CYPRUS
Sidon
Tyre
Darnis
Xerix
Alexandria
EGYPT
R. Nile
RED SEA

Book One
The Abduction

1

Vesuvio planted his feet firmly near the cliff's edge, cupped both hands around his mouth like a conch trumpet and bellowed his brother's name out over the sea. Then, slowly, he lowered his arms to the sides of a coarse weave tunic which cut unevenly around his bare thighs. There was still a protrusion in the back of the brown fabric made by a wooden peg in the gymnasium – Vesuvio had grabbed the tunic to cover his body before rushing to find young Titus.

Now, listening for his brother to answer the call, Vesuvio heard the surf crashing against the rocks far below him; the cries of seagulls overhead as they rose and dipped in the blue Neapolitan sky; the boom of his own voice echoing back from the precipice. But, still, no answer from Titus.

Turning, Vesuvio trudged farther along the cliffside path, one hand clasping the leather thong tied around the opposite wrist, his thick fingers impatiently drumming against the *bulla* he prized even now in early manhood, the Roman amulet he still remembered receiving as a child, a medallion which showed that he was the eldest son and heir to the Macrinus family.

Vesuvio would not ordinarily be worried about his younger brother at this hour, not when the water clock at home had yet to reach the mark of *hora decima*. It was summer now in Italy – *VI ante idus Julius* by the Julian calendar, 854 years since the founding of Rome: the year '101 ANNO DOMINI' according to Christian calculation – and the days were long, sun-filled, languid here south of Neapolis. Not a time for demanding schedules. But a politician from Rome was being entertained this evening at Villa Macrinus and Titus still had not returned home to begin his preparations for the banquet.

Moving up the path which connected his family's villa with the other estates dotted along the coastline of Campania, Vesuvio tried to remember exactly where Titus had said he was going today. He knew that the boy was always sure-footed on the rocky paths which extended beyond the back walls of Villa Macrinus.

Titus never ventured out into the swift currents if he went down swimming in one of the many sandy coves. And there was certainly no question that any of the field or barn slaves on the Macrinus Estate would molest him.

Nevertheless, Vesuvio slowly began to feel uneasy about his brother's whereabouts. Titus had been told the importance of tonight's banquet, that the entire Macrinus family must be present. He was not a disobedient boy.

Stopping on the path and shouting again over the cliffs, Vesuvio tried to dismiss any foreboding thoughts about Titus's safety. But he distinctly remembered telling the boy himself to be at the gymnasium by mid-afternoon.

By plan, Titus was to bathe there with Vesuvio in the porphyry pool, change into fresh linen, and go to the family *lares* to offer incense with their parents. Then Vesuvio and Titus would accompany their father to his library and discuss tonight's special guest from Rome.

When the boy had failed to arrive for his bath, though, Vesuvio's body slave, Sico, had offered to go and search for him. He and Vesuvio were both slippery with perspiration and gulping for air after a strenuous wrestling bout. But telling the slave to prepare the oils for bathing, Vesuvio had thrown the rough-weave tunic over his cincture and gone to look for Titus himself. Sico was strong but no longer a young man; Vesuvio had wanted to spare him a hike after such an exerting match.

Curse banquets, Vesuvio grumbled to himself as he finally turned away from the cliffs. Wishing that he could spend the rest of the day as he pleased, he ran one hand in frustration through the curly tangles of his hair.

Although darkened now to a rich brown by the southern Italian sun, Vesuvio had inherited the fair Etruscan colouring of his mother's ancient *gens* which made him one of the 'light' Romans. He had hair that become more golden with the progress of summer, brilliant blue eyes, a straight nose that flattened and spread only at the nostrils, lips that would be voluptuous without his strong jaw.

Vesuvio's keen dedication to athletics and the physical life in the country had strengthened his tall frame, broadened his shoulders, and added muscle to his arms. His chest appeared to be covered with finely moulded armour but he hoped to boast the real thing very soon, the metal chest plates of a Centurion, when his military sponsor, General Termico, returned from Dacia to give him his formal commission into the Roman military ranks.

Still devoting his early morning hours to reading the Greek poets and works of the Stoic philosophers selected and sent to him by his Uncle Milo in Rome, Vesuvio followed his physical pursuits in the afternoon, wrestling, boxing, learning about combat from Sico who had fought in the Roman arena in his younger days. And, usually, Vesuvio's afternoon hours culminated with a visit to the estate's granary where he satisfied his male appetites with an equally lusty slave girl. He also had inherited an Etruscan's appetite for love-making. Today, though, he would even have to forgo that.

The worst part of this banquet tonight, Vesuvio thought as he continued walking along the chip marble path which curved high above the crashing surf, was that his family did not want to entertain the visitor from Rome. Like Vesuvio, his parents were happy living in the rural isolation of Campania, free from the intrigues of Rome's court life. The Macrinus family was oblivious to the gibes from the more fashionable Roman citizens who lived most of the year in The Imperial City and said that the country nobility were dim-witted morons and fishwives, out-dated relics with a foot in the grave of the Old Republic. The banquet tonight was a highly dreaded – but very important – political gesture.

In recent weeks, Vesuvio had heard his father ranting louder and louder about the ambitious politicians clustering around the Imperial Court in Rome with one eye on the large agricultural estates in southern Italy. His father complained that, whilst Emperor Trajan was far away on the Danube borders of the Roman Empire fighting the Dacians, the haughty court dignitaries were conspiring with greedy members of the Senate to annex many noblemen's estates – and doing so under the false pretence of funding the Emperor's battles!

Vesuvio's father complained bitterly that the antiquity of a land-owner's blood no longer meant anything to the ambitious new breed of politicians now running the Empire. He called the

Empress Plotina a festooned auroch, an ox draped in purple ribbons and garlands of gilt laurel. But instead of being led to a district fair, she was allowed to dictate court protocol in her husband's long absence from The Golden House on Rome's Palatine Hill.

It was because of those scathing diatribes which Vesuvio's father, Aurelius Macrinus, made against the Empress Plotina, certain members of the Imperial Court and Senate, that Vesuvio had to find Titus and take him to the library. Young Titus had also heard his father speak out in near treason. He had to be cautioned not to repeat any of those opinions at the banquet.

Tonight's guest-of-honour was Gaius Lucretius, a man whom Vesuvio knew was not much older than himself but already one of the smoothest – and hungriest – of the new politicians, a man who would not think twice about coaxing stories from a youth who had not even had his first ritual shaving and received the Roman tooga of citizenship. Young Titus was not lose-tongued but he was going through a phase now of wanting all the attention he could get.

By custom, Titus was too young to have a couch placed at a formal banquet table. He would be allowed only to sit on an ivory stool at Vesuvio's feet throughout the meal.

As Vesuvio was the eldest son and heir to the Macrinus family, his formal name was Aurelius Macrinus the Younger. He was known only to his family and close friends by his nickname.

He had been born shortly after the volcano, Mount Vesuvius, had erupted and the Macrinus family's holdings near Herculaneum had been destroyed. Following the devastation of the district around Herculaneum and Pompeii by molten lava, the Emperor – Titus reigned at that time – had extended the Macrinus family's *latifundia* grant to include these rich fields, vineyards, and pasture land along Italy's western coast.

The honour of the *latifundia* grant was Vesuvio's father's main argument against present Imperial annexation. To allow a rising consul, senator, or *aedile* to seize their estate would be a sacrilegious act. Emperor Titus was now deified and to steal land from his beneficiary would be challenging the wishes of a god!

Chuckling how he would argue with Roman politicians in the

terms with which they had burdened themselves, Elder Aurelius Macrinus nonetheless had instructed his wife to prepare a feast with which no Roman could find fault. To show that the stuffy 'Republicans 'still had life in their bones.

Vesuvio had seen only a small part of the last minute preparations for the feast when he had hurried along the marble floor of the *peristylium* from the gymnasium, cutting through the central *atrium* on his way to find Titus.

There had been at least fifty house slaves milling through that hub of activity in Villa Macrinus. Vesuvio had seen a string of kitchen girls walking carefully across the mosaic floor with a murrhine goblet in each hand, the precious vessels worth more than the price of one slave girl's life. A caravan of male servants carried couches inlaid with tortoise-shell from the *triclinium* where the family usually ate dinner, slowly inching the priceless antiques up the marble steps to the top terrace where the banquet could be enjoyed in a cool summer breeze. The gardeners were using block-and-tackle to lift huge pots of palm trees from the *atrium* floor to the tiled opening in the flat roof. And the foreign shrills of the head cook pierced the air as he nervously showed the food-bearers the quickest route to carry the fare from the kitchen to the terrace, a splendid array of delicacies that he and his staff were preparing for the dinner. There would be impressive golden platters of hens stuffed with dates, eggs in jellied pork, oysters, mussels, peppered mice, wild fowl decorated with pistache, tall urns of honeyed *muslum* to be served warm before the Falernian wine was brought to the tables.

Vesuvio also had seen his mother in the *atrium* and, as usual, she displayed her calm manner, even in the midst of the servants' hectic activity. Vesuvio always felt like a barbarian compared to his maternal link to Rome's most noble families.

Cornelia Popiliana Macrinus consoled the Syrian cook in his native tongue, assuring him that his rich *garum* sauce and treasured *muslum* would not turn cold by the time they reached the guests. She talked to the gardeners in the rough local dialect of the Campania district, reminding them to raise the palms slowly and not to crush any of their graceful green fronds. She called to the Greek girls in their Hellenic accent to remember to remove the clay lamps from the niches on the top terrace, replacing them with the more opulent glazed lamps which burned oil from twelve spouts and provided better light for the marble statues of the ancestors which lined the balcony.

Apart from having ancient blood coursing through her veins, Vesuvio often felt that his mother was the mainstay of the Macrinus household. He knew that her cool manner would not change in front of their guest from the Imperial City.

The only costly adornment which Cornelia Macrinus would wear on her *stolae* this evening would be the *fibulae* which she had inherited from her grandmother, Junia Calvina. She would speak calmly – but assuredly – to the guest-of-honour about her lineage, saying how her paternal line went back farther than her august Claudio-Julian blood, that one of her forebears had even perjured himself in an attempt to stop the gossip about Julius Caesar and his unchaste relationship with King Nicomedia of Capadica, the rumour that prompted the quip that Caesar was 'every woman's man and every man's woman'.

Vesuvio knew that if anyone asked his mother about her family's connection to the infamous Agrippina, the mother of the late Emperor Nero, she would dismiss it with a quick shake of her head. Cornelia Macrinus was always protective of her brother, Milo Popiliano, who lived in Rome and – in Cornelia's estimation – reminisced too publicly about his lurid friendship with the Augusta Agrippina.

Whereas Vesuvio's mother was highly selective of her stories, his father often appeared to be verbose. But the long-winded discourses always had an ulterior purpose: Elder Aurelius Macrinus risked appearing the fool to make a point.

Vesuvio had already been told that his father was going to air the dusty tale this evening about the Macrinus family receiving a *latifundia* grant from Emperor Titus when Mount Vesuvius had erupted. He wanted Vesuvio's brother present at the banquet only to stand and recite the praises of his Heavenly namesake.

There was one thing, though, which Vesuvio hoped that his father would *not* do this evening. Vesuvio dreaded his father hopping up from his couch and clutching his crotch through his toga in a gentleman's ancient way of taking an oath.

Reminding his guests about the similarity between the Latin words *testiculi* and *testes*, Elder Aurelius Macrinus liked to call on Vesuvio to clutch himself likewise in a 'testament' to preserve the family line. When he obediently rose from his own couch to do so, Elder Aurelius Macrinus would proudly draw everyone's attention to the potent bulge that showed even in the grip of Vesuvio's clenched fist over his cumbersome toga. His father then would hold out his hand to Vesuvio, embarking on a Roman *pater*'s flowery praise for his eldest son, asking where in all the Empire could you find a young nobleman with such an athlete's body? Skin as smooth and rich as oil from the first pressing of olives? Hair more golden than all the riches in the Imperial Treasury? Eyes as blue as robin eggs? And, most important of all, sexual equipment potent enough to sire an entire legion to defend his family's interest?

Vesuvio was not worried about his mother's presence at such an immodest boast. Cornelia Macrinus had been raised with stories from the Old Republic, a time when Romans made proud – and loud – show of their virility.

No, it was the presence of young Julia Cordonis at the banquet which Vesuvio was concerned about: Julia was the daughter of the nearby Cordo family, the eldest of two girls raised in gentle surroundings. Julia was betrothed to Vesuvio and he imagined how she would blush at the mention of the sturdy equipment which would soon find its way into the equal sacredness of her own body on the appointed night . . . and, Vesuvio hoped, on every night after for many years to follow.

Stopping now by a *maspila* tree growing outside the travertine walls of the Macrinus grounds, Vesuvio picked one of its yellow fruit and bit into its apricot-like hardness. Spitting out the double pip, he looked at the incline of the path, wondering if Titus might have gone down to the next seaside estate, Villa Genitor. He often spent afternoons with the young son from there, Scintus Genitor.

The parents of the two Genitor heirs had died from the Sicilian Fever epidemic. The daughter, Scintilla Genitoris, was Vesuvio's age but she did not like staying in Campania. Preferring the excitement of Rome, Scintilla was part of the Palatine clique who laughed at the old families who lived their full year in the country. But as Scintilla was back in Campania for a few days now, on her way to summer with the Empress Plotina on Capri, she also was invited to tonight's banquet honouring Gaius Lucretius.

Vesuvio hated to go all the way to Villa Genitor to look for Titus. It was not the long walk in the afternoon heat that he dreaded. It was seeing Scintilla Genitoris. She would only want Vesuvio to stay and listen to her boasting, to impress him with stories about the Empress, probably even seizing the opportunity to make snide little remarks about the Cordo daughters, particularly about Vesuvio's betrothed, Julia Cordonis.

Although it was no secret that Scintilla thought that Julia was dull, she also considered herself too worldly to be married to Vesuvio. Yet she liked to flirt with him. She treated him as if he were some lowborn shepherd. And she, a great lady, could tease him in hopes of catching a glimpse of his phallus poking its head through a strip of his cincture in response to her womanly charms, and then sail merrily over to Capri with stories about her naughty escapades in rural Italy.

At her last visit to Campania, Scintilla had drawn Vesuvio's attention to the way in which her *stolae* was draped, a current fashion which exposed one bosom. She had confided that it was called 'the German style', that no smart lady in Rome wrapped her breasts any more with the confining *bandulum*.

Scintilla also painted her face with white lead, darkened her eyes with antimony in the Egyptian manner and made her lips red with cochineal. She copied the Empress Plotina by dressing her hair in a tall mound of curls at the front of her head.

Despite Scintilla's exotic beautification efforts, her growing contacts at Court, and the large dowry which she would bring to her husband – large even after her younger brother took the major share due to the male heir – Vesuvio still felt that she was no better, if as good, as the slave girls who came to the granary on the Macrinus Estate for sex.

Sex. The rough soles of Vesuvio's sandals padded against the rocks as he decided against going to Villa Genitor and, instead, descended the first level of rocks towards the beach. He hopped from ledge to ledge as easily as a mountain goat, regretting that he would not have time for sex this afternoon.

The dark-haired slave girls went to the granary after their work in the olive presses or laundry rooms in the slave complex. They had firm bodies, the hair was soft on the mound between their legs which they eagerly offered to their master, and their ample breasts were kept white as new ivory by their slave mantles – so white that their nipples spread against them like opened roses.

But, lately, a strange thing had been happening to Vesuvio. Whilst he used the slave girls' lusty bodies, his thoughts wandered to the verbena-scented skin and pale brown hair of Julia Cordonis. And, curiously, he had recently begun to feel unfaithful to Julia when he used the image of her body in sexual fantasies with the slave girls. He also sensed that it was doing him no good to be letting the warmth of one female satisfy his maleness whilst his mind imagined that he was laying with someone else.

Many young men Vesuvio's age lay with slave boys to satisfy their sexual needs until they were married, the practice being so common that many men still kept the boys for lovers long after they were married. Although young boys on the estate, as well as soldiers in Rome, Capua, and Puteoli had made advances to Vesuvio, he did not feel a sexual attraction towards males. There was only one person he truly wanted but he had to wait for the day when Julia put on the red mantle of a Roman bride.

Moving from boulder to boulder, Vesuvio was thinking about the six months which still had to pass until he married Julia Cordonis, envisioning the home that he would provide for her on the Macrinus Estate, the sons and daughters they would have.

Suddenly, he noticed something on the beach below him. Shading his eyes against the sun, he saw a small figure dressed in a white tunic running across the small strip of sand in a cove. It was Titus. Vesuvio recognized the tunic worn only by a noble youth and Titus's curly black hair. He had inherited the dark colouring of their father's people.

Next, Vesuvio saw another boy running behind Titus. A smaller boy. Yes. He had been right. His brother and Scintus Genitor were together this afternoon. They both wore their white tunics trimmed by borders dyed purple with the murex ink from shellfish.

When Vesuvio was about to raise his hands to his mouth and shout at the boys, he saw two men on the beach. And whilst he tried to make out who they were, he saw two more men step from behind towering boulders and block the boys' path.

The men were not slaves from the Macrinus Estate. Slaves wore rough tunics, like the garment which Vesuvio had thrown on after his exercises, and wore now. He saw the men on the beach were dressed in brown leather tunics. The sun caught the glint of metallic studs punched around the shoulders and hem.

Vesuvio first thought that the men were wandering *lanistae*, travelling pedlars who sold young men to gladiatorial colleges to be trained for combat in the arena. A *lanista* was a middleman for death, the lowest occupation in the entire Roman empire.

Watching the men move closer towards his brother and Scintus Genitor, Vesuvio's immediate impulse was to shout down to the beach at them. But he checked it and glanced at the rocks tapering around him for a path where he could move quickly – and undetected – down to the beach. He was beginning to have second thoughts about the men being the scum called *lanistae*. They could be marauders or – even – hired abductors.

Falling to his stomach, Vesuvio's mind raced with ways of getting to the boys. Of what to do once he got there. He knew that he was strong but certainly not powerful enough to tackle four men who might be armed. He did not even have a knife with him now. And looking around him at the parched cliffside for a club to bludgeon the strangers with, he realized the uselessness of that, too, against four husky men.

Keeping to his stomach like a serpent, Vesuvio crawled along the shallow stone gulleys and through patches of nettle, stopping only when his body caused a small rockslide.

The rush of pebbles and dirt soon subsided and Vesuvio slowly resumed easing his way farther down the slope, wondering if this action were wise or should he be running back to the house for help. He knew that he and old Sico together could easily tackle the men.

Vesuvio stopped at the sound of another rockslide. But this

one came from behind him. He had definitely not caused those clumps of earth to roll. . . .

Turning his head to look behind him, Vesuvio suddenly felt an arm choking his neck. Clenching both hands on the arm, he reared up with full strength and flung the man over his head.

The man landed in front of Vesuvio with a thud, a stranger who – like the men on the beach – was lean, swarthy, and dressed in a shiny brown leather tunic.

Before Vesuvio could spring upon him, though, one of his arms was gripped from behind by another man. A third man grasped him. Vesuvio was flung to the ground like a calf. They tried to press him into submission.

Struggling to free himself Vesuvio used his legs to fight. He landed the sole of one sandal in a man's stomach and squirmed to knee the other attacker in the groin. As the first man grabbed him again by the neck, Vesuvio thrust back his elbow and then sent his clenched fist flying towards his face – his stomach – the side of his head.

The other two men were back on their feet and, together, tackled Vesuvio. Defending himself as he would against a pack of wolves, Vesuvio threw one off from his arm, bringing a thrust up to the stomach, and spun to hurl the other man by his neck into a heap on top of him.

He was rebounding to charge the third man again when he caught sight of a large object in his hand – a rock or a club – and that was the last thing he remembered.

2

Slowly regaining consciousness, Vesuvio first sensed that he had a splitting headache. He next became aware of a sharp pain piercing his back. Everything around him was dark, hot, stifling, as if he were being smothered under felted wool.

Coming further out of his stupor, Vesuvio realized with a start that his mouth was gagged with a piece of cloth knotted around his head. His hands were locked together with manacles. His feet shackled by irons. He heard chains rattle when he tried to move his legs.

Turning, grunting, Vesuvio struggled to look around him in the darkness and, slowly, he began to see shapes surrounding him . . . 'Where am I?' he thought. 'A cave?'

He sensed dampness now, too. A permeating sogginess. But it was not like dampness from water seeping down the walls of cold rock. No, this dark enclosure was made of wood. He soon began to notice a rocking sensation, a motion as if he were confined in some floating vessel . . .

Vesuvio soon saw two smaller bodies lying next to him. Their clothing loomed like white smudges in the dark and, leaning closer, he recognized the black curly hair of his brother and, next, the dark features of Scintus Genitor. He saw that the boys were also shackled and gagged like himself. But they were motionless, their eyelids closed, their faces covered with dirt, their heads slumped to one side.

'What are they doing here?' he wondered with a half-numb brain. 'Are they dead? What is this?'

Vesuvio strained his eyes to study the boys, wondering if this were some dreadful nightmare.

Struggling to move closer to them, Vesuvio finally saw their chests moving under their white tunics. At least they were both alive. He felt some relief.

As his mind began to clear, he slowly remembered what had happened to him up to the point that he had lost consciousness. He had been looking for Titus. A man had attacked him from behind. Then, two more men had jumped on him. That's right. He had seen strangers in the cove, men in studded tunics surrounding Titus and Scintus.

Straining to raise himself now in a half-sitting position, Vesuvio began to look around him in the darkness but stared in disbelief when he saw a heap of bodies dressed in rags surrounding him.

'No,' he tried to convince himself. 'This is not reality. This is a dream. Or I'm dead. I was killed. I died and no one put a coin in my mouth to pay the Ferryman. I'm crossing the River Styx with beggars and slaves.'

Vesuvio saw – or thought that he was seeing – men, women, children heaped around him like dead animals dumped into a pit. Their faces, arms, legs were cut and bruised. Their wrists and ankles were locked in irons. Their mouths wrapped in cloth.

Slowly, then, he realized the truth. He was not dead but he was close to it. These people – like himself, Titus, Scintus Genitor – were prisoners in a ship. They were not put in the hull of the phantom galley to be ferried across the River Styx to the netherworld of Hades. This was a slave ship and, acknowledging that grim fact, Vesuvio realized that his father had not been wrong when he had talked about the new greed of Rome. Vesuvio was certain that they had been captured in a conspiracy.

Falling back against the side of the ship, Vesuvio began waiting for Titus and Scintus to regain consciousness. When he was not watching them, he looked around him in the dark hull and listened to the pathetic moans and choked cries beginning to rise from the other prisoners.

He also heard a movement above him, the occasional clank of chains and what sounded to him like conversations conducted in whispers. But the overhead darkness kept him from recognizing any shapes.

Although he could not see beyond the blackness at midship, Vesuvio estimated that there were as many as sixty or seventy people packed into the small area around him. A large vessel like a *trireme* would hold many more. He guessed that they were captives aboard a *felucca.*

A fur-covered beast soon caught his eye. No, he next realized the shape was a man dressed in animal pelts. He was moving and grunting in the darkness. At first, Vesuvio thought that the large man was convulsing in pain. Straining his eyes, he then saw that it was indeed a man covered with animal skins but that he was straddling the body of a woman. They were rutting like two animals in the wilderness.

A few of the other captives also noticed the couple. They struggled to crawl towards them, staring to see what they could of the sexual act as the man pulled up his large body to drive into the female. As her groans joined the man's grunting, Vesuvio realized that the female was not being taken against her will.

A mother with a young girl tried to crawl away from the rutting couple, covering her child's eyes from their actions. But more people eagerly pulled themselves closer, holding their heads down to inspect the man's phallus as it penetrated the woman, their heads beginning to bob with the rhythm of his body as he gained momentum, as the female beneath him became more agitated. The sexual act performed within the restrictions of bondage became a focal point, a relief for other people similarly shackled.

Soon, the man in the animal skin lay spent on top of the woman. And as the night wore on, more and more captives fell into limp, motionless heaps.

Fighting a feverish drowsiness, Vesuvio told himself that he must force himself to keep awake until Titus and Scintus began to move. He did not want the boys to awaken without someone to comfort them.

So, keeping himself from dozing off into a stupor like the other captives, Vesuvio began wondering what had happened tonight at Villa Macrinus and if there would be anyone trying to rescue them.

Had the banquet been cancelled when he and Titus did not come home? Had Sico gone looking for them? Was a party of faithful Macrinus slaves now searching the fields and the cliffs? And Scintilla Genitoris, was she hysterical about the disappearance of her young brother? Vesuvio somehow could not imagine that. She would certainly not be as frantic as his parents must be.

Vesuvio jumped as he heard a sudden boom overhead in the darkness. It was a drum. The now steady rhythm came from the front of the hull. He realized that it was the ship's hortator starting to beat a drum for slaves to pull the oars of the ship. They were preparing to hoist anchor.

A lurch of the ship jostled the captives, making them roll to one side in a heap. They began groaning inside their mouth gags, pulling at one another for support.

The ship slowly began to move and Vesuvio saw a line of half-naked bodies above him, oarsmen sitting on benches, dipping and pulling to the beat of the hortator's drum. Their feet were connected by iron chains. They had caused the mysterious noise which Vesuvio had heard throughout the night. Although seeing that this slave galley was not a *bi*, *tri*, *quad*, or *quinquereme* – only a *felucca* – Vesuvio still did not know where it was headed. Even a small ship could travel from one end of the Mediterranean to the other, carrying them anywhere from the Pillars of Hercules to Asia Minor.

The increasing speed of the small vessel did little to lower the humidity inside the hull. Vesuvio remained close by Titus and Scintus, listening to the dip of the oars, their splash in the water outside, the steady pound, pound, pounding of the gavels on the drum.

Also, he heard voices overhead, men shouting in Aramaic. He was straining to understand a few words when he first felt Titus begin to move.

At the same moment, though, he heard a noise midship. He turned and saw a square of faint morning light filling the hull from a hatch.

Both Titus and Scintus were beginning to stir, to look around them, their eyes widening in terror as they saw Vesuvio gagged and shackled like themselves.

Vesuvio shook his head. He wanted to console them. To calm them. But he could not even whisper. He nodded at the sailor beginning to remove the mouth cloths from captives who lay at the foot of the ladder.

Before the sailor came to remove their gags, two more men moved down the ladder, each carrying a large wooden bowl. One man threw wheatcakes to the captives as if he were feeding chickens, the other tossed wet sponges at them.

The sudden scramble for food and water kept the captives from crying out when the cloths were removed from their mouths. Watching the sailor step carelessly through the captives, Vesuvio suspected that the surly man was Moorish. But that still did not explain where they were going, who their captain was.

The surly Moor untied the cloth from Vesuvio's head and

moved towards Titus and Scintus. Vesuvio quickly grabbed wheatcakes and sponges with his manacled hands and held them towards the boys as the Moor progressed down the hull. He still shook his head to keep them from speaking.

Waiting until the sailors had finally gone back up the ladder to the deck, Vesuvio struggled with his hands to wipe the dirt from the boys' faces with his own sponge.

Titus eyed the wheatcake in his hand, the corner of his mouth lowering in desperation. He began to speak but, looking around him at the ragged people, he flung away the wheatcake and buried his face in Vesuvio's chest, his slim body quivering with fright.

Scintus Genitor sat upright. Neither did he lift the food to his mouth. Vesuvio saw that he was trembling, too. He nodded for Scintus to sink against the other side of him.

Now, supporting a boy on either side of his chest, Vesuvio began to see the ship's squalor through their eyes, slowly, realizing the problem of explaining this situation to two virtual children. Scintus was even younger than Titus.

Vesuvio understood that every person in the world went through life with a dim knowledge that, at any time, they could be taken as a slave. Foreign armies could conquer you. The state seize you for debts. A man could be abducted because of political or financial ambitions. But what did a man do when it actually happened to him? How did you prepare children for a totally new life?

Titus and Scintus were accustomed to having a houseful of slaves waiting on them. The idea that they might end up as house slaves themselves would be incomprehensible. Vesuvio feared that becoming a house slave could well be the best fate any of them could expect now.

3

The basis of a plan came to Vesuvio by mid-morning. The *felucca* skimmed over the water as the oarsmen dipped and pulled to the drum's rhythm. The only hint that it was daytime outside the hull was the shafts of light piercing the holes in the bulwark through which the oars were placed.

Studying the other captives, Vesuvio had seen that – except for one female across the hull wearing a white mantle decorated with spangles – the prisoners looked like tenant farmers, peasant women and children, or field slaves. That only his brother and Scintus Genitor wore the murex-trimmed garments of the noble caste. Even Vesuvio himself was dressed like the rest of the captives, still wearing the rough-weave tunic he had grabbed from the peg in the gymnasium, a piece of clothing no better than a slave's brown rag.

Beckoning the boys to him, Vesuvio whispered, 'Titus, you know my amulet.'

Titus blinked his long black lashes. He did not know what a copper *bulla* on a wristband had to do with him being tied and chained in a ship with filthy peasants.

Not waiting for an answer, Vesuvio anxiously continued, 'I am going to roll over on my side, Titus, and I want you to untie the cord of the amulet from around my wrist. Do you think you can do that?'

'Why?' Titus asked, again on the verge of tears.

'Shhh . . . I'll explain later. Just untie the cord. Hold it in your hands until I turn around. Then you give me the amulet and I'll tie it on your wrist.'

Titus began to ask questions but Vesuvio cautioned him about the danger of being overheard. Then, laying quickly on his side, trying not to clank the iron chains connecting the fetters clamped around his ankles, Vesuvio held his manacled hands towards Titus, telling Scintus to lean in front of them to prevent anyone from seeing what they were doing.

Squirming onto his side, Vesuvio quickly worked to tie the

leather thong around Titus's wrist and began to share his plan.

He whispered, 'Titus, from hereafter I want you to say your name is "Aurelius". Understand? Just like Father's name. Aurelius Macrinus. You are to say from now on that you are the eldest son.' He cinched the thong tightly around the boy's slim wrist, continuing, 'You have the family amulet to prove it, too.'

Titus did not understand. The copper amulet did not belong to him. He had always been taught that Vesuvio had inherited it along with the privileges of the eldest son. He knew how much Vesuvio prized the *bulla*.

Vesuvio explained, 'You keep calling me by my nickname. Understand. "Vesuvio". But act as if I'm not your brother. I'm "Vesuvio" . . . your slave.'

'"Slave"?' Titus repeated the word with distaste.

Vesuvio had always worried about the way in which Titus treated and talked about slaves. Even for a young boy, he behaved in the wrong manner concerning slavery, like some upstart who did not understand a master's responsibilities to his people, treating slaves only as underlings.

Vesuvio did not have time to rebuke the boy for that now. He tried to explain, 'Like Sico is to me, I'm your body slave.'

'Why?' The idea seemed repulsive to the boy. He curled his lip.

'Shhh . . . I can't explain it all now. But listen carefully. And you, too, Scintus.' Vesuvio nodded the boys closer to him, continuing in whispers, 'I do not know where we're going. Where we'll land. Why we were taken from home. But when we get to wherever we're going, men will ask you questions. That much is for certain. And, you, Scintus, you must say exactly who you are. Tell them that your father's name was Genitor. Tell them that you have important trustees in Rome. Rich friends. Do not leave out one detail. Even mention your sister, her friendship with the Empress Plotina.'

He sniffed, 'My sister won't help . . . *me*!'

'Of course she will,' Vesuvio said, but he even doubted the fact himself. Turning to Titus, he continued, 'You do the same. But instead of saying that your name is "Titus" Macrinus, swear that you are Aurelius. Tell whoever asks that you are Aurelius

Macrinus the Younger. The descendant of Aurelius Macrinus of Herculaneum and Stabiae. Beneficiary of Emperor Titus. Say that your mother's line is both Claudio-Julian and Popilian. That your father has senatorial privileges. All this is very important.'

'Will they let me go back home then?' Titus asked, his voice breaking. 'When I tell them that, will they set me free, Vesuvio?'

Vesuvio did not want to lie to his brother. But neither did he want to frighten him or young Scintus. He sincerely doubted that they would be ransomed. He suspected that whoever had arranged this abduction had also taken precautions against them being ransomed. That would be too easy. But if Titus were sold into slavery it could prove better for him to be sold as the eldest son and heir of a noble Roman family. Some petty king or rich merchant aspiring to social recognition might buy a noble youth for the pure esteem of ownership. Like a man buys a thoroughbred horse. Titus would not be sent to work in the fields or quarries. A domestic slave always fared better than a labourer.

Also, Vesuvio had visions that, if Titus posed as the heir, he might some day be able to escape from a household position. Vesuvio had to think like that. He had to be realistic about this situation. But he could not expect such optimism from two boys. To be blatantly told that they were being carried away into slavery would be too disheartening now. They would see the ugly facts of slavery soon enough. Vesuvio planned to break it to them slowly, gently, step-by-step before this ship landed at its final destination.

Continuing with the first steps of his plan, he said, 'People will see from your clothing that you're from a noble family. Talk to them about your schooling. Speak in both Latin and Greek. What few phrases of Aramaic, Hebrew, Syrian you've learned. Recite for them. Do numbers. Sing Homer. Don't be humble. But, also, do not be arrogant. Let them see you're of noble birth. Both of you!'

It was Scintus who asked the question. 'What about you, Vesuvio?' His brow wrinkled. 'Won't you get to go home with us?'

Vesuvio was ashamed of his brother for not asking the question. All Titus had asked about was himself.

Smiling at young Scintus, Vesuvio answered as truthfully as he could: 'Fortune is going to take care of me, Scintus.'

Then, hearing the hatch at midship open again, he signalled for the boys to be silent. Whispering to do exactly as he had told them, he pulled them back into the shadows. Together, they looked towards the sound of heavy footsteps coming down the wooden ladder, first seeing a pair of heavy sandals descending from the deck, then the studded hem of a leather tunic.

The sailor stood at the base of the ladder and shouted in what sounded to Vesuvio like circus Latin, 'Where is the woman from Misenum? The woman called Iucunda?'

There was no answer in the hull, only the steady tempo of the drum, the creak of the pulling oars, the sound of the prow crashing through water.

The sailor began to kick at the people lying near the base of the ladder, separating women from the men with his foot, looking for the female he wanted.

A young mother in a ragged mantle begged the sailor to give her another sponge of water for the infant cradled in her arms. But drawing a leather quirt from his belt, he pulled back his arm to beat her clinging fingers from his leg.

Before he had time to strike at the mother, a woman's voice called sharply across the hull from behind Vesuvio. 'Don't punish her, pig! I am Iucunda!'

Turning, Vesuvio saw the female he had noticed earlier, the only other person among the captives dressed in white linen. When she jerked up her head, the mantle decorated with silver spangles fell from her face. Vesuvio saw that she had a smooth complexion, dark eyes, that she was probably only a few years older than he was.

Beckoning with the leather quirt, the sailor called gruffly, 'The captain wants to see you—' He laughed with a sneer. '—Iucunda!'

Falling back into the shadows, the woman answered sullenly, 'The captain will have to come to me.' She arrogantly raised her chin.

Holding back the quirt, the sailor muttered, 'I'll show you who'll wait!'

Becoming more defiant, Iucunda asked, 'How do you expect me to go to your honourable captain?' She jangled her leg irons. She held her locked hands in front of her breasts and, flapping both elbows, she asked, 'Do you expect me to fly?'

Scowling, the Moorish sailor began stepping through the crush of bodies, cursing as he moved towards the woman. He scooped up her body from the grasp of an old crone sitting beside her and hoisted her over his shoulder.

Still cursing to himself, the sailor moved back through the crowded bodies towards the ladder, carrying Iucunda whilst she shrieked at him, 'What do you think I am? A goat you're taking to sacrifice?' She beat her shackled hands against the back of his leather tunic.

Admiring the handsome woman's spirit, Vesuvio whispered to Titus and Scintus as they watched the sailor carrying her past them, 'Do you think we can be as brave as her?'

The two young boys' eyes followed the sailor as he carried the woman shrieking and fighting up the ladder towards daylight.

Vesuvio repeated his question. 'Do you think we can be as brave as that "Iucunda"?'

The boys meekly nodded their heads.

4

The woman named Iucunda did not return to the hull and, as the hours slowly dragged by, Vesuvio remembered her fine features and fulsome body, suspecting what plans the captain and the crew probably had for her. He could see no other woman among the prisoners who came close to equalling Iucunda's beauty.

By the time which Vesuvio guessed was mid-afternoon, he noticed that the rhythm of the drum beats had increased, that the oarsmen obediently rowed at a more rapid pace. Vesuvio knew they were not approaching a storm: the *felucca* was moving too calmly, he heard no whistling winds. If another ship were attacking them, the oarsmen certainly would be showing some panic, he would be hearing shouts up on deck.

No, common sense told Vesuvio that the small vessel was preparing to land somewhere. He wanted to learn where.

Signalling to Titus and Scintus to remain against the curving sides, Vesuvio pushed his way through the other captives, dragging his chained feet until he was directly under a grill he had spotted earlier, an iron grate built into the deck. Wooden planks now covered the latticed ironwork on the deckside. But he knew that, even if the galley had not reached its destination, the captain would have to remove the planks from the grill to allow some ventilation down into the hull. The prisoners were now lying in their own sick and waste. The most cruel slave-master would not risk an epidemic spreading through his cargo. Even if the captain had no concern for his human cargo, he at least would consider the health of his oarsmen.

Vesuvio's supposition was correct. He soon heard the planks being removed from the ironwork. He rose from his spot on the spine of the ship to stand as close to the grill as possible.

When the other captives heard the boards being lifted, though, they began to push at Vesuvio, clamouring and stretching towards the grill as if they could escape from there. They all pulled to topple him.

Defending his position, Vesuvio swung his hands into the grizzled face of a peasant farmer, elbowing the stomach of the man dressed in animal skins. The prisoners were becoming frenzied by the hope of being let out. He could not tell them that, if they were going to be taken from the ship, it would not be through the grillwork, but up the wooden ladder – and to some place where nobody should want to rush!

The voice of a sailor bellowed down at the confused crowd from the ladder. Like frightened animals, the ragged men and women stared at the Moorish sailor and slowly began to draw away from the overhead grill, one by one sinking to the grimy floor, leaving Vesuvio standing alone in a shaft of bright sunlight now streaming through the open grillwork above him.

Stalking towards Vesuvio, the sailor held his leather quirt in one hand. He did not speak, only studying Vesuvio's shredded slave tunic, his perspiration-soaked chest, the scratches on his veined biceps and thick thighs.

'What are you?' he asked in his rough Latin. 'A trouble-maker?'

Vesuvio did not speak.

The sailor persisted. 'Trying to work this scum into a riot? What are you? A slave ring-leader?'

Vesuvio thought more about Titus and Scintus than the sailor, hoping that the boys would not cry out to him.

Grasping Vesuvio by the shoulder, the sailor snarled, 'I think it's time we set some example for you scum. Show slaves what can happen if they start trouble.'

The sailor shoved him towards the ladder, shouting, 'Climb... slave!'

Vesuvio stood at the base of the wooden ladder, his hands locked helplessly in front of him, his ankles held together by the leg irons.

Snapping the cowhide quirt against Vesuvio's back, the sailor repeated louder, '*Climb!*'

Without another moment's hesitation, Vesuvio jumped to grab the highest rung he could reach on the ladder. And grasping it firmly in his clenched fists, he pulled up his weight as if the ladder were a chinning-rod in the gymnasium at Villa Macrinus. Then, swiftly positioning his shackled feet onto a rung beneath him, he gave himself a push with his legs to grab onto the next rung.

Thus, Vesuvio reached the top of the ladder in two quick leaps and now lay with his head, shoulders and chest sprawled half-way out in the sun beating down onto the deck.

But as Vesuvio blinked in the sudden rush of sunlight, gasping to regain his breath, the sailor pushed him on the buttocks, sending him scraping forward out across the wooden deck.

Two more sailors quickly grabbed Vesuvio's arms. After the first sailor explained to them in a rush of Aramaic that he wanted to make an example of this bully trouble-maker, they dragged him across the deck towards the iron grill.

Hurriedly, they freed Vesuvio's hands from the manacles and

unlocked the foot-irons. They laid him face-down across the grill and yanked his arms and legs wide apart. Next, they used leather thongs to tie his wrists and ankles to the four corners of the grill as the prisoners below crowded together in the hull to gawk up at him.

One sailor ripped the tunic from Vesuvio's back whilst the others began to jeer at his skin rippling over his back muscles, gibing that he looked more like a pampered house slave than a field worker. They asked how he got such big muscles – by powdering his mistress's toes? Or was he a catamite to his master?

Through the sailors' crude laughter Vesuvio heard the first snap of a whip in the air behind him, the only warning before he felt a sudden strike against his back. He tensed at the first pain, then felt another strike of the leather whip burn harder across his shoulders.

Forcing himself to hold back his screams, Vesuvio heard the whip slice up through the air again and then whistle down towards him. His entire back felt as if it were on fire.

The whipman did not keep his aim on Vesuvio's upper torso. The next stinging bite of the whip curled around his waist, then catching his biceps, tearing skin from his shoulders.

Vesuvio lost count of the strikes but, still, he did not cry out for mercy. His fingernails tore deeply into the flesh on his palms. The veins stood out on his forearms. His wrists began to bleed when his arms worked against the leather bindings. But he would not plead.

The captives below him cried out with each loud crack of the whip. The sailors now gathered around the grillwork, urging the whipman to strike harder.

One Moor shouted, 'Make the yellow-haired jackal beg for mercy!'

Another cried, 'Show the slave who's his master now!'

'That's the bastard who put up such a fight on the rocks,' shouted the third. 'I want to give him a few lashes for kicking me in the balls.'

As the whip continued to crack across Vesuvio's bare skin, another sailor sniggered, 'Keep your eyes on his buttocks. A flogged man empties his bowels. Watch for the big mess he's soon going to make.'

'A flogging makes a man get *hard*!' called the next. 'Let's roll him over and get a look at his pizzle. Let's tie it with leather thongs and make him ache down there, too. Tie his pizzle to his balls for real submission.'

In the midst of the sailors' abuse and crude urgings, Vesuvio felt his stomach rush up into his throat. Briefly tasting his vomit, he felt it gush from his mouth, then spew down through the grillwork onto the people staring up at him.

Gasping for breath, turning his head to spare the people below the next flood of his sickness, Vesuvio caught a glimpse of Titus and Scintus Genitor looking up at him. He tried to shake his head at them, to signal for them to remain silent. But another lash cut deeper into his raw flesh and the tension in his blood-covered body gave way to limpness.

Vesuvio heard a woman's voice shouting from the end of a long tunnel. A woman's voice scolding someone. He could not remember where he was. He only knew that he was lying on his stomach. That his back felt as if a torch had been put to it.

Finally in his fever, Vesuvio remembered the slave galley, the Moors whipping him. And, now, the touch of a cool breeze across his bare body told him that he was still lying face-down on the deck. He felt no movement of the ship. They had come to anchor.

The sound of the female's voice grew louder and he suddenly remembered the woman called Iucunda. She had been brought up on deck, too. She must be very near. Yes, Iucunda was somewhere close to him now, shouting, 'You plan to sell him, yes? Get a good price, yes? Then why do you mutilate him like this? Stupid camels!'

Feeling the touch of fingers on his back now, he heard Iucunda's voice soften as she whispered into his ear, 'This ointment will sting you, my big friend, but it will help your wounds heal very fast.'

Vesuvio groaned – grunted – to thank her.

'Save your strength,' she whispered. 'I'll explain as much as

I can. You saw when the captain sent that dog of a sailor for me. The captain thought he was going to have a little fun with me! Ha! I fixed that! I know something, too!'

Leaning closer to Vesuvio's ear, she continued, 'The captain is called Sheik Bakir. An Arabian with a crew made up of Arabs and Moors. This ship is called the *Ka'ba*. I know that it means a holy place to the Semites of Arabia. They are cousins to the Jews and will not defile a married woman. Sheik Bakir surrounds himself with golden idols in the prow of the ship like a holy man. We were talking in his tabernacle when we heard his whelps flogging you. Seeing that your body could be ruined by the whip, he stopped the sailors and sent me with this ointment.'

Vesuvio strained to ask, 'Where – are – we?'

'We've anchored to take on fresh water. This is the rocky island called Melita. We're over half-way to Carthage.'

'Carthage . . .' Vesuvio repeated in a weak voice.

'Shhh. Don't speak,' Iucunda cautioned him, then added, 'Carthage is little more than two days away. You might not have time to recover your full strength but this ointment will help you to start healing. When we reach Carthage we will all be separated into lots. You will probably be taken to the men's slave pen. Life will be difficult enough for the women and children. But for a brawny man like you . . .'

Vesuvio tried again to speak.

Urging him to conserve his strength, Iucunda continued, 'I've seen how thoughtful you are to your masters. You have the mild ways of an educated slave. You do not deserve . . .'

A sailor's voice shouted from across the deck, 'Eh, woman!'

Iucunda immediately raised herself to her knees and shrieked at the sailor, 'This poor wretch just asked me if his welts will save him. Save him from you grimy camels buggering him! Ha! I told him not to worry. An Arab shoots his juice before he even gets it in . . . anything!'

Then, chuckling, Iucunda bent down over Vesuvio again. She resumed applying the thick ointment onto his back, whispering, 'These poor dogs. They understand very few words I say to them. But if they did, they would only be bewildered to hear a woman speaking with a tongue of the world. See, they keep their females in veils, demure as white doves. They do not believe that a female has a mind of her own. And never a tongue to speak it.'

The sound of approaching footsteps made Iucunda break off again. She continued to apply healing medicines across Vesuvio's shoulders, down his back, around his waist. But, before the sailor could speak to her, she called to him with another surge of authority, 'Tell your captain we must move this man from the glare of the sun.'

The sailor laughed at her demand.

Speaking more sternly, she said, 'Tell the captain . . . my friend, the Sheik Bakir, descendant of Ibrahim the Wise, that Iucunda wants this slave moved to his tabernacle! It is the only way Sheik Bakir can salvage him.'

A silence followed her stern orders.

Sharply clapping her hands, Iucunda screamed, 'Don't stand there with your mouth open! Waiting to catch sparrow droppings with your tongue! Hurry!'

When Vesuvio heard footsteps slowly retreating across the deck, Iucunda whispered, 'I think we'll soon get you a little more comfort, my big friend.'

5

The Moorish sailors treated Vesuvio more gently now as Iucunda walked alongside them, bossing them not to move him too fast, warning that if they dropped Vesuvio, or bumped him against the mast, they would be whipped themselves.

Sheik Bakir waited behind a tooled leather curtain which separated his tabernacle in the prow from the rest of the ship. He was a tall, slim man, his head draped in a white *kufiyeh* crowned with a red silken rope. He wore a blue *aba* with short but wide sleeves over a long white *kamis* cinched at the waist with a purple silk band twisted with ropes of pearls and gold wire.

Standing in front of golden images fixed into ivory altars, Bakir pointed for the sailors to carry Vesuvio towards the cushions on the far side of the tall, curving prow. Then he himself moved quickly around them to ensure that Vesuvio was made as comfortable as possible, telling the sailors to ignore the likelihood of blood or the thick salve staining the rich appointments of his tabernacle.

After the sailors disappeared, Bakir clapped his hands and a small slave boy with a shaved head appeared wearing nothing but a pair of thin silver hoops through his ears. He bore a small brass brazier which he set in the middle of the cushions which formed a V below the curving prow. The child knelt facing the altar and quietly began to brew a copper of mint tea.

As Iucunda sank to a carpet in front of Vesuvio, Bakir motioned for her to offer his guest some almond paste from a plate of chased silver. But she shook her head. The sweet would be too rich for his stomach.

Soon, though, she held a glazed beaker of steaming tea to Vesuvio's mouth, telling him to drink it, saying that it would help his recovery.

Lounging across from them, Bakir spoke about his vessel, the *Ka'ba*, as if Vesuvio were a friend in his home. He said that he was no pirate but considered himself a 'nomad of the sea', explaining how he was a sheik of the Quraish Arabs, originally of the Red Sea, now putting this *felucca* at the disposal of any country – or man – who could afford his services. He said that he became a slaver as readily as he carried messages or small cargoes that required the speed of this holy vessel.

Despite Vesuvio's curiosity about the Arab sheik's hospitality to him, he could not fight a drowsiness overcoming his body. He suspected that a drug had been stirred in with the mint. But his mind became too relaxed even to question that.

Vesuvio faintly heard Bakir say that the *Ka'ba* would soon be ready to depart from the island of Melita, sailing across the second half of the Mediterranean towards Carthage on the shores of Numidia. And that, so far, they had eluded the ships of the pirate, Lucco, and his wife, Athana.

Iucunda eagerly asked Bakir to tell her all that he knew about the infamous pirate couple. But Bakir raised one long finger to his thin lips, cautioning her against disturbing Vesuvio. He was falling asleep.

The sun's rays glimmering against the gold statuary of Bakir's twin altars first told Vesuvio that it was morning. That he had slept throughout yesterday afternoon and the entire night.

Coming from the deep sleep, he focused on the image of a golden star. Then a camel. A cone that looked like a cypress tree. The crescent shape of the moon. A replica of a flame. A lightning bolt. Even a large gold phallus. Next to it, a vaginal oval. All shapes of nature, each secured to the ivory altars set in front of the leather curtain which gave the tabernacle its seclusion from the rest of the *Ka'ba*.

Iucunda knelt beside Vesuvio, holding another beaker of tea in one hand and a plate of honey cakes in the other. She said, 'You slept well last night, my big friend.'

Vesuvio nodded, reaching for the yellow cakes. He had a ravenous appetite.

Bakir was more nervous today and, pacing the breadth of his tabernacle, he allowed Vesuvio the nourishment before he sank down on the cushions opposite him. The prow curved high above his head, its boards padded in the same tooled leather as the curtains.

He began, 'Tell me about Roman slaves.'

The mention of slavery brought Vesuvio's mind suddenly back to facts. Here he lay in comfort whilst Titus and Scintus were still being held below deck in the heat and stench. He bluntly said, 'You tell me. You've got us here.'

Bakir waved his hand, ignoring Vesuvio's tone. 'No, no. Not a petty raid like this. This is just politics! How can I ever understand Roman politics? I mean slavery as a force. A power.' He looked fleetingly at his altar of golden idols, explaining, 'The religion of my Arab people honours the sky, the earth, the forests. Unlike the Jews, we have not had so many prophets to direct us to unworldly deities. Some say a prophet will come to the Arabs. But I do not await him. I am surrounded by my gods day and night. The facts that make up my life. Your life. So tell me about the great Roman beast . . . their *slaves*!'

Vesuvio was not prepared for such fervour. In no way had he ever seen slavery as being religious. He answered slowly, 'I can only speak about my family.' Then, remembering the instructions he had given Titus, he added, 'The family who owns me.'

Bakir said, 'You were seized on the coastline of Stabiae.'

Vesuvio nodded. 'From the House of Aurelius Macrinus.'

Bakir nodded. 'With his two sons. And getting you was my unexpected profit, my extra reward.'

'Two sons.' Vesuvio considered the words. So Sheik Bakir had been told to capture two brothers. Also, he had mentioned Roman politics.

Vesuvio continued cautiously, 'I am the slave to the heir, Aurelius Macrinus.'

Again waving his hand, Bakir said, 'Yes. But forget that now. Despite the hatred I have for what the Romans call "*res publica*", I am still a man of affairs. I know whom I have been commissioned to grab! But, personally, I am interested in vast multitudes of slaves. The power that puts your aqueducts into place. Builds your temples. Reaps your harvests. Mills your wheat. How many slaves are on your master's estate?'

'More than four thousand.'

Bakir repeated the words, his dark eyes glazing.

Vesuvio contemplated whether to ask the captain who had 'commissioned' him but decided that it was best not to be too inquisitive yet. He could learn more through patience.

Bakir inquired, 'Unlike many slaves in the East, though, your slaves are never freed?'

Vesuvio said indignantly, 'But yes!'

'In which way?'

'Often. By the master. For years of long service.'

Bakir laughed emptily. 'When a man is too old to enjoy life. Scarcely freedom. Not like in Babylonia where a man often is enslaved for no more than four years.'

Studying the long stretch of Vesuvio's body on the cushions, Bakir said, 'Many of the Roman slaves are marked. I noticed, though, that you are not branded. Your earlobe not notched. You wear no collar around your neck. No marking at all except—' He extended his long arm, twisting his spread palm. '—by your golden hair.'

Vesuvio said defensively, 'Some slaves are marked only by their loyalty.'

'Loyalty? I cannot imagine a man remaining loyal to someone who takes away his freedom.'

'My life could be better, true,' Vesuvio began. 'But, also, it could be worse. Like the so-called "free" tenant farmers who starve in the winter and work twice the hours of a slave during the hot summer months. I am a "body" slave. As there are tutors to teach a young master his numbers, how to write with a stylus on a wax tablet, learn the philosophers, there are also men to coach him in athletics. I respect my bondage at Villa Macrinus more than many people can appreciate their freedom.'

'I cannot argue with you about freedom among the low-castes of human life. They are born. Work. Die. I have a cargo of such people under my feet.' He pointed the toe of his slipper towards the layers of silk carpet. 'I was commissioned to take two captives near Stabiae. But to improve upon the profit which the Roman promised me, I sailed up the coastline of Campania and seized any lout I could see. But they are nothing but animals. Thick, dull-witted animals. Let us talk about slavery. Slavery as I worship it. Slavery as energy. Tell me about the city slaves.'

'I have seen very little of them,' Vesuvio said, waiting for the moment to ask Bakir about the Roman who had commissioned him.

'But being a house slave on such a large estate, you certainly hear about Rome. Your master must go frequently to the capital and bring back stories. I have heard that slaves are allowed great privileges in Rome. That slaves are often treated like gods by the Romans.'

Vesuvio nodded. 'Some of the Emperor's slaves have great privileges. Also the slaves of very rich men. But the city of Rome has more than one million people. And more than half of those people are slaves, whilst half that many have been slaves at one time in their life. Not even a Roman can make a god out of that many people.'

Bakir laughed at Vesuvio's irreverence. He asked, 'But the pleasure slaves, tell me about them. I am told that Romans are very corrupt. That the women need love like water. I am also told that the men cannot get enough love either. And this, too, is often supplied by the glory of . . . slaves.'

'I know nothing of pleasure slaves. Our house does not lead that sort of life.'

Bakir nodded at Iucunda. 'The woman here tells me differently.'

Iucunda protested, 'I only said, Sheik Bakir, that this young man could be sold for a pleasure slave – if your sailors did not mutilate him!'

'You hoped!' Bakir said, narrowing his eyes at Iucunda. Then returning to Vesuvio, he asked, 'Are you married, slave?'

Vesuvio shook his head.

'Is that why you have not asked me where we are going? You do not leave a lover behind? A wife? You do not care where you are being taken?'

Forcing himself to show full respect, Vesuvio answered, 'I can only wait for My Lord to tell me.'

'You've got good manners, Golden Slave. What's your name?'

'Vesuvio.'

Excited by the name's connection to yet another natural force, a volcano, Bakir studied Vesuvio's body covered only by the cincture. He said, 'I feel like a messenger of fate when I deliver a fine slave like you to the citadel at Carthage . . . Vesuvio. Who knows what adventures are ahead of you? What distant lands? What powers to see? Or use? Many hunters come to Carthage and buy slaves to take into the hinterlands to catch wild animals for the Emperor's arena. Of course, you could always be sent to the quarries of Simithu, spending the rest of your days cutting their ugly red marble. Or be bought by pirates like that lascivious couple, Lucco and Athana. Or—' He paused, his eyes brightening. 'You might be taken to the East, have your male equipment cut off and be put in charge of a rich king's *houris*.'

Turning to Iucunda, Bakir added, 'But the Orientals mostly come to Carthage to buy women.'

She asked, 'Tell us about the slave yard at Carthage. Are the women divided—'

'Questions!' Bakir said irritably. 'Be like the golden mountain called Vesuvio. Learn through silence.' The Arab turned away from Iucunda and, gazing again at Vesuvio, he said, 'The Romans must do something very good to their slaves to make them as noble as you. What gods do you worship?'

Vesuvio thought about the family *lares* at Villa Macrinus. He lowered his head, answering, 'A slave is not allowed to worship at the domestic shrine.'

'You have your own religions, then? Many Roman slaves do, I am told. Especially the Eastern religions. Like Mithra. Or the new cult of the Nazarene. But don't tell me a fine man like you does not worship some god.' He stretched his hand to his altars, saying, 'The stars. The forests. The sun. The womanly oval.'

Vesuvio could not answer.

Toying with one end of his white *kufiyeh*, Bakir said, 'You are thinking about your young masters now, aren't you? Wishing that you could go back to them. Or is it that you miss the fine palace, the house with the ancestral statuary lining the terrace which overlooks the sea?' He smiled, raising one thin eyebrow.

Hearing his family's home described by this swarthy stranger, Vesuvio angrily blurted, 'Who sent you to Villa Macrinus?'

'Ah! So the slave does have curiosity!' Bakir said, opening both hands. 'Or, perhaps I have talked too much and troubled him. Perhaps I have dishonoured my guest. You see . . . Vesuvio, it is not often that I take captives who talk sense. Most of them are like untamed dogs. But you – and the fiery Iucunda here – can be my two pets for this voyage to Carthage. Both of you. And don't worry about your young masters, Vesuvio. They must learn how to live in bondage. The youths will be slaves soon enough.'

Bakir then clapped his hands again for the child in silver earrings to bring them more refreshments, osier boxes of grapes, bracelets of figs, some pomegranates.

As the sun climbed to its zenith, the *felucca*'s curved prow continued cutting through the waves, sailing southwesterly towards Numidia. A fine ocean mist occasionally sprayed over the tabernacle, the sun catching a spectrum of colours in the fleeting needle-points of water.

Vesuvio lay back under a saffron-coloured awning now unrolled as protection against the day. The refreshing mist tingled his face and a wind gently tossed his hair. Iucunda had just finished applying a new layer of salve to his wounds and his main thoughts now were about talking to Titus and Scintus, preparing them for the slave market in Carthage.

Sheik Bakir still lounged across from Vesuvio and Iucunda, finally breaking the sound of the hortator's pounding by saying to Vesuvio, 'You are a thinking man. I can see your brain working.'

Vesuvio shook his head, his eyes closed. He appeared to be enjoying the sun filtering through the saffron awning but he really was thinking about Titus and Scintus locked below in the stifling heat of the hull.

Bakir continued, 'I can also tell that you are a very potent man. That you have known many women.'

Vesuvio did not like the new tone of the Arab's voice.

Bakir held his hand towards Iucunda, continuing, 'I took this woman from a trader in Misenum. I don't know how much she has whispered to you about herself. I don't even know if she is aware that I possess knowledge of her background.'

Iucunda gasped, 'You know Fortunato? That I belong to Fortunato?'

'You were that rich merchant's concubine for the last five years – yes, I know Fortunato of Misenum.'

'But Fortunato is my protector!'

'Is he also the man you claim to be married to?' Bakir asked smiling.

Iucunda lowered her head.

'You are not married at all, are you?' Bakir demanded. 'That was only to keep me from . . . raping you.'

She protested, 'I *am* married!'

'Do not excite yourself, beautiful Iucunda. It does not matter to me one way or another if you're married. I do not want you for myself.' He lay back on his cushion.

Rising to her knees, Iucunda shrilled, 'If you wanted me for those pig sailors of yours, you are mistaken! I'd jump into the sea—' She pointed towards the carved prow. '—before I'd lay with them!'

'Iucunda! Beautiful, artful Iucunda. I beg you to control your vile tongue. To share some of the grace of your fellow traveller! In fact, Iucunda, to acquaint yourself more closely with the slave, Vesuvio. I want you to study him. Study him very carefully. More closely. You do understand me, Iucunda . . . Concubine of Fortunato.'

She slunk back on the carpet.

Moving to the edge of the cushion, Bakir began, 'The gilded slave wears only his cincture. See. And he cannot move because he still has much pain. So, I do not tell the precious Vesuvio to move. But I *do* want to see the famous powers of the concubine, Iucunda, at work! I have heard much talk about you from my friend, Fortunato. I want to see you perform with my own eyes. He told me you have powers to raise mountains.'

She screamed, 'I will kill Fortunato.'

Laughing, Bakir said, 'That is exactly what Fortunato feared. That you were going to murder him. That is why he paid me to abduct you. Fortunato and you spent too many happy hours together for him to kill you himself. He thought that it would be easier if I just helped you . . . disappear from his life.'

Then, shaking his head, Bakir said, 'But I was talking about you and Vesuvio. I was telling you to remove his cincture. You see, Iucunda, I want to watch you be his slave. I have heard what you can do to a man. Now I want to see this with my own eyes. I want you to restore his masculinity.'

She sniffed, 'I do not know what craziness you are talking about.'

Reaching under his cushion, Bakir produced a small whip with an ivory handle. The long tail was made of plaited red silk, a silver pin glimmering in its tip. He quickly flicked the whip at Iucunda.

Holding the spot on her arm where the tip had pricked her, Iucunda gasped.

Bakir said more coldly, 'I do not want to order you again, Concubine of Fortunato.'

Slowly, obediently, Iucunda fell in front of Vesuvio's cushion. She did not raise her eyes to him, only moving her hands slowly, careful not to hurt him as she reluctantly began to remove the now-soiled cloth encircling his groin.

Soon, the cincture was peeled away. Iucunda dropped it behind her on the carpet, hesitating then in front of Vesuvio's naked body.

'Continue!' Bakir shouted.

Taking a deep breath, Iucunda still did not raise her eyes to Vesuvio. She slowly reached towards his phallus with one hand and began to stroke the blond hair on his thigh with the other hand.

Vesuvio did not look at Bakir, only staring at Iucunda, wondering if the story the Arab had told about her was true. Was she a concubine? A famous whore from Misenum?

Soon, he felt her fingers gently lift his phallus. She reached for his scrotum with the other hand, adeptly cupping it so as not to press his testicles.

As much as he tried, Vesuvio could not keep himself from becoming aroused. His phallus began to harden in the palm of Iucunda's hand; she removed her other hand from his scrotum and moistened the fingers with her tongue.

Replacing that hand on the now throbbing crown of Vesuvio's phallus, she moistened the fingers of the other hand, placing it on the phallus behind the first and began to work the saliva down to the root of his phallus.

Finally, she moved her head forward.

Raising to his knees, Bakir marvelled at the thickness to which Vesuvio's phallus had swollen, whispering about his magnificent crown, the artful way in which he had been circumcized.

Soon, Vesuvio felt Iucunda's warm mouth encircling his crown, her agile fingers now working the moisture on his scrotum.

As Vesuvio watched Iucunda's face rise and fall into his crotch, he felt his excitement increase. Also, he saw her breasts now hanging freely from her *stolae*. She was pressing her breasts against his inner thighs, rubbing them against his bare legs as she took him deeper into her mouth. She worked at him with the pressure of her lips and also her quick darting tongue.

Vesuvio's whole body began to tighten. The pain in his back gave way to this excitement. Iucunda worked her mouth harder, faster on him; her breasts brushed closer against his thighs.

Raising himself by his elbows, Vesuvio made his first move to reach down to her, to fondle her pendulous breasts, hoping to pull her up to him. He wanted to roll onto her, plunge deep into her body.

Then, fleetingly, he remembered the man covered in animal skins who had mounted the woman in the hold. Did he have no more control over his passions than some rustic peasant? The question lingered only momentarily in his mind, though, the sensation in his groin becoming sharper as Iucunda took him deeper into her throat. He forgot about distinctions between men and followed his base instinct to consummate his lust, to draw Iucunda's body under him.

As Vesuvio now gripped for her arm, though, Bakir stopped the action. He pushed Vesuvio down to the pillows. Next, forcing Iucunda back on the carpet, Bakir knelt where she had been only a few seconds before.

Thinking that the Arab was going to continue Iucunda's work, Vesuvio immediately clasped his legs together.

Slowly shaking his head, conducting himself as if he were in a religious trance, Bakir parted Vesuvio's knees with his hands, keeping his eyes fixed on the still erect phallus.

Vesuvio looked quizzically at Iucunda who, in turn, nodded at the altar of golden images in front of the leather curtain. Sheik Bakir had found a phallus even surpassing the richness of the one he treasured in his tabernacle.

Bakir's words almost became a chant as he knelt in front of Vesuvio and gazed at his maleness – 'The master of many men . . . You belong to a slave . . . The master of the living . . .'

Slowly, Bakir lowered his palms to the carpet, his arms placed in prostration as Vesuvio's phallus lay erect on the trace of hairs which spread up his flat stomach, the crown stretching towards the neat tuck of his navel.

6

'*Aurelius?*'

Cornelia Macrinus stood anxiously in front of the locked doorway to her husband's library, calling louder for him to answer. Two nights had passed since her sons had vanished from the estate and Cornelia's thin face was lined with worry. She had not slept one moment since then. But worse, she still did not know where Vesuvio and young Titus had disappeared.

Holding a small stone lamp in one hand, Cornelia beat again on the locked door of the library. And when she still did not receive an answer, she nodded at the servant to force open the door. He was Sico, Vesuvio's body slave, the Corsican who had been loyal to the Macrinus family since he had left the Roman arena.

Lowering one shoulder, Sico began to throw his muscular body against the door. The wood creaked but, still, the lock did not give way.

Cornelia murmured to him, 'I will call more men. You can ram it with a pole. I *know* my husband is in there.'

Determined to assist his mistress immediately, Sico threw himself harder against the lacquered wood.

Looking nervously around the dark *atrium* behind them, Cornelia saw a house she no longer recognized. She remembered the recent preparations for the banquet, the care and pride that had gone into arranging a feast for the Roman, Gaius Lucretius. But those hours all now seemed as if they had happened in another *domus*, preparations supervised by another wife and mother.

The nightmare had begun when Vesuvio did not bring Titus to offer incense at the family *lares* before the guests' arrival. The slave, Sico, had reported that Vesuvio had left the gymnasium to find Titus, that he himself had gone looking for both of them and found only footprints in a cove, the traces of a small boat in the sand.

It was from Sico's report that Cornelia and Aurelius Macrinus first feared that their sons had been abducted. But it was not until the guests began to arrive for the banquet – neighbours such as the Cordo family bringing Vesuvio's betrothed, Julia, and her sister, Lucia – that a messenger galloped down the cypress-lined driveway to Villa Macrinus with a dispatch saying that Gaius Lucretius would not be attending the banquet that evening at Villa Macrinus. No explanation was included.

The pieces of the puzzle soon began to form a grim pattern. Aurelius Macrinus's worst fears were quickly becoming fact. The first guests returned soberly to their homes and slaves were sent to inform the others that the dinner was cancelled. The house-servants began their work quickly, clearing away the murrhine goblets, silver, glazed lamps from the upper terrace, then they retired quietly to their quarters.

A foreboding gloom soon crept over the house, spreading the next morning to the slave barracks and small white stucco houses which formed the slave settlement beyond the stables. No worker went to the fields, vineyards, presses, or mills. The women kept the children indoors.

The estate bailiff, Vitalis, came to the house to report the slaves' curious behaviour. But Aurelius Macrinus told him not to force the people to go to their work. He reminded Vitalis about the fright which some animals show before a calamity of nature, such as cattle lowing, or dogs barking before an earthquake devastates a district. Aurelius Macrinus solemnly said to his bailiff that people also can perceive such catastrophes. Perhaps the slaves did. The only order he gave to Vitalis was to bring the list of the men, women, and children he owned up to date, making certain that any newly born infant was assigned to his rightful parents. He wanted the names of all the slave families in their correct groupings. He did not give his reason.

A loud crash now drew Cornelia's attention to the library door – Sico had finally forced it open. He worked quickly now to break away the splinters for his mistress to enter.

Holding the stone lamp in one hand, Cornelia lifted the long skirt of her *himation* in the other to step over the jagged debris and cautiously entered the dark library.

She called, 'Aurelius! Are you—'

Suddenly she stopped. She stared at a flood of moonlight, seeing her husband's body lying face-down on the floor. The silver handle of a knife protruded from his back. His white toga was covered with blood, a red pool spreading across the tessalated floor from both the wound and his open mouth. The doorway to the library's garden was open, one of the small panes of *lapis specularis* broken near the latch.

Rushing past Cornelia to the body, Sico stared at the knife and then, asking his mistress to turn away, he quickly knelt to the floor and jerked the knife from the corpse.

Cornelia now stood behind Sico, looking from the knife in his hand to her husband's smeared body. She recognized the weapon. Aurelius Macrinus himself had given the Damascene *gladus* to Sico many years ago when the slave first came to the estate. It had been a symbolic gesture towards the veteran gladiator that he was now trusted in their household, a token for Sico to teach Vesuvio the athletic skills which he brought from the arena.

Sico's face looked up beseechingly at Cornelia, still holding the long knife in his quivering hands.

Cornelia began soberly. 'Someone who knows our house well, Sico, has helped plan this crime. They knew that there is one slave here who possesses a weapon. And with proof that a slave murdered his master, then every slave on the estate can be put to the sword. They know Roman Law.'

Lowering her sober eyes to Sico, she put her hand on his broad shoulder, assuring him, 'You are the last man to betray this family, Sico. I am not thinking about that. I am remembering that my husband mentioned the possibility of such a plot to me. He talked about it again only two nights ago. After Vesuvio and Titus disappeared. He knew even then that the action against us had begun. The male heirs to the estate had vanished. He could be next. Of course, Aurelius could not see the exact way in which our enemies would strike. But he knew that his own life was in danger. That his disappearance or destruction was the next logical step in disguising greed for a succession of catastrophes.'

Taking a deep breath, she continued in an even voice, 'Now,

the implication of your knife will be interpreted as the seeds of a slave revolt. Every man, woman and child can be killed. Or only a token few. But whatever the outcome of that punishment, the land will still remain rich and fertile. There will still be this land for somebody's taking.'

Setting the lamp down on a table, Cornelia spoke more quickly now to Sico. She said, 'But Aurelius also took precautions against such action. Quick! Go bring Vitalis to me. Then I want you, Sico, to go to my brother, Milo Popiliano, in Rome. As a woman, I am allowed no part in legal matters. But Milo can act as executor. As a Knight of the Roman Empire, he should be spared from any of the scurrilous actions now plaguing this household.'

Slowly shaking his head, Sico asked in his hoarse voice, 'Can you send somebody else to Rome, Mistress Cornelia? Even Vitalis? We do not—' He hesitated. 'You do not know what plans your enemies have for you, Mistress. I want to stay by your side. Or let me take you from here to safety.'

Cornelia said firmly, 'I cannot leave this house until I dress the body of my husband. My grandmother's grandmothers did the same for their husbands. Even if I have to light the pyre myself, and crawl all the way to Rome to put his ashes in the vault on Via Appia, I will see that my husband receives honourable rites.'

Sico began, 'But, Mistress—'

Cornelia was adamant. She told Sico to bring the estate bailiff quickly to the library. They must also send word to their trusted neighbours, the Cordos, that blood was spreading in the neighbourhood. At the same time, Sico must ride to Rome to inform Milo Popiliano about the disappearance of his nephews, the assassination of his sister's husband, whilst Cornelia Macrinus stayed in Campania to perform the duties of a noble Roman wife, stopping only to pray at the *lares* that her two sons had been spared death, that there was a favourable god somewhere in the world looking after their safety.

Sico's mind was a blur of duties, stations, responsibilities, and, now, the sudden news that he was to be a free man. Cornelia

Macrinus had told him to deliver the message to Milo Popiliano in Rome and, after that, he was free to return to his homeland. She had even given him a pouch of coins to begin his new life, forbidding him ever to return here to Campania.

Hurrying now from the dark stables, Sico wondered if he really wanted to be a 'freedman' . . . the first step towards achieving citizenship of Rome. How would that better his life?

Sico was proud of being owned by the Macrinus family. They belonged to the highest order of Roman citizens, outside the Imperial family. They possessed the one million *sestertii* – and a great deal more – which was required to be classified among the senatorial elite.

Vesuvio had explained many times to Sico how his uncle, Milo Popiliano, had kept his stature as a knight bestowed upon him long ago as a young man. A knight was a lesser position than a senator but often safer politically because everyone feared to conspire against a man who had military affiliations. Sico had always known that fact.

If Vesuvio's father had been a knight, he, his wife, and sons might not be suffering these catastrophes, Sico suspected. Belonging to the senatorial order was dangerous in many ways. A senator could be attacked on political grounds but a knight's danger lay on the battlefield. There was even a saying in Rome that an old knight had the freedom of 'Caesar's wife'.

Riding away from the stables in the dark hush of night, Sico thought about honour, and also how the Macrinus family had spoken many times about the meaninglessness of honour nowadays in the Roman Empire. Aurelius Macrinus had always ignored his rank of senator, scoffing that being a senator meant nothing any more, not since Nero had begun raising rich merchants to senatorships during his reign. Nero had elevated ruffians for the money they would pay him. The truly noble Roman citizens – those families with ancient blood in their veins and promising young heirs to raise – lived in the Italian countryside. They tried to ignore the shallow arrogance of the city people just as the country slaves felt superior to the town slaves – braggarts, liars, and villains.

The many levels of Roman citizenry had always confused Sico.

He knew that distinctions between Romans were often sharper than the caste differences among slaves.

All people born free in the Roman Empire were called *ingenui.* Apart from the senators and the knights, the upper classes included army men and their families, as well as all government officials living both in and outside the Imperial City. The lower classes were 'plebians', shopkeepers, tradesmen, even freeborn farmers who had abandoned small plots of land in the countryside and flocked to the Imperial City, preferring to receive free wheat from the public charity, the *Annona*, rather than working for their livelihood. Most slaves looked down at this new breed of free Romans who lived a leech's life in the city. Nobody respected them . . . except the politicians when they wanted their votes.

Since his childhood long ago on the island of Corsica, even an uneducated man like Sico had seen Rome change drastically since the reign of Nero. In one year there had been three emperors – Galba, Otho, Vitellus. Then had come Vespasian, Titus, and Domitian, followed by the first of the successful 'military' Emperors – Nerva.

Now, the military emperors gave more strength to the throne than the old noble blood. The present emperor, Trajan, was also a soldier, a foreigner who had risen to power through the army. It was said that Trajan's adopted son, another soldier named Hadrian, was marked to follow him.

A military emperor like Trajan was a relief to the Treasury of Rome in conquering distant territories which brought booty home to Rome and expanded the might of the Empire.

Colonials who went to live in the far-off provinces were made honorary citizens of Rome; provincials who accumulated more than one million *sestertii* sat side-by-side now in the Senate with the old Republicans, foreigners who often were unable to understand eloquent Latin, to converse with the senator sitting next to them. Sico used to joke with Vesuvio that maybe even he – a Corsican slave – might some day be made a Roman senator himself.

To be a Roman meant either one of two things to Sico: a rich citizen who paid exorbitant taxes or a poor citizen living well off other people's taxes. More and more Romans were refusing to work. Able-bodied Romans were leaving labour to the hordes of slaves which Emperor Trajan was sending home as war-prisoners. No, Sico was not eager to become known as a 'Roman'. He was more proud to belong to the Macrinus family.

Suddenly, hearing the laughter of men ahead of him in the night, Sico reined his horse. Laughter was unusual at night in Campania. All the field and mill slaves were long ago asleep in their dormitories, having to rise for the next early work day. Sico realized that the revellers were some kind of free men.

Sliding off his horse, Sico slowly led the animal through a roadside ditch by the reins, now seeing the outline of five men standing around a bonfire beyond a break of cypress trees. He saw their metal helmets catching the glint of the flames. They were speaking Latin. Coarse Latin no better than his own. As many cautious citizens were now paying mercenaries to provide them with security, though, it was difficult to tell which military men belonged to the Emperor and which armies were privately supported.

Next, a girl's cry suddenly rose from the midst of the five men. Their voices grew louder. They became more animated as they kicked and prodded at a half-naked body at their feet. Sico listened as they spoke.

'This wench doesn't look as if she wants our love, Scarpa.'

'That's only because she's never had a good man before.'

'She's going to take five of us tonight if she likes it or not.'

'Why shouldn't she like it? I know a senator's wife in Rome who'd give us each a gold *aureus* if we drilled her with half as much meat as this lucky wench is going to get!'

Although Sico could not see the features of the girl – not able to tell if she was a free woman or a slave – he felt like a coward for not rushing to her defence. Such an act would be stupid, though, he tried to convince himself; he had important duties to carry out for his mistress. He had to think only about the Macrinus family.

Nevertheless, the nearness of this bonfire to the neighbouring villa made Sico wonder if the girl belonged to the Cordo family. If she might be Vesuvio's betrothed, Julia Cordonis? Or her younger sister, Lucia? But how had these vipers seized the girl? Had one of the daughters been abducted from the grounds of the villa? Could that be possible?

Also, Sico asked himself, 'Why are these Romans acting so openly? Are they the same men who killed Master Macrinus? Part of a mob now ravaging the local nobility? Why? Who's paying them? What's happened to the orderliness of this district?'

Creeping slowly past the soldier's small fire, Sico next wondered if the estate bailiff, Vitalis, had been able to warn the Cordo family yet. Then he thought about Vesuvio, wondering if he should try to get a closer look at the girl to see if she was young Julia. But what could he do if it were?

Telling himself again to pursue his own business, Sico stealthily moved through the long shadows of the cypress trees, wondering if Vesuvio would ever return to this land. Sico hoped that he would be near to help Vesuvio if he ever did come back to seek his revenge.

The Macrinus family had always been very good to Sico, treating him not as a slave but as a man. He did not want to ride out of their lives, never again to show his gratitude for their many years of kindness.

What future waited for him on Corsica, an island only distinguished by the honey and wax it supplied to Rome? Sico had been taken away from there as a child. Sold to Rome. He had grown strong but his best years were not spent in the sports arena. He had been an animal there. The Macrinus family had elevated him to a human being. He would like to remain their slave forever.

7

Sheik Bakir pointed towards land on their second morning in his tabernacle. Vesuvio first only saw a grey-brown strip rising against the horizon like a sandy island in the sea. But as the strong winds filled the *felucca*'s tri-cornered sail, and the drum grew louder in the hull, the *Ka'ba* sped southward and, soon, they were in sight of the stone walls surrounding the city of Carthage.

Vesuvio and Iucunda flanked Bakir in the prow. There had been no reference to Bakir's adoration of Vesuvio's phallus since the Arab had risen from his knees yesterday afternoon. The slave child had lit incense in front of the golden images on the ivory altars, and then, when he brought the brass brazier to the tabernacle and began to boil mint, the conversation was dominated by Bakir reminiscing how his tribe, the Quraish, had been masters to nomadic peoples for more than one thousand years.

Not knowing what waited for him in Carthage, Vesuvio could not be patient for the wounds on his back to heal. He forced himself to stand today, making every effort to be strong. The salve which Iucunda had used on his back was slowly beginning to work its promised miracle. Even Vesuvio's pain was disappearing.

The sunlight now filtered through the saffron awning stretched over the prow. And as it flapped in the breeze, Bakir pointed at the city walls, explaining, 'The tall towers of Hannibal once stood on that shore. The Carthage you see now is not even a shadow of the proud city that Rome destroyed more than two hundred years ago. Everybody in the world today has a grievance against Rome. But the Carthaginians are the most bitter. Every child is told how the buildings of their city were razed by Rome, the fields sowed with salt, the land dedicated to the infernal gods of Rome. All human habitation was forbidden in Carthage for two generations. The citizens were carried off in chains. The few survivors fled to caves as far south as the Atlas Mountains. Only jackals and leopards roamed in the rubbish which had once been a great capital.'

Now within sight of their destination, Vesuvio became more worried about talking to Titus. He had not seen the boy for two days now.

He called now to Bakir, 'Do you unload the captives at our arrival in Carthage?'

Not looking from the circular harbour they were approaching, Bakir answered, 'Do not spoil my memory of you, Golden Mountain. Slaves do not ask questions.'

'Memories!' Vesuvio did not care what memories the Arab took with him from this voyage. He demanded, 'When are the captives unloaded? The people in the hull?'

Still not turning to face Vesuvio, Bakir said, 'Do you so desperately want to join your young masters?' Slowly shaking his head, Bakir said, 'No. You stay with me in the tabernacle until the end.'

Soon, small vessels began to swarm around the *felucca*, open boats filled with dark-skinned men and boys screaming for news of the cargo, the adventures at sea.

Bakir pointed for Vesuvio to look at a larger boat being rowed towards them by twelve oarsmen. A man in metal armour stood in the prow of the open boat. He held a Roman standard in his hand, bright purple and yellow ribbons fluttering from its brass cross-arm.

Bakir said, 'There is the Consul's man coming to clear us.'

Seeing the standard's eagle, Vesuvio quickly wondered if he should seize this chance to make himself known, to shout out to his fellow countryman.

As if Bakir could read Vesuvio's mind, he added, 'As Carthage is now a Roman province, all ships must be cleared by the Roman officials. The authorities are expecting the *Ka'ba*. So do not try anything stupid, golden slave. It will not be you who dies. But the two youths in the hull.'

Vesuvio's body tightened with anger and he moved towards Bakir.

Seizing Vesuvio's elbow, Iucunda pulled him back and shook her head, also warning him not to do anything foolish.

As the Moorish sailors shouted down to the Roman boat, or exchanged stories with the men crowded into the swarm of smacks, Bakir explained, 'We will spend only enough time with this Roman to report that we carry no plague or sickness. That we sighted no pirates. From then on, slavery in Carthage is conducted like everywhere else in the civilized world – the Greeks control it. They have contacts here as they have all over the Roman Empire. I suppose that that is Rome's paltry repayment to yet another nation it has squashed under its heel.'

The oarsmen in the Roman consul's boat now rowed towards the harbour, officially leading the *Ka'ba* towards a mooring on the stone port.

Shading his eyes against the sun, Vesuvio saw white cubicle-shaped houses rising behind yellow stone walls. The drooping tops of palm trees swayed with the breeze. The cries of harbour birds joined the din from the brown men in the small boats. Then, as the *Ka'ba* drew closer to its stone mooring, Vesuvio caught the first whiffs of decaying fish, offal, the stench of foul garbage. But underlying the sickly smell of rot and refuse was a heady aroma – the taint of strange spices and exotic herbs, a pungent scent that told Vesuvio that he was indeed arriving on a shore very far away from home. The Romans now called this distant place *Africanus*.

Book Two
Slaves of Carthage

8

Beggars and urchins crowded the stone wharf of Carthage, jeering the chained captives being led from the *Ka'ba*, grabbing and prodding at the separate columns of men, women, and children as they were hurried into long lines by the Moorish sailors' quirts.

Although Vesuvio wore manacles and leg irons again, no clothing covered his body except for the scant cincture. Some old women in black mantles reached to feel his blond hair, others tried to pet his bulging biceps or stroke the yellow down that curled on his thighs. But most of the crowd only reached to pinch or scratch at him, spitting globs of saliva in his face, trying to slap at the welts on his back as his leg irons were attached to the last man in the line of male prisoners.

A guard beat back the crowd with a cudgel. But when he hurriedly joined the other guards to lead the slave column from the wharf, the crowd also armed themselves with weapons, now flailing dried reeds, bamboo canes, spidery palm fronds at the captives. They shrilled in Aramaic, Hebraic, Punic, Greek, a babble of languages and dialects which soon gave way to the one word they had learned from their conquerors – *Servus! Servus!* – the Latin word for slave. As a mounted soldier now rode through them, snapping a long bullwhip to start moving the male column, the tattered onlookers marked a rhythm with the rustle and snaps of their makeshift lashes, chanting louder, '*Servus! Servus! Servus!*'

Moving from the wharf, the male captives led the procession towards the yellow walls of the city. A mounted guard waited at the tall wooden gates as another guard rode at the lead. The slaves were soon driven between the first rows of flat-roofed houses. Women and men leaned from the slit windows in the stark white buildings, hurling garbage at the prisoners, joining the cry of '*Servus*' as, first, the men, then the women and children clanked through the downfall of over-ripe fruit, food slops, human waste.

Stumbling along a narrow street at the end of his column,

Vesuvio held his shackled arms to his face as protection against the putrid missiles. When he gained enough slack in the iron chain connecting his ankles to the man proceeding him, he turned to try to catch sight of Titus or Scintus in the column behind him.

A guard snapped a bullwhip over Vesuvio's head and, again, he faced towards the front, being pulled along by the prisoners' chain up a narrow alley.

Through the onslaught of jeers and rubbish, Vesuvio caught only a glimpse of the town which had replaced the fabled city of Carthage. The buildings were drab, having no decorations, and the bleak taverns were filled with sinister-looking men, a populace composed of the dregs from the Mediterranean world.

The name 'Carthage' had always conjured up the image of power set amidst distant splendour for Vesuvio. The city he now saw was not that place. Gone were the historic citizens dressed in colourful robes, the legendary temples which had once terraced the Punic capital, the cultivated gardens and streets adorned with marble statues, twisting alleyways redolent with sweet spices and lit by tinted lanterns. Rome had obliterated all the mysterious richness which the poets had inspired every schoolboy to associate with Carthage in its prime.

Reaching a marketplace, Vesuvio saw fruit and vegetable stalls surrounding him. Both customers and vendors joined in the abuse of the captives; a herdsman sent his flock of goats into the midst of the men's feet, the crowd laughing at the confusion which the animals caused amongst the long, connecting chains.

On the far side of the square, the alley became steeper, spaces appearing between the houses. The shout of '*Servus*' was replaced by another word – '*Byrsa*'. The slave column was approaching the only remains of the old city, the quarter of ancient Carthage known as 'Byrsa', the name now only applied to the grim citadel which had been spared destruction because of its distance from the main centre of original Carthage.

The front guard galloped back to the guard behind Vesuvio. After shouting an order, he returned to his lead position.

Hearing cries rising from the women and children, Vesuvio turned and saw their column being separated from the men. The foot-guard snapped his whip over Vesuvio's head. Reluctantly, he trudged onwards, wondering if he had missed his last opportunity of catching sight of Titus and Scintus Genitor.

Detached from the women and children, the male prisoners soon passed under the iron gates of the fortress, the thick black walls rising high above the outside houses. Dragging his feet in the dust, Vesuvio felt a chill over him as he passed from the light of day into the darkness of Byrsa.

From a dirt courtyard the men were herded down a dimly lit passageway to emerge in an enclosure which looked and smelled to Vesuvio as if it also served for a stable in the fortress: straw covered the ground and the air was thick with the smell of horse manure.

A wooden door slammed behind the men and a small number of new guards surrounded them, some carrying wooden buckets in their hands. As the guards from the wharf began unlocking leg and hand irons from the captives, the new men shoved their way between them, carefully studying their bodies.

Suffering the dark prodding hands and sharp black eyes estimating the strength of his body, Vesuvio did not flinch when he felt fingers poke at the welts on his back, squeeze the firmness of his limbs, pull back his cincture for a glimpse at his maleness. A guard spun him around whilst another man dunked a rag-covered stick into a bucket and made a white 'X' across his chest. Next, he was shoved towards a far wall.

Not knowing what the chest mark meant – whether it was a distinction or condemnation – Vesuvio looked at the other men also being dabbed with white paint and now pushed towards him. He realized that the 'X' was a mark to designate the strong.

Then they, too – this new brawny elite splattered in white paint – were moved through a second door, pushed down another low-ceilinged passageway, emerging in a large yard with no roof.

Other prisoners were already there, males from many nations. Young Sicilians with olive-skinned bodies made hard by farm work. Burly Thracians scowling under curly black hair. Southern tribesmen with ebony skin and glistening white eyes. Tawny men from Asia Minor with high cheekbones. Flat-faced Armenians. Sinewy Arabs. They squatted in small groups, sprawled on the dirt floor, sat on stones which bordered a sand pit lying in the middle of this yard deep inside Byrsa.

Without warning, a large hand gripped Vesuvio by the shoulder and pulled him around. A big-bellied man wearing nothing but a soiled loin cloth and a spiked helmet now leered at Vesuvio, snarling in Greek, 'Your back tells me a story, slave. It tells me you are a trouble-maker.'

Vesuvio remained silent.

Taking off his spiked helmet and handing it to another guard, the large man said, 'Let's see how well you can fight.' The words were no sooner out of the Greek's mouth than he pushed Vesuvio on the chest, forcing him to tumble over the stone border, falling into the sandpit as the Greek came hurtling after him.

The fine grains of sand stung Vesuvio's back wounds. But quickly rolling onto his side, he jumped to his feet as the Greek landed on his fat stomach.

Rushing towards his sprawled body, Vesuvio straddled his back, gripping him around the neck, beginning to twist it as if he were killing a hen.

Quickly, two other guards in spiked helmets rushed forward to grab Vesuvio, pulling him off by both arms.

Rising to his feet, the Greek brushed the sand off his hairy belly, shoulders, and face, saying, 'That slave can fight. He goes there.' He nodded towards the left of the yard.

Immediately, the guards pushed Vesuvio towards a lewen, a small alcove providing the only shade from the sun in the yard. He stood facing the lewen, seeing a line of surly men sitting along the length of the grey wall. They made no room for Vesuvio to sit amongst them. A faint smile spread over a Moor's face. A Hispanic leaned back to enjoy more shade. An Arab hardened his fist and slowly began pounding it into the palm of his other hand.

Panting, looking at the row of cold eyes studying him, Vesuvio finally strode forward. He quickly kicked the Arab's foot from the dirt and knocked away the bent knee of a monkey-faced youth sitting next to him. He took his place amongst them.

9

Life at Byrsa was filthier than in any swineyard which Vesuvio had ever seen back in Campania. The food consisted of scraps that swineherds at home would not toss into a sty. The men slept on stone floors and wore only the tattered rags which they had arrived wearing. The few questions asked were for the specifics of their origin – Vesuvio still held to his story of being a young nobleman's body slave – and from then on all words were orders. The slaves' sole activity concentrated on overpowering one another: hourly contests took place during the day in the open sandpit of Byrsa in which the brawny men did nothing but fight.

Vesuvio had been trained by Sico to use the javelin, trident, the leaded net of the *restarii*, a contest with swords. Here at Byrsa the confrontation between the men was strictly hand-to-hand, a barbaric mixture of wrestling and boxing – but boxing without the leather *caelum* wrapped around the pugilist's fists, and wrestling with the goal of seeing which man could survive, in any way possible, stopping only the moment before death.

To Vesuvio, his first days at Byrsa were no better than being a mongrel in a dog fight. Yesterday he had seen a Thracian lock an Egyptian in his arms, then sink his teeth into the man's jugular vein. And, when a thick geyser of blood began spurting from the Egyptian's yellow neck, drenching the sand of the pit with a dark red river, the Thracian released the limp body.

He rose smiling, eager to receive congratulations for his victory. Instead, he was led to a post in one corner by a Greek in a spiked helmet, his arms tied around the post, and flogged with a cat-o'-nine-tails for killing a man who would fetch a high price at the slave auction. Vesuvio quickly changed his opinion – life at Byrsa was worse than a dog fight. No cur would ever be punished for winning.

Vesuvio now counted the passing of fifteen days and, still, he had not seen nor heard word of Titus or Scintus Genitor. Nor had he seen the men who had been eliminated the first day from the column on their arrival from the wharf. Vesuvio was confined to the surly and pugnacious, the angry and desperate, a group of barbaric slaves who would be auctioned for their sheer brawn power.

His body – like the bodies of the other men – quickly hardened at Byrsa. Despite Vesuvio's vigorous exercises with Sico, there had always been generous helpings of roast kid and fowl every evening at home, the thickly crusted bread and lemon cakes still warm from the bakery. But no prisoner's body had any respite from the pressures of a strenuous way of life at Byrsa. The shoulders that had been broad on arrival soon showed only epaulets of bare muscle. Hands became filth-encrusted paws for destruction. Either flaccid or hard at the outstart, every stomach now rippled with lean definition. Thighs were transformed into bulging pads of armour. The daily grapplings of the hungry, embittered and virtually naked men in the sandpit quickly produced satisfying results for their temporary Greek masters wearing the spiked helmets. Every day took a slave one more step in his preparation for the auction where he would be sold.

The only man in his group to whom Vesuvio spoke regularly was a black giant named Balthazar. Having been brought to Byrsa a week before Vesuvio, Balthazar felt more at ease in the citadel's dingy atmosphere and made the first nod of friendship.

Vesuvio soon learned that Balthazar had spent half of his childhood and all of his adult years so far as a slave. Balthazar did not know how old he was but believed that he was in his twenty-sixth year.

Balthazar told Vesuvio that he remembered a distant childhood in a tropical land beyond the great desert to the south of Numidia. Many slave raids were made against his people by the lighter-skinned and more powerful tribe called the Garamantes. The black captives from the inland were taken to an oasis called Kufra where they were sold to passing caravans. Balthazar said that so many of his people had been taken to that one particular caravanserai over the years to be sold that they were known for as long as any man could remember as 'the Kufra' tribe.

From a second trading post located on the sea, Tripolitania, Balthazar had been sold to work in the silver mines of Hispania.

After the depletion of its ores, he was next sent to the wheatlands of Baetica in the same region and, later, transported south by his master to another estate beyond the Pillars of Hercules in Mauretania. He had come to Byrsa after marauders swept down from the Atlas mountains, killing the weak slaves, selling the others to colonial agents.

Despite Balthazar's difficult life, he had a healthy, upright body. He even towered over Vesuvio, the tight black curls of his closely cropped hair forming a skullcap on his strong head, the whites of his eyes glistening from a blue-black face. Vesuvio marvelled at how a man could spend his life in slavery and still be able to smile so much.

Balthazar's sense of survival quickly won Vesuvio's admiration. When the food had been particularly bad one evening at Byrsa, Balthazar nodded Vesuvio into a corner of the damp cell where they slept. In the flickering light of a torch, he pointed towards a scorpion slowly crawling across the dirt. Vesuvio quickly stepped back. But motioning for him to remain beside him, Balthazar grabbed a handful of straw from a corner and placed it in a circle around the scorpion. Then, reaching to light a few shafts of straw in the torch, he set the circle ablaze. As the fire surrounded the scorpion, its long tail raised over its body and, seconds before the fire reached the scorpion, it stung itself. Prodding the scorpion, making certain that it was dead, Balthazar quickly gathered more straw and proceeded to roast it on the ledge of the barred window in their cell. Soon, he and Vesuvio were gobbling the stringy but nourishing meat.

Today was Vesuvio's seventeenth day at Byrsa. He and Balthazar sat in one corner of the open-air yard, enjoying a break from the sand-pit. They devoured a midday meal of bread, green olives, and goats' cheese.

Biting the hard white cheese, Balthazar said, 'The food is getting better. The next thing we'll get is a bath.'

Scratching at the lice bites on his shoulder, Vesuvio grumbled, 'About time.'

'That means the auction is near.'

Startled, Vesuvio looked at Balthazar. He had been so despondent with the squalor of Byrsa, and the likelihood that he might never get to see his brother, he had even forgotten about soon getting out of here.

Dipping a bread crust into the bowl of olives to sop up the oil, Balthazar continued, 'I hope my next master will be better than the last. I haven't had your luck so far. Not a considerate master. Not a master who will let me learn three or four different languages. Live like a man. I've been bought and sold like a camel. The fact is, that's the history of most of the men here. Except you.'

Vesuvio sat soberly on the ground, his bare shoulders hunched forward. He felt like a liar now, having stuck to his story that he had been born and raised a slave on Villa Macrinus in Campania.

'Just hope your good luck keeps up, friend,' Balthazar said, moving to slap Vesuvio on the back. But remembering that he had been whipped, he stopped to examine the welts.

Carefully prodding the scabs forming over Vesuvio's last marks, the second, third, or fourth encrustments for some wounds that had been roughened in daily combat, Balthazar assured Vesuvio that they were well past the danger of festering.

Then, squeezing Vesuvio's biceps, prodding at his ribs, feeling one thigh, he said, 'You've tightened up since you've come here, friend. You arrived strong. But strong like a man. Now you're sinewy like an animal.' Nodding his head, Balthazar said, 'You'll get a good price.'

'I now know why they turn us against one another. But what do they do with the women?' Vesuvio asked. 'And the children? Where do they keep them? I haven't seen anybody but us and the guards since I've been here.'

Pointing at the ground, Balthazar said, 'I have heard that Byrsa is like a beehive down there. Divided into cells and dungeons and torture chambers like honeycombs. We are just lucky we get exercise. And see daylight. Some slaves are brought here and never seen the sun for the rest of their days.'

The shout from a guard disturbed their break, a call for all the men to congregate by the only door leading from the yard.

Balthazar whispered as he rose on to his long legs, 'I'll bet you a scorpion for supper tonight that we're getting that bath now.'

*

Balthazar had been right. The men were told that the time had come to wash a few layers of dirt and sweat from their stinking bodies.

Escorted by guards bearing short swords and pine torches, they were led down a long spiral staircase that pierced deep into the black core of the old citadel. The stone stairway abruptly stopped at a round pool of water reflecting the torch flames. The guards' voices echoed overhead as they shouted to the men to take a plunge into the inky pool in turns, but to hold securely onto the rope secured to a stone pillar. They warned that no one at Byrsa knew how deep this cistern sank into the earth.

The water was icy cold and the sinister warning that the pool might be bottomless obliterated any enthusiasm which the men had anticipated for a bath.

Soon they were glad to be led back up the winding stairway, but still muttering amongst themselves about being cheated out of a swim, drying their naked bodies as they climbed with the scant rags they had worn down from the yard.

But the escort halted the column before they reached the top landing. A doorway was open now which no one had seen on the way down the dark stairway. A Musulami stood in the open door, asking the escort how many men he had in his charge.

'Eighteen.'

The Musulami muttered, 'We only have eleven women. Seven of your animals will have to wait. Do their business quick before the next crowd arrives.'

The news that they were going to be allowed women spread quickly down the winding staircase of naked men. Loud whoops and cries echoed in the stone chasm as they tried to push at one another to get to the door.

But as order was quickly restored by threatening prods from the guards' blades, the men quieted and, soon, were led in groups of four through the small door.

Vesuvio was included in the second group, following the Musulami down a narrow passageway, stopping when they reached a corner.

A second hallway with four doors stood in front of them. The Musulami pointed at an old hag wrapped in black cotton. She waited with a ring of keys dangling from one withered hand. And, as each man walked towards her, she nodded him into a separate cell, closed the door, and locked it with a large key.

Vesuvio now stood inside the door, listening to the key click behind him. Looking around the small vaulted room, he soon heard a low whimpering in the far corner. He saw a narrow shaft of light pouring through a slit in the wall. A woman was crouched at the base of the faint light with a mantle pulled around her head, cloth that had long ago been white.

Moving closer, Vesuvio kept his eyes on the woman. He whispered, 'I will not hurt you . . .'

Her whimpering became louder.

Dropping to his knees beside a straw pallet, Vesuvio put his hand on her shoulder, asking compassionately, 'Have they not fed you? Were you beaten? What is the matter? Please, speak. You can talk to me.'

There was a pause in her crying. Her slim body momentarily stopped shaking under the mantle.

By now Vesuvio had no intention of laying with this defenceless woman, even if she had been the most beautiful creature he had ever seen in his life. He would not inflict himself on someone if it only increased their misery.

Instead he tried to console her. He said, 'Don't be frightened of me, woman. We'll just talk. Just you and I. Maybe I can – help you.'

He heard the woman begin to sniff back her tears, saw her move one knuckle to wipe the moisture from her eyes.

Allowing her the one small privilege of composing herself in private, Vesuvio rose to his feet.

He called from a short distance, 'Perhaps you can help *me*. Are the women here imprisoned with the children—' He stopped, seeing the woman making an effort to move.

Slowly Vesuvio continued, 'I am trying to find a young . . . Roman . . . boy . . .'

Then, before Vesuvio realized what was happening, the woman threw down her mantle and she was facing him. He saw that she was not a woman at all. But a girl slightly younger than he was himself. She had fine features, a slim body, but her eyes – her eyes were unnaturally large. And wild.

As the young girl looked at Vesuvio, her pale hands slowly rose to her gown, pulling at her bodice one moment, ripping at the skirt the next, all the time moving closer to Vesuvio.

He knew now that the young girl was not here against her wishes. She eagerly rubbed her body against his bare leg, reaching to feel his face, to run her hands over his naked shoulders, down his broad chest. She stared at his mouth, licking her thin lips. And as she now freed her body from the gown, she rubbed her small breasts against Vesuvio's chest, his stomach, trying to straddle his knee with the furry patch between her legs.

Vesuvio held one hand to the girl's naked shoulder. She was being the aggressor. He did not want that. But pushing her away from him, he felt the softness of her skin, a silky feeling that he had forgotten. He looked down at her breasts and saw that, although they were not pendulous, they stood with a neat firmness. Her nipples were pink, taut, inviting.

Falling to her knees on the stone floor in front of Vesuvio, the girl pulled frantically at his cincture. She muttered words which he could not understand.

Aroused now himself, he reached down to drag the girl onto the pallet. But she moved faster than he did and, soon, she was laying on her back, holding her legs wide apart, fingering the lips of her vagina with both hands, anxiously beguiling him.

The girl screamed – whined – as Vesuvio made his first blunt jab into the warm patch between her legs. But gasping after a momentary pause, she quickly began to pump her thighs against him, accommodating him to sink deeper into her. She covered his face with kisses, pulling feverishly at his hair, frantically exploring his neck, his shoulders, his chest. Then, working her tongue against his bare arms planted alongside her body, she pumped her hips for him to drive deeper and faster into her.

Too soon, Vesuvio felt himself reaching an explosion in the tightness of her vagina. He did not want to finish so soon but the girl squeezed him so desperately, gyrated with such hunger, that he could not fight the explosion.

She opened herself wider as he moaned with excitement, trying to take his final drives deeper inside her. Then, even after Vesuvio lay satisfied on top of the girl, she continued working her small body under him, as if enjoying the remaining stiffness of his phallus more than before, as if its thickness and length was pleasure only for herself.

But as the girl persistently worked herself on Vesuvio, he soon felt himself becoming excited again. This time, though, he wanted to be more in control. He held her down to the pallet by both arms as he plunged deeper into her, watching her toss her head frantically from side to side.

Soon she tried to raise her head, attempting to take bites at his chest, to chew into his shoulder and arms with her sharp teeth as he pumped into her.

Slapping her into submission with the flat of one hand, Vesuvio continued driving his groin as the girl now moaned pleasurably from the slap; then she began laughing, squeezing for him to stir deeper and wider.

The first pounding on the wooden door behind Vesuvio began as he felt himself nearing his second explosion. The moisture of his previous seed – and the girl's voracious appetite – kept him from knowing if she had reached one or one thousand orgasms.

The pounding sounded louder on the door. But Vesuvio could not stop. He continued pumping into the girl. She hungrily squeezed for him. Neither of them could stop.

Even when the thick wooden door swung open, Vesuvio continued thrusting into her and she pumped towards him. Two guards dragged Vesuvio away from her. The old hag and another guard held the girl to the pallet as she struggled to follow Vesuvio's hard phallus. She fought them, stretching her arms to the phallus being dragged farther and farther away from her . . .

. . . Vesuvio was in the first stages of his orgasm. Even as the guard held him back by the arms, his midsection jerked. His phallus bobbed up and down. His seed spewed through the air in long spurts . . .

. . . The girl cried for it. Tore to get to it. Fell to lick it from the stone floor . . .

. . . Vesuvio was edged out into the hallway and, as he looked down at his phallus, he saw blood – the blood from breaking the hymen of a virgin.

Later that night he heard that the young girl – like each of the girls which the men had enjoyed this afternoon – was a sacred virgin from the Temple of Isis. Their head priestess had fallen from political grace with the Governor of Carthage. But because it was contrary to law to kill a virgin anywhere in the Roman Empire, the young girls were brought to Byrsa, heavily drugged with the aphrodisiac, *satyrion*, and given to the slaves to be made impure for their execution.

10

Hasdrubal was a small, pinch-faced man who had been put in control of Byrsa by the Romans. A Carthaginian by birth, Hasdrubal possessed the brooding temperament of the Hamitic people who had originally settled this shore of Numidia – long before the Romans, Greeks, or Phoenicians invaded from the north.

On the night before the slave auction, Hasdrubal received a visitor in his tower room high above the main courtyard of Byrsa. The room was sparsely furnished, the darkness lit only by two torches flanking the low-padded wooden bench on which he sat.

The visitor was Sheik Bakir, captain of the *Ka'ba.* Although they were not close friends, and their eastern blood bond was distant, they were allied by their innate distrust of Rome. They knew they could trust one another if, not like brothers, then, like understanding cousins.

Sheik Bakir did not plan to stay at Byrsa for the auction tomorrow. He had only come to see Hasdrubal tonight with a message which concerned them both, a scroll heavily sealed – but the waxes already broken by Bakir's own dagger because the message had first come to him from Rome.

With the sides of his *kufiyeh* swept back over his shoulder, Bakir sat facing Hasdrubal. He held the scroll in one hand as he, first, proceeded to ask the Commander-in-Chief of Byrsa for a favour, an action involving a captive whom he had recently brought across the Mediterranean from Italy aboard the *Ka'ba.*

Bakir explained, 'The woman's name is Iucunda, a concubine of a wealthy trader of Misenum. The man is an old acquaintance of mine. When he felt that his concubine planned to poison him, he asked for my help.'

Hasdrubal impatiently nodded his head, wanting the Arab to proceed quickly with the story.

His black eyes glistening in the torch light, Bakir slowly continued, 'The woman is attractive but not a beauty. You could sell her for breeding although her womb is not young.'

Still eyeing the Roman scroll, Hasdrubal nodded.

'We have a custom in Arabia. It was devised to punish Quraish women who speak profanely. This Iucunda, she is an unclean woman. My friend in Misenum, Fortunato, told me that her mouth gave him much pleasure. But he was not talking about the words which spread like pestilence from it. I saw her applying her mouth to a man in the manner which Fortunato had described to me. She was accomplished, true—'

Pausing, Bakir lowered his eyes and explained, 'However, the woman talks in the common manner of the lowest prostitute. I heard her say things to my sailors which—'

Hasdrubal could wait no longer. He blurted, 'You want me to cut out the slut's tongue.'

Nodding, Bakir said softly, 'It will not detract from her selling price.'

Hasdrubal laughed, 'From what you tell me about this woman's other talents of the mouth, such an act might even enhance her selling price!'

Pausing, Hasdrubal asked, 'She is a Roman, yes?'

'A Roman slave. She wears the gold slave chain around her waist. But wait. There is more. Not only would I like you to sever her tongue but I would also like you to lay the tongue on a stone. In the hot sun. And when it is completely dried – like a fig – I humbly ask you to send it to me in Alexandria.'

Hasdrubal looked puzzled.

Smiling, Bakir explained, 'That is a Quraish custom for dealing with blasphemous slave women. We cut out their tongues. Dry them in the sun. Stretch them over the end of a stick and make us a . . . pizzle!'

'A phallus? With the head of a tongue?'

Bakir nodded, continuing, 'The skin from the tongue that spoke so many profanities becomes the crown of a phallus, a toy to give the pleasure which the woman brazenly spoke about.'

Flicking his hand that the request was easily granted, Hasdrubal eyed the scroll and asked, 'Now what news do you have for me there?'

Holding the scroll towards him, Bakir said, 'This is a message from Rome. Sent by the man who paid me to kidnap two heirs of a rich estate on the coastline of Campania. I suspected that something was wrong when I interviewed one of the captives during the course of our journey. He was like no slave I have ever met. And now—'

Bakir held out the scroll. 'This document says that the heir to the Macrinus estate is in full maturity. That he is not a boy but has reached manhood. And, I swear by it, the heir himself is posing here at Byrsa as a life-long slave. He denies being a born nobleman.'

'A Roman noble? Posing as a slave? Why?'

Bakir shrugged. 'He is not like any Roman I have ever met. He is handsome in a most unique way. Virile and young. Yet . . . he has the pride and assurance of a much older man . . . I suspect that, rather than save his own neck, he has given his name to his younger brother to ensure that the boy might find a lenient master. That he is willing to suffer the hard life and let his brother be spared.'

Hasdrubal scratched his hollow cheek. 'That doesn't sound like a Roman's action.'

Waving the scroll, Bakir explained, 'But the important misunderstanding, the subject of this parchment, is that another young boy – a youth named Scintus Genitor, was kidnapped in the same raid. By error. My client, a politician by the name of Gaius Lucretius is in daily contact with the boy's sister. But she is not troubled by her brother's disappearance at all. Quite to the contrary. She now stands to inherit his full share of the property. To make certain of this, she asks through my client that the boy be . . . decapitated. And his head sent to her in Campania. This woman, Scintilla Genitoris, wants proof that her brother is dead.'

'Now that *does* sound like a Roman!'

'Will you comply?'

Narrowing his eyes, Hasdrubal asked, 'Does this noble lady offer me a reward for the head of her brother?'

'Ten thousand *sestertii.*'

'How old is the youth?'

'No more than ten years.'

Quickly calculating figures, Hasdrubal said, 'A boy of ten years – he would fetch around five thousand at the auction. Seventy-five hundred at the most. But the lady is offering ten thousand. Yes, she gets her brother's head. It shall be dispatched to her on the first galley north.'

Rising, smoothing the folds of the *burnous* he wore to protect him from the night air, Bakir bowed, saying, 'Hasdrubal is always honourable.'

Looking Bakir straight in the eye, Hasdrubal said, 'Before you leave, let us return to the subject of the Roman nobleman posing as a slave. How much extra did your patron pay you to *keep* the true heir away from Italy? To make certain that he does not return to his estate?'

Sheik Bakir's confident façade momentarily shattered. His dark eyes widened at Hasdrubal's direct question. He quickly composed himself, saying with a thin smile, 'You are a credit to your Hamitic blood, Hasdrubal. You do not miss one chink in the commercial wall which surrounds slavery. The fact is, my patron has included an additional five thousand *sestertii* for me to make certain that the Roman heir is kept here. I was only now going to tell you that I was also instructed to pay you half that sum.'

Hasdrubal slowly nodded, suspecting that Bakir was a liar, that if he had not asked about the money he would have never heard about it.

He said blandly, 'Half of five thousand added to my ten thousand for the other boy's head makes a decent sum. Not magnificent. But decent.'

Softening his voice, Hasdrubal continued, 'Now if I could impose on you for some free advice, Sheik Bakir, perhaps you might tell me how you think this Roman heir posing as a slave should be sold.' He was giving Bakir the opportunity to regain his pride. As he wanted to continue doing business with this Arab, he could not allow him to leave now feeling shamed.

Putting his hands into the wide sleeves of his *burnous*, Bakir began modestly, 'That is your decision, Friend Hasdrubal. But if it were myself, I would say to let the pantomime continue. He is a slave now anyway. Low-born or noble. And, besides, his brother is young and still impressionable. You could well get a high price for him for some pederast. Or a new-rich merchant who fancies a noble heir to decorate his household. But the true heir – No, he is too old to be trained into a house pet. Even the most ambitious man would quickly see that he would have trouble breaking *him*! No, Hasdrubal. Let the true heir be sold as a man slave. And he is a magnificent specimen. You will not lose on that accord. He could easily sell for a stallion and, you know as well as I, those buyers don't care what kind of blood flows, not as long as it keeps hot.'

'What is he called?'

Smiling, Bakir said, '"Vesuvio". He has hair as golden as the wheat fields of Mauretania. He is built like a gladiator. And speaking purely as a spectator of life, I would enjoy pondering in future years about whatever became of that gilded mountain. What adventures he was having. What successes he enjoyed. The punishments he endured. Oh, such thoughts are sweet to a mind like mine, Hasdrubal.'

Raising himself between the pair of torches, Hasdrubal confessed, 'I do not share your romantic view of a slave's life, Sheik Bakir. But you are a shrewd business man. I know for a fact that the slave market is now short of good men. Strong male slaves. Like this – what is his name? Vesuvio? On the other hand, the auction blocks from here to Emesa are crowded with pieces of fluff for the bedchambers. So, to raise the price of the young boy, I shall let him be sold as a noble heir. But the stallion, he goes as brawn.'

Bowing low, Bakir said, 'And you will not forget the head of the other boy to be sent to his sister, Scintilla Genitoris, in Campania?'

'My blade is sharpened more quickly with silver,' Hasdrubal said holding out his hand. And whilst Bakir dug into a pouch to extract the coins, Hasdrubal added, 'But the slut's tongue will be sent as my compliments to you in Alexandria. To be made into a sexual toy for you to use in good health with an obedient *houri.*'

Bakir confessed, 'Rather than the knobbed pleasure-stick which the blasphemous tongue will soon help to create – with the blessings of the sun – I would prefer the real phallus of Vesuvio. But . . .'

Holding up his hands, Hasdrubal said, 'No. You ask too much of an old friend, Bakir. Too much.'

Sheik Bakir quickly explained, 'But I do not ask for that! To defile him would be a sacrilege to all nature! His sacred proportions are too monumental even for a holy man like myself to keep in one isolated tabernacle. The world is the altar for his maleness.'

Holding up one of his golden neck chains, Bakir confided in a whisper, 'His phallus is this richly skinned . . . like gold!'

Nodding impatiently, Hasdrubal moved his hand again for the money. He was eager to count every coin of the payment, not wanting to waste time listening to zealous talk about the sexual equipment of slaves.

11

Vesuvio decided to tell Balthazar the truth about his identity. The black giant had not only become his only friend at Byrsa but to persist in telling him a lie was to show doubt of Balthazar's integrity as a man.

Apart from paring down his body to an animal leanness at Byrsa, Vesuvio was beginning to see more clearly than ever that the gulf between a master and a slave was not a distinction made by nature. Wars, greed, politics were what sat people on thrones or locked them in chains. Vesuvio was still the same person that he had been as a master, the heir to Villa Macrinus. The only difference now was the denial of his freedom.

The man that he would become in the future was another matter, he realized. He could transform into a hardened, bitter creature like the majority of the male slaves at Byrsa or exist in bondage like Balthazar, looking for small amusements, hoping for the best in a miserable life, setting the basic fact of survival as his goal.

Somehow Vesuvio doubted that he could develop a carefree attitude. Apart from not having such a nature, he knew that he would always harbour anger against the injustices done to his family, keep brooding about the man – or men – responsible for his abduction.

For the moment, though, Vesuvio tried to convince himself that a large gap lay between himself and the future, that it would do him no good to think about his destiny until he was auctioned to his future master, whoever he might be. His only responsibility now was to correct the false impression he had given to Balthazar.

On the morning of the auction, the area around the sandpit was transformed into a series of stations for the men to prepare themselves for the sales block. Hemp mats were spread along the walls where old women and children distributed earthen jars of water for a farewell dowsing, palm oil to shine the captive's bodies, clean loin cloths to wrap around themselves, herbs for disguising their body odours.

As Vesuvio and Balthazar progressed through the preparatory steps, Balthazar spoke lightly about the advantages and disadvantages of being purchased by a female. He said that he had always hoped that his next owner would be a woman. He added, 'But a woman who buys a slave usually wants him only for one thing. That can tire a man very fast. Especially the kind of woman who has to buy a slave to give her love.' He held a jar of water over Vesuvio's head.

Spluttering, rubbing himself around the neck, under the pits of his arms, palming the water down the muscle of his abdomen and around his crotch, Vesuvio said, 'I suppose there is no perfect master for any slave.' He in turn threw water onto Balthazar's naked body.

Dipping the wide expanse of his black shoulders to catch the full wash of the cold water, Balthazar joked, 'Maybe the answer is to be sold to a eunuch!'

Looking how the water beaded on the tight curls of Balthazar's thick hair, Vesuvio said, 'A eunuch would have his advantages.' He added, 'By not having them.'

Bending to work the water between his toes and the bottoms of his feet, which were calloused but pink compared to the rest of his skin, Balthazar reconsidered. 'But then a eunuch can be as evil as a man and a woman put together. They scream. They're suspicious. They plot. They scheme. They make a slave work twice as hard as an ordinary man.'

'Fortunately there aren't that many eunuchs in the world.'

'Many? The world is crawling with eunuchs! And very rich ones! Powerful ones! They hack off a man's balls in the East as soon as talk to him. Half the men there are eunuchs. But because they don't spend all their time worrying about sex, they have time to make life miserable for other people.'

A sharp grunt from an old woman standing nearby called for them to take a handful of palm oil.

The oil glistened on Balthazar's skin as he rubbed it into his arms, chest, legs, face. He proudly held up both arms in the sunlight and admired them. 'The good thing about this dark skin of mine is the shine! Just look how I shine!'

Turning back to the old woman, he held out his hand and

asked, 'Give me some more, Mother. A dab to rub here – ' He held out his phallus by the purple-black foreskin enveloping its head.

The old woman gave him a shove, slapping the next measure of palm oil into Vesuvio's hand.

'Why not?' Balthazar joked to her. 'A little shine there might catch the eye of a very rich woman! Somebody who will appreciate me! Spoil me like I'm meant to be spoiled.'

As Vesuvio rubbed his own body with oil, he walked alongside Balthazar to the next station – a small boy sitting on a hemp mat and handing out sprigs of fresh mint. The prospective buyers might want to examine the teeth of their potential property. The mint would sweeten their breath.

Chewing the fresh leaves, Vesuvio began, 'We don't know if we'll see each other after today. Our whole lives will suddenly change. And look at you! You're happy. Making jokes.'

'I've been through this before, friend. I know what people look for. I know when to appear tame. When to flex the muscle in my arm. When to look sullen or flash them a smile. But for you—'

Balthazar shook his head, continuing soberly, 'For you, this is something all new. You were born to your last master. You grew up on the estate. But don't worry. You've got a fine face. That is very important. Almost more important than your strong body. Plus—' He smiled and tousled Vesuvio's blond hair. '—you've got all that golden stuff growing on your head. Buyers in these markets like your colouring. They get very few light-skinned, yellow-haired people from the north. Even in Italy you must be a rare slave.'

Vesuvio squared his jaw. Then, taking Balthazar by the elbow, he confessed in a hushed tone, 'I have not been truthful with you, Balthazar. There is no reason to tell you this now. I probably will never see you again after today but—'

Raising his head to look Balthazar straight in the eye, he confessed, 'I am not a slave. Not up to now. It was a lie I made up before I arrived here. I was captured from my family's home in Italy. Me and my brother. He is much younger than I am, though, and I thought—'

'That's why you keep asking about the children. Where they are kept.'

Vesuvio nodded. 'Our family is a noble line. I gave my insignia to my brother. I thought it might help him secure a better future than just being sold as a youth.'

Putting his hand on Vesuvio's shoulder, Balthazar said soberly, 'You are very honourable.'

Vesuvio shook his head, denying, 'I am not honourable when I lie to the one man who is my friend here. Helped me live through these wretched days. Each time I heard you speak about the generosity of my "master" I felt a sickness and not because of what I lost. Of course, my first anguish was about being here. Being taken away from home. But the more you talked about my good luck in the past, the worst I felt for deceiving you. I was never owned by a master. I was a master myself to more than four thousand slaves!'

Looking at Vesuvio in bewilderment, Balthazar said, 'And you entrust me with this story?'

Vesuvio nodded. 'I couldn't leave you with a lie.'

'I have never met a man like you before, Friend.'

'If anyone is rare,' Vesuvio began, 'it is you. Surviving the silver mines. The wheat fields.'

Grinning widely, Balthazar said, 'I would be more rare if I could be sold in Rome! As you are different here, so would a black man be there.'

Nodding, Vesuvio said, 'There are only a few black people in Rome. They are very prized. And not only as slaves. Up to now, though, I always heard it was for sexual reasons. But I know that that does your people a great injustice.'

The two men — Vesuvio, his fair hair glistening in the sun now; Balthazar, looking like a statue hewn from ebony — held one another's hands firmly before being parted by the Greek guards in spiked helmets.

The first buyers, or their agents and stewards, were coming to inspect the men slaves to gauge their strength, to hear about their backgrounds, to examine their teeth like horses, to order their loin cloths to be removed for an inspection of any deformation, inflictions, or masculine distinctions. The auction was now less than two hours away.

The auction was held in the main courtyard of Byrsa, conducted from a small wooden platform built at the far end of the iron gates opening into the citadel. A semi-circle of stones was piled into three tiers around the platform for seating.

Vesuvio was led along with the other men slaves to slat-fronted pens behind the platform, given a number tag to wear around his neck, and both feet were brushed with white chalk – the Roman custom of denoting that someone was for sale.

There were five pens behind the platform and, as midday approached, Vesuvio still sat soberly on a wooden bench in the fourth pen, listening to the calls of the Greek Auctioneer.

Having heard at least seventy-five slaves being sold so far, Vesuvio still tried to make a connection between the physical characteristics which the Auctioneer called to his audience and the physical attributes of Titus. But either the slave was too old, the wrong sex, the wrong-coloured skin, or lacking in education.

When he heard the Auctioneer extolling the virtues of a black man, he immediately knew it was Balthazar. The Auctioneer listed his past services, drawing attention to his towering height, his obvious strength and, after some shrill calls from the crowd, the Auctioneer begged them to view his praiseworthy maleness.

Vesuvio sat in the cell, listening as the bids climbed for Balthazar. Finally, the Auctioneer's mallet pounded. But as Vesuvio strained to hear the name of the person who had bought him, the crowd laughed and cheered, drowning out the words.

It was next that Vesuvio heard a curious announcement. The Auctioneer called that he would skip the next number, that the youth of noble Roman birth had been bought prior to the auction.

Vesuvio sat to the edge of the bench. 'Youth'? Of 'noble Roman birth'? Was it Titus? Had he already been sold? Why?

Rushing to the slat gate of his pen, Vesuvio wanted to hear who had bought his brother. But the guard stepped up to the gate. As he reached to pull back Vesuvio by the leather thong around his neck, he glanced at the number tag. He nodded at the two escorts marching from the platform and called to them, 'Number Eighty is in a rush. He's already waiting.' The gate swung open and Vesuvio was led out into the sun.

The expanse between the auction platform and the stone tiers was now filled with tents, awnings, panoplies – a small, brilliantly coloured city which had been erected there in the few hours since the slaves had been taken to their pens.

Standing on the platform with his hands bound in front of him, Vesuvio ignored the whistles and comments rising from the benches, looking instead at the conical and quadrangular-shaped roofs which protected richly dressed people from the hot Numidian sun. These privileged classes sat on cushions or thrones, lounged on divans, in the openings of their tents. Many of them were cooled by slaves gently waving fans made from ostrich feathers or dyed reeds. Their stewards stood closely at hand, flanked by body guards armed with daggers, scimitars, spears. Vesuvio saw Berber chieftains, their desert-baked faces draped with *kufiyehs*, intricately wrapped turbans crowning the proud heads of young princes, ornate clusters of pheasant feathers towering above the sober features of black men, rich merchants wearing golden bibs set with glistening gems, and people who wished to conceal their identity by covering their faces with clay masks painted in either the benign or terrifying tradition of old Punic gods.

The Auctioneer announced that he would take bids only in gold currency for this slave, the *aureus* worth twenty-five *denarii*, one hundred *sestertii* – and that he would accept them only in multiples of ten.

Reaching to lift Vesuvio's chin with the butt of his mallet, he said, 'Not only are you offered a fine body with this slave but look at that exceptional face. Notice the brilliant blue eyes. The fine golden hair. Surely there's someone—'

A voice called from a scarlet ciborium near the platform, 'Fifty *aurei*!'

The Auctioneer nodded graciously at the person who opened the bidding, an obese man ensconced on a chair, his jewelled fingers working eagerly on the gold dolphins forming the arms of the chair.

From a much larger but less ornate tent set a few rows back from the scarlet ciborium, another voice called, 'Sixty *aurei*.'

Before the Auctioneer had time to accept the bid, the fat man in the dolphin chair called, 'Seventy!'

Vesuvio raised his head to look more closely at this person so eager to buy him, seeing a smooth pink face, pendulous breasts hanging inside an elaborately embroidered bolero, and a necklace of dew-claws set with garnets. He remembered Balthazar's remarks about eunuchs.

The voice from the back tent called, 'Eighty!'

The rich eunuch raised his hand again and impatiently shrilled, 'One hundred golden *aurei*!'

Vesuvio realized that the bidding was only between the eunuch and the one other person – a man he now saw sitting in a slung iron-and-tigerskin chair amidst a group of veiled girls. They clustered around the chair, keeping their eyes on Vesuvio. And when the man now bid again – one-hundred-and-twenty *aurei* – the girls hugged one another in excitement, jumping up and down on their knees.

But before the eunuch had time to raise his last offer, another voice joined the bidding. It was a white-robed steward bidding on behalf of a masked person lounging on a cushion under a tangerine cotton pavilion supported by long, twisting narwhal tusks. The clay mask and voluminous robes hid the gender of the new contestant who now had ordered the bid to be raised by another ten golden *aurei*.

Next came the fifth, sixth, and seventh bids from other tents and baldichins in the courtyard, climbing by tens toward two hundred *aurei* until a voice boomed from the centre of the courtyard, calling an offer which topped the last bid by fifty, an extravagant sum that produced gasps and moans of withdrawal from other contenders.

The bid came from a shamiana composed of long and multi-coloured pennants draped over brass rods, by far the richest and most spectacular construction in the courtyard, each pennant divided into alternating chevrons of red, yellow and black silk.

A man dressed in silver-and-gold chest plates sat on a carved cedar chair placed alongside a divan with clawed feet. But the divan's tall back was positioned towards the Auctioneer's platform, obstructing any view of the person who lay upon it.

Accepting the overly generous bid, the Greek Auctioneer smugly reviewed the other contenders with a quick sweep of his eyes.

The eunuch's round face flushed with anger. He began to open his small mouth but, shuddering with anger, he jerked at a cord and the flap of his scarlet ciborium flapped quickly down in front of him.

The eager girls surrounding the man in the iron-and-tigerskin chair looked anxiously towards him. But he shook his head.

The sexless person wearing the clay mask withdrew the steward, motioning now to a slave to bring an ivory goblet of wine which she – or he – drank under the slight lifting of the mask.

The Auctioneer nodded towards the shamiana of pennants and called, 'A bid of two-hundred-and-fifty *aurei*. Will there be another offer?' Not even bothering to consult the people crowded on the stone benches, he surveyed the variously shaped and coloured tents.

There was a silence in the courtyard. The ostrich fans continued to dip slowly. Pinions fluttered from spear shafts supporting some awnings, banners and long ribbons flapped from the central pikes of others. The sun glistened on golden necklaces, rare gems, silken robes, aigrette feathers, and the immobile masks. Women stroked the heads of Abyssinian cats. Boarhounds pulled at chains which held them to ground pegs. A panther chewed on meat held to a carpet by his front paws. But no one spoke.

Finally, raising his mallet in the air, the Auctioneer began, 'This Roman slave is sold then to Lord Lucco. Or—' He suddenly paused, stopping the mallet before it reached the table. He called to the shamiana, '—is it the Eastern general's wife, Lady Athana, who is spending two-hundred-and-fifty golden *aurei* at Byrsa today?'

A murmur finally rose from the benches, an amused response

to the Auctioneer's reference to the man as an 'Eastern general' – a well-known synonym in the Mediterranean for a pirate.

Ignoring the whispers and laughter, Vesuvio studied the opening of the extravagant shamiana. He saw an arm slowly rise from the depths of the divan. He heard the jangle of bracelets as a woman's slim arm waved its denial – that, no, 'Athana' was not buying the slave. He remembered Sheik Bakir speaking about the pirate couple, Lucco and Athana.

The pound of the mallet echoed through the courtyard as the Auctioneer called, 'Sold! To Lucco . . . the Eastern general. For two-hundred-and-fifty gold *aurei.* Six-thousand-two-hundred-and-fifty silver *denarii.* Or twenty-five-thousand *sestertii.* A Roman slave named "Vesuvio"!'

Book Three
The Pirate Galleys

12

The black galley lay at anchor this humid afternoon in a small cove to the east of Carthage, its one-hundred-and-twenty oars slanting into the water like the drooped wings of a giant dragon-fly. The name of the majestic vessel was the *Ceres*. Its prow curved gracefully upwards, the bulwark stretched wide and strong. Although Roman-built, the *Ceres* now served as the lead ship in Lucco's pirate fleet.

The oarsmen from the *Ceres* lay scattered across the rocky slope above the inlet, seizing this respite from a journey back to Lucco's headquarters to stretch themselves in the southern Mediterranean sun. Many members of the slave crew had peeled off their tunics and run down to the clear blue water, diving from tall boulders, wrestling in shallow pools, racing one another at swimming across the cove.

Vesuvio remained on the rocky slope, relaxing in the sun rather than joining the raucous men who cavorted in the water. Although having been in slavery for three years now, Vesuvio had only been an oarsmen aboard the *Ceres* for ten months – time enough to learn that these swims often led to sexual encounters amongst the oarsmen, that the carefree games and playful gropings frequently culminated in abandoned orgies on barren shores and hidden inlets. Such perverse activities did not appeal to him. He preferred to remain as far away from them as possible.

Except for his unkempt appearance, Vesuvio had little in common with the pirate slaves with whom he had been living for the last three years. His blond hair now fell to his shoulders. A full beard covered his face. The pierce of his blue eyes was sharpened by the deep bronze of his skin. He saw himself as a mangy wolf remaining aloof from the pack.

Despite the exorbitant price which Lucco had paid for him at the Byrsa slave auction, Vesuvio's first duties in the pirate encampment had been menial. He had gathered sea salt from square pans cut into the rocks; built stone walls for the pirate barracks; picked olives from wild groves; hunted for game; performed any chore, large or small, in whatever location Lucco had chosen to make his headquarters.

Lucco's method of enslavement was not what Vesuvio had anticipated three years ago. The only ropes or chains which Lucco attached to his men were put on them for their own safety, as in the war galley, the *Ceres*, when the crash of a wave against the longest oars could fling a man across the width of the hull. Lucco chained a slave to an oar to save his life. He also moved his men at fixed intervals from the left to the right of the galley to keep their bodies from becoming lop-sided with muscle – the constant pulling of an oar on only one side of the galley quickly deformed a man.

Vesuvio had been surprised how Lucco kept his slaves' obedience. The pirate lord offered every man the privilege of buying his freedom, paying for it from the gold seized from unguarded fortresses or towns which they looted along this southern shore of the Mediterranean: the booty was divided amongst the pirates by their rank and station.

Lucco's pirate soldiers – the 'Marines' – were men who had amassed enough wealth to buy their freedom but still remained with their master to accumulate a fortune which they could never hope to possess in the outside world. Every new slave – whatever price had been paid for him – had to work his way up through the ranks of the strict hierarchy which Lucco set for his men. Lucco's promises of gold only whetted a man's greed to want to become a Marine, to stay with the pirate horde until he was either killed in battle or had his throat slit by another pirate in a dice game.

The alternative of escaping from Lucco to some other life was rare. Vesuvio had seen in the last three years that an escape led only to the desolate Libyan desert to the south . . . or the sea. He recognized that the pirate slaves were virtually trapped by their own vagabond life.

For many men, though, the life with Lucco improved upon the conditions they would have known as free men. The majority of the slaves were low-born peasants originally brought from uncivilized lands by the Romans as prisoners-of-war. The oarsmen who had been raised in slavery were mostly field workers, men born of slave parents or abandoned as infants by peasants who could not afford to feed another child. The foreign captives, the field slaves, the foundlings, all spoke a mixture of Latin, Greek, and Arabic, a coarse language peppered with profanities.

Vesuvio often heard men bragging about the high price which Lucco had paid for them at the slave markets of Emessa, Smyrna, Alexandria, or Byrsa. It was a custom for Lucco to offer a lavish bid at a slave auction for a man he wanted, a price which made some slaves swagger and feel important. The higher a slave's price, though, the longer he had to wait – saving his small share of the booty to reach the equivalent sum – until Lucco offered him a formal choice of 'buying' his freedom or becoming a Marine.

During his first year with the pirates, Vesuvio had begun to understand how a high purchase price was a formidable shackle to Lucco, a fact which some men refused to accept. The slaves often interpreted their cost as proof of their own importance. Vesuvio had originally argued with his fellow slaves, trying to make them see that they were being duped by Lucco's promises. Such arguments only led to fights and, after four or five physical encounters with the other slaves, he learned to keep his silence. He quickly realized that the pirate slaves preferred to feel important at the cost of remaining ignorant.

Apart from the wealth which Lucco gathered for himself, his main interest was the legend he kept alive of being the one pirate whom the Roman fleets had not driven away from the Mediterranean. The other pirate ships now haunted the safer shores of the Black or the Red Sea. Vesuvio saw irony in the fact that the Romans themselves had made the Mediterranean a more profitable place for Lucco.

Lucco was a Sardinian, a noble-looking figure in his early fifties. His black hair was silver at the temples and his complexion always weather-beaten. Dressed in his fine armour, he presented a dignified contrast to the ragged men who eagerly listened to his promises. More than a pirate, Lucco was an orator, a political leader, a master who could wring zeal from his slaves.

The only person whom Vesuvio had seen who was not mesmerized by Lucco's lavish promises was the pirate lord's young Hispanic wife, Athana. Although Vesuvio had only caught brief glimpses of Athana in the last three years, he had seen enough of her to recognize that she was a haughty female, an enigmatic woman who was totally detached from the magic which Lucco cast for his bedraggled men.

Vesuvio knew that Athana was an independent force, quite distinct from Lucco in many operations. She commanded her own galley, the *Lupa*. She had formed her own pirate élite, men whom she called her 'Military', fighting sailors who wore red woollen capes over their unkempt tunics. Athana worked independently within the power structure which Lucco had built as a pirate navy.

Athana and her red-caped men often attacked targets which Lucco ignored or did not think worthy of his military genius. She sent out spies, learning which fortresses were not heavily guarded, taking chances which her husband considered to be too risky for the treasures promised. She also allowed her men to chew a resin called *charas* before some attacks. As Lucco did not permit his men to use any drugs, there was little talk about that fact.

Because Athana did not mingle at night with the men by their bonfires, many rumours spread through the camp about the private life of the tall, slender, long-limbed woman. Men joked about Athana not making love to her husband. That she was without passion. Other stories told that she paid for the sexual services of a free man; that she refused to make love to any man who was a slave. The pirates also passed around rumours that Athana like to lay with other females; that her Syrian slave girl, Lita, was her present lover.

The only consistent story which Vesuvio had heard about Athana in the last three years was that she was of Hispanic blood, and that she had fought as a *gladiatrix* in the colonial city of Leptis Magna before Lucco had purchased her. No one knew if Lucco had freed his wife from bondage since then or if Athana was also saving to accrue the price of her own freedom like the other pirate slaves.

In recent months the headquarters of Lucco and Athana had been on a barren island called Platea, a rocky knoll located south of Greece and lying off the coast of Cyrenaica. Platea had been colonized eight hundred years earlier by a Greek sect which had sailed south on the advice of the ancient oracle at Delphi. The colonials built a temple on the small island but when they did not prosper there they sent an emissary back to Greece with a complaint to the Delphic Oracle about the soil. A new order returned to Platea, saying that the Oracle had meant for them to settle on the mainland. Thus the temple was abandoned and the island left unclaimed, even avoided as an ill-omened spot. The pillars of the temple eventually collapsed and, washed by years of rain, became only more chunks of stone strewn across the sun-bleached island.

Today the *Ceres* was headed back to Platea. A small Roman patrol had earlier given Lucco chase from a seaside villa of a provincial governor. And having finally diverted the Romans north towards the Aegean, Lucco had circled back to southerly waters, now making a way home to Platea. He had stopped at this cove to give his men a much-needed rest.

Vesuvio looked forward to having a good rest tonight in the barracks at Platea. After rowing in the *Ceres* for almost a year now, he still had not learned to sleep in a hammock whilst at sea. He could only relax when he stretched out on a straw pallet in the barracks, feeling the warm body of a Berber girl curled next to him, the ground solid beneath his tired body.

Now, letting his sinewy legs and arms stretch in a spread-eagle position in the sun, Vesuvio thought about returning to Platea. His thoughts were wandering to his Berber concubine when, suddenly, he heard the voices of two men on the slope next to him. They discussed the group of swimmers gathering on the shore below them. They laughed at a young German slave who knelt in the middle of the naked men.

Raising himself to his elbows to look down the hill, too,

Vesuvio saw that the muscular German youth was kneeling on the ground like a dog whilst a succession of men formed a line behind him waiting to drive their sexuality between his buttocks. Vesuvio had heard about the German youth's prodigious appetite for unnatural sex but he had never before seen a performance of it. He watched the act with curiosity, wondering how a slave could allow himself to be more debased than he already was.

The licentious behaviour spread quickly amongst the naked swimmers. A man with a mop of greasy black hair soon knelt in front of the young German and held his phallus to the boy's mouth. The slaves standing around the spectacle began to grope one another, working the next man's maleness with their hands as they watched the succession of oarsmen satisfying themselves with the handsome youth.

Puzzled by one male's attraction for another, Vesuvio lay back down on the slope and began drifting into a nap when he next heard the slapping of bare skin next to him.

Turning his head sideways, he saw one of the two men – a Numidian – kneeling behind the plump buttocks of the other man, a bearded slave from Gaul. The Numidian slapped the Gaul's buttocks with the flat of his hand as he drove his hardened phallus into him. The loud groans and coaxings told Vesuvio that the Gaul enjoyed both being smote and buggered simultaneously, that the two men were well-matched in their taste for punishment and pain.

Lying back down on the pebbles, Vesuvio shaded his eyes against the sun and thought about slavery, debasement and punishment. Why did men want to be struck for enjoyment? Was life as a slave not bad enough? What kind of slave would want to be abused, pummelled, disciplined by another slave?

Next, Vesuvio wondered if life was as sordid as this in the free world. Was he a misfit only here amongst the pirate slaves? Or was this all some form of play for the men? A release that he did not understand? Having seen many of the pirate slaves enjoying themselves with both males and females over the last three years, Vesuvio wondered if he would soon become confused about what was the norm for human beings and what were the exceptions. When he allowed himself to dwell on the miserable conditions of his life, Vesuvio saw that he existed in an immoral and scurrilous world. He found his existence only bearable when he accepted it on a day-to-day basis. He had to discard all the values he had learned from childhood, the preparations he had made for his adult years.

As a young man on his family's estate in Campania, Vesuvio had possessed hope for his early years of manhood. Now at the age when he was supposed to have been a Centurion in the Roman army, his body was no better than a shell to him. His mind was a confusion of personal values and methods of survival.

Slavery had robbed Vesuvio of something far more important than his physical freedom. He had been taught to respect reason. Living amongst the pirates, though, he could only rely on his physical senses. He often felt that he had nothing to look forward to except an ignominious death. As much as he tried, Vesuvio could not convince himself that he was only passing through a sordid phase of his life. He felt hopelessly trapped in a netherworld fouled by every excess man had ever practised.

The straw pallet that night in the slave's barracks on Platea did not feel large enough to hold two people. Vesuvio and his Berber concubine – a short, ripe girl called Jebel – had made love once already and, although Vesuvio was tired, he still had not fallen asleep.

Love-making with Jebel precluded any active involvement for herself. Although she was more preferable than a male to Vesuvio, she was far from his ideal of a lover.

Even love-making had become debased for him. As he should have been a Centurion now in the outside world, he also should have had Julia Cordonis as his wife. He tried to forget that fact along with the idea that he might also have been a father by now. Vesuvio used the Berber girl merely to slake his physical needs.

Offering her body for Vesuvio's sexual enjoyment, Jebel always kept her eyes shut as he drove into her slit thick with coarse black hair. She stifled all passionate cries or gasps, checked any protests when he worked her enormous brown breasts, pulled her hips closer to him, or pushed her face-down on the pallet, dragging her onto his maleness as if she were made of rags.

Jebel was like many of the Berber girls who left the poverty of their families' tribes for Lucco's well-stocked pirate camp. For Jebel and the other women, love-making was a female's duty to a male. She saved her responses for Vesuvio until he had satisfied himself with her body, waiting until a man's needs were accommodated before she began to shower her generous affection on him.

Jebel now lay alongside Vesuvio in the darkness of the stone-and-canvas barracks, petting his shoulders, running her fingers through the thick growth of his beard, playing with a lock of his long hair.

Tossing restlessly on his back, Vesuvio edged his arm under Jebel's neck and brought her close to his chest. He hoped to keep her still and give himself some peace. He was not so heartless, though, as some men in the barracks who pushed their women to the floor after they had finished with them.

Now, as Vesuvio tried to sleep, Jebel began to kiss his beard, to work her tongue around his neck like a cat.

Sighing, Vesuvio feared the reason for Jebel's attention. He knew that she did not want him to make love to her again. She had confessed to him many times that no other man could make her happy, that she longed to bear his children, to serve him as a wife. Jebel wanted Vesuvio to marry her.

The gentle brushing of her lips against his beard was next accompanied by a roving hand. She traced her forefinger down Vesuvio's stomach muscle, twisted the hairs at the base of his phallus, then quickly moved her hand up to his chest to feel for any pumping of his heart.

Vesuvio turned abruptly on his side.

Curling around him, she whispered, 'Is Master comfortable?'

Vesuvio grumbled, 'Let me sleep.'

Jebel meekly offered, 'Perhaps Master wants me to sleep at his feet tonight.'

Vesuvio suddenly sat upright on the pallet and held his head with both hands. He had almost fallen asleep, slowly slipping into a dream he had been having repeatedly lately. It was almost a nightmare in which he saw himself in his room in Campania. The sunlight was streaming through the window, lighting the green, blue and yellow wall mosaic of a hunter and his boar-hound. The dream was both pleasing and disturbing to Vesuvio. He saw no beauty here on Platea. The last three years as a slave had all been sharp contrasts between the shabby and the garish. The brilliant and the profane. The discomfort of thin pallets and the glitter of stolen gold. Chunks of fresh meat turned on an outside spit in a welter of green flies. Casks of raw wine drunk from the jewel-encrusted chalice which had once belonged to a prince. Vesuvio was convinced that he would never see Villa Macrinus or his family again. He only wished that he would stop having these dreams, nightly visions which only worsened his present conditions. He could control his thoughts during the day. He wished that he could now dispose of all the dreams which conjured up his past.

Jebel asked in a loud whisper, 'Does Master want me to sleep at his feet?' She accompanied the question with a poke at Vesuvio's ribs.

He said gruffly, 'I am not your "master". Go to sleep.'

Surrounding voices in the dark of the barracks called to Vesuvio and Jebel to lower their pitch or go outside to have a fight, that some of the other people wanted to sleep, too. Many of the men in this barracks also had Berber women, females who now also called for Vesuvio and Jebel to be quiet. The men sharing pallets with one another grumbled for peace, too.

Sidling up to the warmth of Vesuvio's naked body, Jebel whispered, 'You are a master to me. Some day I know you will buy your freedom from Lucco. Then you and I will go back to my tribe. You will meet my father. He and the chieftain will give me to you.'

Slowly Jebel's fingers began to inch up Vesuvio's chest again, her other arm finding its way across his tapering back as she continued in a soft voice, 'I will wear my mother's blue mantle for the wedding. My grandmother's silver bracelets. My two sisters will weave me a bridal skirt of yellow, red and green wool. My brother will pierce my nose and his wife will give me . . .'

This talk about her family both maddened and frustrated Vesuvio. He did not know what had happened to his own brother, Titus, and here he was listening to a Berber girl talking about *her* brother piercing her nose for bridal chains! She talked freely about her father giving her away whilst Vesuvio had almost driven himself crazy worrying about his own mother and father! He did not want to hear about Jebel's relatives. He did not care how pleased they would be to see *their daughter* married.

Pushing her down to the pallet, Vesuvio said, 'Go to sleep.' Then he fell down beside her, turning over on his stomach, and laid one arm across her breasts. He hated to be cruel to this simple nomad girl but he could not sleep with her talking about a wedding which he knew would never take place, children he did not want to sire.

After a short time he heard her whispering soft words again in the darkness. He could not understand the words but he suspected they were more claims of love. He could tell by her tone. His heart sank at the idea of this love. Jebel was a loyal girl, pretty girl. She would make some man a very devoted wife. She had a strong body to bear her husband many children. But not his . . .

'I was betrothed once,' he told himself. 'That is over now. Life has changed for me. I am a slave. A pirate. An animal.'

At the far end of the barracks, a pitch torch suddenly glowed in the darkness. A voice boomed, 'The oarsman Vesuvio! Wake up! Where is the oarsman called Vesuvio!'

Groaning, raising himself up on one arm, Vesuvio blinked at the smudged brightness of the torch and irritably called, 'Down here. What do you want?'

Voices in the barracks began to grumble again as the guard strode down between the row of pallets. He held out the torch to see Vesuvio's yellow hair and full beard, saying, 'You're the one with hair like straw. Come on. Throw your wench out of bed. Lucco wants to see you.'

Vesuvio blinked. 'Lucco? Now?'

'Now,' the man repeated. He looked from Jebel back to Vesuvio and added, 'Put some clothes on your stinking body. Lucco's woman is with him. He wouldn't be much pleased to see you parading what you've got in front of her.'

As Vesuvio reluctantly rose naked from the pallet, Jebel wrapped her arms around his muscle-hard legs, begging, 'What have you done, my Master? Why are they taking you away? Why are you going to be punished?'

'I'm not going to be punished,' Vesuvio assured her, pulling a woollen tunic over his head. 'I haven't done anything . . . not that I can remember.'

Running one hand through his leonine mane, he looked down at Jebel kneeling at his feet. Her black eyes were wide with fear. He could feel her small body quivering against his leg. She was not feigning her love for him.

Nodding towards the pallet, he murmured, 'Go back to sleep.' He threw the felted covering over her naked body and turned to follow the guard outside to the dark sky glittering with stars.

Vesuvio walked soberly up the hill to the spot where the Greek temple used to stand. Now Lucco's headquarters held this highest point of the rocky island, commanding a sweeping view of the moonlit sea.

As he trudged along the chip path, Vesuvio remembered another part of his half-dream – his mother and Julia Cordonis had been carding wool in the *atrium* of Villa Macrinus. Sico had been working alongside them. Vesuvio smiled to himself, thinking how absurd dreams were, that his long-ago slave, Sico, would ever be doing a woman's job.

13

Waiting for the oarsman, Vesuvio, to be brought to his tent, Lucco picked through the heap of correspondence and military information which had travelled through intricate networks of messengers to reach Platea and had awaited him on his return. He glanced at an offer from a merchant in Syracuse to sell him fifty slaves; a brief note from a scribe in Carthage who intimated that he was willing to sell Lucco information about a villa which could be easily plundered. Next, a wax tablet too smeared to read. Then Lucco broke the seals on a scroll dated three months earlier.

'*The slave I have asked you so many times in the past to purchase on my behalf,*' Lucco began to read by the flickering oil light on his desk, '*still has not arrived at the Royal Palace here in Samosata. To refresh your memory of my requirements, the slave must be a male who has reached manhood, possess a smoothly skinned but manly body, show the qualities of leadership without being offensive in personal habits, yet be quick to cultivate the refined habits of court life preserved only here in the East. I confess that it might seem a small matter to you, My Cherished Friend and Illustrious General, but it is most important to me that this slave be not dark skinned but instead possess the light hair so frequently attributed to the tribes of . . .*'

At the sound of footsteps outside his tent, Lucco dropped the scroll to the heap of other correspondence beside him and leaned back in his cedar chair to wait for the guard to bring Vesuvio into the first vestibule of his tented headquarters.

After dismissing the guard, Lucco waved Vesuvio to come across the layered carpets into the well-lit section of his canvas warren. He saw a man who was young enough to be his son, a well-muscled slave who, despite his unkempt hair, full beard and careless tunic, was nevertheless handsome. A male who would be striking if he lived anywhere other than a pirate's hideout.

Lucco thought of two things. First, he wondered why his followers always bedecked themselves in gold like pantomime actors or, in the other extreme, let themselves become slovenly. He had noticed on occasions before tonight that Vesuvio was not among the most unkempt but still the Roman slave was never shaven and tidy.

The second thought was of the last letter he had read, the request from an old friend to send him a slave of light colouring. He saw that Vesuvio had all the physical characteristics required by the court official at Samosata but he suspected that Vesuvio was too roughly hewn to adapt to the necessary refinements of a king's palace. Never willing to sell one of his men, anyway, Lucco forgot about the letter from Samosata. He had his own plan for Vesuvio. He had caught glimpses of him in the hull of the *Ceres* and decided that he could trust him.

Before speaking to Vesuvio, though, Lucco quickly looked to see if his wife had taken any notice of this burly oarsman. Athana lay on a couch next to the desk. She was dressed tonight in a white gown, a plum-coloured robe draped around her reclining body as protection against the chill in the island air. Her long black hair was pulled to the top of her head, falling over one shoulder in a long sweep.

Continuing to toy with the end of the sweep of black hair, Athana studied a leather map spread on a fur rug in front of her couch. She did not even glance at Vesuvio.

Athana's coolness pleased Lucco. Although this yellow-haired slave held no high position in the encampment, he possessed a strong masculine presence, a handsomeness despite his shabby appearance. Lucco relaxed, realizing that Athana was still devoted only to him.

He began his late-night business in a terse voice. 'Little more than two days from here is a coastal city called Darnis.'

There were many towns and cities along the coast between Carthage and Alexandria which had been named and renamed by the Romans. Vesuvio could not keep track of them. He listened for more details.

'Darnis is Roman. But in command only. A legion is seldom

there and recently—' Lucco pointed to a document flattened on his desk by lead weights. '—someone has sold Athana proof that Darnis has a very rich temple.'

Like Rome, many provincial cities kept their treasures in a favourite temple. Also, it was not unusual for Athana to buy information from citizens within a town; men willingly opened the gates, too, for the right bribe. Vesuvio still remained silent, not even looking at Athana reclining on the couch.

Lucco continued, 'Athana will lead an attack on Darnis. She will sail in her galley, the *Lupa*. But as she has recently raised many men to her Military, she is in need of oarsmen. I want you, Vesuvio, to suggest replacements for those men. Oarsmen from the *Ceres*.'

Noticing the quizzical wrinkles in Vesuvio's brow, Lucco explained, 'Nobody knows men like someone who works alongside them. I've watched you. You don't talk much but you're always looking. Observing. I don't think you're waiting for ways to escape. You were with me at Nula. Remember Nula? Ten men tried to escape when we watered there. I admit, they had a good chance. You were near the forest with them. You could have run, too. But you didn't.'

Vesuvio slowly said in a flat voice. 'Those ten men failed.'

Lucco conceded, 'But they could have escaped. They had a very good chance. Even I didn't know that the woods there led down to the inlet where we trapped them.'

'But if they had escaped,' Vesuvio asked, his piercing blue eyes fixed on Lucco, 'where would they have run? South to the Auris Mountains? And if they could have made it across the desert that far, what would they have done once they got there?'

'They did fail. They are dead. But you – you obviously use your mind,' Lucco said. 'That's why I'm asking you to help me pick out fifty good men to sail with Athana to Darnis.'

Lowering his eyes to a small map spread on the desk to his left, Lucco pointed a stylus towards a dot that represented the island of Platea. He said, 'I will stay here in camp for a few days. In that time, Athana will move down the coast—' He pushed the stylus eastwards. '—and strike at Darnis. Then turn . . . here.'

Vesuvio began, 'If you are able to spare fifty slaves from the *Ceres*, I can help you choose them.'

Lucco held the stylus in the air, twisting it over his shoulder as he asked, ' "Slaves"? Why do you use that word? I call you "men". Yet, you say . . . "slave".'

Holding Lucco's inquisitive stare, Vesuvio answered, 'It is the correct word . . .' Vesuvio added with due respect, 'Sir.'

'Aren't you also a man?'

Vesuvio paused. He did not want to argue the points of freedom with the master who owned him. But neither did he want to pretend he enjoyed liberties which he did not have. He wanted to keep some facts certain in his brain.

Vesuvio's voice remained even as he continued, 'You are generous with your – "men", Sir. Very few leave you. Even when they can afford to . . . buy their freedom. But we are still bound to you.'

'Not by chains!' Lucco boomed.

Vesuvio lowered his head, apologizing, 'It was wrong of me to have spoken to you that way. It shall never happen again.'

'You have been educated, haven't you . . . Vesuvio?'

He answered, 'One more reason for me to recognize the importance of your authority.' He stopped himself from saying that he had tried to forget his education, that Stoic teachings confused his mind now.

'I am glad all my men aren't as pensive, as brooding, as mysterious as you, Vesuvio. I might not sleep nights.'

Vesuvio did not speak. He refrained from telling Lucco how he could not sleep at nights himself. That often the stench of the men in the barracks, the sounds of them rutting with their Berber women, the dreams he had of his family, made him wish that he would go to sleep and never awaken in the morning.

Lucco continued, 'The thing about you that troubles me, Vesuvio, is that you are the rare kind of man who *does* save to buy his freedom. You do not throw your money away on the first woman you see. You do not drop the jewels of an empress into the bosom of some camel girl.'

Smiling for the first time, Vesuvio said, 'A few months ago I was gathering salt crystals from the sea pans for you, picking olives from the wild orchards. I have not yet rowed far enough to see these garnets and sapphires I keep hearing about!'

'You will win much, Vesuvio. Your treasure will be kept safe in the strong box for your eventual decision. You can join my fighting ranks to increase your fortune. Or you . . . But I do not like losing men like you, Vesuvio. Fortunately, you are in a minority and . . .'

Shaking his head, Lucco said, 'This talk does not take us any closer to Darnis.' He looked fleetingly at Athana, who still lay engrossed in her map, fingering her long fall of black hair.

Not glancing towards the couch, Vesuvio asked, 'When does your wife plan to sail from Platea, Sir?'

'Athana departs tomorrow morning. Shortly after dawn. But the attack will not be until the following day.'

'Then the men must be picked tonight.'

'Tonight,' Lucco said, unrolling another scroll onto his desk. Beckoning Vesuvio to step alongside his carved cedar chair, he explained, 'Here are the names of all the oarsmen from the *Ceres*. See if you can put faces and abilities to each name. Choose fifty for me. I will notify them myself.'

Without looking up from her map, Athana spoke for the first time. She called in a disinterested voice, 'Lucco?'

He looked at her.

Athana nodded at Vesuvio and said, 'Forty-nine men, Lucco.'

'Oh, yes.' Lucco looked back to Vesuvio and explained, 'You will make number fifty. You go on the *Lupa* with Athana, too.'

14

Vesuvio had heard about the desert tribesmen smoking the dried leaves of the hemp plant for its intoxicating effect. He also remembered hearing as a boy about the herb called '*cannabis*'. The foreign words of '*bhang*' and '*charas*' meant little to him, though, when a few of Athana's oarsmen began to whisper them the next morning aboard the *Lupa*. He only knew they were the names for a drug which caused a strange behaviour in a man. He had not yet been informed how Athana allowed the drugs to be used for her raids – or why.

Athana descended the ladder into the *Lupa*'s hull as the men were finally settling onto the benches behind the leaded handles of their oars. Day was only breaking and many of the oarsmen from the *Ceres* were still grumbling that they had to row for Athana, preferring to stay on Platea for a rest. No amount of *charas* or gold was as tempting as three days' sleep.

Walking down the narrow wooden ramp which ran between the top tiers of oars, Athana inspected the men with a military eye. Unlike them, she was wide awake and fully dressed in her ornate battle uniform.

Athana's black mane was completely hidden now by a brass helmet fronted with a silver visor which rested on her forehead, a shining head-piece which was majestically crested with a plume of scarlet feathers. Her eyebrows were thin slits across her sun-washed face, her cheeks and jaw line strong inside the masculine contours of the brass-and-silver helmet.

Wearing a tunic made from the same red stuff as her Military's capes, Athana had cinched it tightly around her waist with a copper belt. A leopard skin was tied around her shoulders. Long leggings covered her calves and knees, over which were laced the sturdy thongs of her black leather sandals. A dagger hung in its silver scabbard from one side of her copper belt, a black leather whip coiled on the other.

Pacing down the ramp, Athana began, 'This is the first time for fifty of you men to sail with me. There are few differences from sailing with Lucco. Forget what happens on deck. My Military does the charge. In the rare chance that you are called upon to take a sword or spear, follow the same tactics you have been taught aboard the *Ceres*.'

Stopping on the ramp, she said, 'I expect no trouble from either weather or the Romans. We are sailing for a town with no garrison. A town called Darnis. My Military will conduct the fighting – but I am assured by my informer there will be no resistance.'

Looking at the oarsmen on the lower benches, she continued, 'But that does not mean you won't get your share of the spoils. I will take my customary half. The same as Lucco. A quarter will be given to my Military. The rest will be divided amongst you. You can also keep what you manage to find yourselves. If there are any women or boys that you want, you can enjoy them in Darnis. Only if time permits. Like Lucco, I take no prisoners. There is no need for prisoners. Also, those of you who chew *charas* are as responsible for your actions as those who don't.'

Walking towards the prow, she said, 'You can leave the *Lupa* and come to the harbour when you hear my Military blow the horn. You will come by groups in long-boats. At no time will this galley be unguarded. For a safeguard, I will leave one boat at sea to sound a warning in case of a Roman prowler.'

Standing with one foot on the ladder, she said, 'I mean to reach Darnis tomorrow at dawn. I warn you now that if there is any trouble, disobedience, squabbling – the same holds true on the *Lupa* as on the *Ceres*. I toss a sheep's knucklebone for your punishment. One side says "decapitation". The other, your body is flayed of its skin.'

Nodding at the hortator, Athana quickly climbed the ladder. The drum began to boom from the platform as the oarsmen slowly pulled the *Lupa* from the island harbour of Platea.

Athana had made adequate allowances for weather but the winds were behind the *Lupa*, a strong gust that eased the slaves' toil. The first night, the oars were fastened to their stays inside the hull and, after food provisions were distributed on deck, the men returned to the hull and stretched hammocks between the benches.

At that time, one of Athana's Military distributed small chunks of black resin to those oarsmen who asked for it. When the new men from the *Ceres* inquired about it, they were told that Athana allowed her men to chew this resin from the *cannabis* plant on occasions when they did not have to obey strict discipline. They could chew *charas* tomorrow.

Vesuvio took a small piece of the black drug in his hand and was told to keep it until they reached Darnis. He suspected that

Athana had personal reasons for allowing her men this liberty. He had learned that she and Lucco had ulterior purposes for everything they did. He doubted if the drug was some small concession to ease the work of their slaves.

Early the next morning, the *Lupa* moved along the sandy coastline of Cyrenaica and, as the first sunlight lit the rippling water, the pirate galley crept into the small harbour of Darnis.

As Athana had predicted, the walled town lay unprotected. No warning trumpet sounded an alarm from its parapets at the sight of the pirate galley. No balls of fire were catapulted towards the sea. Athana and her Military rowed quietly to shore in long-boats. It was at that time that some of the oarsmen first began to chew the bitter-tasting *charas*. Vesuvio was one of them.

There was no immediate effect of the drug. The men who had taken it now awaited it more eagerly than for the shrill of Athana's *litui*, the horn that would call them to share the spoils of Darnis.

A Bedouin looked out of the hole through which his oar was placed. Finally, he shouted that he saw six of Athana's Military running to a long-boat below the city walls. The horn sounded. The time had come.

The first group of galley slaves moved from their benches and climbed up the wooden ladder, swarming across the deck to descend the ropes to the long-boats which would take them ashore.

Vesuvio stood in the first crowd of pirates, crushed alongside an Athenian named Hector, a broad-shouldered man who had become one of Vesuvio's few friends in the last three years.

Hector had also chewed *charas*. He asked Vesuvio if he felt any reaction yet. Vesuvio shook his head.

The long-boat reached the shore as a group of sober-faced citizens emerged from the city's clay walls. They wore strange conical-shaped felt hats and leather skull-caps decorated with small brass bells. Their arms were piled high with offerings for the pirates, some holding golden platters and silver vessels, others bringing reed trays of fruit, vegetables, cakes.

Clambering from the boat, Hector said, 'Pay no attention to them. The good stuff is probably locked away.'

First, Vesuvio looked at the citizens grouped along the shore and, then, glanced towards the open gates in the city's wall. He saw Athana striding down towards the shore. The Military followed her with large bulging bags. Vesuvio guessed that they were carrying the riches from the temple.

He next saw Athana's men sliding her long-boat into the water. She did not glance towards the citizens, even ignoring her oarsmen flocking towards the gates. Vesuvio continued staring at her as she stepped into the boat. For some reason, he could not take his eyes from her.

Athana suddenly looked radiant to Vesuvio. Almost like a goddess. She was the most exciting female he had ever seen. He wondered why he had not noticed this before. She was desirable.

'Is this the effect of *charas*?' he asked himself. 'Why have I never seen her like this before? How can that cold, ruthless woman look so beautiful to me?'

It was then that Vesuvio felt a strange feeling spread over his entire body. His mind began to turn. The desire for Athana became mixed with other feelings. He felt as if his feet had to run with the rest of the men. He had energy that was both wild and carefree. He, too, wanted to shout. He was both happy and reckless.

The next thing that Vesuvio knew he was racing towards the cries rising inside the town. He saw a blurred flash of sienna-coloured walls, narrow streets, smashed wooden doors.

Reality became a whirlpool of images for Vesuvio. He saw oarsmen hurling pallets, benches, cushions from windows onto the cobbled alleyways. He watched old women being shoved to their knees. He stared at girls and boys being grabbed, kissed, fondled in front of their parents. He felt detached, though, from what was happening all around him.

He watched as one young father resisted three oarsmen trying to break into his house, trying to keep them from defiling his family's home. Vesuvio stared as the oarsmen began to beat the man, pounding their fists against his face until his eyes were swollen and his nose broken into a bloody pulp.

The crack of a leather whip behind Vesuvio made him turn. He saw a bearded Sicilian snapping a whip near the feet of two pale-faced women. The Sicilian called, 'Jump, you bitches!' He raised the aim of the whip towards the skirts of their linen robes.

The two women jumped.

Snapping the whip at them again, the Sicilian called, 'Start dropping your robes now. Let's see your titties bounce!' He snapped the whip again.

Slowly, the two frightened women began to reach to their shoulders.

Vesuvio moved on from this scene when the smirking Sicilian reached under his ragged tunic and began to fondle his maleness.

The narrow streets and alleyways of Darnis provided an arena for Athana's oarsmen. Vesuvio stumbled through the curving alleyways, listening to raucous laughter cut by piercing wails. His mind was too foggy to feel disgust for his fellow pirates – or have compassion for the helpless citizens.

He saw a pirate reach both hands towards a woman's ears and rip away a pair of gold rings pierced through her lobes. He slowly shook his head in astonishment as he saw a group of Athana's Military rush through a flock of hens, laughing as they stepped on the chickens as if they were ants. He wondered if he were hallucinating when he watched a pirate ram the spearhead of his shaft into a yellow dog and pitch the animal into the air.

Next, Vesuvio saw a young girl dash from the side door of a small white clay house. She had long black hair which reminded him of Athana. Or was she Athana? Was he seeing a girl of Darnis, or Athana? What was the drug doing to his mind?

Standing momentarily motionless, Vesuvio struggled to remember how he had watched Athana board the long-boat like a goddess. He recalled his lust for her.

Athana . . .

Before Vesuvio realized what he was doing, he was chasing the young girl. He did not know if he was chasing Athana or a stranger. His mind was becoming more crazed by the drug.

Catching the girl in a small stable attached to the house, he fought to keep her from escaping. She kicked at his shins. She dug her sharp fingernails at his face and arms. She pulled his hair and beard. Struggling bravely like this, though, the girl assumed more of Athana's characteristics in Vesuvio's mind. She was strong. Athana was strong . . .

Vesuvio slapped her into submission. His phallus hardened with the violent act. He laughed as she fell to the ground. Yes, he was eager to conquer Athana this way. To overpower her.

Ripping at the girl's coarse clothing, Vesuvio kneed open her legs and thrust his erect phallus downwards. Straddling the girl, he voraciously began making love to her . . . or Athana.

Athana.

Vesuvio had to make love to Athana. He pulled the girl up to him now, pressing her hips against him by one hand and holding her in submission by her long black hair, still pushing into the tightness of her vagina, not thinking of this act as rape. No. He was mastering Athana . . . Athana . . . *Athana!* He laughed louder. He shouted.

Vesuvio remained in the stable, enjoying himself as the girl struggled and fought him until he heard the *litui* first shrill outside the walls.

Next, the sound of pirates rose from the alleyways. The men were going back to the long-boats.

Panting, laughing to himself, Vesuvio joined the other men as they flocked to the harbour. He felt as if he had shared a true victory.

It was not until Vesuvio was sitting on the benches in the hull of the *Lupa* that the drug began to wear away. He was pulling at the oar but each stroke seemed more difficult than the last. His mind was becoming sober.

For the return voyage to Platea, Athana had stationed a whipman on the ramp between the oarsmen's benches. She had given him orders to lash any man who did not use all his strength to pull the oars. The cracking whip soon obliterated the carefree spirit caused by the *cannabis* resin.

Vesuvio then slowly began to suspect why Athana allowed her men to take the drug. They became crazed for sex and destruction when they were under its influence. The pirates spent little time in search of treasures. The drug heightened their appetite for violence and rape whilst keeping them from searching for extra gold, silver and jewels to put towards the price of their freedom. They would be dependent on the meagre share of the temple booty which Athana would dole out to them.

Worse than Lucco, Athana mastered her oarsmen's minds as well as their bodies. Vesuvio hated himself for falling for this ruse.

15

After the *Lupa* returned to Platea from the raid against Darnis, Athana continued to lead what she believed to be a boring, humdrum existence. She felt more miserable than any slave on Platea. She felt imprisoned by the rocky island and frustrated by her need for a sexual release from boredom. These feelings were only worsened by Lucco's ambition to be more than a pirate, to become a great military legend. He craved recognition from all the world.

Athana was thirty years younger than her husband and interpreted his hunger for greatness as the first signs of senility. She saw his diminishing appetite for love-making as an omen of impotency.

Understanding that she and Lucco could not share the same passions which they had enjoyed when he had first purchased her from the gladiatorial stables in Leptis Magna, Athana still expected some show of sexual excitement from him these days.

Lucco was built like a bull but, like many overtly masculine men with whom Athana had lain, he had let himself be sexually conquered by her. When Athana had seen that the almighty Lucco truly adored her, she was able to dominate him completely, to make him kneel between her naked legs and beg for her love, obey her commands, become passive as if he were her slave.

Then even that had stopped. It was as if Lucco had caught himself losing his masculine pride to Athana. Although he still showed respect and affection towards her, he had not come to her couch for over a year now, not even for warm fondlings or a natural consummation between husband and wife. Athana diagnosed this as Lucco desperately clinging onto his waning potency.

She had noticed, too, that Lucco was becoming more jealous of her. He did not care how she used other women. Lucco was only worried about Athana giving herself to men. As there was no one on Platea but slaves and her uncouth Military, Athana was not tempted by unfaithfulness. She saw no man whom she could respect.

Athana had changed in the years since she had been a slave at Leptis Magna. Her own ambition had become more fierce since she had entertained the provincial Romans in the arena there. In those hateful days, Athana had learned how to accept the idea of being a misfit – a woman who fought in the arena like a man needed a strong man to remind her that she was a female. It was at Leptis Magna that she had acquired her first passion for power. Lucco had helped her to nurture those seeds.

Like their counterparts in the Imperial City, the provincial Romans went to the arena for sexual titillation as well as to watch sport events. The *lanista* who owned the young but statuesque Hispanic slave-girl, Athana, believed that the sexual attraction outweighed the athletic.

The *lanista* carefully chose Athana's wardrobe for the arena. He dressed her lower torso only in the black cincture of a male and covered her on top in a thinly-ringed plate of armour which formed cups for her breasts and left her back exposed. Like a Roman soldier, Athana wore metal shin and wrist guards, and the red-plumed helmet of a Centurion. She presented both a threatening and erotic vision in the arena.

Rigorous exercises had made Athana an expert with a *gladus* but, as the city *lanistae* vied with one another over the unusual acts they could provide for the arena, other colleges began training more exotic females than they had done in the past.

Word reached Athana's college that there was a new woman being groomed to challenge her, a slave-girl who had originally worked as a *popina* in a tavern. The next report claimed that the new gladiatrix had injured herself in accelerated training to match Athana's expertise. The rival college quickly substituted another woman but, so far, neither Athana nor the *lanista* knew anything about the replacement nor her skills.

The day of the Games arrived and still no information about Athana's new opponent had reached the college. The first glimpse which Athana got of the woman was when the contestants followed the white-robed priests to the platform in front of the official podium, a ritual in which the contestants – both male and female – offered their loyalty to die in the arena in service to their governor. They next followed the priest to a central altar and stood soberly as a sheep was sacrificed to see if the omens were auspicious for the Games.

Athana immediately knew that today would be a fight without rules when she saw the large blue-black Negress glowering at her. They stared coldly at one another through the sacrificial rites, knowing that one of them had to die.

Their contest came fourth on the bill. Dressed only in a leopard skin, the black woman drew more applause from the crowd than Athana did in her glittering armour. Black slaves were rare even on the northern coast of *Africanum.*

The Negress showed little sign of gladiatorial skills. She came hurtling at Athana like a wild animal freed from its cage. Her black hair was shaved closely to her skull like a young boy-slave. The muscle bulged in her arms and naked thighs like that of a fully grown man. The only sign that she was a female was the bulge in the scant yellow-and-black animal hide tied around her torso, her breasts threatening to overflow the fur.

Athana caught the Negress's first thrust with her own sword. The two women quickly came into a hand-grip. The Negress's strong arms began to power Athana down to the sand as perspiration beaded on her inky skin.

Breaking the lock, Athana stepped to one side and the Negress fell forward to the sand. Spinning with her sword ready, Athana expected to make an easy kill, to pin down the Negress as she fell to the ground.

Having caught herself, though, the Negress crouched like a jungle cat and sprang on Athana with her blade thrust forward, this time drawing blood from Athana's arm.

Realizing that the black woman had a natural appetite for battle, Athana quickly forgot her formal *lanista*-training and prepared herself for a struggle of brute power, a raw contest for life or death.

The two women charged one another. Their swords clanked in the sun. They muttered obscene words in their own tongue. The crowd roared as Athana's foot gave way. The first nick was made against the Negress's bare shoulder. The perspiration poured from both their bodies. Drops of blood began to stain the sand.

Soon, Athana saw that her opponent was beginning to take deep gulps of air, that the Negress had not learned the importance of conserving her breath.

Pacing slowly around her, wasting more of the black woman's wind, Athana finally made the important lunge – she sliced the Negress's wrist which held her sword.

The blade fell to the ground. The Negress darted to retrieve it. Athana's foot clamped down on her hand and she moved quickly to jab the tip of her sword towards the Negress's throat.

Holding the blade there, Athana looked to the officials' podium, waiting for the Governor to signal whether the black woman should live or die.

The crowd cheered for the Negress's life. She had given them a fine show. Their response pleased Athana. Winning was enough for her today. She had hardened herself against killing but she did not want to run her blade through this particular opponent. Athana could not help but admire her. The savage woman had had little training but she possessed powers which many men even lacked. The Negress showed a passion to win, to be superior. Athana even felt a perverse sexual attraction for the powerful black woman, an inexplicable curiosity to know who would dominate whom in a love match. What kind of battle would that become? Athana could not fight someone in an almost naked state and not feel a sexual curiosity about them.

The Governor turned down his thumb, signalling for the black *gladiatrix* to die. The crowd roared its displeasure with the ruling.

Athana still waited to make the fatal stab. It was unusual for a dignitary to go against the crowd's wishes. She waited for him to reverse his position.

When the Governor did not relent, Athana firmly gripped the hilt of her sword and sent the blade through the woman's neck. Then, after quickly withdrawing the bloody weapon, she reached down and yanked the leopard skin from the Negress's twitching body.

This surprising gesture of disrobing the black woman immediately lightened the mood of the crowd. They rose to their feet and cheered, trying to catch a glimpse of the naked black woman still spurting blood in the arena.

Ignoring their wild applause, Athana strode quickly towards the exit known as 'The Gate of Life'. She had not bared the Negress's body for the crowd's pleasure. She had wanted some token from one rare female she could respect.

The leopard skin soon showed a magic for Athana. Lucco had been sitting that afternoon on the marble podium with the dignitaries. He made arrangements to buy Athana from the *lanista*. She still wore the Negress's leopard skin to this day, wrapped around the shoulders of the red tunic of the uniform she always wore on a pirate raid.

Athana saw little courage on Platea these days. Her Military lusted after gold like petty merchants. Lucco talked nonsense about becoming a military legend. Also, after the plundering of Darnis, Athana became more impatient as she listened to Lucco complain about Libyan raiders moving from the desert towards the coastline. Rumours increased about the Libyans throughout the summer and Lucco became more vexed that they would attack Platea.

Libyans! Athana fumed. Nothing but nomads! Five – even

two – years ago, she knew that Lucco would not have given even a second thought to a renegade tribe. Now he was talking about moving down the coast towards Alexandria to avoid any surprise attack by . . . Libyans!

As the summer days cooled into autumn, though, Lucco agreed that it was too late in the year to move their headquarters. They would stay in the present encampment until springtime.

Athana dreaded spending the winter on Platea but, soon, the cold winds whistled down from the north and, as Lucco still did not come to her couch, she spent the long nights with the Syrian girl, Lita, who acted as both her body servant and her lover.

Spring approached and Lucco talked again about where their next headquarters would be. He grew intent on locating now near Antipyrgus. He had received reports about a cove protected by tall boulders jutting out into the sea like impregnable towers.

The plan was ludicrous to Athana but she did not argue with her husband about running away from Libyans. She was waiting. She knew that an opportunity would provide itself as it had five years ago in Leptis Magna.

Then, just as Lucco was preparing to sail to inspect the possibility of making a new encampment near Antipyrgus, Athana heard of a fortress named Xerix. It had also been troubled by the Libyan nomads. The Roman garrison had left Xerix to pursue them into the desert.

Knowing that she must act at once, Athana carefully but quickly planned her attack against Xerix. The walled town stood on a rocky knoll overlooking the sea to the east of Platea. Athana would lead half of her Military on foot to the back walls of the town whilst her galley swept into the harbour to divert the citizens' attention. She again asked Lucco for the use of oarsmen from the *Ceres* to supplement her own galley slaves.

Lucco was planning to search out a location for the new headquarters at this same time. He needed oarsmen, too. As he also had been training new men from the labour squadrons to graduate into galley slaves, he allowed Athana to take the same fifty oarsmen she had used for Darnis.

He made only one stipulation. Since his oarsmen had last sailed with Athana, many of them had spoken about the resin she allowed them to chew. He ordered Athana to refrain from giving the *charas* to any man on the attack against Xerix. Lucco believed that even an oarsman should always be in full control of his senses.

16

When Lucco informed the fifty oarsmen from the *Ceres* that they would sail with Athana on her attack against Xerix, Vesuvio thought only about the drug which he had taken on the last expedition with Athana. He had decided never again to allow anyone to take control of his brain. The erotic image of Athana which the *charas* had awakened in Vesuvio still troubled him. He knew that it was futile to think that he could consummate his fantasy with his master's wife. He foresaw his role at Xerix as being insignificant. He did not expect to act as anything but an undistinguished galley slave. He promised himself, though, that he would keep in control of all his natural faculties. He was pleased when he heard about Lucco's stipulation.

The winter months on Platea had seen many changes in Vesuvio. He had sent Jebel away before the first cold winds began to blow from the sea. Having watched her fervour for him grow daily, Vesuvio had decided that it was both pointless and cruel for her to remain as his concubine.

Since chewing *charas* at Darnis, Vesuvio had realized what little pleasure he derived from Jebel. He was ashamed of himself for raping the girl in Darnis but the drug had also taught him that he wanted a woman with sexual vitality.

During the last days of October, Vesuvio withdrew a handful of silver from his small jar in the treasury tent and took Jebel with him on a boat which was going to the mainland to hunt for the winter fuel supply. He paid a nomad to escort Jebel to her people's tribe, giving her the silver and explaining that he could not foresee a happy future for the two of them. He insisted that it was useless to think they could live out their life as husband and wife. He could not envision himself eventually dying as a nomadic tribesman, his corpse painted red and buried in the curled fashion of the Berber people.

Vesuvio tried to explain to Jebel through her sobs that he was from a faraway land, that he had been raised to a different life. When her crying grew louder, he nodded for the muleteer to take her away into the desert.

The pirates on Platea were not possessive of their women, trading them amongst one another as readily as lewd tales. Vesuvio spent the cold winter months in promiscuity, trying new women, discovering the physical joys of laying with a corpulent girl, sometimes bedding with three different females throughout the course of one day, pursuing every sexual variation except the Eastern Vice.

Vesuvio did make one drastic change, though, in his life during the last months. At the onset of Spring, he cut his hair and began shaving his beard. The process was both slow and painful. His face was deeply scratched from the shaving but, once having obtained the former smoothness of his skin, he shaved himself regularly, the salt water and warm spring weather soon healing his scars.

Now, he regularly scrubbed his body with wood ash; he enjoyed the feeling of working a cleanliness into his face, arms, chest and legs. He dutifully laundered and mended his slave tunic. He sailed to Xerix a different man than he had been on his last voyage with Athana. His physical cleanliness and tidy clothing gave him a new confidence. He told himself that, if he had to be a slave, he did not have to be a slovenly beast. He was the master of his mind and wanted to control as much of his body as he possibly could, too.

The city of Xerix – even without the Roman garrison – quickly armed itself for a battle against the pirate galley creeping into its harbour. Fire balls sizzled into the sea around the *Lupa*.

Archers gathered on the high, white-stone battlements of the city. Athana's *litui* had not yet sounded to call the oarsmen ashore to plunder Xerix but two of her red-caped Military were bringing the slaves up on deck in anticipation of a victory.

Such conduct was foolish, Vesuvio thought. He immediately saw that it was a bad stratagem to gather the oarsmen on deck so soon. Although the *Lupa* was too far from the city for a storm of arrows to reach it, he knew that the mere sight of the oars locked in a harbour position and oarsmen gathering on deck would tell Xerix that the ship was not planning to come any closer to the wharf. Someone in Xerix might guess the truth, that Athana was leading a surprise attack at that very moment against the back walls of the city.

As a slave, though, Vesuvio could not argue with the two superiors whom Athana had left in charge of the *Lupa*. He kept his silence as the Military guards hurried to bring up the rest of the oarsmen from their benches in the hull.

Studying the grave faces of the slaves around him, Vesuvio saw that every man was sombre this morning. The atmosphere was tense. There were no drugs to raise their spirits. They waited anxiously for Athana's clarion of victory.

When Vesuvio first smelled the fire, he thought that one of the pitch balls catapulted from the city had landed aboard the galley.

Pushing towards the oarsmen clustered around the hatch, he looked frantically for a Military and began to shout, 'Fire! There's a fire on deck!'

The galley slaves began to panic at the report of fire. They could see the burning missiles landing closer to the galley. They could smell a fire smouldering but no flames rose among the ropes and sails. Everyone saw that the wooden galley was highly volatile.

Looking around him in the growing confusion, Vesuvio spotted two white figures he did not recognize running quickly along the carved railing. They wore white *djellabahs*. Each man carried a torch.

Forgetting about his low position in the pirate hierarchy, that he had been given strict orders to wait by the hatch, Vesuvio rushed after the two men. Guessing what they were, that they had probably climbed up from the harbour on the slanting oars, he shouted 'Libyans!'

He then saw the blaze that the Libyans had started. Although it was small, the flames were spreading towards the mast. He heard the confused voices of the men behind him. No one knew how to react to this surprise attack against the pirate galley itself.

Yanking the leather curtain which hung from Athana's quarters and calling for men to join him, Vesuvio rushed to beat out the flames with the curtains. He also ordered someone – anyone – to pursue the Libyans. They were scrambling down the harbour side of the *Lupa*.

Raising his eyes, Vesuvio saw a third white-clad figure crawling up the mast with another torch in one hand. Instantly, Vesuvio turned to Athana's quarters and seized the first weapon he saw – a long, leather bull whip.

'*Slave!*' a voice boomed behind him.

Hesitating, Vesuvio saw one of Athana's Military climbing up the ladder from the hull. The soldier's steel sword was drawn from its scabbard. Before Vesuvio had time to explain about the fire and the Libyans, the guard lunged towards him.

Side-stepping the blade, Vesuvio caught the man on the back of the head with the butt of the whip. He levelled the cut of his hand against the Military's neck, too, making certain that he would lay temporarily unconscious. He could not be concerned now with rank or superior officers. He had to follow his natural instincts.

Looking above him towards the Libyan scaling the mast, Vesuvio unfurled the whip over his shoulder and sent it flying upwards. The whip cracked. The leather tip caught the Libyan on his bare leg. He fell screaming from the mast, his *djellabah* fluttering like the plumage of a white bird, and then the bones of his body cracked as he hit the bank of wooden oars.

'Grab swords,' Vesuvio called to the other galley slaves who were now gathering around him. He pointed towards the strong box in Athana's quarters and, wrenching an iron rod from between the wooden dowels which separated these quarters from the deck, Vesuvio began to batter the iron lock on the weapons chest.

The air was thick with smoke as the second Military appeared from the hull. Vesuvio shouted to him, 'Libyans – They started a fire – Some have just escaped overboard.'

The second Military did not contest Vesuvio's sudden leadership. He joined in the handing-out of weapons to some of the slaves, ordering others to lower long-boats from the stern to pursue the Libyans now swimming ashore.

Still armed with the bull whip in one hand and holding the iron rod in the other, Vesuvio reached the dowel railing as more Libyans – he counted eight – were scaling the oars with daggers in their clenched teeth. He stabbed the rod at the first of them, casting his whip at the others as they scurried along the banks of oars protruding from the galley's bulwark; they balanced themselves by their hands as their bare feet clung to the oak shafts like claws.

A high-pitched warble filled the air. One of the Libyans threw back his head and made the eerie noise by both wailing and working his tongue between his lips. Vesuvio looked from him to the other men in time to see a dagger flying towards him.

He side-stepped the dagger's aim and slashed the whip farther out over the side of the galley. His mind raced with the facts of this surprise attack. He realized that the men represented only a small corps of Libyans. The Roman garrison were most likely chasing the majority of them into the desert. These nomads had planned to harass Xerix themselves in the Romans' absence but, instead, they had found the *Lupa* in the harbour. Although the pirates greatly outnumbered the Libyans, they could cause serious damage to the galley if they were allowed to scale the slanting oars.

Turning to the galley slaves on deck, Vesuvio shouted, 'Go below to your benches. Don't row! Just heave! Heave the oars up and down! Chop them in and out of the water! Now!'

As the men quickly ran to the ladder, Vesuvio snapped his whip towards the oars again, still trying to keep the Libyans at bay. A swarthy man in a *djellabah* rushed at him. Vesuvio only saw the silky black of his moustache before he swung the rod of iron against his chest, sending him clattering down the oars.

As more of the nomads now began to cry in the piercing warble, inching their way closer towards the bulwark, the oars finally began to rise from their downwards position. The movement became faster. Soon, they were chopping up and down, tumbling the Libyans into the water. They continued to rise and fall even after the Libyans had splashed into the sea, catching their bodies now with all their forest of oars.

From the deck, Vesuvio also saw that Athana's long-boats had circled around both the stern and prow of the *Lupa*. The Military wielded swords and lances, slicing at the Libyans. The clear-blue water of the Xerix harbour quickly began to darken with pools of blood.

Turning from the railing to look across the empty deck towards the city for any sign of Athana and her men, Vesuvio froze when he saw the crouched body of a man. He wore a red cape. He was kneeling over a sword. It was the same man – the red-caped Military – who had tried to stop him from first leading the slaves in the protection of the *Lupa*. He had killed himself on his own sword. Vesuvio knew that his fortune was changing. A free man had committed suicide rather than face the consequences of having tried to stop a slave from saving the pirate galley.

Athana soberly studied the ten Libyans whom the pirates had not killed but brought to the deck of the *Lupa* for her inspection. She had left Xerix when the oarsmen had not come ashore at the sound of the *litui*. Athana's attack had been successful but that glory was now overshadowed by the report of the Libyans' surprise attack against the galley. Even worse news for Athana was that one of her élite red-caped soldiers had committed suicide during battle whilst a mere galley slave led the men. She had already ordered the coward's body to be thrown overboard in the harbour of Xerix.

Looking at the shambles on the deck, then back to Vesuvio, she asked, 'What is your name, oarsman?'

'Vesuvio,' he answered, realizing for the first time that he had endangered his life for Athana. He had never suspected that he would go so far beyond his lowly duties. He only knew that he had acted as if for himself.

'"Vesuvio",' she repeated. 'You're from the *Ceres*. One of Lucco's men. I remember now. You were with me at Darnis. But—' She hesitated, saying in a softer voice, 'You had a beard. Your hair was long.'

Nodding, Vesuvio turned back towards Athana's quarters to explain why he had torn down the leather curtain, that he had also taken one of her whips to stop a Libyan from crawling up the mast. He had broken the lock on the weapons chest, too, and spoiled the dowelling.

Holding her arm to Vesuvio, Athana said, 'All that is nothing. You have saved much more. You do not have to go to the city with the rest of the men . . . Vesuvio. I'll give you my share of the spoils. That is my contribution to a man who has acted bravely for me. Lucco will want to do even more.'

Letting her eyes drop down his heaving chest, his large hands hanging by the uneven hem of his tunic, the brush of yellow down on his brawny thighs, she said soberly, 'You did not act like a slave at all, Vesuvio. You have the soul people look for in a . . . master.'

17

Athana's galley returned to Platea late the next afternoon and, although Lucco was still away on the *Ceres* searching out a new headquarters, the island encampment soon became alive with activity. Night-time came and fires blazed in front of the many stone barracks. Festive lambs slowly turned on the spits, their juices dripping and sizzling on the embers. The air was filled with laughter, the jangle of tambourines, and songs from the Berber concubines who were jubilant to have their men safely home from Xerix.

The presence of ten Libyan prisoners in camp also added to tonight's excitement. Athana had ordered her Military to decapitate the Libyans at tomorrow's sunrise. She would string their heads together on a rope like pearls on a wire, put the rope around the head of a horse and take the animal to the mainland where it would be sent into the desert as a warning to all tribes planning any attacks against the pirates.

Before the horse was strung with its bloody garland, though, Athana told her men that they were free to amuse themselves with the Libyans. Prisoners were rare on Platea and Athana gave the pirates permission to satisfy their appetites on them, mutilating, flaying, disembowelling their bodies in whatever manner they chose – but to leave the heads undamaged for the beading of tomorrow's rope.

Vesuvio sat alongside Hector the Athenian on a log in front of a fire. They had only briefly witnessed the initial flaying of the Libyans' skin, watching how each prisoner's legs and arms were pegged down to the ground and his body dowsed with a cauldron of boiling water. Next, large boulders were placed on the screaming victims' bodies, the sharp edges of the rocks making the initial cuts into the skin softened by the boiling water.

The pirates eagerly tossed coins to see who would enjoy the first removal of the skin with a knife – 'heads', they could peel the hide from the flesh like dried skin off sun-blisters; 'ships', they would have to wait until a body was half-flayed before they could slit open a Libyan's stomach, cut-off his testicles to use the pouch as a treasure sack, batter a victim's knees to rip-off the shin- and feet-bones more easily from the legs and use them for making musical instruments.

A frenzied madness spread through Platea tonight as the pirates vented their appetite for cruelty. Vesuvio had seen that the oarsmen were the most savage of all the pirates, men usually kept in a galley's hull and away from the main action of an attack. He felt ashamed when they praised him for first spotting the Libyans aboard the *Lupa*. They said that without him they would not be enjoying these pleasures.

'You are a hero,' Hector said to Vesuvio as he passed him a wineskin in the light of their fire.

Listening to the distant shrieks of agony intermingled with the gay songs rising from the many bonfires, Vesuvio confessed, 'I don't much care for the victory cries. I keep wondering if this would be happening if Lucco were here.'

'Lucco doesn't approve of torture,' Hector said, holding the wineskin above his mouth. After swallowing a red jet of wine, he wiped his lips and said, 'But he also would have felt very humiliated if he lost a ship to a band of Libyans.'

They both looked across the flames of the fire as one of Athana's Military stalked towards them.

The red-caped pirate grunted, 'Vesuvio? Athana wants to see you.'

Nudging Vesuvio, Hector joked, 'She wants to start giving you your reward.'

Rising from the log, Vesuvio said, 'Count the heads strung around the horse's neck tomorrow morning. See if mine is there, too.'

Vesuvio left Hector, following the guard through the patches of fire, climbing the hill towards the dark outline of the spreading canvas walls and pegged roof of Athana's tent.

Entering the first section of the dimly lit tent, Vesuvio saw Athana lying on a couch beyond a curtain of ribbons. The guard nodded for him to proceed alone from this point. Parting the ribbons with one hand, Vesuvio smelled sandalwood perfume. He saw a large tray of meat, fruits, almonds and cakes laid on the floor next to Athana's couch. The mood here was calm compared to the wild abandon of the camp; the music and shouting down the hill were barely audible.

Athana motioned to the tray of delicacies, asking, 'Have you eaten?'

Vesuvio nodded, transfixed by the difference in Athana now as she lay on the couch and the woman he remembered from the *Lupa*. Her black hair fell to her shoulders, her breasts hung free under a thin white robe, and her legs and feet protruded temptingly from under the clinging fabric.

Holding a silver goblet to him, Athana said, 'The wines here are new and green. Have some with me, anyway.' She held out her goblet towards a brass flagon, saying, 'Refill mine, too.'

Squatting beside the couch to fill both the goblets, Vesuvio gave one to Athana. He took the other for himself and said, 'Thank you.'

Raising the goblet to her lips, Athana sipped as she kept her dark eyes on him. Lowering the goblet, she asked, 'Do you know what you'll do if you can buy your freedom . . . Vesuvio?'

The sound of his master's wife saying his nickname so casually was strange to him. He answered, 'Your husband paid a large price for me. It will take a long time before I see that much gold.'

'I offered you my share from Xerix.'

'Even if it's enough to repay Lucco for my freedom, I wouldn't have anything left to equip myself for the world. I don't mean to start out life again as a beggar.'

'Wouldn't you consider staying on with us? As a free man, you could amass a great fortune.' Athana rose.

Also rising to his feet, Vesuvio said, 'Your husband will have to decide that.'

'Lucco will be grateful for what you did at Xerix. He was the one who dreaded the Libyan scum. I told him . . . '

Momentarily, Athana looked as if she was about to divulge a secret to Vesuvio but, stopping, she reached to fill her own goblet.

Setting down the flagon on a small brass table, she said, 'We are alone, you know.'

Vesuvio knew that Athana meant more than the words she had just said. He waited for her to elaborate.

'Leaders,' she explained. 'People who know how to excel in a crisis. There are very few of us in the world.'

He did not speak. The only thing he knew was that his phallus was hardening under his cincture. If she had invited him here to arouse him, she was very successful.

Looking at him and then down to her goblet, she quietly asked, 'Do you want more wine?'

'I can wait for wine . . . Athana.'

Slowly setting down the goblet on the table, she said, 'You are a very confident man.'

Then, raising her eyes to him, she slowly fell back on the

couch and murmured, 'I admire confidence, Vesuvio.' She held one arm to him, inviting, 'I would like you to share it with me.'

As Vesuvio sank down on top of Athana's warm body, she immediately wrapped him in her arms, whispering, 'I need a man like you. I need a man who is strong. I know you are very strong, Vesuvio.'

He was kissing her cheek now, brushing the smoothness of her face with his lips as one hand began to explore her breasts and he pressed his groin against her body as she raised herself towards him. The wine he had been drinking all evening obliterated any concern about Lucco, only fuelling a passion to enjoy the one woman on Platea he had ever wanted.

Their tongues met, Athana's mouth tasting sweet to Vesuvio as he explored deeply inside it. Her body thrust harder up against him. Her robe opened and her breasts spread between them.

Vesuvio's mouth moved from Athana's lips, kissing the skin on her neck, down her throat, and finally to the fullness of her naked breasts. He knelt back on the floor to lift the tunic over his head and then returned to her body, circling each nipple with his tongue, listening as she groaned pleasurably with each nibble of the dark pinkness.

Vesuvio's phallus was now throbbing for love. He moved assuredly over Athana's body, spreading her legs with one knee and holding her breasts as he resumed kissing her mouth. She held him in her arms, her legs wrapped around him, repeating, 'I need a strong man . . . a very strong man.'

Vesuvio began to sink his first drive into her, excited to have a woman at last who responded to his sexuality, became an active partner in the union.

Taking him with increasing excitement, Athana whispered into his ear, 'I want Lita to join us for a while . . . only a short time . . . Do you mind?'

He answered, 'Anything you want. Anything you need.'

Athana called in a soft voice, 'Lita! Lita!'

The young servant girl appeared quickly from behind a curtain and, shedding her robe, she moved obediently towards the couch.

Holding one arm to the sober girl, Athana pulled her towards them, saying softly, 'Lita, I want you to help me make this man very happy. He is very strong, Lita.'

Pulling Lita down farther between herself and Vesuvio, Athana whispered to him, 'I want Lita, my slave, to feel your power.' Moving over on the couch without allowing Vesuvio's phallus to fall from her, Athana embraced Lita with one arm and held the other arm around Vesuvio. Lita's small mouth joined theirs in a kiss. The three tongues intertwined, licking at one another. Lita soon fell deeper in between Athana and Vesuvio.

Soon, Athana allowed Vesuvio's hard phallus to slip from her own warm moisture and made room for Lita to lay in her position on the couch.

Lita now rested under Vesuvio, catching his phallus between her small brown legs as Athana knelt beside the couch, watching the act and asking, 'Are you enjoying the beautiful man, Lita? Do you like him overpowering you? Do you like his thickness? He is not too big for you, is he, Lita? Do you like your mistress's new lover using you for his slave, too?'

With her eyes closed, the girl slowly nodded her head.

Vesuvio drove deeper into the girl. She was very small to accommodate his large proportions but she did not complain or cry for him to stop. When she opened her eyes it was only to look devotedly towards Athana as Vesuvio slicked deeper into her tightness.

'Come kiss your mistress now, Lita,' Athana urged as she rose towards the couple.

Lita immediately wrapped her arms around Athana's neck, covering her face with desperate kisses.

Athana asked the girl, 'Shall we show the strong man how you serve me?'

Looking intensely at Athana, Lita did not answer.

Rising to stand next to the couch, Athana protruded the brown patch between her legs towards Lita's mouth. She ordered, 'Taste where the man drove into your mistress. Moisten me with your own mouth, Lita. Eat from your mistress. Prepare me for my new master.'

As Lita obediently moved her mouth towards the vagina, Athana leaned forward to join Vesuvio in feverish kisses as he continued to drive his phallus between the slave girl's legs, and as she performed oral satisfaction on her mistress.

Pulling her mid-section back from Lita, Athana said, 'You can go now, Lita. Return to your pallet behind the curtain. Lie there and listen to this beautiful man making love to me. Listen to your mistress give herself to this man like you give yourself to me. Go. I want my new master alone.'

Taking Athana's hands and kissing her fingers, Lita slid out from under Vesuvio. She surrendered her position to Athana and crept quietly away from the couch.

Before Vesuvio slid his hardness back into Athana, she called to the slave girl, 'Watch me eat this man's strength, Lita. Watch Athana become a slave like you.'

Vesuvio raised himself for Athana to take his phallus in her mouth. She swallowed the taste of Lita's femininity from him, and, after smearing him with more saliva, she joined her own mouth to his.

Their bodies were once again locked together in a tight embrace, their mouths pressed together, their arms encircling one another.

Athana began whispering to him again, confessing, 'Your strength is power to me, Vesuvio. I need to feed on you. I needed someone like you for a long time. You are no slave. You are a master. My master. I need you . . . Vesuvio.'

Clamping his mouth to hers, Vesuvio stopped her words as he felt his maleness gripped tighter by the warmth of her vagina. He did not want to hear her speech. It was enough that they should share the same dream, that he should finally overpower the aloof and almighty Athana.

Sitting on a rocky knoll in the morning's faint light and overlooking the small harbour at Platea, Vesuvio watched the sentinels at their posts waiting to see the sails of the *Ceres*. He had not gone back to his barracks after leaving Athana's tent only a few hours ago.

Vesuvio felt spent this morning but not tired; he was exhausted from long hours of love-making with Athana but revitalized by the excitement of laying with a woman with such sensual expertise. There was no comparison between her accomplished love techniques and the awkwardness of Berber girls. Vesuvio had forgotten what it was like to be with a woman who wanted more than conjugal love – or gold – from a man. Athana had reawakened the powers of being a man in Vesuvio.

Having always trusted his intuition, Vesuvio listened to the voice inside himself this morning. He knew that his life was going to change in the very near future. He did not know if that change involved being raised to Athana's red-caped Military. He doubted it. Neither did he think that Athana was going to become his permanent lover. Such an arrangement would be too dangerous for a slave. Regardless of what Athana had told him on her couch, he was still in bondage to her husband. He was master only in Athana's mind.

Vesuvio had long ago suspected that Athana had an appetite for danger and he wondered this morning if that excitement included making love to him the night before her husband was due to return to Platea.

Athana was perverse by most women's standards. Vesuvio remembered how she had included the Syrian slave-girl, Lita, in the first stages of their love-making last night. Thinking back now to the sight of the two naked female bodies pressing together, then pulling him into their embrace, made his maleness stir again in his cincture as he watched the golden dawn spread on the Mediterranean. He realized that he had never been with a female so totally uninhibited as Athana.

Vesuvio knew that some women liked to be taken by force, even physically abused, to achieve sexual satisfaction. He had not beaten Athana, not inflicted physical pain on her. She had not wanted that. She had only wanted a man to dominate her. She was a very strong woman. Her strength had strangely revitalized Vesuvio's powers, too.

A trumpet sounded on a far promontory of the island. Vesuvio looked towards the rising sun and saw the square sail of the *Ceres* approacheing Platea, the three banks of oars lifting and lowering in neat precision. He thought how not long ago he had manned one of those very oars – *Why do I think those days are over?*

A succession of trumpet blasts soon spread the announcement of Lucco's arrival home. Bleary-eyed pirates staggered from their barracks. Tousle-haired women followed the men with blankets thrown around their naked bodies. Dogs began to bark. The encampment quickly awakened from its stupor to greet Lucco and hear the news of where they would move from here.

The *Ceres* soon lowered its oars at the mouth of the rocky harbour, a rowboat bringing Lucco to shore. Calling greetings to the people waiting for him on the bank, Lucco assured them that he had good news to tell, that he would share it with them when he removed his armour, bathed, had some breakfast in his tent.

Vesuvio remained at a distance, watching Lucco climb the steep hill to his headquarters. He did not see Athana throw open the front flap to welcome him. That did not surprise Vesuvio. Athana never behaved like a devoted wife.

Vesuvio was surprised, though, to see the Syrian girl, Lita, emerge from the crowd of people following Lucco to the flaps of his hilltop tent.

Watching Lucco put one arm around Lita's neck, Vesuvio saw him stop for a brief moment to listen as the girl spoke to him.

After Lita hurriedly departed, Lucco turned one last time to wave to his pirates and, pulling back the flap, he entered the tent.

Smelling smoke from the early morning fires being built around the camp, Vesuvio decided that he should eat his breakfast now, too. He doubted if Lucco would give his announcement until midday.

He stopped. He felt his face. He had stubble on his cheeks and chin. Yes, he would shave and bathe, wash the perspiration from his hair before he ate his breakfast. Regardless of what happened to him in the next few days or months, he must remember that he was – apart from anything else – a man.

*

A slack mood began to spread through camp during the ensuing hours, an uncharacteristic lack of order even in the pirates' preparations for breakfast. Vesuvio sensed this feeling of uncertainty. That nobody knew about the future of their lives. Where they would go from Platea. He remembered that this was always the mood during the time when Lucco disrupted one camp and moved to another.

As the firesites were still strewn with food from last night's debauched festivities, many men swatted away the swarms of green flies and sated their hunger with chunks of bread, cheese, greasy meat left exposed throughout the night. Soon, the pirates and their women began to take positions on the hill in front of Lucco's headquarters, making themselves comfortable on goatskins for the long wait for the midday anouncement.

Clean-shaven, with his hair dried by the sun in curling tangles against his skull, Vesuvio took a lone position back from the main throng of men and women. He sat on the weathered capital of a Doric column from the ancient temple of Platea. He could see both the rear and front flaps of Lucco and Athana's headquarters. He spotted two of Athana's Military enter the tent through the rear flap. They soon departed and, only moments afterwards, the front flaps of the tent were thrown open.

Lucco emerged from the tent. He had an angry expression on his face. Seeing the crowd of devoted followers waiting on the hillside, his scowl quickly changed into a strained smile.

But even when the people cheered him, Lucco did not acknowledge them with his usual aplomb. He looked disturbed, suddenly vexed. Also, Athana was not beside him as she always was on such occasions. Vesuvio first became alerted to trouble by this fact.

Keeping an eye on the back flap of the tent, Vesuvio listened as Lucco began to address the men.

He called in a clear voice, 'It is selfish of me to keep you good people waiting. I will tell you the news now.' He silenced their cheers with outstretched hands, calling, 'The Roman fleet has been divided! Emperor Trajan has called for more Roman ships to aid him. To put an end to the long war with the Dacians. But—'

Lucco raised his arms again as he strode down the hillside between the crowd, '—But across the Mediterranean, to the north, an uprising of Cilician pirates has diverted the remaining patrol . . .'

The men and women began rising to their feet, crowding around Lucco, eagerly listening for details.

Lucco explained, 'The Romans are chasing the Cilicians around every island in the Aegean. Probably all the way to Sicily. We have their coast – and the entire coast of Lycia – all to ourselves!'

A cheer surrounded Lucco.

Holding up his hands, he called, 'So here are my plans. I will leave Platea immediately! Tomorrow! The *Ceres* will take the coastal route along Alexandria, Caesarea, Tyrus. And after the camp here is dismantled, the *Lupa* will cut directly across the Mediterranean, sailing north to Cilicia!'

A louder cheer went up from the crowd, '*To Cilicia!*'

Lucco raised his hands to quiet them again. 'We all will meet in Cilicia. We will have a distribution of gold!'

The surrounding cheers grew wild.

Lucco boomed, 'But the good news is not only mine. Athana tells me . . . My wife just told me about the success at Xerix. A success of plunder and . . . *and* you have brought me Libyans! I hear I have my slave "Vesuvio" to thank for spotting a fire aboard the *Lupa* – for leading a brave defence. I want to repay that slave!'

'Slave'? Vesuvio tensed at the mention of the word. He remembered Lucco asking him why he insisted on calling himself a 'slave'. What had Athana told him? Why was Lucco suddenly calling him a 'slave'?

'To show my gratitude to Vesuvio – as well as to my other brave men who rowed for the *Lupa* – they all will sail aboard the *Ceres* again – but not as oarsmen! I am making plans to incorporate them into a new group of fighting men – the Military of Lucco!'

The crowd cheered Lucco's announcement. He quieted them again, though, continuing, 'We first have work to do this morning. To dispatch the heads of the Libyans back to their people. To show them – and all the desert marauders – that Lucco's men are strong. And . . . unified!'

Vesuvio felt a hand on his shoulder. He turned and saw a guard in a red cape who announced soberly to him, 'Athana wants you in her tent.'

At that moment, Vesuvio knew his premonition would prove to be true, that his life would soon be changing.

18

The interior of Athana's tent was in shambles. The couch lay on its side. The carpet had been kicked into heaps and scattered with a disarray of cushions. Bowls and jars had been smashed into bits. Pieces of dead charcoal from the brazier were spread across the floor.

Athana stood in the midst of the confusion, her black hair spreading wildly around her face, her black eyes crazed with fury. Her appearance – like the condition of the tent – had altered drastically in the few hours since Vesuvio had left here.

Seeing Vesuvio move towards her from the back flap of the tent, Athana ran to throw her arms around him, crying, 'He knows! Lucco knows! I do not know who told him we made love last night but he knows everything!'

Unclasping her arms from behind his neck, Vesuvio said, 'It was foolish for you to send for me.'

'No. We are safe. He has gone to look at the Libyans.'

Clenching her hands, Athana wailed, 'He even got angry about the prisoners! That I allowed the men to punish them! He struck me! Lucco struck *me*!'

Vesuvio said, 'He didn't seem angry outside.'

'Ha! I heard that speech! Cunning but cowardly. Lucco is

nothing but a coward . . . a coward . . . a coward.' She began to kick at the cushions, throwing silver goblets, ripping at silk panels richly embroidered with Egyptian motifs.

Grabbing her by the wrist to subdue her, Vesuvio said, 'Keep calm. He has spies. He will know I'm here now. I can't stay with you.'

She scoffed, 'I know who his spies are. They are in my pay, too. No, there is only one other person who knew you were with me last night. Only one person.'

'Lita.'

'Yes. But Lita is too loyal to betray me. She would never tell anyone about me. You saw for yourself how Lita worships me. She's my adoring . . . slave!'

Vesuvio remembered seeing Lita approaching Lucco this morning on his arrival at the tent. He decided to omit that detail. What would more revenge serve?

Instead, he said, 'You heard Lucco say, then, that I am to sail with him again on the *Ceres*.'

'Yes! And that I am to take another course across the Mediterranean. He will take the long coastal route and I am to sail due north.'

'You will only make him more angry if you fight him.'

'Fight him? He has already threatened to *sell* me!'

Vesuvio finally knew that the story he had always heard about Athana still being a slave was true. Lucco owned his wife as if she were his chattel.

Wringing her hands in frustration, Athana paced around the tent, ranting, 'What proof do I have that I earned my freedom from Lucco? Are there law courts for pirates? Laws to uphold the fact that I bought myself back from him a thousand times over?' She drove the heel of one bare foot at the brass table, sending it flying across the tent.

Looking back to Vesuvio, she threw her arms around him again, pleading, 'I want us to stay together. Just the two of us. Two young, strong people commanding our own entire . . . fleet!'

Unclasping her hands again from around his neck, Vesuvio said, 'That would be impossible.'

'Impossible at the moment, yes. Lucco would even bribe my own men to turn against me now. He is determined to punish me. He knows I have been unhappy here. That jealous pig knew for a long time that I would form an alliance with another man as soon as I found one. And I have!'

Raising both hands through the tangle of her black hair, she mused, 'Athana and Vesuvio! Vesuvio and Athana!'

Vesuvio glumly added, 'Vesuvio and Athana . . . two slaves.'

'Slaves? I hate that word. I hate slaves! I am a master! A mistress! I am Athana! And I will kill . . . I will kill because of this. I will kill . . . She reached for a dagger and began slashing at the sides of the tent.

Vesuvio shouted, 'Athana! Control yourself. We must think about our lives!'

'My life?' she asked bitterly, still holding the dagger in her hand. 'What does my life matter if I'm a slave? A slave to an impotent master? No, I will kill. I will . . . kill. But, first, I will do as the stupid, impotent Lucco commands. I *will* sail across to Cilicia. I *will* meet him at that northern coast. But I will get my revenge. You will see. You will see, Vesuvio. By the time you arrive with Lucco aboard the *Ceres*, I will be waiting. I will be ready for him. I will have my men totally devoted to me. To Athana! I will be stronger than Lucco ever hoped to be! There will be a battle between us. A battle – oh, such a battle . . .'

Stopping, lifting the knife, she shrieked, 'Lucco! How I hate his impotency. His vain dreams. His cowardly honour.' She began slashing the walls again, cursing Lucco, his failings, his treachery, his jealousy.

Backing away from Athana, Vesuvio moved towards the rear flap and left her raging in the tent.

19

The *Ceres* set out from Platea the next morning, travelling along the southern periphery of the Mediterranean. Vesuvio noticed that Lucco kept his oarsmen at a leasurely pace, that he always stopped before sundown, never charting a course by the stars, showing no anxiety to reach his ultimate destination of Cilicia on the northern shores of the Mediterranean.

No further word had been mentioned about raising Vesuvio and the other oarsmen to a new fighting corps. Neither did Lucco send them below deck to take a place again on the benches of the *Ceres*. Vesuvio slept in the sailors' berths, spending the days like an idle passenger.

The first two days of the voyage, Lucco stayed alone in his cabin, seldom mingling with the sailors on deck and always avoiding Vesuvio. He still had not thanked him personally for the defence of the *Lupa* at Xerix.

This solitude gave Vesuvio time to contemplate Lucco's curious activities, wondering why he had evacuated Platea so hurriedly, leaving Athana and her crew to dismantle the encampment, and now keeping the *Ceres* at a snail's pace.

The third day at sea, the *Ceres* moved northward from Alexandria, their water casks and provisions replenished, sailing towards the city of Tyrus on the eastern shore.

Vesuvio was standing alone on deck, the yellow coastline of Syria now visible from the railing. He did not hear Lucco approach him.

Lucco's first words gave Vesuvio a start. He looked to his right and saw Lucco gazing mistily towards the shoreline, saying, 'Trajan hopes to push the border of the Roman Empire past Syria. To encompass the greatest area Rome has ever known. Trajan has dreams of becoming mightier than Alexander the . . . Great.'

Lucco stood motionless, his thick arms folded over his brass chestplate as he continued to stare into the distance. Vesuvio had never seen the pirate lord looking so alone, so desolate, so old and forlorn.

Speaking in the same lost vein, Lucco continued, 'Men like Trajan and Alexander, even Hannibal – they never allowed themselves the luxury of love. Like Alexander, Trajan is married. That is expected of a great man. Also, like Alexander, Trajan satisfies himself with boys. But true love?' Lucco shook his head.

Vesuvio asked, 'Are you saying that a man who loves cannot also be great?'

'Love saps energy. Neither does love endure.'

'Where is the empire of Alexander today?'

Gripping his fists, Lucco said in a surge of passion, 'But Alexander knew greatness. He tasted power. He went beyond Syria. He conquered Mesopotamia. Persia. So will Trajan.'

Vesuvio calmly said, 'Trajan has to finish what he has begun in Dacia before he can start marching eastwards towards Persia.'

Lucco shook his head. 'Trajan is left only with small matters in Dacia. Like settling differences between the princelings. Trajan knows that he has defeated King Decabulus.'

'So why divide his fleet?' Vesuvio asked. 'Rally half of the ships through the straits of Babylon?'

Lucco sneered, 'Trajan did not divide the Mediterranean fleet.'

Staring at Lucco's placid face, Vesuvio realized what Lucco was implying. He slowly began. 'Then Athana is sailing directly into a trap which . . .'

Stopping, he turned away from Lucco and said, 'I see. You are trying to free yourself from love.'

Lucco did not immediately reply. The waves tossed gently around the *Ceres*, an empty silence echoed beyond the steady dipping of the oars.

Finally, Lucco spoke. 'Some slaves are marked with hot irons. I fell in love with a woman who did the same to me in her way. A branded slave can be set free. He can try to hide his gruesome mark. But he still knows it's there. He knows that he is imperfect. Incomplete. Marked.'

Lucco clasped his hands behind his back, continuing in a sombre voice, 'I always knew that Athana would betray me some day. I was not jealous of her body. It was her devotion I guarded. At one time I knew that I was the only man who could give her what she desired. Even as a slave at Leptis Magna, Athana was magnificent. She was neither man nor woman, male nor female. She became my soul mate. I even encouraged her hours spent with slave-girls like Lita. She used women as an outlet for her masculine tastes, objects for her dominance. They were food for her, like they are to men.'

In growing agitation, Lucco faced Vesuvio and said, 'You see, Lita was more jealous of Athana's body than I was. I only wanted Athana's trust, her total devotion and loyalty. But Lita became jealous when she saw a man use Athana in the same way that Athana used her.'

Vesuvio asked, 'That is why Lita told you about Athana and myself.'

'Lita was jealous of you using her mistress's body.'

Vesuvio calmly asked, 'And you?'

Letting his arms fall to his sides, Lucco said, 'Even as I talk to you now – you, the only man who has ever made a cuckold of me – I cannot get angry at you. Not angry like a jealous husband. Yet—'

Vesuvio waited.

In a firmer voice, Lucco said, 'Neither can I give you your freedom. You have more than earned it by your actions at Xerix. But I cannot allow you – the one man who is able to give Athana satisfaction she no longer finds with me – I cannot allow you your freedom . . . slave. Especially not after Athana served you as her master. I have been betrayed personally by the pair of you.'

Vesuvio stood staring at the waves. The coastline of Syria looked closer to him now. Instead of wondering if the *Ceres* was making its way to the shore, he thought about his slavery. Had he really expected to be offered freedom?

Lucco explained, 'Nor can I allow you to remain in my fleet. The mere sight of you would only remind me that I had suffered a private defeat. That I had been discarded by Athana. That I am getting old. That soon I will . . .'

Vesuvio waited.

In a firmer voice, Lucco said, 'Athana will sail directly into a Roman fleet. If she has guile, if the *Lupa* and her leopard skin are truly lucky for her, she will escape the trap.'

'You are willing to sacrifice those men, the galley, the equipment and gold aboard—'

'And Athana!' Lucco shouted, glaring at Vesuvio. 'I am risking her life, too!'

Then, turning back to the sea, Lucco said, 'As for you, Vesuvio – the first slave to conquer my wife, the only man to give Athana enough strength to think of abandoning me – I have had very serious thoughts about you. There is no question that death is the only way to deal with a traitor.'

Vesuvio stood solemnly.

Lucco continued, 'Death is the only way to repay a traitor . . .' Turning to Vesuvio, he said, 'But you did not betray me in battle. No, in fact, you helped to add to the glory of my fleet. But then you involved yourself in my private life. And, consequently, as a man who's always held the greatest esteem for military principles, I am not going to condemn you to death. I am going to deal with you in another way. I have made arrangements for you to be sold. I have an acquaintance in the Court of King Abgar in Samosata. He is meeting us at Tyrus. His name is Zeno. He is the Chief Eunuch for the great king called Abgar. You will be sold to Zeno the Chief Eunuch. No one will ever know that you have been taken across the Syrian desert to Mesopotamia.'

Turning away from Vesuvio, Lucco walked back to his cabin, leaving Vesuvio staring at the orange parapets and high towers of Tyrus now in view from the *Ceres*.

Book Four
Mesopotamia

20

Zeno the Chief Eunuch could not understand how his pirate friend, Lucco, had thought that this ruffian slave could possibly be of any use to his ruler, the Great King Abgar. The dusty caravan had been travelling for five days now since leaving the port of Tyrus. The camels and oxen-drawn carts had inched their way up the eastern shore of the Mediterranean; cutting away from the sea, they headed northeast across the Syrian desert on their way to Mesopotamia – the valley of the Tigris and Euphrates Rivers . . . and the Royal Palace at Samosata.

During those five days, Zeno still had not recognized any remarkable attributes in this strangely named Roman slave, Vesuvio.

Zeno was at least thankful for the season. Summer was near and the King always suffered his vapours in the summer. Zeno might not have to produce Vesuvio to the King immediately on their arrival in Samosata. He could keep the yellow-haired slave in seclusion, spending more hours in an attempt to polish him for his intended position in King Abgar's court.

In more desolate moments of the caravan's trek through the Syrian desert, Zeno wondered if he had been too eager to accept this golden-haired brute from Lucco. He had been sending dispatches all around the Mediterranean to Lucco for the last ten years to find a man fitting certain requirements. Now he wondered, 'Is this yet the right slave?'

On the sixth morning of the caravan's slow journey to Samosata, Zeno waddled from his own cart with the decision that today was the day to find out if Vesuvio could be of any service at court. If not, he would fling him out of the cart and let the blackbirds feast on his blue eyes.

A slave bearing a sun-shade hurried behind Zeno, trying to keep up with the quick-stepping eunuch as he now hurried past a howdah swaying on top of a camel. The yellow curtains were drawn all around this tent borne by the oscillating animal. Brass bells jangled from blue silk ropes hanging from its four corners and a small, golden palm tree rose from the centre, glittering in the sun, marking that this was a royal transport.

Hearing a woman's irate voice complaining inside the swaying *howdah*, Zeno smiled as he continued past the camel. The journey to Tyrus had been solely because of the Royal Princess Nunar. She was to meet Prince Cholam in hopes that he might marry her. By the time the caravan had reached the coastal city, though, the Prince had already chosen his first bride. No daughter of King Abgar could become a secondary wife. Nunar's hopes for marriage were dashed.

Although life at Samosata would have been much easier with Princess Nunar out of the way, Zeno was ironically pleased that she had not got a husband. He secretly hoped that she would spend the rest of her life as a spinster. But he knew that, somehow, he had to find an eligible husband for the wretched woman – a female with a face like a crow and a bark like a jackal. He told himself to worry about a husband for Nunar later. He had other problems now.

Reaching Vesuvio's cart, Zeno waved his pudgy hand to the driver to slow the oxen and reminded the bearer of the sunshade to keep walking behind the cart in readiness for his departure. Then, lifting one leg to climb over the tailgate, he heard the giggles and unbridled laughter from the front wagons, the conveyances which carried the harem.

The harem was another bother for Zeno. The Second Eunuch in Command at Samosata was Zediciah. He was the puppet of Princess Nunar – or, rather, in Zeno's estimation, it was often the other way around. The Princess Nunar had insisted that Zediciah make the journey with her to Tyrus, so Zediciah had thought it was necessary to travel with his female charges from the Royal Harem. Zeno hated pleasure-women as much as he loathed Zediciah. Their presence only made the caravan more vulnerable to bandits.

Panting when he climbed into the back of the cart, Zeno saw his newest slave lying on a deep mound of cushions. Vesuvio was trying to steady a carved ivory tablet in his hand, attempting to read the Mesopotamian histories which Zeno had given him to study whilst the cart bumped over the desert. They were written in Greek, a legacy of Alexander the Great; Zeno was pleased that the Roman slave could read both Latin and Greek.

Looking at Vesuvio sprawled back on the cushions, Zeno had to admit that he was a striking-looking beast. His blond hair flowed from his face like thin twists of gold. His eyes looked like brilliant blue stones in rich bronze. He had a fine nose. A strong chin. The silken robes which Zeno had given him to wear clung perfectly to the brawny proportions of his body.

Checking his admiration for the slave's appearance, Zeno proceeded to make himself comfortable against the padded walls of the wagon, reminding himself again that today was the day that he had to discover if the Roman was indeed the man he wanted. It would be futile to take him any farther if he were not. He would dispose of him at once.

Leaning his head to one side, Zeno looked sharply at Vesuvio and asked, 'What are your experiences with horses?'

'I ride. I drive a chariot and four. And, although I have never before driven a cart and oxen, given a chance, I'm sure that I would do better than—' He nodded towards the front of the cart.

Zeno was not interested in prattle. He asked, 'Are you a hunter?'

Vesuvio began, 'Every man hunts . . .'

'So you are acquainted with the manly life?'

A smile broke over Vesuvio's face. 'I did not spend my time with Lucco shuttling a cotton loom.' Lucco had told him that this eunuch had been spending the last ten years looking for a man whose description he himself fitted. After five days, though, he still did not know for what reason he had been purchased, what job he was meant to do.

Surveying Vesuvio's reclining body, Zeno asked, 'Are you a military man? Have you ever been a soldier?'

Vesuvio thought back to days long ago, remembering his intended conscription into the Roman Army. But he would not mention that fact, nor his military sponsor, General Termico, to this prying eunuch.

He answered, 'If you call an oarsman in a pirate galley a soldier, the answer is yes.' His eyes narrowed, wondering exactly what Zeno was trying to find out about him.

Reaching to his neck, Zeno's pudgy fingers nervously toyed with one of his long golden necklaces as he next asked, 'And you are built like a man, too? Big?'

Vesuvio slowly began to realize where these questions were leading, the talk about horses, hunting, a military life. Now – if he understood the question correctly – the size of his masculinity. He asked cautiously, 'You want me to tell you how I'm . . . built?'

Zeno's small eyes suddenly flared. He kept toying with his necklaces and snapped, 'I want more than to know. I want to *see* your manliness.' He quickly raised one finger, adding, 'But just a sight. Just proof that you do not have a body of a man with the equipment of a boy!'

Vesuvio's first reaction was to ask Zeno to show him the wounds of a eunuch. He had never before seen castration marks. Thinking better of it, though, he obediently reached down to the hem of the silk robe. He soon lay unashamed as Zeno stared at his phallus, his scrotum hanging limply over the front of his thigh like a wineskin.

Keeping his eyes on Vesuvio's naked crotch, Zeno began to speak. He cleared his throat. Then he started again. 'And . . . and . . . and *that* becomes even larger?'

Lowering the robe down his legs, Vesuvio said, 'Given the right partner, yes, "that" becomes larger.'

Looking at Vesuvio's face again, Zeno began in a lighter voice, 'We have been talking the last few days about you living in the Royal Palace. Your position in the River and Mountain King's Court.' Zeno nodded at the chain of ivory tablets. 'I am glad to see you taking an interest in our histories so soon.'

Vesuvio waited. He knew he was hearing more than a compliment. They had talked about Vesuvio living at the Royal Palace, true, but the interviews had seldom gone any further than asking if he knew such basic manners as not to urinate in corners or drop his piles of waste on marble floors. Vesuvio had yet to hear about the specifics of his role at Samosata.

Zeno continued, 'You know we are travelling with the King's harem. Part of it. You have made no advances towards them in the last few days. No approaches to their wagons. That is very wise of you. I gave orders at the outset of this journey for you to be killed instantly if you merely walked past the wagons of the harem.'

Vesuvio still waited for what Zeno really wanted to tell him. Having become despondent about being carried like a prisoner – albeit in great luxury – to some arid land, he could not think much about the particulars of his future.

Reaching for one of his golden neck chains, Zeno said, 'I am glad to know you have no interest in women, Roman. It will make your life at Samosata much easier.' Raising his forefinger, he warned, 'But you must not let the King know that you do not *like* women. He will have no interest in you at all. None whatsoever.'

Vesuvio's mind suddenly reeled. He could not believe what this fat eunuch was telling him. Zeno had jumped to the conclusion that he did not like females and now was charging him to pretend that he did. These words could only mean one thing.

Vesuvio blurted, 'You want me to be a stud to your King!'

Zeno gasped, 'You are talking about the King From The Sun and The Heir To The Moon!'

Vesuvio rose to a sitting position on his cushion. He thought about the Roman soldiers who had eyed him as a youth in towns like Puteoli. He remembered his distaste for male slaves who had offered themselves to him on his parents' estate in Campania. He recalled the repugnant male orgies amongst the pirate slaves. He also remembered with a start, though, that he was a slave. That he must do whatever his new master ordered him to do.

His brain churning, trying to think of some way to escape the role of a palace stud, he asked, 'But you told me that your king is a father. That he has a daughter, the Princess Nunar. He also has a son, young Prince Abgar. He obviously has a taste for women himself. Why does he need a . . . stallion?'

Zeno began to sputter, looking nervously to the tailgate of the wagon for spies listening to the conversation. Seeing only the bearer of his sun-shade trekking dutifully behind them in the dust, Zeno waved him to lag farther back.

Vesuvio was gaining more confidence. He asked, 'And what about that giggling and laughing I hear from the harem wagons? That's not the sound of old crones! Those are young girls I hear up there? Who are they for?'

Raising himself to a full sitting position, Zeno said proudly, 'Every great king has his harem!'

'Even if he never enjoys them?'

'The Great Abgar shows generosity to the chiefs of his district. Only in Samosata does a satrap enjoy the King's royal harem.'

Vesuvio could not resist saying with distaste, 'So your king panders for his wives!'

Zeno pulled back his hand to strike Vesuvio, hissing, 'Do not be disgraceful . . . slave!'

'Slave, yes. But a stallion to—' Vesuvio's blue eyes flared. His chest heaved with anger.

Zeno coldly studied him. His small hands were locked into pink fists. He said in a hard voice, 'Do not be disrespectful, slave. Do not overstep your bounds. I am your master. I can throw you out into the desert like an orange peel! A beetle plucked from a cushion! A troublesome dog!'

Despite his own anger, Vesuvio knew that what the eunuch said was true. He was at Zeno's mercy. He had obviously been purchased to be a pleasure slave and, if he did not fulfil his duties, he could be disposed of in any manner which his new master chose.

Taking a deep breath, Zeno said slowly, 'You talk about being a stallion. Fine. I will treat you like an animal. I will start being gentle. I will not get angry. I will not have you flogged straightaway. A master does not start by flogging his young colt. He shows kindness at first. I will do that by telling you a story.'

His brain numb, Vesuvio watched Zeno as he began to compose himself, smoothing the skirt of his robe over the gold rings of his sandals, rearranging the chains around his neck, straightening the gems on his stubby fingers, preparing to tell his story.

*

Zeno began, 'There was once an Armenian prince brought to King Abgar. A captive. That was more than twenty years ago now. He was a magnificent man. He had been conquered and brought to the Palace at Samosata as a tribute to the Great King. For the King to do whatever he wished with him. To use him as his huntsman. Put him into his army. Send him to supervise the date orchards. Anything he wanted. But the Great and Truly Good King kept the Armenian in his palace. He kept this conquered prince beside him at all times. They became friends. Closer than brothers. Even sleeping together like boys.

'Also at that time, the Queen was still young but had not borne any heirs for the King. So—' Zeno opened his hands. '—Abgar recognized that the blond Armenian was a gift sent to him from the bountiful skies. He had learned from his nights spent with the Armenian that they themselves fitted together like a man and wife. He also learned that his own manhood became very hard throughout the act of the Armenian lying astride him. He realized that when the Armenian used him as a woman he also could penetrate his own wife. So you see, the All Wise King was very pleased. The Armenian *did* provide a cure for Abgar and his wife. Soon Her Magnificence was with child. The first-born was the Princess Nunar. Finally the Queen of the Mountain Pools gave the King a male heir, the young Prince Abgar. There were other children in between but, as they were all girls, the royal nurses smothered them with pillows. One Princess is enough in Samosata.

'Following the birth of the young Prince, the Queen was allowed to expire. We call it "protected". Protected from giving birth to any other man's son. There are often attacks from the desert. The first woman to be raped is the King's first wife. She has the royal womb of heredity. That is how pretenders to the throne are bred.'

Zeno's small face became sad, his voice almost weak, as he explained, 'Now that the king is old, he wants to enjoy the remaining pleasures in the gardens of this world. In the last ten years, though, he has found nothing to equal the blond prince. The Armenian was killed by an attack of Berbers. Since then the King has only found reed-thin boys and heartless sycophants. He strongly desires warm satisfaction once again before he dies. From a man who is strong and golden like his Armenian . . .' He stopped, his eyelids lowered.

Vesuvio lay studying the fingers of his hands locked together on the flat of his stomach. He began calmly, 'I do not mean to be impudent with you. Only honest. And, if I understand you correctly, your King could not become sexually aroused by his wife to make love to her. The only way he could perform the act to procreate children was if someone – a man – was giving him his own pleasure. From . . . behind. Your obedient Armenian did just that. But to do that feat, your Armenian had to be aroused himself. Have a taste for such an action. And don't you see . . .' Vesuvio opened his hands, confessing, 'I could not do that. I would not be aroused by your king. Not by any man.'

Zeno's eyes began to narrow. He asked, 'So what arouses a slave like you?'

Nodding towards the harem wagons in front of his cart, Vesuvio answered, 'If I told you, you would cut off my head.'

'A woman?' Zeno flicked his hand. He was regaining his animation. He said, 'That is easy. You will have a woman near you. Someone desirable posing as a bed attendant. You will be allowed to see her and—' he pointed to Vesuvio's crotch. '—your manhood will become firm for the King. His Majesty need never know that it is not himself who has aroused you!'

Vesuvio began, 'I think the problem is more difficult than that . . .'

Zeno smugly interrupted, 'Nothing is difficult for me to arrange. I was granted my freedom many years ago by King Abgar for solving much more difficult problems than making you . . . big. And I will remain in Abgar's service, and the service of his heirs, only because I dedicate my life to solving difficult problems.'

Turning to the tailgate, Zeno quickly clapped his hands for the sun-bearer to come closer. The slave hurried towards the cart and Zeno ordered, 'Have the male-slave Diod brought here from the silver wagon. Then go to Zediciah and tell him that I need . . .'

Hesitating, Zeno turned to Vesuvio and asked, 'What kind of woman pleases you, slave?'

Vesuvio looked at him in astonishment. Zeno was going to have him attempt a coupling now!

'Speak! I do not have time to waste. What kind of woman pleases you? Tall? Plump? Raven-haired? A woman of your own colouring? Tell me before I decide to throw you to the vultures!'

Slowly shaking his head, Vesuvio answered, 'If you are going to do what I think you are . . .'

'Slaves do not think! They obey!' Zeno snapped. He turned back to his sun-bearer still trekking behind the cart and ordered, 'Tell Zediciah to send me a comely woman with black hair. Someone pleasing to a Roman. If he protests, tell him that I do not require a virgin. Tell him to send a woman already defiled by a satrap. A hand-maid. A cosmetic slave. Anything. Just make certain she's attractive.'

Turning back to Vesuvio, Zeno folded his arms across his chest and said, 'Now we'll see how difficult your problem is. If you go any farther on this journey or if I pierce your eardrums with long needles, sew your lips together with black hairs from a horse's mane, and leave you in the burning sun covered with the fat of a goose!'

He threw back his head and laughed.

Vesuvio looked from the honey-skinned girl now kneeling demurely at the back of the bumping cart to the young male-slave, Diod, who lay face-down on the floor cushions. Diod had dark hair which curled around his neck into long ringlets like a female but his back and legs were too well muscled for Vesuvio ever to fantasize that he was a woman. His buttocks were extremely curvacious, almost plump, and Vesuvio guessed that that was the reason why Zeno had chosen him for the experiment.

After Zeno explained to Vesuvio that he must imagine that the young man was King Agbar, careful to add that the King, of course, was older and demanded supreme respect, he ordered the girl to shed her spangled robe.

Obediently removing all her clothing except for a gossamer mantle which fell over her black hair, the girl held her eyes to the floor cushions. She sat with her small hands primly folded over the furry patch between her bare legs, the movement of the wagon making her breasts bounce with each jolt.

Zeno said to Vesuvio, 'Don't sit there like an idiot, Roman. You must take off your clothes, too. You don't expect to mount the King like that?'

Looking from Zeno to the naked man lying face-down on the cushions, and then to the kneeling girl, Vesuvio next glanced out of the back of the cart. He saw two guards mounted on black horses. They were following the cart. One guard held a lance in his hand; the other, a bow with an arrow positioned in the string.

Taking a deep breath, Vesuvio pulled the silk robe over his head. He slowly folded it on the cushion and knelt naked between the young man's outstretched legs.

Looking at the girl, Vesuvio saw that he would be eager to make love to her at any time. Her soft brown skin clung tightly to her body. She looked like a man's fantasy of an Eastern slave-woman, obediently waiting with downcast eyes to serve her master. Vesuvio felt himself becoming aroused as he studied her light brown skin.

Hoping to fix her image securely in his mind, he reached towards her to have only one slight touch.

Zeno slapped at his hand and railed, 'Do not touch the woman, slave! Just look at her. You will not be able to touch females in the Royal Bedchamber. The King must believe that it is his body which is seducing you!'

Remembering the armed guards following the cart, Vesuvio did not argue. He closed his eyes and tried to fix the image of the slave-girl in his mind. He envisioned her oval face, her small tender mouth, her spreading breasts with their rosy nipples, her small hands gently folded across the dark patch between her legs . . .

Feeling the hardness beginning to build in his maleness, Vesuvio slowly opened his eyes and told himself that he was seeing the girl on her stomach, that the naked buttocks belonged to the young girl, that a female now lay on her stomach for him to mount her from behind.

When Vesuvio moved his phallus forward, though, the young man raised his buttocks from the cushions to meet Vesuvio. His testicles hung in full view.

Pulling back, Vesuvio's phallus immediately softened.

Zeno whispered with sudden eagerness, 'Should the slave-girl sing? She knows Persian love songs.'

Shaking his head, Vesuvio closed his eyes, trying to recapture the erotic image of the harem girl. He tried to see in his mind how she would spread her legs for him, cradling him between her soft thighs, wrap her small legs around him.

Moistening his fingers now with saliva, Vesuvio worked the wetness onto his phallus and told himself that he had to achieve hardness. If Zeno would be this perverse, Vesuvio was convinced that he would throw him out into the desert for the birds of prey or whatever painful torture his perverted mind could devise.

Before opening his eyes the next time, though, he whispered to Zeno, 'Tell . . . him to lie still. Not to raise himself towards me this time.'

Zeno tapped the male slave on the elbow, ordering, 'Lie still.'

Although never enjoying the act of masturbation, Vesuvio continued to work himself with one hand, telling himself that it no longer mattered what he liked or did not like. He was a pleasure slave. He rationalized that he had suffered worse degradations on Platea, that this was a purely sexual act, a way by which he could survive. He could still maintain his personal respect. Many good men partook in sodomy.

Zeno said to him as if he had just remembered the fact, 'Roman, you do realize that no one dares to order the King. If King Agbar wishes to twist, squirm, or jump up and down, he can – and will do it.'

Vesuvio went soft again. He opened his eyes. He looked hopelessly at Zeno and then down at the male slave.

Zeno said blandly, 'Your performance is not very impressive, slave.'

'Could you go and wait outside. Shut the flap. Leave us three alone?' Vesuvio asked.

'Leave you alone? With the . . . King? You are making a joke! No man is ever left alone with the King. There will be attendants in the Bedchamber with you. Many more servants and slaves than just—' Zeno quickly gestured to four of them in the small, bumping cart.

Again, clenching his eyes, Vesuvio tried now to remember the slave girls whom he used to meet in the granary on his family's estate. He had used fantasies with them. That was too convoluted for his mind, though. He had made love to those girls whilst often thinking of his betrothed, Julia Cordonis. She had represented a beautiful happiness to him, a complete fulfilment. No, he did not want to use her for these lustful images. He wanted to keep something sacred.

Looking again at the harem girl, Vesuvio conceived another image. A better idea. He tried to convince himself that, after he satisfied the King, he would be allowed to make love to a woman. He would not explode his seed into the King but save his orgasm for a female. That a woman would be his reward for pleasuring a man.

The idea worked. He felt himself hardening again. He thought how he would have a harem girl every night, every afternoon, whenever he wanted. She would be young. Smooth-skinned. Obedient. Exactly like this honey-skinned girl with him now. She would surprise him, though, and transform herself into a hot-blooded tigress once she crawled onto his couch. She would be like Athana, squeezing him . . .

Without opening his eyes, Vesuvio moved his hardened phallus towards the male slave. He looked only to see where the man lay. He centred himself on him.

The man twisted on the cushions. Vesuvio saw the muscles move in his back. His shoulders spread wider. But telling himself to forget that he would be laying with a man, urging himself to keep thinking about the harem girl he would enjoy, Vesuvio directed his phallus towards the buttocks with one hand and prodded with the other to find his orifice.

After locating the tight opening between the man's buttocks,

Vesuvio removed his hand to moisten a finger for spreading the hole for an easier entry.

Then, holding his erect phallus in his other hand, Vesuvio leaned down closer over the waiting body.

Finding the man's anus again with his finger, he tried to guide the thick crown of his phallus towards it. The man slave was very tight. Also, the bumping cart made Vesuvio's attempted drives more difficult. He poked. Jabbed. Tried again. He hoped he would not suddenly become impotent as he tried to perform for his new master.

Suddenly above him, Zeno clapped his hands. He said, 'Stop! I see you are willing. I see that with more practice you can possibly serve the Great Abgar, that my search has not been entirely in vain. But these conditions are difficult. We will resume later when we're not being jostled in a cart.'

Waving his hand at the harem girl and the man slave, Zeno said, 'Hurry! Dress yourselves! Back to your wagons!'

Then, looking at Vesuvio, Zeno said coldly, 'You have no reason to feel proud, slave. I have seen dogs do better than you.'

21

Vesuvio waited in dread that night for Zeno to come to his tent and order him to embark on another sexual ordeal with the male slave, Diod. By nightfall, though, Zeno still had not appeared and Vesuvio told himself to forget about the fat eunuch, not to torture himself with the unexpected threats which Zeno had made this afternoon.

Tomorrow would be the seventh day since the caravan had left Tyrus. Vesuvio had spent his time comfortably up to now in the cushioned wagon during the day and a luxurious tent at night. He decided that there was no reason not to continue enjoying his hours alone. Why dwell on the ugly aspects of his new life? He certainly was more comfortable here than on Platea. He had even been given the ivory history tablets to read. He had not read one word as a pirate slave. He must enjoy the reading. He could learn to use his mind again.

Vesuvio was curious by nature. He followed that natural inclination and thought now about his environment. One point which puzzled him was where – and how – they camped each night in the desert. Although not knowing who was responsible for organizing the nightly encampments, Vesuvio admired the person's ingenuity and sense of detail.

Every evening, a tented city awaited the arrival of the caravan, a forest of poles prodding up sloping roofs, the smell of roasting lambs, aromatic vegetable dishes, rich savoury stews tempting the dusty travellers.

The same mystery prevailed at the morning departure: the caravan never lingered for the tents to be struck and provisions packed. The armed escorts mounted on horseback, the harem wagons, the *howdah* of Princess Nunar and the rest of her party travelling on camels, the slaves on donkeys or on foot, all the court personages in oxen-drawn carts left last night's shelters behind them, only to find them miraculously waiting for them the next evening.

Also, there was never any variation in the decorations and furnishings. Tonight, as for the last six nights, Vesuvio found the same ornamental hangings in his tent, the same blue, red, and yellow carpets strewn on the floor, the same brazier to warm himself against the desert's cold nights, the same long sleeping cushion he had known every night since he had left Tyrus.

Vesuvio lay awake tonight long after the chatter and giggles had subsided in the harem tents, when the shrill orders of the cantankerous Princess Nunar finally gave way to the clanking of armed guards settling around their fires, the distant howling of the wind, the sound of sand gusts blowing against the sides of his tent.

Reclining on his cushion, Vesuvio stared into a small flame in a brass oil-lamp and thought about the intrigues with which these people filled their lives. He somehow could not believe that they would ever leave Syria, pass into the land called Mesopotamia, and reach the city. Samosata, on the banks of the Euphrates River. He thought that Samosata, its palace, even King Agbar himself, were all part of a mirage in these Orientals' perverted minds.

Lulled into a tranquility by a flagon of chilled wine, Vesuvio again reconsidered Zeno's reason for purchasing him from Lucco, that he was meant to be a pleasure-slave to the King. Zeno was so intent on it that – Vesuvio could even laugh now about this afternoon's debacle – that he had ordered him to practise the act in the bumping wagon.

Rolling over on his back, Vesuvio locked his hands behind his head and thought about Zeno's devious character. He remembered the personable black slave at Byrsa, Balthazar, telling him how eunuchs possessed the bad habits of males and females, that a freedom from a sexual life gave them time to plot and make mischief. Also, he remembered the eunuch in the scarlet ciborium at the slave auction who had so desperately wanted to buy him.

Thinking about the auction and slavery, Vesuvio's mind wandered to the pirate slaves on Platea. He remembered how he had tried to dissuade them from feeling proud over the high price which Lucco had paid for them. That it would only lengthen their time in slavery. He wondered now if he worried and argued too much, became too vexed about slavery. Other people accepted it as a fact of life. Why did not he? He did not know the reason why – or when it had begun – but he was beginning to think more and more that there must be another way of life. Not only for him but for all men and women in bondage. Was slavery really necessary? For anyone?

Suddenly, a distant sound disturbed Vesuvio's thoughts. He sat upright and listened. He recognized the sound of – yes – the thunder of galloping horse hooves against the earth. The noise told him that there were not many riders, probably no more than six or eight. Therefore it was unlikely to be an attack by a band of raiders.

Rushing to the flap of his tent, Vesuvio listened as the galloping grew closer. When it stopped, he heard running feet and excited shouting in the camp.

Lifting the flap of the tent, Vesuvio stepped outside into the night but was immediately halted by two guards crossing his path with their steel lances.

Moving back into the tent, Vesuvio heard the cries of women, the wail of agony, a cacophony that sounded as if the entire camp was suddenly thrown into a turmoil. But, then, through the midst of the inexplicable disturbance, he heard laughter – a strident laugh which sounded like the hysterical shriek of a hyena.

Again, Vesuvio lifted his flap. The crossed lances still blocked his exit. He had learned from the previous nights that the guards would not speak to him. He did not press them for an explanation.

The wailing continued for a long time after Vesuvio lay back onto his cushion. The flame flickered out in his lamp and it was only when a voice shouted at him in the darkness that he realized that he had somehow fallen asleep.

Raising himself to his elbows, Vesuvio blinked at the flap of his tent being held open for him. He saw the bulky outline of his covered cart waiting outside the tent in the darkness. Dawn was not yet approaching but he heard the rumble of other carts. He knew that the caravan was preparing to make an early start.

Grabbing the silver chain strung with the ivory history tablets, Vesuvio moved quickly past the guards towards his cart. He climbed over the wooden tailgate and saw a small light flickering at the rear of the cart.

Stopping, he stared at Zeno sitting on the floor cushions. He held a taper in one hand and motioned impatiently with the other hand for Vesuvio to come towards him.

He wants me to try another male-slave, Vesuvio immediately thought.

He was wrong.

Zeno whispered, 'King Abgar is dead.'

Vesuvio listened soberly as Zeno explained that the disturbance last night in camp was caused by Throne Guards who had ridden from Samosata to bring word to Princess Nunar that her aged father had died. Zeno explained that the Princess had laughed when she had heard the news. Vesuvio remembered the strident screech he had heard cutting through the wails of mourning.

In a confidence which Zeno had not before shown to Vesuvio, Zeno explained how King Agbar had sent Nunar to Tyrus to marry Prince Cholam. He said, 'King Agbar did not want the Princess Nunar to marry a satrap called Cleon. He is one of the king's richest viceroys, a man with many trading caravans and slaves. But Agbar did not want his daughter to marry this wicked person.'

Vesuvio wondered why Zeno was suddenly talking to him as if he were a confidant. He resisted asking the question and inquired instead, 'What are the Princess's alternatives for marriage now?'

'Her brother, the Prince Abgar. Or, as he will be known, the new "King" Abgar. His hand will be joined to Nunar by their father.'

Vesuvio was more puzzled. 'I thought – How can a dead man—'

'It is part of the philadelphic tradition. The sacred priests can place a deceased father's hands on the male heir to marry his sister.'

Vesuvio knew the term "phildelphia", the Greek word – ΦΙΛΑΔΕΛΦΙΑ – for the incestuous love between a brother and his sister. He asked, 'But isn't the new King much younger than the princess?'

'Age is not a problem. A boy-child can take his sister for his first bride regardless of the age difference. The problem now is a political one. An uprising among the satraps.'

'The man Cleon?'

Zeno nodded glumly. 'He is presently carrying on a persecution against the Jews in our land. The Palace priests are behind Cleon in that matter. At the moment, young Abgar's tutor is a Jew. His name is Reuben ben Sahm. I have already sent word to Samosata to have him removed from the Palace.'

'Killed?'

Zeno shook his head. 'Reuben ben Sahm is more than a wise man. He maintains peace among his people. To execute him would cause a revolt in their districts. But I dare not keep him in the Palace. Cleon is a man with his eye on both today and the future. He would claim that young Abgar is being beguiled by the Jews through Reuben ben Sahm. But I have thought of a way to challenge that. Cleon also fears that the Roman Emperor will soon bring his war machines to our land.'

Vesuvio nodded. 'Your friend, Lucco, told me about Trajan's ambitions.'

'The Roman Empire has been looking towards the Euphrates and the Tigris Rivers for a very long time. But we know nothing about them here. That is why *you* will be installed as the successor to Reuben ben Sahm when we reach Samosata. You will be young Abgar's Roman tutor.'

'You now want me to be a . . . tutor?'

Reverting to his usual sharpness, Zeno snapped, 'Why not? You have been raised in the Roman Empire. You have knowledge of their ways.'

Vesuvio sank back into the darkness of the now rumbling wagon. He was relieved that he had been spared playing the role of a pleasure-slave. He knew he should be jubilant. Yet he could not forget what Zeno had just told him about the powerful satrap named Cleon, a man who sought revenge.

He asked, 'What if this Cleon finds out I am not qualified to teach your new king?'

'"Qualified"!' Zeno dismissed the idea with a flick of his chubby hand. He explained in a more intimate voice, 'Besides, Abgar is not yet crowned. The marriage according to philadelphic rites has to wait before it is accepted formally by the Council of Twelve. It also might take some time to force Princess Nunar into accepting it, time for her to learn if she is supported by any military strength. You will go unnoticed at Samosata for many days. People will be too occupied with the changes to notice the arrival of one mere slave.'

Stopping then, Zeno smiled for the first time at Vesuvio. The corners of his small mouth lifted as he leaned closer into the light of the small taper and said, 'Why do you look so disturbed? Isn't this much better than your original duty, my sand-dusted slave?'

Vesuvio soberly nodded at his castrated master, realizing that it was not impossible for him to become a eunuch, too.

22

The Palace at Samosata gloried through the funereal observances for King Abgar. A city within a city, its yellow walls rose higher than the boundaries of Samosata itself. Whereas the town walls ran flat-topped and at irregular angles, the Royal Palace stood like a magnificently crowned cask within the city, its turrets looking towards the Antitaurus Mountains in the north, the Euphrates River snaking from the east, and the goldenness of the surrounding fields, low hills, deserts and valleys.

The main entrance to the Palace was arched, its thick doors reinforced with square iron studs, and led into an extensive courtyard floored with *pavimenta punica.* A square fountain stood in the middle of this large central space, its shallow pool glimmering with schools of silver fish swimming against its green tiling. The fronds of gracious palm trees drooped over the surrounding arched porticoes, and four pairs of tall brass-and-silver doors opened onto the shady avenues which led to four outlying courtyards.

To mark the death observances of King Agbar, the floor of the main courtyard, and all its tributaries, were layered with thick carpets to soften the echo of camels, horses, donkeys and oxen which brought mourners to Samosata. Also the fountains throughout the Palace were ritually perfumed to sweeten the decaying flesh of the deceased, filling the environs of the Palace with a heady reminder that their ruler was passing into a sweeter paradise. Cages of white doves were freed in the cavernous marble hallways inside the Palace itself; the thinnest scrims of almond-dyed silk were suspended from the curved arches to keep the white birds from escaping until the King was officially interred.

The distant wails of the harem continued day and night from behind the gold wickets which separated their quarters from the activity of the Palace. White-robed priests, high Palace dignitaries, consolatory satraps came and went in the Royal Quarters.

A line of scribes from the Treasury sat solemn-faced under an awning outside the death room. They carefully valued the worth of each funeral gift, entered it on their parchment records, and only then allowed the mourner to peer through a notch in a thick cedar door to view the sarcophogus of the King before it was borne to the Royal Temple.

Vesuvio heard the news of all these happenings from Reuben ben Sahm who came to visit him on the third week after the caravan had reached Samosata.

Reuben ben Sahm, born into the Hebraic religion, was cautious how he answered Vesuvio's eager questions about the funeral, the burial, the philadelphic marriage of young Abgar to his sister, Princess Nunar – all pagan practices to the laws of Reuben's own religion.

The two men met in the small quarters where Zeno had hurriedly installed Vesuvio on arrival at Samosata. It consisted of one room sparsely furnished with cushions and a low ivory table, a marble bathing closet, a latrine which opened into the sewerage system, and a minuscule garden planted with dwarf palm trees and flowering vines, a courtyard setting like a tiny box in the mazework of the spreading Palace. Fresh clothes arrived daily for Vesuvio, mute slaves also bringing regular trays of food, wine, water.

Vesuvio now shared a bowl of dates left from his breakfast with Reuben ben Sahm. They sat on a stone bench in the garden, the solemn Jew holding a staff in his hand, speaking stiffly as if his visit was nothing more than a formality.

Vesuvio finally said, 'Zeno told me you must leave the Palace. What are you going to do now?'

'I am staying with friends in the Jewish section. For a position, I have been made Custodian of the Old Sepulchres. As I am approaching death myself, that is the safest place for me.'

'Cleon won't bother you?'

Reuben turned slowly to look at him. 'How do you know about Cleon?'

'Zeno told me about him. He is the man who wants to marry Princess Nunar.'

'That is what some people believe. And in many ways it would be good. At least, for young Abgar, if Cleon does marry Nunar.'

'Why?'

'I am a Jew. I have my scriptures and also the beliefs of a sect called the Essenes. That is the main reason Cleon wants to be rid of me. The Essenes do not believe in slavery. We differ from the established Hebraic tradition in that way. We even differ from the young cult called the Christians or Nazarenes. But the satrap, Cleon, is rich in many ways. Especially with his slaves. He fears that I will spread the Essene belief—'

Hesitating, Reuben said, 'You asked me about the young King and his sister. I divert to tell you about my beliefs. Let me keep the subject to young Abgar. The political dangers.

'I believe that if the boy marries his sister he will not remain King for long. The Princess has a close ally in the eunuch, Zediciah. He is second in command to Zeno. But also being the Guardian of the Harem, Zediciah extols sexual pleasures. The Princess Nunar listens to him. She is driven insane by the physical joys he describes to her. She feels she is missing much of life, a satisfaction which she envisions only the barbaric satrap, Cleon, can provide for her.' Shaking his head, Reuben said, 'You probably see that I am not sad to leave the Royal Palace. Even for the Old Sepulchres.'

'But how is young Abgar in danger?'

Fixing his eyes on the ground, Reuben explained, 'He will either be fatally removed to make room for Cleon. Or he will learn the only way he can survive. And that will put blood on his hands before he reaches manhood. If a woman becomes unchaste, if Nunar lays with Cleon, Abgar can have her executed. It would take only one accusation in the ear of the young King—'

'But certainly a mere boy does not know, or can possibly comprehend the ways of an adult body. And certainly not . . .'

Fixing an eye on Vesuvio, Reuben said, 'You are foolish to underestimate an Oriental child, Roman. Very foolish indeed.'

'I'm beginning to think that the fool is Zeno to consider that I – a slave bought from a pirate – can replace a wise man like you.'

Raising a finger, Reuben warned, 'Also, do not underestimate Zeno. He can be your most dangerous enemy. But he can be your best ally, too. As a free man, Zeno enjoys the position as the Administrator of All Protocol. The second eunuch, Zediciah, loathes Zeno. As does the Princess Nunar who has tried to have him poisoned three times. Also, the Satrap Cleon threatens to raise an army against the Palace if Zeno is allowed to keep his position under the new kingship.'

Supporting himself on his staff to stand, Reuben said, 'I am only sorry to see a young man with your stamina, your obvious zest, be caught in such a putrid atmosphere as this. Roman, you look as out of place here as a wild horse in a silk bazaar.'

Vesuvio contemplated confiding in Reuben ben Sahm what his original role was meant to be at Samosata but, suspecting that the wise Jew might know about it already, he decided against sullying his ears with more talk of physical excesses.

Accompanying Reuben ben Sahm from the garden to the door of his sitting-room, Vesuvio tried to eke some small bits of information from the old man about when his duties as tutor would commence, how he should teach his pupil, what the child was like.

Reuben smiled as he reached for the door with his staff and beat on it to announce to the hall guard that he was ready to leave. He said to Vesuvio, 'Rome! That is all they want to hear about. Rome! How they can protect themselves from . . . Rome!'

The door opened and Vesuvio moved to bid Reuben ben Sahm a warm farewell. But both men faced a young girl standing in the hallway. A messenger hovering behind her said, 'For the Roman!' He pushed the girl towards Vesuvio, adding, 'A gift purchased especially for the Roman.'

Looking furtively at Vesuvio, Reuben ben Sahm shook his head and, turning, he followed a guard down the long marble corridor.

The young girl now stood inside the closed doors of Vesuvio's room, her head lowered and both slim brown arms hanging gracefully to the sides of a diaphanous fabric flowing from the gold slave belt encircling her bare hips.

Vesuvio's passion had multiplied since he had been confined to this remote section of the Palace. After his talk with Reuben ben Sahm, though, he told himself to proceed cautiously with this sudden gift.

The messenger had said that she had been purchased especially for him so Vesuvio knew that she was not from the harem. But he wondered who had bought her? Who had sent this unexpected gift? Also, since listening to stories of poisonings, murders and conspiracies, he wondered if the donor was a friend or an enemy. Could this tiny, harmless-looking girl have been sent here to kill him, even now be concealing a sharp blade?

Raising one hand to the girl, Vesuvio beckoned her to step across from the closed doors.

Obediently, her bare feet slowly glided across the white marble floor. And as she moved, Vesuvio quickly stepped behind her to survey her lithe body for any concealed weapon.

Closely studying the girl, he saw that her slim waist amply curved into voluptuous proportions. Her long black hair was twisted with red ribbons into a myriad of plaits, falling like a million snakes around the chains of gold bezants which jangled from her long neck. She was even prettier than the girl whom Zeno had summoned to the cart on the journey from Tyrus.

Now, putting a hand on her slim shoulder, Vesuvio stepped in front of the door leading to his garden. He gazed down at this tiny but exquisite creature's face, seeing how her long lashes brushed against her golden complexion as she held her head respectfully low. He caught the sweet perfume wafting from her body. He lowered his hand from her shoulder and began to stroke her bare skin.

His only thought was about hurting the girl, about driving his phallus into her vagina and possibly ripping someone so delicately made. His phallus was already lengthening under his robe. He could feel the crown inching up the inside of his thigh with excitement.

From the soft skin covering her shoulders, he moved his hand towards the twist of blue silk gathered around her small breasts. Cupping his fingers, he reached to feel her breasts . . .

But his fingers cupped nothing! He felt only bunched fabric where there should be breasts. And, alerted by this, he held her neck by one hand and reached towards the gauze suspended from her slave belt.

Raising his middle finger to probe the slit of a vagina, Vesuvio felt a satin pouch holding the small but definite equipment of a male.

Misunderstanding the gesture, the young slave moved closer towards Vesuvio, sidling his small body against Vesuvio's legs, easing his curved buttocks closer to the stiff protrusion of Vesuvio's phallus under the robe.

Shaking his head, Vesuvio began to murmur, 'No . . . no . . . no . . .'

The words became louder as he pushed the boy slave towards the door. Soon, he began pounding on the door with one fist.

When the guard slowly opened the door, Vesuvio pushed the boy slave out into the hallway and slammed the door. He stood now with his back to it, wondering what he was going to do for sex in this strange land where people kept thrusting males at a man. His phallus was throbbing under his robe. His hand moved to ease the passion. His fingers curved into a fist to relieve the tension but he fought the temptation. No. He would wait for a woman. Not a boy. Not a man slave. Not his own hand. But a female.

23

'*You did not like the gift I sent you!*'

Vesuvio stared at a child dwarfed by the tall doorways of his new quarters. He had been moved to these more spacious apartments a few days after Reuben ben Sahm's visit and had been waiting more than a week now for the arrival of his royal pupil.

Striding across the peach-coloured marble floor with the authority of an adult, young Abgar surveyed Vesuvio's body and asked sharply, 'Did the slave offend you? If he did, I shall have the wretch whipped myself!'

Assuring him that the slave had not offended him, Vesuvio bowed and said, 'I did not know Your Majesty had sent the gift.'

'That slave was very costly. He would have gone to my Father. But—'

Pausing, the boy's petulant expression turned into the face of a child as he asked, 'Are boy slaves like girl slaves?'

Trying to stifle a smile, Vesuvio said, 'There are a few differences between them.'

Continuing past Vesuvio, Abgar said, 'That's what Zeno told me. But he couldn't explain it any better than you. But I thought somebody should have him.'

Stopping, turning to look at Vesuvio, he reverted into a child again, asking, 'But wasn't all that hair funny? Plaited with ribbons! Long and twisty like red-bellied snakes! Did you get to pull it? I did!'

Smiling broadly now, Vesuvio confessed, 'No. He didn't stay with me long enough for that.'

Motioning to the sober guards flanking the tall doorway, Abgar said, 'They have to stay with me. I'm the King now. I can't go any place without guards.'

Stopping and squinting his eyes at Vesuvio, he asked, 'You do know I'm King, don't you?'

Bowing again, Vesuvio said, 'Yes, Your Majesty. And you

look like a very fine king.' He felt as if this was more of a game, an extension to the mirage of Samosata.

'You're a Roman, aren't you? And you're going to teach me all about Rome.' Abgar passed two divans and stood staring now at long sheets of parchment glued together, held to the floor by brass lamps placed at each corner.

He asked, 'What's that?'

Walking alongside him, Vesuvio said, 'It's a map I made for you. To show you how the Romans build a camp. I drew it with charcoal.'

'Is it in Rome?'

'No,' Vesuvio answered, walking over and crouching next to the young boy. 'A camp like this is built when the Romans go on a military expedition.'

'But how is Rome defended itself? Rome the city?'

'Well, there are the Praetorian Guards. They are the special soldiers of the Emperor. They camp outside the city walls.'

'Why outside?'

'Because the people of Rome are frightened that they might turn against the city. The Praetorians are very strong soldiers. And evil men in the past have been known to bribe them to turn against the government.'

Abgar sniffed. 'They don't sound very good to me.'

'Ah, now! If you want to hear about good ones . . .' Vesuvio said, turning his head to Abgar. 'They are called the "Vigilis". Everyone likes them. Whenever a fire breaks out in Rome they rush to put it out. And they patrol the streets after dark to make certain that no thieves or ruffians attack the citizens in dark alleys.'

Abgar tried to pronounce the name.

Vesuvio repeated slowly, 'Vi-gil-is.'

Wrinkling his brow, Abgar asked, 'What are people doing out in the streets of Rome at night?'

'That's when Rome is the busiest. Even noisier than in the daytime. See, there is a law in Rome that says that no supplies can be brought into the city by carts or wagon after dawn. The streets are too narrow and they would run over the people. So that business must wait until night. Rome gets very noisy after sundown.'

'When do Romans sleep?'

Vesuvio laughed. 'Some Romans get very little sleep because the noise is so bad.'

'So when do men make love to their wives?'

Vesuvio pondered the question.

'Husbands!' Abgar explained. 'Men like me!' He thumbed the gold bib hanging over his small chest.

Again, Vesuvio tried to keep himself from smiling. He said, 'Oh, a Roman manages to find time for that.'

Sitting down on a cushion in front of the map, Abgar said, 'That's what I want you to tell me about, too. I want you to teach me how Romans make love to their wives.' Then, leaning closer to Vesuvio, he whispered, 'Have you ever made love to a wife?'

'I don't have one.'

Sitting back on his haunches, Abgar bragged, 'I do!'

Vesuvio graciously nodded.

'I've got a wife but I've never made love to her. Or to any woman. You must teach me all about that, too. Love-making.'

'There are certain . . . requirements.'

'I've got that.'

Vesuvio eyed him.

'I've got the biggest bed in the country. Probably the whole world. It belonged to my father. My father is dead now. But I've got the bed he was lying on when he joined my hand to the hand of the Princess Nunar.'

Stopping, lowering his eyes, Abgar corrected himself, 'Or my father's hands were placed on ours. He was dead. His hands were like cold wax. I remember that. But by touching them meant that I was to be married. The Princess Nunar, oh, she fought it. And she shrieked like she always does. She hates me. I've only seen her three times in my whole life. But that doesn't matter. I'm the King now. And she'll have to be my wife or . . . or . . . or something very bad will happen to her!'

Listening to the small boy, Vesuvio felt an urge to put his arm around him. To tell him that he did not have to be so gruff. That he could forget about wives for a few moments and think about being a boy.

The intricate charcoal lines on the map suddenly caught Abgar's eyes and, holding out his hand, he asked, 'What do they mean?'

'Those four lines there,' Vesuvio explained, pointing to his drawing of a Roman camp, 'that's where the legions sleep in their tents. And the foot soldiers, they sleep in those long lines there, the barracks. The oblong tents. But their horses are kept between them – in those there.'

Soon, the boy was kneeling over the map, listening intently as Vesuvio explained how a camp was laid out by a strict rule made by the Roman general, Marius, who had reformed the army of the Old Republic.

During the following weeks, Vesuvio kept young Abgar interested not only in the camp of General Marius but also told him about Lucullus, the general who had invaded Armenia, the country to the north of Mesopotamia, almost two hundred years ago now. He also talked about Pompey, the Roman who had conquered Syria to the west. He drew another map to show the plan which Julius Caesar had used to scale the walls of Avaricum when he had invaded Gaul.

Despite all his interest in the Roman armies, the parade costumes of the soldiers, the stories of Roman generals, Abgar always manouevred the conversation back to the subject of beds, wives and the duties of husbands. Also, Vesuvio noticed that the young boy had a precocious interest in breasts.

Abgar surprised him one morning by arriving with a chain of ivory tablets jangling from his small hand. They were yellow with age and more delicate than the history tablets which Vesuvio had read on the caravan journey from Tyrus. Abgar did not even trust his guards to carry them.

Drawing Vesuvio into a corner, he whispered, 'I took these from the Indian Love Mistresses. They counselled my father. Look . . . these are all the positions how a man can make love to his wives . . . look at them.' He studied the small figures carved into ivory like any other boy would examine a bug or brightly speckled stone. As some of the figures were so minute and contorted, they often confused him and he had to ask which one was the man and which was the woman. Vesuvio pretended that he was also unable to comprehend the pictures in which two men were coupling. He thought that the boy's life would only become more complicated with an explicit discussion of the Oriental Vice. That would undoubtedly come soon enough. The artful depictions of a man holding a woman's breasts as he penetrated her interested Abgar more than those showing a purely coital union.

Vesuvio was only able to divert the boy's attention from sex that day by, first, telling him about the young girl slaves whom the Roman soldiers took on long expeditions and, then, cautiously changing the subject to a battlefield or a province of Rome. He found that his own mind drifted back to the explicit Indian love carvings, his sexual appetite at a burning point.

He kept trying to keep the subject away from the female anatomy and love-making as the weeks passed but the more that he tried to hedge Abgar's questions the more he began thinking about sex himself.

It was almost two months now since Vesuvio had been with a woman. After he had rejected the young transvestite sent to him by Abgar, no more bedmates of any description had been offered to him. The boy's obsession with sex soon began to take its toll on Vesuvio.

Finally, he thought of a ploy that would get him out of the palace, a way in which he could slip away from Abgar for an afternoon and, hopefully, find a bordello in the city.

Late one morning after they had finished discussing the athletic contests at the Flavian Amphitheatre and the Circus Maximus in Rome, Vesuvio announced brightly to Abgar that it would be nice to have plaster to build a replica of the Imperial City. He told Abgar that he could study the model and really see how Rome looked. He could even help to construct it.

The idea excited the boy so much that he immediately jumped to his feet to call for a messenger to fetch whatever materials Vesuvio needed.

Putting his hand on the boy's shoulder, Vesuvio explained that the best building plasters were the most difficult to recognize. That he would have to test various plasters in the shops and find the correct one for the construction of their model.

Abgar munificently offered to have all the plasters available in Mesopotamia brought to the Palace. They would examine them together.

Vesuvio insisted that, no, it would be quicker if he went into the city to look for them himself – and immediately this afternoon.

The boy was crestfallen. His lower lip protruded and he mumbled, 'Then I can't go with you.'

Although Vesuvio's mind quickly strained for a reason why Abgar could definitely not accompany him, he was beginning to feel worse than a liar. He felt as if he was betraying a new friend. He imagined someone befriending his young brother, Titus.

Abgar moped, 'I'd like that, too. To go looking for plasters with you. But I can't. Princess Nunar and I have to sit with the Council this afternoon.'

Breathing more easily, Vesuvio promised the boy that he would bring the building supplies back to the Palace and would not start to construct the model without him.

Watching the child now walking slowly towards the door, his head drooped forward in a pout, Vesuvio tried to convince himself that he was doing the right thing, that he must not devote his entire life to the childish moods of the young King. But he did begin to understand now how slaves developed loyalties to certain masters.

24

Leaving through a postern in the Palace walls, Vesuvio showed his ivory pass to the guards and then tucked it into the pouch where he also carried money to buy the plaster. Abgar had been more than generous with him: Vesuvio had enough shekels in the pouch to buy every prostitute in Samosata – plus enough plaster to build a full-scale victory arch. He laughed to himself about a child doling out money to him.

The afternoon wind blew bits of sand through the narrow streets and Vesuvio pulled a hooded cotton cloak around him as he hurried between the stone and mud buildings, not lingering to look at the shiny and colourful wares spread on hemp mats along the narrow passageways. He only had one image in his mind.

His sandals clattered up stone steps as he thought about someone who could direct him to a bordello. He decided that the surest way to find a respectable establishment was to locate a gem merchant, a man who dealt with rich and discerning customers.

Soon, Vesuvio saw a square at the end of the street. He quickly turned, taking his bearings to find his way back through the *zouk*, then continued towards the opening in the crush of flat-topped houses.

A horse charged in front of Vesuvio as he turned the corner into the square. Its surly rider cracked a long whip at a line of slaves chained together as they slowly dragged their bleeding and calloused feet over the cobblestones.

Stopping, Vesuvio stared at the slave column, remembering how he had been led in a similar manner through the alleys of Carthage. He looked at the crusted blood and deep lash marks on the slaves' bodies and, then, feeling the soft silks and cottons against his own skin, he realized how many years had passed since that time, how his life had so radically changed, how a slave was so much at the mercy of fate.

A second rider galloped across the square towards the slave-driver. He was a large man, dressed in a scarlet red *burnous* embroidered with gold thread and with a full hood pulled down over his face. As the man drew nearer to the slave column, he swore in Aramaic at the driver for whipping the slaves.

'Good for you!' Vesuvio said to himself and continued along the side of the square to find his way to a gem merchant.

With information from two litter-bearers, Vesuvio soon headed towards a small niche in a street slanting off the square. The merchant in a gem shop there readily gave Vesuvio the names of three respectable bordellos, particularly recommending an establishment called 'Palmyra's', but adding that it only catered to men who liked the pleasures of females.

Grinning, Vesuvio assured the merchant that he had seen enough of the Oriental Vice, saying that Palmyra's sounded as if it were exactly the place he wanted. Then, after listening closely to the directions, Vesuvio promised the merchant that he would return – if not today, some day very soon – to buy one of the finest gems he had for sale in gratitude for this information.

Vesuvio saw the oil lamp, the carved lictern over the doorway which the merchant had described to him. Also, he found a brass door-knocker in the shape of a lizard. Lifting the ornamental reptile by its head, he gave it a loud rap.

Soon, he saw a small slat open in the wooden door and next he heard the inside locks being unbolted. The door slowly opened and Vesuvio faced a pale-white slave with small pink eyes, his head glistening with pure white hair.

The Albino slave bowed hospitably to Vesuvio and, leading him across a small courtyard, he held out his hand towards an old woman reclining on a couch by a small pool and lisped, 'Mistress Palmyra!'

Looking at Vesuvio from head to foot, Mistress Palmyra said in coarse Latin, 'I haven't had a Roman here for years. But I know just the girl who'll please you.'

'How do you know I'm Roman?' Vesuvio asked, lowering his hood and smiling at the woman garishly dressed in a peacock blue *himation*, a tatty wig of yellow curls sitting askew on her head.

'How does a fine lady smell a fart?' she asked, laughing,

showing a mouthful of black teeth. Then, clapping her bony hands, she shouted, 'Esmid! Esmid, you bit-titted wench. Come out here!'

Turning back to Vesuvio, Mistress Palmyra said, 'Esmid's not a cheap piece. And I won't have you leaving her all marked with bruises.' Eagerly holding out her hand to Vesuvio, she said, 'Also, you'll have to pay me in advance. Come on! Fifty shekels!'

'Fifty shekels?' Vesuvio gasped in mock horror. He knew enough to bargain. 'I could probably buy her freedom for that.'

Looking at him with one thin eyebrow arched, Mistress Palmyra conceded, 'Forty. But you can't bugger her for that. I have too much trouble finding a good physician to heal the wenches if they get badly buggered.'

'Bugger? Who wants to bugger this Esmid if she's as fine as you say?' He was preparing to reduce the price by half.

Smiling, Mistress Palmyra held her thin arm towards a balcony and, turning, Vesuvio saw a young woman dressed only in widths of sheer yellow gauze hanging from her waist. Her naked breasts hung full over the curve of her bare torso. Vesuvio had never seen such pendulous but firm breasts . . . nor such nipples as large as fully blown roses.

Giving Vesuvio a faint smile, Esmid languidly combed both hands through her long black hair, slowly extending one hip.

Quickly digging into the money pouch, Vesuvio tossed forty shekels in a clatter towards the Mistress Palmyra. And already peeling off his cloak, he bounded up the steps towards the slave prostitute.

The young woman slowly moved down the balcony, disappearing through an open door as Mistress Palmyra laughed in the courtyard below, cackling to her Albino servant that it was a good thing that Esmid had not seen the Roman before he paid – that Esmid would have probably given herself to such a fine-looking young man for nothing.

When Vesuvio reached the room, Esmid's skirts already lay on the floor. She stood naked, holding her arms out to Vesuvio, welcoming him into the room lit only by daylight pouring through a thin pane of alabaster in the ceiling.

As soon as Vesuvio could shed his clothes, he and Esmid fell together onto a soft pallet placed on the floor in the flood of rich lighting. He was surprised to find how sweetly Esmid's mouth tasted, how warmly she returned his kisses, as if they were established lovers. Vesuvio's phallus was aching to move towards the rich mound of hair rising between her legs. But as if Esmid sensed his long period of celibacy, she whispered into his ear, tickling him with her breath as she said, 'Why don't we do the first one quick? Then we will play. Then . . . Then we will . . . ' She drew out the words. '. . . make real love.'

Vesuvio agreed immediately, holding her in his arms, moving his phallus directly to the warmth between her legs, tonguing her mouth as she squeezed him between her soft thighs.

Intent on easing Vesuvio's pent-up sexuality, Esmid lavished her caresses on him, the pressing of her breasts, the warmth of her mouth, the contracting tightness of her femininity, drawing him quickly to the gasp of his first explosion. She accompanied his thrusts and grunts with an even more expansive consideration and warmth until his face now lay motionless next to hers, resting in the soft veil of her hair.

Laughing softly into his ear, Esmid whispered, 'Now we will stop being animals. Now I am a woman. And you—' She pulled Vesuvio closer towards her. '—you are the most beautiful man I have ever seen.'

Kissing him on the forehead, she promised, 'I will treasure you like gold. Just you see . . . *domine*.'

25

Walking happily down the sloping street from Palmyra's, Vesuvio wished now that he had had time to make love with Esmid for the fourth time. As she had promised, their second coupling had been prolonged, passionate, a physical act that passed into the realms of artistry.

Esmid had met every hunger that Vesuvio showed, a heated encounter which culminated with Vesuvio kneeling on the pallet, his mouth ravishing the fullness of her breasts as she straddled his midsection, working, twisting, squeezing an excitement for both of them until they finally burst in unison, grasping one another like desperate lovers.

But it was the surprise of the third encounter that had been the most spectacular for Vesuvio, when he and Esmid lay side by side, beginning to explore one another's body yet again. They let first their hands, then their lips and tongues feel, lick and explore. Eventually, they lay facing in opposite directions, Vesuvio tonguing the richness of Esmid's soft femininity as she eagerly took his thick maleness deeper into her throat.

Soon, they approached another pitch, drawing tighter and closer together into a naked ball of two bodies until – as if by some unspoken cue – they spread out on the pallet, holding one another in their arms once again, sharing the tastes lingering in their mouths as they rushed for completion.

It was Mistress Palmyra's shrill shriek from the courtyard below that brought Vesuvio back to his senses. She shouted that she would soon start charging him for lodging if he stayed any longer.

Reluctantly, Vesuvio dressed himself, promising Esmid that he would return to her at the first opportunity. Then, giving her one last smile before he left the room, he remembered through his daze that he had an errand to do . . . What was it? . . . Oh, yes . . . The plaster.

At the foot of the steep street, Vesuvio decided to go to the gem merchant yet again, asking the good man if he could suggest a shop where he could find plaster. Hurrying before the merchant pulled his blind, Vesuvio thought how he would think what a strange fellow he was: first a bordello, now plaster to build a toy city.

Seeing the doorway still open. Vesuvio quickly entered the small shop but saw that the merchant was sitting on floor cushions with a customer.

Not wanting to disturb the man at business, Vesuvio was about to turn away when the merchant waved him back into the shop.

Vesuvio began to say that he was in a hurry, that he was only seeking more information, when, suddenly, the customer turned from the merchant to look at Vesuvio, too.

First, Vesuvio recognized the red *burnous*, the same garment with elaborate gold embroideries that he had seen earlier in the square. Next, seeing a black face smiling at him, Vesuvio realized that he knew him, this man who had shouted at the driver whipping the slaves.

'Balthazar!' Vesuvio shouted.

Jumping to his feet, Balthazar held out both long arms to Vesuvio, 'My friend from Byrsa!'

Warmly embracing one another, the two men flooded one another with simultaneous questions. What were they doing here? Where had each gone from Carthage? Who had bought them? Why was Balthazar looking so rich?

Balthazar explained that he had finally achieved his dream, that he had been purchased by a master who appreciated his worth. Or rather, that he had been bought by a Cypriot merchant whose *wife* appreciated him for what he was. And, on his master's death, the woman had not only freed Balthazar but took him for her legal husband. Together, they now ran a trade route from Cyprus to Persia. Balthazar occasionally accompanied his caravans and he was on the way back from Persia now, returning to Sidon, from where he would sail home to Cyprus. He had stopped in Samosata to learn the value of some strange-looking gems he had found in Ecbatana.

Digging into a pouch for a handful of white stones, Balthazar produced one of the gems for Vesuvio to examine.

Holding the faceted stone up to the light, Vesuvio studied the yellow, blue, even purple light that its clearness refracted like fire. He asked, 'What's it called?'

'That's what I'm trying to find out. I have more. Look . . .' He emptied the pouch in his hand, the gems trickling out like small chunks of ice, some cut into many facets, others still in rough form like rock salt crystals.

As Vesuvio continued to examine one, Balthazar said, 'You must keep it as a gift. Here! Keep a handful!' He grabbed Vesuvio's arms and emptied more into his palm.

Vesuvio began to refuse.

But shoving back Vesuvio's hand, Balthazar insisted, 'They might be worthless. Who knows? I got them from a cameleer who had brought them from near the Kistna River. But I can't interest anyone in them. Everybody is like this good trader here. They want nothing but pearls or carbuncles – garnets, rubies, sapphires.'

Still sitting on the cushions behind them, the merchant shrugged, shaking his head, smiling helplessly.

Putting his arm around Vesuvio's shoulders, Balthazar said, 'I am staying at a caravanserai by the Occidental Gate. Come. Visit with me for a few hours. As the days are so hot now we are waiting for moonrise before we leave.'

Sobering, Vesuvio said, 'I'm not as lucky as you. I'm still – a slave. I'm owned by a man called Zeno.'

Before Vesuvio had time to explain, Balthazar blurted, 'Not Zeno the Chief Eunuch at the Palace?'

'How do you know about him?'

'This part of the world is filled with nothing but talk about the Palace at Samosata. You have a new King now. A young boy who's supposed to marry his sister.'

Vesuvio was surprised that Balthazar knew so much about the remote life in Mesopotamia. He listened as Balthazar told him that he had heard many stories about the young King and his sister on his way back here from Persia. There were even rumours about a satrap, a man named Cleon, who was making preparations to march on Samosata.

Leaning forward, Balthazar whispered, 'I saw some of his soldiers myself. At a caravanserai not three days east from here. An army being formed to ride here.' He tapped Vesuvio on his chest, saying, 'You be careful, my friend. I don't want you becoming a eunuch yourself.'

As Vesuvio was making a mental note to tell Zeno this news about Cleon, Balthazar cautiously added, 'I said I am leaving tonight. There is room for you to hide in my caravan . . . if you want to escape.'

Vesuvio paled.

Balthazar continued, 'I remember the story you told me in

Byrsa. How you were abducted from your home. Do you want to return there?'

Vesuvio said, 'If someone would have asked me that question three months ago, a year ago, three years ago, I would not have hesitated. I still long to know what happened to my family. If they are still alive. Nevertheless my father raised me to respect honour and I somehow feel a strange duty—' He faltered.

'I always remember you as honourable, Vesuvio.'

Vesuvio shook his head. 'No, that sounds sham. But I feel that if I leave now—'

Balthazar raised his hand to Vesuvio's shoulder. 'I will not tempt you now. I will be through here again. Perhaps the next time you will consider my proposition. It will still hold.'

So, promising to meet one another at some unfixed time in the near future, Vesuvio and Balthazar parted. Vesuvio then forced himself to cast Balthazar's kind offer out of his mind. He could not dwell on it. He might think that he was a fool. He deeply believed, though, that he could not abandon young Abgar.

It was then that the merchant told Vesuvio the bad news, that the suppliers of building supplies and plaster only opened their shops in the morning. Vesuvio had to go back to the Palace without material to build a model of Rome.

Although the sky was darkening, Vesuvio managed to find his way back to the Palace, by the way which he had noted in the *zouk*. Walking quickly towards the postern, he dug amongst the shekels and mysterious stones which Balthazar had given him, producing the ivory pass to show to the guards.

Darting across the back courtyard, he began thinking of a story to tell Abgar if he should meet him. He did not want to disappoint the boy.

Once inside the vaulted corridors, Vesuvio heard a distant sound of sandals clattering along the marble floors. He saw a cluster of men coming towards him through a series of arches. Not wanting to answer any questions as to why he was so far away from his quarters, Vesuvio quickly flattened himself behind a pillar.

Seeing Zeno leading the small group of men, Vesuvio stepped out of the shadow, moving towards him to report the story about Cleon's soldiers which Balthazar had told him.

Zeno paled at the sight of Vesuvio. He gasped, 'I thought you might be dead, too.'

Vesuvio looked now at the men behind Zeno. They were carrying a litter between them.

Gripping Vesuvio by the arm, Zeno pulled him towards the litter and, as the men parted, Vesuvio saw a small body covered with a blood-drenched white pall.

Zeno said grimly, 'It is young Abgar. The blood is the work of the Princess Nunar.'

'Abgar – dead?'

Zeno nodded. 'He and Nunar went to have their marriage approved by the Council of Twelve. She waited until then to show her displeasure with the act. That she intends only to marry Cleon.'

Vesuvio remembered the child saying that he had to go to a meeting, sulking that he could not accompany him into the city.

Quickly clapping his hands, Zeno told the men to continue carrying the litter down the hallway. As Vesuvio now hurried alongside them, Zeno whispered to the men, 'Take the body to the cellar. Guard it there.'

Having collected himself now, Vesuvio said to Zeno, 'Cleon is on his way here. With an army.'

'How do you know that?'

Hurriedly, Vesuvio told Zeno about his excursion into the city this afternoon, how he had accidentally met an old friend who had seen the soldiers on his travels west from Ecbatana.

'Then this assassination was planned,' Zeno said slowly. 'Cleon must know. He and Nunar . . .'

Gripping nervously at the gold chains around his neck, Zeno suddenly began to panic. 'Murder. Upheavals. And I don't even have a place to inter the boy's body!'

'His sister will not allow him a burial?'

'Princess Nunar? She would certainly not allow his spirit in the family vault. And if young Abgar were to be buried beside his father, Cleon would desecrate the tomb to defile the Succession of All Abgars.'

Vesuvio remembered something he had heard when he had first arrived at Samosata. He asked, 'What about Reuben ben Sahm? Perhaps he can help?'

Zeno suspiciously eyed Vesuvio.

He explained, 'Reuben ben Sahm has the keys to a place called the Old Sepulchres. He told me that when he first came to visit me.'

Pondering the idea, Zeno said, 'The Jew was always very fond of young Abgar . . .'

Vesuvio said quickly, 'Also, if the Princess is as spiteful as you say, we should warn him that his life might also be in danger. You told me that Cleon is persecuting the Jews.'

Looking at Vesuvio, glancing next to the small blood-stained bundle on the litter, and then to the white-robed men holding it, Zeno said, 'These slaves are mine. Like you, I can trust them. They can take the boy to the cellar. Prepare his body for burial. In that time, you and I will go to Reuben ben Sahm.'

Quickly giving the instructions to the litter-bearers, Zeno grabbed Vesuvio by the sleeve and hurried him through the back gate of the Palace.

26

Night was enveloping the city as Zeno and Vesuvio passed through the *zouk*, rushing on foot to the Jewish quarter of Samosata. They soon stood in front of a tall white house with no windows facing the street.

Zeno said, 'Stand to one side. The servants will recognize the purple of my robe. They will not refuse me entry. But they might be frightened if they see two of us.'

The night sentinel readily answered Zeno's pounding on the door. But when Vesuvio stepped from the shadows, he reached for a sword.

Zeno announced imperiously, 'I know the good Reuben ben Sahm is a guest in this house. Tell him that his trusted friend, Zeno, is here. Our business is very urgent.'

The sentinel began to protest but, seeing the stubborn expression on the eunuch's pink face, he reluctantly allowed Zeno and Vesuvio to enter the house and then left them alone in the courtyard as he went to fetch Reuben.

Sinking down onto a stone bench by a vine-covered pillar, Zeno said, 'This is all happening so fast, I wonder if I am making the right decision.'

Vesuvio said, 'You can't very well leave the boy's body exposed to the crows.'

Leaning his head back against the wall, Zeno said in a softer voice, 'Young Abgar was becoming very attached to you, Roman. He told me so only this afternoon. He even seemed to be in a pout that you hadn't taken him with you on some errand.' Looking at Vesuvio, he asked, 'Where did he want to go with you?'

Vesuvio hated to say it now. 'To find some plaster. We were going to build a model city of Rome.'

Shaking his head in bewilderment, Zeno said, 'Who would have guessed it? Who ever would have guessed it? I spent years – *years!* – trying to find a golden-haired man for his father. And what do I get? A playmate for his son?'

The sound of footsteps made Vesuvio turn. He saw Reuben ben Sahm hurrying across the courtyard.

He called to Vesuvio, 'You are foolish, Roman. Very foolish to come here.'

At that moment, Zeno rose from the bench, saying, 'The Roman slave has come with me. Young Abgar has been murdered. Assassinated by his sister. I fear that she and Cleon – along with Zediciah – are in some sinister collaboration.'

The old man's hand went to his chest. 'They killed ... the boy?'

Zeno nodded. 'Princess Nunar. With her own dagger. She slit open his stomach like a lamb. Only a few moments after they left the Council of Twelve.'

Wringing his hands in confusion, the old man asked, 'Then why do you come to me? What can I do?'

'We need a place to inter the boy's body. The Roman here tells me that you now hold the keys to the Old Sepulchre.'

Reuben gasped, 'You mean Princess Nunar will not even allow her brother to be interred in the family vault?' Then, shaking his head, he murmured, 'Of course not. She would be frightened of his spirits.'

Zeno was impatient. He snapped. 'Do you have the keys or not?'

Slowly nodding his head, Reuben said that he did have the keys explaining that many Jews had fled the district because of Cleon's threats and there were many sepulchres available for the asking. He reached towards the folds of his robe.

Vesuvio finally spoke. He said to Reuben. 'You are not safe here either. Cleon is headed towards Samosata with an army. A friend of mine told me this news in the city. My friend has a caravan leaving tonight for Tyrus. You could travel with him to there, sailing from there to Cyprus. Or go . . .'

The old man's eyes suddenly sparkled. '—or go south to the Red Sea. Sail south to join my brethren at the Essene community.'

'Yes,' Vesuvio said, remembering Reuben telling him about the religious sect which did not believe in slavery. 'You could join the Essenes.'

Hesitating, Reuben looked at Zeno.

Flicking his pudgy hand with impatience, Zeno said, 'Don't be stupid! Leave this place! Go!'

Vesuvio urged, 'If you stay, you will only be killed.'

Holding the iron ring of keys in his hands, Reuben began, 'These have been entrusted to me. I cannot—'

'Bah!' Zeno said, snatching the keys from him. 'I can return them to this house. They are good people here. They will find another custodian. Who knows? I might even convert to Judaism and beg for the job if Cleon comes into power! Now you listen to this Roman. He has a very good plan for your escape. And you have my pledge of silence!'

Reuben ben Sahm looked slowly from Zeno to Vesuvio.

Zeno urged, 'And if you don't hurry, you will not meet the caravan. It will leave Samosata as soon as the sands cool.'

The old man began to weaken. 'I have very little to take with me. I could sail south from Tyrus.'

Zeno slid the iron rink of keys over his small fist as if it were one more bracelet to wear. Then, removing a gold chain from around his neck, he tugged at it with both fists. Finally the chain broke.

Handing the chain to Vesuvio, Zeno said, 'This is for your loyal services. You also leave Samosata on the same caravan with Reuben.'

Then, urging them both to hurry, Zeno waddled towards the door and disappeared into the night, the iron keys clanking from his wrist.

Vesuvio stood alone in the courtyard with Reuben ben Sahm. Looking from the door to the gold chain which Vesuvio held in his hand, Reuben explained, 'Your bondage is broken, Roman. Zeno has freed you. The broken chain testifies that you are no longer a slave.'

Book Five
The Imperial City

27

The cool island winds of Cyprus had been refreshing to Vesuvio after the stifling heat of the Syrian desert and the sultriness of the sea voyage from Sidon. Now, bouncing up and down on the wooden seat of a two-wheeled cart, he filled his lungs with the sweet air of Italy and was thankful that he had seen the last of all foreign lands – even that hospitable island named for its copper, Cyprus.

The Italian sun was fading in the countryside north west of Brundisium, painting the olive orchards a soft violet hue. As the cart passed through the first terraced vineyards of Campania, Vesuvio became more anxious about arriving at his final destination. He had been away from home now for more than five years.

The Greek ship, the *Salamis*, had harboured last night in Brundisium. The voyage from Cyprus had been lonesome without the friendly chatter of Balthazar. Vesuvio had enjoyed his company from the night they left the caravanserai in Samosata five weeks ago now, throughout the sea voyage from Sidon, and during the entirety of his stay on the island of Cyprus.

In any other circumstance, Vesuvio would have enjoyed lingering in the seaside city of Paphos with Balthazar and his wife, Yianoulla. But he was a free man now and eager to return to his own family.

Although older than Balthazar, Yianoulla was pretty in her plump, jovial way. She greeted Vesuvio as if he were a brother to her black-skinned husband, telling him that he was welcome to stay in their home at Paphos. Balthazar immediately directed Vesuvio to a barber and put his servants to work making Vesuvio a wardrobe of colourful robes in the Greek merchant fashion.

When Yianoulla saw the handsome transformation in the travel-weary Vesuvio, she clapped her hands with delight. She not only called Balthazar's attention to the fact that they needed a dashing young representative to handle their business in

Athens but also reminded him about her sister being well past the marriageable age. Yianoulla generously said that if Vesuvio – she called him '*Chrisos Aedos Mou*', My Golden Eagle – did not like her sister then he could also meet some of her cousins. Like Balthazar, Yianoulla did not want Vesuvio to leave Paphos, the birthplace of the Greek love goddess, Aphrodite, where he would have no trouble in finding a bride, as well as building his own fortune.

A merchant vessel, the *Salamis*, was soon to depart for southern Italy. Vesuvio did not want to wait for the next ship sailing west. He graciously thanked both his host and hostess for their hospitality, as well as for the clear white gems which they still insisted he kept. Promising Balthazar and Yianoulla that he would write to them from Rome when he learned if the jewels had any worth, Vesuvio boarded the *Salamis*, looking like a prosperous Cypriot businessman voyaging to the markets of Rome.

The captain of the *Salamis* had assured Vesuvio at their departure that the voyage would be free from pirates, explaining how the Roman fleets had demolished the galley of a pirate witch named Athana.

Laughing at the oddity of a female leading such a coarse life, the talkative captain explained that Athana had, nonetheless, led the Romans a wild chase. But in the end, six warships blocked Athana into a cove near Magydus in Pamphylia and catapulted her with burning missiles until the only thing left floating in the sea – the captain sniggered – was a leopard skin from her battle uniform.

Vesuvio listened soberly to the account.

Finally, the captain saw that his story about the defeat of Athana – a tale which usually captivated every audience – was not being enjoyed by his distinguished-looking passenger. So, passing Vesuvio a wineskin, the captain embarked on a subject which he knew every gentleman loved: the wretched specimens of manhood now being offered for sale in the Mediterranean slaveports.

It was nightfall when Vesuvio reached the end of his cart journey from Brundisium. He paid the driver from the money he had obtained in Paphos in exchange for the shekels which young Abgar had given to him. Vesuvio had withheld one of the Eastern coins from the dealer, wanting to keep it as a memento of the young king. He carried the shekel with his other money in the waist pouch, along with the broken gold chain from Zeno and the gems which Balthazar had given him – all treasured keepsakes from the last five years.

Vesuvio thought about Carthage and the Arab, Sheik Bakir, in his ship, the *Ka'ba*, as he trudged along a dirt track now in the moonlight.

Carrying a single bundle of clothing in his hand, Vesuvio was thinking about his brother, Titus, and Scintus Genitor. Where were they tonight? Had his plan to disguise Titus as the heir to the Macrinus *gens* been successful? Had Titus been saved from some short-lived life in a quarry or as a field slave? Had he managed to escape? Would he be home when Vesuvio got there? Home ...

The iron gates hanging from their hinges on the entry arch to the Macrinus Estate first warned Vesuvio about his homecoming. He saw weeds growing through the driveway which had once been scrupulously paved.

Approaching the gate in slower strides, Vesuvio next noticed that the family *nomens* was gone – had been ripped-off from the stonework. He saw patches of dried tar where an edict had been posted but now even that had been washed away by the rain, torn by the wind, or ripped down by vandals.

Vesuvio stepped towards the jarred, rusty gates, raising the bundle as he slipped through the narrow space.

Inside the crumbling walls of what had once been rich farmland, he looked at the cypress trees lining the approach to his family's villa. They stood now like death pikes in the moonlight. The fields showed no signs of planting or harvest. He looked at a clump of buildings in the distant which he remembered to be the slave quarters. But no light flickered in any of the niches, no smoke rose from the squat stone chimneys.

Keeping to the shadows of the trees on one side of the driveway, Vesuvio heard only the sound of his sandals crunching on the gravel. Then, soon, he heard the surf of the sea washing against the cliffs below the back walls of Villa Macrinus.

The cliffs. The path adjoining the seaside estates. Vesuvio remembered the hot afternoon when he had gone to find Titus. The banquet being prepared for Gaius Lucretius arriving that evening from Rome. His mother's calm manner with the excitable house servants. He remembered his body slave, Sico. The porphyry pool in the gymnasium. The library. His father's rantings about the Roman politicians who wanted the estate.

His father. Vesuvio knew intuitively, even before he reached the portico of the villa, that his father was now dead. That Elder Aurelius Macrinus was no longer living.

But, then, the house itself, the grounds, everything about Villa Macrinus looked dead to Vesuvio in the moonlight. The gardens had run wild with weeds. The shrubs were twisted into grotesque shapes. The marble floor of the portico was cracked and littered with dried branches.

Suddenly, Vesuvio saw a movement between the darkness of the Doric columns that led into the *atrium*. He fell against the wall of the portico, now hearing the sound of sharp nails clicking against the cracked floor. He thought that he saw a wolf. No, it was a dog. Yes. A young dog. Little more than a pup.

Recognizing the animal's fair colouring, Vesuvio remembered their hound, Albucia. But she must be dead now. This young dog would be the offspring from one of her litters, an animal that was growing up like a wild dog.

Vesuvio moved from the wall towards the *atrium* when he saw another shape. Stopping again, he saw the figure of a boy creeping from inside the abandoned house, trying to coax the young dog by clicking his tongue.

Immediately, Vesuvio thought about Titus. Then he quickly realized that this boy was even younger than Titus had been when Vesuvio had last seen him.

Hearing the boy now calling to the dog, Vesuvio could tell by his rough accent that he was a slave boy, or the son of a nearby tenant farmer.

Vesuvio kicked a rock with his sandal, the first signal to the child.

Jumping at the sound, the boy looked in Vesuvio's direction.

Stepping out from the shadows, Vesuvio called in a soft voice, 'Don't be frightened, *puerulo.*'

Backing away, the boy began to stammer, 'I'm not doing anything wrong.'

'I know. You just want to play with that young dog there.'

'He doesn't belong to anyone!' the boy said defensively, looking at Vesuvio's foreign clothing.

'What's your name?'

'Primo,' he stammered.

Vesuvio nodded at the house. 'What happened to the people who used to live here, Primo?'

The boy shrugged, 'I don't know—' He now added respectfully, '*—domine.*'

'You look old enough to remember them, Primo. They couldn't have been gone that long. How old are you?'

The boy said more brightly, 'Eight!'

'Have you always lived in the neighbourhood?'

'My father is a farmer!'

'His own farm? Or a tenant?'

The boy lowered his head.

Vesuvio knew that if the boy's father owned his own piece of land that he would brag about it. He asked, 'Has it been a good year for your father's people, Primo?'

Slowly shaking his head, the boy looked at the dog again.

Vesuvio understood more. He said, 'So, your father has sent you out tonight to be a hunter. You are supposed to bring home the meat!'

Primo confessed, 'That's what *he* wants. But . . .'

'But you want the dog for a pet.' Vesuvio nodded, offering, 'Well, maybe your father can have meat for the family and you can still have a pet.'

Reaching into his pouch, Vesuvio pulled out five *asses* and said, 'I'll pay you, Primo, if you can tell me as much as you know about the Macrinus family.'

'The . . . who?'

Vesuvio realized instantly that the boy knew nothing about his family. He asked, 'Don't you ever see anyone coming in here? Horses or carts or wagons coming or going? Do you see any activity?'

'I just know . . .' the boy began excitedly, 'I just know . . .'

'You know what, Primo?'

He blurted, 'I just know that I'm not supposed to be here. Because this big, old house is . . . cursed!'

' "Cursed" is it?' Vesuvio said slowly.

'This and all the land, the houses all the way from here to, to, to—' He held out his arms wide in both directions.

'Does anyone live in the other houses,' Vesuvio asked, thinking of Julia Cordonis and her family.

He shrugged again. 'Just the ghosts, I guess.'

'Ghosts?'

Nodding, Primo said, 'My father says all these big empty houses are cursed and controlled by ghosts. That it is dangerous to come here. Except—' He looked at the dog now sitting by a pillar and cocking its head at the boy.

Holding out the coins to him, Vesuvio said, 'Here, Primo. Give this money to your father. Tell him that you earned it by helping a traveller. And why don't you leave the dog here? That way, there won't be any temptation at home to toss him in the stewpot. He looks like quite a smart dog. I'm sure he can find enough food for himself in the fields. And if you visit him, who knows? He might even become your friend.'

Gripping the coins in his small grimy fist, Primo asked '*Domine*?'

Vesuvio nodded.

'What is your name? My father will ask me who gave me so much money.'

'Just say that I didn't tell you my name.'

'Where are you from then, *domine*'

Patting the boy on the head, Vesuvio said, 'Tell your father that I didn't say where I was from either. Tell him that all you know is that I was on my way to Rome.'

'Rome?' The boy gasped, his eyes widening. 'You're going all the way to Rome? That far from here?'

Vesuvio nodded. 'That far from here.'

28

Vesuvio rested on a bundle of rags that night in a corner of the *atrium*. Although he could not sleep, he lay down after looking at as much of the empty house and neglected grounds as he could bear to see.

Staring through the square opening in the roof of the *atrium*, he gazed at the brilliance of the stars and remembered this home as he had last seen it. He remembered the serving girls walking carefully with a murrhine goblet in each hand on the afternoon of the banquet. He remembered the men slaves moving the couches from the *triclinium* to the top terrace. The cook being so nervous about the urns of honeyed muslum. His mother speaking to all of them in their own language and dialects.

Sitting upright and wrapping his arms around his knees, Vesuvio thought, 'But they couldn't have all just disappeared! There must be a trace of somebody! Something!' Then, remembering how he had even found the slave barracks and animal stables in total delapidation, Vesuvio's stomach churned with anxiety.

Lying back down on the rags, he locked his fingers behind his neck and realized that there was only one man who could give him a clue to what had happened to his family and this land. That is, if he was not dead, too.

Milo Popiliano had been an old man even five years ago but, if he still lived, Vesuvio knew that he could learn all he needed to know from his Uncle Milo in Rome.

The sky turned orange as sunrise drew near. Vesuvio dressed himself the next morning in the plainest of the tunics made for him in Cyprus and strode quickly along the cliffside path, his cape of indigo-dyed blue wool fluttering behind him.

He knew that this path was not the quickest way to reach the road to Misenum – where he could secure a horse from a stabler and exchange it for fresh mounts at wayside posts until he reached Rome – but he wanted to see with his own eyes if the neighbouring estates were as derelict as the boy, Primo, had told him last night.

This morning Vesuvio did not dwell on the past. He set out with determination from the shambles of Villa Macrinus. He had sworn to the household goddess, Vesta, that he would sleep in his family home again – and not on squalid rags in some filthy corner. He would reinstate Villa Macrinus to a respectable condition. He did not yet know how he was going to achieve this, what opposition he might meet. But Vesuvio had made the vow and he would honour it with his life.

He regretted that he could not make any pledges to reunite his family. He had to wait to hear who lived and who died. When he thought about Julia Cordonis, though, his mind became a jumble of emotions. He remembered being in love with her five years ago. He remembered longing for the day of their marriage. But he knew he had changed since then. And Julia might . . .

Suddenly pausing for the first time on the path, Vesuvio stared in horror at Julia's house. Tiles were missing from the *peristylium*. There was no longer any demarcation between garden and field. The doorways were opened only to the wind. Vines withered on the top terraces. Like Villa Macrinus, the slave stables here were also vacant.

Trying to contain his anger, Vesuvio proceeded along the path, climbing to the crest where Villa Genitor stood. He stopped when he saw that, athough the large home looked uninhabited, the stone walls were all standing. The shrubberies were clipped, the shutters neatly bolted on all windows.

Seeing the contrast between the fine condition of Villa Genitor and the shabbiness of the Villas Corda and Macrinus, Vesuvio realized that two things were possible. Young Scintus had returned home and now oversaw his inherited property. Or Scintilla Genitoris's influence at Court had spared her land from Roman annexation – or whatever blight had been suffered by the other families.

'Why am I standing here?' Vesuvio asked himself and hurried now towards the stone buildings which stood on the far side of the villa. He knew that if this estate had not been abandoned there would certainly be some slaves about to maintain it.

Stopping next to a white-washed well, Vesuvio shouted and, when he received no answer, he shouted louder.

The crow of a cock was his first response and next he heard the padding of bare footsteps on the dirt behind him.

Turning, he saw a young man dressed in a slave's mantle. He remembered how country slaves were always wary of strangers. And so, gallantly tossing the long cape back from his shoulder, Vesuvio said warmly, 'Good morning, Friend!'

The slave suspiciously eyed Vesuvio's clothing. The tunic was sewn from plain weave but the border was ornately stitched in red-and-gold threads – a pattern which no Roman would wear.

Vesuvio said brightly, 'A family called Genitor used to live here. Can you tell me it they are still the owners?' He had decided that it was wiser not to identify himself.

Digging one bare foot into the dirt of the yard, the slave glumly answered, 'The Lady, she lives in Rome.'

'Is that the daughter, Scintilla Genitoris?'

'She's the wife now to Gaius Lucretius.'

The name stung Vesuvio. Dropping the friendly voice he had assumed, he gasped, 'Scintilla married . . . Gaius Lucretius?'

Nodding, the slave said, 'They spend most of their days in Rome. At their home, The Palace of the Dolphins. Or—' He nodded towards the sea, in the direction of Capri. '—they go out there. Neither the lord or lady has much use for this old place any more.'

'Then what happened to her brother? Young Scintus?'

'There's never talk of a brother,' the slave murmured.

Vesuvio pressed, 'The boy? The son who was kidnapped by marauders?'

Lowering his head further, the slave continued to dig patterns in the dirt with his foot and asked, 'Is that what happened to him? I never did hear.'

'What about the families down the way? The Cordos? The Macrinus?'

Shrugging, the slave said, 'All I know is that our Lady sold off most of the slaves. Those of us left, we don't bother her with questions.'

Vesuvio saw that the man feared for his own well-being. So, wishing him a good morning, he moved up the path, climbing in wide strides, more anxious than ever to reach Misenum and ride as quickly as possible to Rome.

29

Milo Popiliano was still alive, living at the same house on the Esquiline Hill which Vesuvio remembered. But he had forgotten about his uncle's eccentricities. The additional years had only added to the old gentleman's unorthodox habits: Milo Popiliano's mind was lucid but, without warning, he would break off into a tangent totally unrelated to the subject he had been discussing and usually choosing a prurient diversion, most likely recounting his distant youth when he had been a lover to Nero's lustful mother, Agrippina.

Like Milo Popiliano, Rome too had changed. Vesuvio had never looked forward to coming to the Imperial City, except for the athletic shows he had seen as a youth at the baths. Rome had always been too congested, too noisy, its inhabitants always pushing and shoving one another. And that had only worsened in the last five years.

The streets were still narrow and steep but also much darker now because of the new apartment blocks which had been built, the *insulae*, to house the growing population of people who flocked there from the countryside. The streets were often only wide enough for a cart to pass through, and the new apartment blocks rose to heights of six, eight, even ten stories above the ground.

Vesuvio had arrived in Rome at nightfall and, having surrendered his horse to the stables at the Ostiens Gate, he engaged a public litter to take him to his uncle's house across the city. But as the streets were already filling with vegetable carts, freight wagons, plodding conveyances never allowed in the city during the daytime, he soon abandoned the litter on Via Sacra and proceeded on foot.

Vesuvio saw that many of the new apartments were built with peperino, and had *tabernae* crowding the ground floors where men stood drinking wine or eating quick meals. There was no visible difference between slaves and the 'freedmen', men who had once been slaves, nor the 'freemen' – people of Rome who could vote. They all dressed in similar robes of cotton weave but Vesuvio noticed that both the males and females now were dyeing the fabric or sewing fringe on the hem. He did not remember this fashion. The official 'toga' was in little evidence.

Also, Vesuvio had forgotten how the Romans revelled in loud noise, and seemed impervious to the disarray, the cramped darkness, the putrid smells of their city. Their eyes were in constant movement, sizing up passersby for their visible worth. They also had sharp elbows, not hesitating to prod someone from their way, mindless of a wagon rushing perilously down the narrow street where they were walking.

The public display of wealth in the Roman streets came as another surprise to Vesuvio. He saw private litters carried by eight slaves, accompanied by four torch bearers in front and four behind the litter, lighting the way even in twilight when there was no need for such illumination.

This time of evening also brought out the elaborate wagons of the tradesmen who had recently made fortunes importing oils, silks, ivories, spices – any luxuries for the Roman markets. These new vehicles vied with one another in ornateness, not only in the carving and painting of their framework but also in the richness of the curtains which the passengers could part with one hand to see – or be seen by – the other people riding in the streets at this busy hour.

The Romans loved the streets. They gathered in throngs to hear a story-teller sitting on a carpet to entertain them for only a *quadran*. Vesuvio saw a giant Nubian attracting a crowd as he swallowed a burning stick, then spat out the flames above the onlookers' heads. Another man called for people to see his trained vipers. An old woman shouted her services for reading good fortune in the stars.

Vesuvio passed a family sitting in front of a tall *insula*, visiting the neighbours across the way and, when a flock of sheep was herded between them, the entire family stood to continue their conversation in shouts over the top of the flock. Men idled at the sidewalk jars, the public latrines, and even after they had stopped making water their robes were still tucked into their belts as they discussed the topics of the day.

Jumping, Vesuvio avoided a cascade of human waste tossed from the attic window of another *insula*. He dodged a bucket of kitchen slop hurled from the next.

Finally reaching Via Esquilina, he looked eagerly for his uncle's *domus*, one of the two thousand private houses in this city of over one million inhabitants.

A surly slave woman answered Vesuvio's sharp rapping, suspiciously eyeing him when he told her that he wished to see the master of the house, saying that he was the nephew of Milo Popiliano. She began to shut the door on his face so he blurted, 'Tell Uncle Milo that "Vesuvio" is here!'

The woman's face suddenly lost its colour. Her eyes widened at the mention of the nickname. Both hands flew to her mouth. Then, bowing low, she held out her flabby arm for Vesuvio to pass through the *portus*.

Milo Popiliano's reception of his nephew was not so awe-struck. He did not question Vesuvio's identity. But, noting the width of his shoulders, the girth of his thighs, the bronze colour of his skin, he said, 'There is no doubt you have our blood. But I did not dress so effeminately as a young man. Agrippina – the *Augusta* Agrippina—' he added majestically '—she did not take warmly to young men who feathered themselves like peacocks. She liked a man's clothing on her men.'

Shaking his head at the memory of Agrippina, Milo immediately began, 'One of the best laughs I had was the night that Empress Agrippina asked me if I could bring another Centurion with me to the house she kept in Subura for our assignations.

She wanted two men poking inside her at the same time. So, off we went – this friend and myself – to Subura. You know Subura. Nothing but beggars live there. No place you'd expect to find a lady. Especially not the noble Agrippina who – besides being the mother of Nero, sired by Cnaeus Domitius – was the wife of Claudius. She poisoned poor old Claudius. Which is how I learned to protect myself from poisonings. I learned from Agrippina to take a little poison every morning. A small daily dosage works as an antidote. But that is another story. Now, what was I saying?'

Milo still had not invited Vesuvio to sit on a couch in the *atrium.* Although Vesuvio did not care about the small lapse in hospitality, he was anxious to hear about his family.

He said, 'You were telling me about my mother, Uncle Milo. Your sister, Cornelia Popiliana. And my father, Aurelius Macrinus. And our home, Villa Macrinus in Campania.'

'*Campania*!' Milo gasped, suddenly blinking his watery eyes. Then, looking at Vesuvio as if he were seeing him for the first time, he flung both arms around him and pressed his cheek to Vesuvio's. He shouted, 'My nephew! You've been delivered! You've been delivered from the dead, my nephew!'

Vesuvio slowly helped the old man to a couch and, holding his hand between both of his, he began, 'I am glad I find you in good health, Uncle Milo. But it is concern for my mother and father that brought me directly to you from Campania. I arrived back in Italy only two days ago and . . .'

Looking into Vesuvio's eyes, Milo said, 'You were kidnapped, weren't you? You and your younger brother?'

Vesuvio nodded.

'A plot to seize the estate?'

'That's what my father believed when I last saw him.'

Rising from the couch in a sudden rage, Milo raved, 'I know so! Your noble father's suspicions were correct. He took every step he could to thwart those lily-faced thieves! Those murderers! Those plunderers in purple! But—' He stared at Vesuvio. '—but that did not save Aurelius's life.'

'Father is dead?' Vesuvio was relieved that he had prepared himself for that shock.

Milo nodded.

'And my – mother?' he asked more warily.

Sitting back down on the divan, Milo reached for Vesuvio's hand and said, 'You have travelled many miles, Son. I can tell that by the dust on your clothes. Also, I see you have hatred seething in your eyes. I might be an old man but I still know about vengeance. It still flickers in my body, too. So I will not – I cannot – flood you with the entire story about your family and have you running out into the street like a wild man. I will feed the pain slowly to you. Like I take my daily drops of poison. My antidote. I will tell you about the fate of your family in bits. In pieces. It is the only way to protect your own life. Because – ah! – you still have enemies about!'

Squeezing his uncle's hands, Vesuvio pleaded, 'My mother? Is she still alive?'

Milo nodded. 'Cornelia lives. But . . .'

Rising to his feet, Vesuvio said, 'If Mother is dying, I must see her immediately. Don't you know—'

Shaking his head, Milo said, 'You are behaving exactly as I feared. You would do your mother more harm if you went rushing to her tonight than if you waited.'

Kneeling in front of Milo's divan, Vesuvio said, 'Just tell me a few things, Uncle Milo. I give you my word that I will do nothing rash tonight. I promise you.'

Putting his hand on the side of Vesuvio's face, Milo said, 'Son, your mother – the noble Cornelia Popiliana Macrinus – is a slave. She is in fact worse than a slave. She tends a *columbaria*. She is the mistress of the "dove-cotes", sitting in a dungeon and putting the ashes of slaves into jars. Then, after setting the jars into the niches in the walls, she waits in darkness for the next ashes to arrive. Your mother is a "dove-mistress".'

Sinking his face in the folds of his uncle's toga, Vesuvio could no longer contain his emotions. His chest began to heave as his first tears came from deep inside him.

Putting his hand on Vesuvio's shoulder, Milo said, 'Only a truly great man can weep. And it will take a great man – a great and strong man – to revenge the injustices done to your family. You must live for us all, Vesuvio. You must restore your name.'

30

The noise of Rome's night traffic – the rumble of wooden wheels, the sound of logs scraping over the cobblestones, distant crashes of pottery, raging arguments, laughter – only added to Vesuvio's misery, keeping him awake on a divan in the room which Milo had assigned to him. He became more bitter as he lay thinking about his mother living at this very moment as a slave in a *columbaria*, a woman with the country's noblest blood in her veins now barely existing in one of the city's lowest positions – a 'dove-mistress'.

Throughout the din of the interminable night, Vesuvio fluctuated in opinions about his Uncle Milo. First, he became angry at him for not having done anything to help his own sister to escape from her loathsome position.

Then, realizing the old man's helplessness against the tyranny of political powers, Vesuvio tossed on his bed and told himself that he had been away from Rome for many years – that he had forgotten the strict divisions between classes. Whereas his father had held a senatorial rank, Milo was a knight. There were limits to what he could achieve, restrictions to how much Milo could do for his sister. Vesuvio also knew that he had his uncle's knighthood to thank for the old man having been spared. He remembered the saying about a knight enjoying the freedom of 'Caesar's wife'. What would he have done if Uncle Milo had been enslaved or killed himself? No, he must not complain. He must remember that Uncle Milo was a well-meaning person. In throes of impatience, though, Vesuvio cursed the old man for not immediately telling him in detail about the Macrinus family.

Vesuvio was already sitting in the garden the next morning, impatiently picking at a bowl of plums when Milo finally emerged from the archway of his house. Quickly rising from his seat inside a pergola, Vesuvio saw that his uncle was carrying an armful of military equipment – chest plates, a crested helmet, leg greaves, a red woollen cape.

Although wondering why the old man was bringing equipment of the Roman Army out into the garden, Vesuvio quickly moved to help him with the awkward load.

Cautioning Vesuvio to handle the equipment carefully, minding not to scratch it, Milo sank down onto a seat in the pergola, explaining in winded gulps, 'I've had a man slave keep the metal polished and the leathers oiled. You'll find it all in perfect condition.'

'Whose is it?' Vesuvio asked, examining the fine metal craftmanship.

Looking at Vesuvio in astonishment, Milo explained, 'Yours! Whose do you think? Your commission came from General Termico shortly after your disappearance. Old Termico, he's dead now and you've never been appointed to a post. But you're still a Centurion in rank.'

Vesuvio looked from his uncle, down to the pile of armour, recognizing the helmet with the sideway crest as, indeed, the regalia of a Roman Centurion.

Still, he was confused. 'A Centurion is one thing, Uncle Milo. But such uniform and armour is costly. And paid for—'

'By your family!' Milo said quickly.

'*You* had all this made?'

'Termico was an old friend of mine. I could not very well let him make my nephew a Centurion then dishonour him by not ordering the equipment from his cousin!' Waving his hand, Milo added, 'You know Rome. As soon as a man is made a general, all his relatives become dealers in armaments.'

Now, spotting a slave girl bringing his breakfast from the house, Milo sat up higher on the bench and puffed, 'There's a parade spear and a shield in the house somewhere. I thought it was foolish for you to trouble yourself with them now. Even the armour is not necessary this morning. But a man should always know what battle equipment he has. Even if you'll just be wearing the plains today.'

'Today?'

'You can't go around Rome looking like some foreign catamite.' Milo shook his head in disgust, staring at the embroidery on Vesuvio's tunic. 'Dress like a man! Shed those Greek frills!'

Vesuvio fell back onto his bench in a daze. He was distraught with the news about his family but – at the same time – he could not believe that he had achieved a childhood dream – he was a Centurion in the Roman Army!

Inspecting a trayful of small cakes and fruit which the slave girl held in front of him, Milo said, 'You haven't already forgotten about seeing your mother today, have you?'

'Uncle Milo! You can't possibly mean that!'

'Good. I thought you'd be raring to go this morning.'

Selecting a plum from a bowl of water, Milo studied it and quickly dropped it back into the bowl with a plop. Next, he surveyed a plate of sesame cakes, saying, 'You have yet to tell me how you fared in the last five years. You survived. That's the important thing. But your brother never came back.'

Finally, choosing a cake, Milo bit into it and chewed for a few moments before adding, 'Don't be concerned about mentioning your father when you talk to your mother. Cornelia has lost many of her old ways but she still has fortitude. She was found dressing your father's corpse at Villa Macrinus when the soldiers came to seize him. That's why she's in a *columbaria*. A perverse position devised by Gaius Lucretius. Perverse, yes, but he also is very cunning. You must give him credit for that.'

Holding both hands to his uncle, Vesuvio implored, 'Please, Uncle Milo. Please, slowly. Tell me the entire story slowly. First, was it really Gaius Lucretius who was behind the plan to seize Villa Macrinus?'

'Aided by that trollop down the cliffs from you.'

'Scintilla Genitoris. She married him. I heard that.'

'A whore!' Milo boomed. 'Before the slaves from your estate were disbanded, they told stories about Scintilla Genitoris that would . . .'

Vesuvio gasped, 'Our people were – disbanded?'

Chuckling, Milo said, 'That was one of your father's cleverest moves. He had drawn up documents proving the manumission of all his slaves. He knew what was happening. He had even taken precautions for his own assassination!'

Vesuvio paled. 'Who assassinated my father?'

'A dagger, reportedly belonging to one of your slaves, was found between your father's shoulder blades the night following your disappearance. I do not recall the slave's name. He was from Corsica, I believe. I know that's where he is now. He was your body slave. He first brought the news to me.'

'Sico?'

'Something like that. Yes, it was Sico. He turned out, of course, to be quite innocent and totally dedicated to your mother's plight. A good sort. But, ah!'

Milo raised his hand for Vesuvio not to disturb him, continuing, 'Your father had weighed every possibility of attack. He might have spent too much time in his library but he was a shrewd man. He knew Roman Law. He knew that if a slave murdered his master – or was even accused of the act – that the entire slave population on the estate could be put to the sword. But to prevent such an atrocity, he back-dated their manumission papers. Thus, on his assassination, they were no longer his property. All four thousand slaves were free! Or was it more?'

Pausing, Milo cocked his head to think of the number. Then, shrugging, he continued, 'It hardly matters now. They're gone. But it was a busy time for me. Your father did not want to set four thousand people out into the world with no money, no positions, no shelter. Nor did he want them drifting to Rome and becoming idlers, living off the *Anonna* and waiting only for the next circus. So, I went to Puteoli. I rented a small office in that awful little town. I distributed the money your father had set aside for their assistance. And I made suggestions as to where they should go as freedmen, what jobs they were qualified to seek. Cobblers. Bakers. Farmhands. Fortunately, harvest time was close at hand and, as you know, all the labourers that can be found in southern Italy and Sicily at that time of year are immediately put to work.'

Vesuvio knew that his father had suspected some nefarious action but he had no idea that the man had been so well prepared for it. Even taking into consideration his own murder.

Now, he was torn between asking for more news about his father's assassination, the dealing with the slaves, or hearing more about his mother.

He began, 'Why is my mother a slave? What laws hold her?'

'The Roman Law that takes five per cent tax of a slave's price at manumission. Your father left funds to cover this, too. But Gaius Lucretius had a friend in the Treasury demand an inflated sum. Without giving your mother or myself time to raise it, he had her seized by the state and then bought her from them.'

'That man owns my – mother?'

'Yes, renting out her services. All because of the manumission. But it still remains his trouble spot. He could not challenge the manumission because it would attract too much public attention. Secondly, he didn't have his eyes on your estate for the Emperor at all. With no heirs, the estate would be auctioned. Court connections would allow him to place the only bid. But, ah! Suddenly there were no slaves! Wheat lands take great armies to work them. That many slaves runs into fortunes. He terrorized your neighbours, beginning by slowly forcing them to sell him their slaves at a much reduced price. He beguiled the whore down the cliffs to marry him. But still – to this very day – he has not raised the money to restock your estate with slaves, let alone wring a profit from it. I even heard that he is still trying to secure the title! That's why I wonder about his other activities. I hear, firstly, that the man needs money. Then I know, next, that he is sponsoring the Games. But that does not make sense to me. How does a man with no money sponsor a day at the Amphitheatre?'

'Gaius Lucretius is now sponsoring the Games?'

Nodding slowly, Milo said, 'That's where he is clever, too. Getting public opinion. He is obviously trying to win some well-paying public office. The Empress has not helped him so now he is after the votes of the apartment dwellers. All the patricians know that he is nothing but a scoundrel. They also agree that he wants to line his purse through politics. But to do it, I suspect that he has had to borrow money to the hilt. Even his wife, Scintilla Genitoris, is said to have gone through her fortune.'

Then pausing, looking at Vesuvio, Milo said bluntly, 'It is getting late in the morning now. I don't think you should be idling here in the garden, gossiping with me. You should be on your way to Via Ostiensis.'

'What's on Via Ostiensis?'

'Your mother! That's where she is in the *columbaria.* And on second thoughts, I do think you should continue wearing that disguise. At least for today. If there are any spies lurking around Via Ostiensis, they might wonder why a Centurion is going to see the poor old "Dove-Mistress" down in the *columbaria.* Everyone knows, though, that foreign catamites are likely to do anything. Yes. The more I think about it, keep wearing your disguise.'

Next, pointing to a small door in the stone wall surrounding the garden, Milo said, 'You can go to the stables through there. That entrance is not used much any more. As a young man, I used to slip out through there when I went to meet Agrippina. She loved me arriving with the smell of manure on my body. Agrippina used to swoon that I smelt just like a stable boy. One night, I remember—'

He chuckled, saying, 'You'll like this story. One night, Agrippina and I started talking about horses. She said that it was one thing for me to be built like a horse. But she wanted to try the real thing and—'

Vesuvio could no longer pretend to be interested in his uncle's lewd memories. He jumped up from the bench and ran across the garden towards the stable door.

Vesuvio knew the direction in which to ride towards Via Ostiensis. Once outside the Old Servian Wall, he stopped a slave woman carrying a large bundle on her head and learned that the entrance to the burial cellar lay in a field beyond a group of warehouses.

Vesuvio slowed his horse to a canter as he passed between the low storage sheds interspersed with fields of refuse.

The morning sun was hot, putrefying the garbage heaps. But ignoring the odour, Vesuvio increased his gallop when he saw the small greystone structure which the woman had described to him: a portal flanked by two urns filled with withered cypress branches – the symbol of death.

Tying his horse to a shrub, Vesuvio approached the portal leading to the underground *columbaria*, wondering for the first time if he was prepared to see what he might find.

An empty basket waited on the threshold. Vesuvio knew that a funeral society sponsored these burial spots known as 'dovecotes', slave fraternities existing on meagre alms. He guessed that someone from the society brought a daily basket of food to the 'Dove-Mistress'.

Stepping into the dark portal, he looked down at the moss-covered steps descending into darkness. Preparing himself for the reunion, dreading the condition in which he might find his mother, he soon saw faint lights flickering along the steps in the blackness. They were torches attached to the wall.

Without further hesitation, Vesuvio slowly began to descend, his footsteps echoing as he moved deeper into the *columbaria*. Not wanting to frighten his mother, he tried to think of some way to prepare her for the reunion, too.

Remembering that many Romans referred to old women as 'mother', Vesuvio decided to act, at first, as if he was someone coming here to inquire about the burial of a slave.

He called once, listened, then continued descending deeper into the earth. Wide gaps of darkness lay between the wall torches and, as Vesuvio fumbled his way in the intervening spaces, he smelled a musty dampness collected over many years.

Stopping at a level section between the steps, he thought that he saw a light moving in the darkness far down below him.

He called again.

The light bobbed closer, a frail voice answering, 'Do you come from the society?'

Vesuvio moved down the next steps, calling, 'I come from a friend!'

'You must go to the society,' the woman's voice said. She coughed and continued weakly, 'The offices are across the river in Transtiberina. Go to the society—'

Vesuvio stood on another landing between the steps. He watched the torch rising nearer and, by its smudged light, he saw a black mantle wrapped around an old woman's face. He was momentarily speechless. But more concerned than ever about not frightening his mother, he continued, 'I do not come about death . . . Mother. I'm here with news of life. Good news.'

The torch moved slowly up in the darkness, coming closer towards him. After coughing again, she said, 'I do not understand your words. But you would not come down here if it weren't important. Wait there. I'll find a bracket here to—' She groped on the stone wall for a place to set the torch.

Stepping closer, Vesuvio spotted the iron ring which she was trying to find. Taking the torch from his mother's hand, he secured it into the ring, desperately trying to think of what he would say to her when they came face to face in this light.

But before Vesuvio moved his hands away from the torch, his mother reached forward. She put one hand on his shoulder. She whispered only one word.

'*Vesuvio . . .*'

Grabbing for his mother, Vesuvio held her frail body in his arms, patting the back of her head, feeling her sobbing into his chest. He felt tears welling into his own eyes. He tried to gulp them back at first, but then he let them fall down his cheeks. All the words he tried to speak only caught in his throat.

Pulling back from him, Cornelia Macrinus wiped a knuckle in the corner of each eye, staring up at Vesuvio in the torch light. Then, when she saw him gaping at the iron bracelets locked around her wrists, she began to shake her head, to explain.

Grabbing her again in his arms, Vesuvio held his face down to her head, begging, 'Mother? Mother, what have they done to you?

'I'm alive, Vesuvio,' she assured him. 'I lived to see you again.'

Pulling back from him, she gazed up at his face and said, 'Fate has dealt us cruel blows, Vesuvio. But you are alive, too.'

Vesuvio took her iron-cuffed wrists. Holding them in his hands, he protested, 'But—'

She withdrew her hands, repeating, 'I live.'

'Live? *Live?*'

Reaching for his face, she consoled, 'We must remember your Father's spirit, Vesuvio. And your Father is smiling at this moment. Smiling through the atrocities and bloodshed and losses we have suffered.'

Stopping, Cornelia wiped tears away from her thin face with the edge of her mantle, saying, 'You went to Milo's house.'

Vesuvio nodded.

'Be patient with him. Your Uncle Milo is an old man. He helped me as much as he could. Poor Milo often tried to aid me more than he should have. I asked him to stop. To be more cautious. I knew you would come back. I prayed you would go to Milo. His knighthood has spared him so far but I suspect that spies watch this place. In the same token, Vesuvio, you must also move cautiously.'

'Spies? What do I care about spies? I want you out of here.'

'There are laws, Vesuvio. Unjust, cruel laws. If we fight them, there will only be more deaths.'

Grasping her again, he said. 'I *will* fight them, Mother. I will not leave you here in this . . . this . . . ' He looked around him in the darkness. And when he heard her begin coughing again, he cried, 'Listen to you! You're not well! No! I will not leave you here, Mother! I will not!'

Smiling pitifully at him, she asked, 'Would you rather see me executed for running away? And you also killed for assisting a slave to escape? No, Vesuvio that would only please our enemies.'

'But, surely, the society, the slave fraternity which supports this place will not execute you!'

'The society is only a concession to poor slaves. A token allowance. These dove-cotes serve Rome well. They keep the streets free from rotting flesh.'

Looking up at him, she insisted, 'No, Vesuvio. You must not be rash. You must recognize the fact that our lives have changed. No longer are we the masters. We now—' She held out her wrists, showing the iron bracelets. '—we now are the slaves.'

Taking both of her hands in his own, Vesuvio kissed them, whispering. 'Come! Let us go sit!' He moved to lead her down the steps.

Pausing, Cornelia straightened the ragged mantle around her head and said, 'It would please me, Vesuvio, if we did not. I do not want my son to see . . .'

'It cannot – be – that – bad!'

'It is not "bad", Vesuvio. But it is not how you remember me. I don't want you leaving here today with hateful images in your heart. No more than you have already.'

Lowering her head, she continued, 'Also, I don't know how much Milo has told you. But your brother . . . Titus has still not appeared.'

'I know.'

'Vesuvio, I can confess this only to you. I never expected to see Titus again. He was much younger than you, true. But a mother can often see things. And I saw a weakness in that poor child. A delicateness that you never showed. It was you I knew who would return, Vesuvio. And you have!'

He assured her, 'I have not only returned, Mother, I have come back strong. Determined. After I slept in our old house two nights ago—'

Her eyes lit up. 'You've been to Campania?'

Nodding, Vesuvio said, 'I slept in the house. Long enough to know that it would be restored again. And soon, Mother. Soon!'

'The house is still standing?'

'It is a strong house, Mother. It will take many more years of neglect to destroy it. The fields are not ploughed or planted but neither are they barren. The land is still very rich.'

'And did you go to Villa Corda?' she asked hesitantly, holding her eyes on him.

He waited.

'Do you know about Julia?' she asked.

He shook his head.

Taking a deep breath, she said, 'Julia . . .' She stopped, bending to cough.

'Julia is dead?'

She nodded.

'When? Why? How did it happen?'

'Julia was noble. The Cordo family was fine. Her young

sister disappeared the night your father was killed. Julia provided strength for her family. But then when . . . she also was . . . defiled . . . and her body . . .'

'Gaius Lucretius?' Vesuvio asked, his face pale.

'His mercenaries. They struck like beasts. The Cordos . . . all are gone.'

Clenching his fists, Vesuvio looked into the darkness above his mother's head and tried to control the blasphemies rising in his throat.

Putting her hand on his forehead, she said, 'Your life has been spared, Vesuvio. You still have health and strength. You must not burn out your soul with hatred. Hatred only destroys the spirit. Be strong and sharp. And, above all, be cautious.'

He murmured, 'It will be difficult, Mother. It will be very difficult.'

She asked, 'Does Gaius Lucretius know you are back? That you did not disappear from the face of the earth as he had planned?'

Vesuvio shook his head, his eyes closed.

'You must move carefully, then. You must plot every step. You are the heir now. The *pater familias*. But most important, my son—' She grasped his hands. '—you live!'

Slowly sinking to his knees in front of his mother, he pressed her cool hands against his face and again began to weep. Cornelia Macrinus drew him closer against her mantle and, wrapping one arm around him, she began running her gnarled fingers through his thick golden hair. She repeated his name over and over.

31

The next morning, Vesuvio rode to The Palace of the Dolphins on the Palatine Hill. He gave the reins of his horse to the groom, marched up the steps with his red Centurion cape flowing behind him in the breeze, and announced to the major-domo that 'Centurion Aurelius Macrinus' demanded an immediate audience with Gaius Lucretius.

Watching the haughty servant walk down the arched *peristylium,* Vesuvio carefully noted by which statue he turned – it was Mars – and next listened to hear how far his footsteps went before there was the sound of a knock, then the opening of a door. He wanted to know the exact whereabouts of Gaius Lucretius. If he refused him an interview, Vesuvio would know where to find him.

Returning a few minutes later, the major-domo bowed, saying, 'My master regrets that he is in a meeting. But he bids you to call back tomorrow.'

As the slave spoke, Vesuvio kept looking towards the statue of Mars. He had suspected that Gaius Lucretius would put him off until tomorrow. It would allow him time to verify Vesuvio's identity, check on his whereabouts, perhaps even dispatch an assassin.

But Vesuvio had also surmised that Gaius Lucretius's curiosity would be so great that he would not allow Vesuvio to leave The Palace of the Dolphins without trying to catch a glimpse of him.

He was right. Before the major-domo returned to full standing position, Vesuvio spied a man peering around the corner of the *peristylium.*

Quickly moving past the major-domo, Vesuvio strode down the marble floor, ignoring the sudden protests of the slave behind him.

'Lucretius!' he boomed. 'I thought you and I should meet as soon as possible.'

Although seven or eight years had elapsed since Vesuvio had

last seen Gaius Lucretius, he saw that the man was still handsome. But his swarthy features had become leaner over the years, his brown eyes having lost the boyish guile which Vesuvio remembered. Yet he still looked powerful – tall, well-exercised, his skin bronzed by the sun.

Lucretius sobered as Vesuvio approached him. He called, 'I gave the slave a message for you.'

'He delivered it. But I see you aren't too busy with your meeting to catch a glimpse of "Aurelius Macrinus".'

Lucretius stood erect in his spotless white toga, his dark eyes blazing with anger.

'What occupies you today?' Vesuvio asked, holding his hand towards an open door down the hallway to the left. 'Am I disturbing preparations for the Games? Or a meeting with your bankers?'

Ignoring the questions, Lucretius demanded, 'When did you return to Italy?'

'Ah! So you know I was travelling?' Vesuvio laughed.

Looking at his uniform, Lucretius said, 'What I did not know was that you are a Centurion – if indeed you are.'

Vesuvio boomed, 'I do not pretend to be what I am not.'

By now, three short, balding men in togas stood in the open door, staring down the hallway at the confrontation.

Waving his hand at the men, Lucretius called firmly, 'Go back to your papers. I'll join you in a moment.'

Vesuvio had heard last night from his Uncle Milo that Lucretius was indeed having money problems. Milo had confirmed the rumour through his network of friends. Lucretius's patronage for the games had been posted but the costs were rising daily. Vesuvio knew that he was meeting today to raise additional money.

Looking at the three short men, Vesuvio said, 'Perhaps your learned colleagues should stay to listen. I haven't been in Rome for many years now but I would say that they are bankers. They might learn something that could be useful to them.'

'Say what you came to say,' Lucretius snapped, 'then leave my house.'

'To you, Lucretius, I need not say anything. You see that I

am alive. You know that I am the heir to the estate in Campania you want to buy.'

Lucretius said quickly, 'I warn you to watch what you say. I have witnesses. You could end up in the courts.'

'There is only one thing I would like better!'

Lucretius waited.

Vesuvio half-smiled as he began, 'As sponsor of the Games, you must have a great love of sports.'

Blandly, he said, 'There will be games, true.'

'Rome loves a blood spectacle, Lucretius. And you are making a bid to win the plebian vote. To become a hero. So why not go all the way? Why stop at only uncaging a few animals from *Africanus*? Allowing a cell or two of criminals to execute one another?'

'You're speaking in riddles. I have important business to do. These men have come here to my house to meet with me and my wife, Lady Scintilla.'

Vesuvio threw back his head and laughed.

'What strikes you as being so funny?'

' "Lady" Scintilla!'

'I warn you, Vesuvio . . .'

'Oh! So you know the name my family calls me! Do you want to tell me how well you know my family these days? And the family of the Cordos?'

Vesuvio's face was beginning to harden. He continued, 'Or do you want to show the people of Rome your true heroism? Will you follow an ancient custom of entering the arena yourself?'

The defiance came easily for Vesuvio. His family losses, coupled by his five years in slavery, justified the idea which he had stumbled upon last night with his Uncle Milo. Blood feuds in the Old Republican days had often been settled in the arena. And, although Milo Popiliano had no proof of Vesuvio's capabilities, he had agreed that the safest way for Vesuvio to remain in Rome was to meet Gaius Lucretius in the amphitheatre. The sponsor of the Games could hardly afford to have his opponent assassinated before the contest. It would lead to rumours of cowardice and defeat the purpose of the costly spectacle.

Now Lucretius asked in astonishment, 'You are challenging me?'

Controlling his voice, Vesuvio said, 'You are the sponsor of the Games. I can only honour an invitation to meet you there.'

The three bankers had come further out of the room, listening more avidly now.

Narrowing his eyes, Lucretius said, 'My sport is the chariot. Driving a span of four. I do not think—'

'Do not "think", Lucretius. Your thinking only makes misery for others. If you drive a chariot and four, then so do I!'

Studying Vesuvio, Lucretius said in a firm voice, 'Fine. I challenge you, Aurelius Macrinus. I will meet you in the Flavian Amphitheatre. At the Ludi Lucretius. I will surrender my position in the podium next to the Empress Plotina. I will post new bills on the walls of Rome announcing a chariot race as being added to the entertainment.'

Vesuvio asked, 'Are you in a position now to place a wager on yourself? Or should I—' He looked towards the three men. '—should I be asking your bankers that question?'

Lucretius sneered, 'I think we can leave wagers to the betting shops.'

'Not even if I want nothing more from you than the freedom of one female slave? One of my blood now held in your bondage? A noble woman descended from the Claudio-Julian line but who is condemned to work as a "dove-mistress"?'

Lucretius's thin lips curved into a smile. He said, 'The woman of whom you speak, Centurion, is no chattel of mine. She belongs to the slave whom you rushed past to speak to me.'

'My mother belongs to your – slave?'

'You certainly have heard about a "*vicarius*", the slave of another slave. My major-domo, Kirnus, owns quite a string,' Lucretius said, now in full command. 'If you remember, a slave to another slave in Rome is often a gift from his master or mistress. Or from some of their grateful friends. But I must warn you, Centurion, that Kirnus does not sell any of his slaves. He only rents out those of . . . inferior quality.'

Moving to strike Lucretius, Vesuvio caught himself.

Smiling at his sudden loss of confidence, Lucretius said, 'Do

I still have the honour of contesting your skills at the Flavian Amphitheatre?'

'You do! *You do!*'

Vesuvio turned, striding quickly down the *peristylium*, not looking at the slave, Kirnus, who stood smiling by the open portal of The Palace of the Dolphins.

32

Milo anxiously waited for Vesuvio to bring back news of his confrontation with Gaius Lucretius. But when Vesuvio returned to the house that afternoon he glumly repeated the news about Cornelia Popiliana Macrinus being enslaved to a slave.

Milo remained momentarily silent. He finally said, 'I would think the same standard will apply to your mother as to you. She is momentarily safe during the period before the Games. Especially if I spread it around town that Lucretius's major-domo owns the mother of his rival in the races.'

Nodding his head, Milo became more confident. 'Yes, this might even help your mother's case for manumission. If there's one thing that the Romans love more than blood, it's a mother!'

Vesuvio reminded his uncle, 'But, according to Lucretius, this Kirnus never sells his own slaves.'

Milo waved off the report with a flick of his liver-stained hand. He said, 'Leave that to me. I'll mention it to my friend, Pliny. He does not take lightly to slaves owning slaves. Also, there is a movement to stop the renting-out of slaves by contract. And after talking to Pliny, I will put a few words in the ears of some banker's telling them that there is a panic among the creditors holding Gaius Lucretius's notes.'

Looking at Vesuvio, Milo said, 'This morning, while you were at the Palace of the Dolphins, I went to see General Termico's cousin. The man called "Old Termico". He can train you on his track outside Porta Latina. You have a month. That may sound like a long time to you. But it's not when you're dealing with a team of four strong beasts.'

Patting his uncle's shoulder, Vesuvio said, 'I'm becoming more and more dependent on you. I don't like that.'

'Yes, I've been thinking about your independence, too. You haven't had much of it lately.'

Vesuvio began, 'I didn't mean like that . . .'

'Forget how you meant it. When was the last time you had a woman?'

Smiling, Vesuvio realized that he had not made love to anyone since returning to Italy.

Milo said, 'You would be stupid to waste the energy during your training. Old Termico will send you home exhausted every night. You will have to go to him before dawn. There's more to driving a chariot than guiding a plough-horse, you know!'

Now tugging on Vesuvio's red Centurion cape, Milo said, 'I think you've had enough service out of this for one day. Change into something less conspicuous for your visit to one of the bordellos. But don't wear those Greek clothes. You'll be flocked by every pervert in Subura.'

'Subura?' Vesuvio asked. 'Is that where I should go?'

'As a horse goes to a trough for water, a man with a stiff pizzle points it in the direction of Subura.'

Located to the northwest of the Esquiline Hill, Subura was a squalid district of Rome. The dark, narrow streets were cramped with shops and vendors selling bread, meat, vegetables, olives, sour wine – the provisions to feed the city's poorer classes.

By late afternoon men, women, and children thronged the streets whilst cobblers hung sandals in the doorways of their shops for the afternoon business hours, barbers began sharpening their blades, and butchers dragged squealing pigs across the cobbled streets.

Walking deeper into Subura, Vesuvio was both amused by the sights that he saw – children poking their fingers into wicker rabbit cages – and repelled by the sour odour of this impoverished section. He hurried towards the 'Street of the Lanterns', heading for a bordello which his uncle had recommended to him. By coincidence, it had the same name as the bordello which he had visited in Samosata – Palmyra's.

Vesuvio knew that he had passed into the prostitute quarter when he saw women with white lead on their faces lingering under dark archways; passed boys still in puberty wearing cochineal on their eyes, their tunics hitched up to a leather belt to show the roundness of their buttocks; heard the rattle of brass curtain rings from windows, a whore trying to attract a customer from the coolness of her room. The people on The Street of the Lanterns were as eager for business at this time of day as the cobblers and vegetable pedlars.

Seeing a wooden shape of a palm tree hanging above a door, Vesuvio hurried his step. He was only a short distance from the blue-fronted house when a crippled man tugged at his arm.

Turning, Vesuvio saw a twisted shape leering up at him. The man asked, 'Do you want the best suck in Rome?'

Vesuvio continued towards the blue-fronted house.

The cripple was persistent. He hobbled behind Vesuvio, saying, 'She will charge you only a few *asses*. Look! You can see her there behind the jars! She will hold your phallus in her mouth for free. She will let you feel the deepness before you decide.'

Vesuvio did not want to brush the man rudely aside but neither did he want to waste precious time with him.

The cripple urged, 'Just try her, *domine*. Iucunda has a secret. She has a mouth like no woman in Rome. Come with me. Feel Iucunda's secret mouth.' Leaning closer to Vesuvio, he divulged, 'She does not have a tongue . . . aaah!'

Reaching towards the brass knocker on the door of Palmyra's, Vesuvio said, 'I need more than a mouth today.' He beat on the door.

'Then use her hole!' The cripple spread his arms. 'But I tell you, you haven't had pleasure if you haven't enjoyed Iucunda sucking you with – no tongue!'

The door to Palmyra's opened. Vesuvio stepped inside and, as a female slave led him across the paved atrium, he fleetingly thought about the name. Iucunda. He had known an Iucunda once. But where?

Vesuvio forgot about the crippled pimp and his 'Iucunda' as he saw a line of girls lying on divans by a pool. The mistress of Palmyra's was a Syrian woman, wearing a yellow *stola.* She led Vesuvio towards the line of girls sprawled on their upholstered divans and nodded approvingly as Vesuvio chose a black-haired girl with an oval face and fulsome body. Beckoning the girl, the mistress told Vesuvio that her name was 'Mira'.

Vesuvio asked her if 'Mira' had endurance, saying that he would need her services for more than a few moments, that he had been without a woman for a long time.

Again, the mistress nodded. She said that Mira came from the same province as the Emperor himself. Hispania. That she was also as indefatigable as Trajan. That Mira would keep Vesuvio busy for as long as Trajan was warring the Dacians. Like the Emperor, too, she only required the money.

After paying the mistress, and following Mira to a cubicle under a stone stairway, Vesuvio quickly undressed and lay down on a pallet. He was already aroused when he took Mira in his arms.

Lying Mira on her back, he immediately began to penetrate her with his stiff phallus. He dismissed her first moans as the sounds simulated by all professional women. But soon Vesuvio knew the gasps were becoming more genuine. Her body joined his in the heated rhythms.

Moving his hands towards Mira's breasts, he repositioned her sideways on the pallet and began to twist deeper inside her. He felt his manhood slowly returning to him. He was glad that he had warned the mistress about his appetite. Better than sensuous now, Mira was durable. Vesuvio knew that he would stay with her for many hours. He needed to lose himself in passion.

Only one question inched its way into his mind that night: *Am I destined to find satisfaction for the rest of my life only with prostitutes?* He had no betrothed now. No wife. No prospect of heirs. Only the companionship of pleasure-women.

33

Old Termico – the cousin of the deceased General Termico and proprietor of the track outside Porta Latina – was part of the set of aging gentlemen in Rome who preserved the conservative spirit of the Old Republic. Termico – like his friends – felt that the Empire was becoming weak, its armies lacking discipline, the officers effete. They considered the citizens to be lazy, too dependent on the public distribution of wheat from the *Annona*.

Also, this conservative group loathed the direction in which the Games were headed. Although they were mostly old knights like Milo Popiliano who had spent their youths in promiscuity, they felt that decadence was becoming too public in these modern days, that too much emphasis was being put upon sex in the arena.

The Roman Games had been instituted three hundred years ago by two brothers after the death of their father. The brothers were members of a wealthy family. They wanted to better the funerals usually given for a *pater familias*. The Roman custom at that time was to sacrifice an animal as a tribute to a great man. Determined to revive a noble practice from ancient Etruscan days to honour their esteemed father, the two brothers commanded two manly slaves to fight to the death in public as a blood remembrance.

The populace of Rome enthusiastically responded to the funereal show. Soon generals commemorated victorious battles with combats between slaves. Politicans tried to win attention by setting slaves against one another with swords, spears, and tridents. The popularity of fighting slaves quickly grew as the crowd became more addicted to the thrill of seeing mortal combat.

Exotic animals from foreign lands were soon added to the events, also colourful clowns, juggling acts and ancient plays staged with elaborate costumes and tedious speeches deleted from the texts. The floor of the amphitheatres was flooded for full-scale naval battles. Nero brought elephants to Rome to trample the Christians when the crowd grew weary of watching them being torn apart by lions. Gorillas attacked maidens who had been smeared with reproductive juices which the animals recognized as a cue for mating. Horses and bulls were manually excited by slaves and directed towards young girls pegged out on the *harena* – the sand of the amphitheatre.

Old Termico, Milo Popiliano and their small circle of friends knew that the crowd was becoming increasingly jaded, that there was little hope of these patterns changing in Rome. Although Emperor Trajan was away at war, the country was represented at the Games by the Empress Plotina and Trajan's adopted heir, Hadrian.

Despite Plotina's pretensions to integrity and honour, she allowed the politicans to present the bloody spectacles. Private sponsorship saved her husband the cost of amusing his subjects and to eliminate the Games could easily excite the plebian crowd to riots. The Romans had become addicted to their entertainments of death.

Old Termico was pleased that Vesuvio was entering the Games on behalf of his wronged *gens*. He also approved of Vesuvio not being the product of a club which trained contestants for the Games. The chariot races especially had become a debacle to the old conservatives' way of thinking.

There were four popular racing teams in Rome, athletic clubs recognized by their colours – the Blues, the Greens, the Reds, the Whites. To Termico and Milo Popiliano, the sportsmen of those clubs made a sham show of manliness. The veteran knights felt that the young charioteers strutted around Rome like peacocks, behaved like pompous fools when they were chased by females and celebrated in drunken revelries by their male fans. Termico was pleased to hear that Vesuvio was prepared to meet his death in the Flavian Amphitheatre for the sake of family honour.

Termico was a bald, barrel-chested old man whose age belied the stamina still raging in his thick-set body. He would be shaved, dressed in a leather tunic, and waiting for Vesuvio every morning inside the walls of his dirt track beyond Porta Latina.

His main lecture to Vesuvio concerned form. Although

cursing the rules set down by the now popular racing teams, Termico was wise enough not to ignore them. He told Vesuvio that he had seen Gaius Lucretius race a few times and, on each occasion, Lucretius had not only been the victor but drew the loudest cheers from the upper seats of the circus.

Lucretius usually raced as a 'Blue'. The supporters of that team were particularly unruly. Termico warned Vesuvio that he must drive not only to win but also to overcome the handicap of not having the sponsorship of a college – to be prepared for the mockery of the Blue supporters in the stands.

Termico began Vesuvio's training by leading him through a progression of one, two, three, and, finally, four horses pulling a light training-chariot made of pine. He watched with approval as Vesuvio quickly learned the role of an *agitator*, gauging the strength of the *funales*, the outside horses which were not harnessed to the chariot like the two middle animals.

He told Vesuvio that a chariot had to avoid racing too closely to the inside wall of the arena. That if he hugged the wall too closely he could become smashed. To the extreme, though, if a charioteer drove too far out he could quickly lose a lead position.

An *agitator* must continuously be on guard to gain on his opponent, even if that gain was minimal. Termico told Vesuvio that many Roman *miliarii* – charioteers who had won more than a thousand races – had achieved that distinction by winning only by short distances.

To acquaint Vesuvio with the spirit of a chariot race, Termico did more than just to teach him the handling of the four horses, the *quadriga*. He tutored him in the background of the four chariot teams.

The more time Vesuvio spent in Rome, Termico said, the more chance he would have to see slogans scrawled on its walls about the heroes of each team. Rome was covered with love poems written to the charioteers, elegies were even composed by court poets at the death of a favourite. The more vulgar and ostentatious the charioteer was, the more the people adulated him. Rome adored her athletic figures.

*

Vesuvio saw an example of the hostility between the racing clubs when he was taking a break for a midday meal at the end of his first week. He was listening to Termico explain how the *Circus Maximus* in Rome held the strictest form of racing in the Empire: it was a rule that never more than four chariots raced at one time. In a provincial arena, though, sometimes as many as twelve chariots participated in a race. The inhabitants of Rome were beginning to demand such racing spectacles, too.

Termico was drawing a political parallel between the dangers which the provincial influence was having on Roman politics as well as on chariot ruling when one of his slaves dragged two young boys across the dirt track.

The slave was a burly, shaven-headed Thracian. He held each boy by the scruff of his neck and reported to Termico, 'I found these two rowdies lurking around the walls. Do you think they're spies?' Termico had given his men strict orders to be on guard against agents of Gaius Lucretius. He knew they would want to learn as much as they could about Vesuvio's training and equipment.

Termico eyed the two youths. They were dressed in rough tunics and had pimply skin. He said, 'They must be supporters of the Greens. Only a Green would be courageous enough to come nosing around where he didn't belong.'

The taller and more thuggish boy spat defiantly on the ground. He snarled, 'The Greens be damned! The Blues are the best and bravest team.'

He had fallen for Termico's ruse. He had come from Lucretius's college, the Blues.

Smiling, Termico said, 'The Blues are also as dumb as jackasses.'

Seeing his mistake, the boy began to sputter. His curly-headed friend looked angrily at him.

Studying the two boys, Termico demanded, 'Did Gaius Lucretius send you here to spy?'

They did not answer.

'Maybe he thought we'd let two children like you pass without any questions. Whatever his reason, we'll give you something to report back to him,' Termico said. Then turning to the Thracian slave, he ordered, 'Tan their backsides. They're too young for whipping but not too old to have a rosy butt. Use some leather harnessing on them.'

'I'm the son of a free man,' the second boy wailed. 'My father's a baker in Via Triana!'

'Then you should be there helping him,' Termico barked. He nodded for the Thracian to drag them to the stables, saying, 'Grip that leather strap and make a few good welts on these hooligans. Then send them home. Their mothers can dry these two cry-babies' tears before they go back to report to the Blues that Termico will really flog the next snoopers he finds around here.'

Settling back down beside Vesuvio on the ground, Termico said, 'You see now what I mean about the different clubs. Those two youths would rather betray themselves as spies than be mistaken for Greens.'

Loud wailings began to rise from the stables. Termico looked fleetingly towards the canvas flap of the flat-roofed building. He muttered, 'Brats! They should get the same at home. Parents don't discipline their broods today like in olden days when I was a boy.'

Turning back to Vesuvio, he resumed talking about his passion – the arena – saying that there was a maxim for a man like Vesuvio, a charioteer not favoured to win a race but who could ultimately become the victor . . .

'*Erupit et vicit.*' Termico thought the words were fitting, too, for a young man named in honour of a volcano.

The practice with Termico's horses continued for only ten days. Towards the end of the second week Vesuvio began to acquaint himself with a new span of horses, a gift to him from Milo Popiliano.

The fine animals were Arabian, the colour of desert sand. Milo had purchased them under the pretence of sending the horses to a sheik in Damascus. He explained to Vesuvio that they could not be too careful. The city walls were plastered with announcements that Gaius Lucretius was to race an unknown charioteer called 'Aurelius Macrinus'. Gossip was rife about Vesuvio's identity. The Imperial City was crawling with spies to find any details about this mysterious *agitator*. Since the two youths were strapped with horse-harnessing at Termico's stables, though, no one else had been found skulking about in the shadows. Vesuvio practised in guarded privacy with his new team.

Knowing that his Uncle Milo was not extraordinarily rich, Vesuvio repremanded him every evening for spending so much money on the team of golden steeds.

Gripping his toga, Milo bragged, 'For every inch of pizzle that I gave Agrippina, she rewarded me in her august way. Does it bother you to be the beneficiary of my immoral earnings?'

Swatting his uncle playfully on the shoulder, Vesuvio answered, 'That doesn't mean you have to put your money back into stallions!'

Despite his light-hearted manner with his uncle, though, Vesuvio wondered how he could repay him for the steady outlay of cash – money he had spent on his Centurion's equipment, the endless hospitality on the Esquiline, and, now, the four golden Arabians, a chariot built from citrus wood, his equipment for the arena.

As Gaius Lucretius was participating in the race, he could not offer a money purse for the winner. The prize was only to be the honour of victory. Vesuvio could not challenge that but neither could he use it to pay the legal fees to prove that Villa Macrinus belonged to him.

The little money which Vesuvio possessed was still in the waist pouch he had worn from Cyprus. When he remembered that leather pouch, he suddenly thought about the gems which Balthazar had given him in Samosata. During all his training with Termico – long days followed by nightly visits to his mother in the *columbaria* – Vesuvio had completely forgotten his promise to Balthazar and Yiannoulla. He had given his word to them that he would try to find out in Rome if the stones had any value.

Before leaving the house one morning for Termico's track, Vesuvio dropped a pouch into his uncle's lap. The old man was eating his breakfast in the *pergola*.

Vesuvio said, 'Here! Show these to your cronies and find out if they have any worth!'

Milo waited until Vesuvio had gone out through the postern to the stables before he closely studied the clear stones. A sly smile spread over the old man's face as he watched the morning sun sparkle a myriad of colours in their facets.

34

Whilst Vesuvio trained with Old Termico beyond the Porta Latina, activity was reaching a pitch on the Palatine Hill in The Palace of the Dolphins. Gaius Lucretius trained at the Blues course in the Tiberian District of Rome. And as the games were scheduled for the colossal Flavian Amphitheatre – and not the Circus Maximus, the oblong theatre where the races were generally held – Lucretius had also devised obstacles for the race which would add amusement for the crowd, and put Vesuvio at even more of a disadvantage.

Although keeping his plans a secret, he sent a message to Vesuvio at Milo Popiliano's house, only telling him to have his horses well blinded.

Scintilla knew little about her husband's games, except that it was a bid to win the office of *aedile* in Rome. That was all she cared to know. She was not feeling healthy these days.

Sleeping behind the locked doors in her private chambers in The Palace of the Dolphins, Scintilla continued to have the same horrible nightmare, visions of her young brother appearing in her dreams and staring accusingly at her.

At first, the nightmares had left her brain slightly addled the next morning. A drink of unwatered wine put her at ease, or the anticipation of what Praetorian guard she would secretly meet in the afternoon for a sexual assignation.

But now Scintilla's nocturnal phantoms were beginning to take toll on more than her nerves. Dark circles were appearing under her eyes. She ate gluttonously out of frustration. She was gaining weight. She knew that she would be seated on the Imperial podium at the Games, in full public view. She was not greatly worried about being fat and puffy-faced for that important occasion. She could disguise her obesity with flowing robes, artfully apply thicker cosmetics to her eyes, lips, cheeks and chin.

Scintilla feared the most that, soon, no man would want to lay with her, that she would not longer have any of her lovers – not even for money. A Praetorian had his pick of any woman in Rome.

Scintilla and Gaius Lucretius seldom made love any more, not with one another. He had his concubines and she her Praetorian guards. Their liberal arrangements had bothered Scintilla in the first years of their marriage. Now, seeing that love-making for her husband was only an outlet for his ambitions, she knew that she had no cause to be jealous. She would not lose him to a lover. Only to Rome.

Scintilla had always been ambitious in her own way, having hated to go to Campania as a young girl after her parents had died, always conniving a way to remain in Rome and be invited to banquets given at the Golden House of the Empress Plotina, or join parties visiting the Imperial summer residence on Capri.

Gaius Lucretius had suited Scintilla's tastes in those early days. Also, she knew that she possessed powers which would be useful to him. When her brother, Scintus, had been abducted with the Macrinus sons, Scintilla had told Lucretius how she would inherit the entire estate if her brother was dead. The money from the patrimony could help finance Lucretius's ambition to own the Macrinus estate.

The plan had gone well in the first stages of its execution. The initial problem arose when they discovered the precaution which Elder Aurelius Macrinus had taken. Without an heir, the Macrinus Estate could be forfeited to the Empire and sold to Lucretius. He had originally planned to auction half of the Macrinus slaves to finance his first years of being an absentee farmer.

To this day, though, the Macrinus Estate belonged to no one. Gaius Lucretius had spent the last of his own inheritance to buy this house in Rome, The Palace of the Dolphins, when he had not received a consulship in Dalmatia as he had hoped, a stepping stone towards a more powerful position. He had to put on a show of wealth to prevent anyone from surmising that he was becoming insolvent. A poor man would never receive an appointment in Rome.

Now, he was spending the last of Scintilla's money to finance the Games. They were his last hope of becoming elected to a public office. Neither his nor Scintilla's ardent attention to Empress Plotina had produced any Imperial favours. Scintilla spent as much time as possible with the Empress but she secretly hated her, especially when she carped on 'justice'.

Justice! How Scintilla loathed the word. She had been present at the meeting with the bankers when Vesuvio had come storming into their home.

Unlike the grubbing bankers, Scintilla had not rushed to the door to witness the disturbance. She remained on her couch, her fingers curling with anger that Vesuvio had not died in chains. That he could now very well ruin her husband's chance of winning the aedileship. She and her husband both desperately needed the office for their social standing in Rome.

She had heard Vesuvio laugh, too, when Gaius had called her 'Lady Scintilla'. Instead of becoming angered at his disrespect, though, the laugh had secretly thrilled her. It was the same laugh she begged to hear from her afternoon lovers. Scintilla had discovered the act of being debased by a man, by acting as his slave and having a man not only abuse her with words but also to defile her body as if he were her master and she no better than a slave whore.

Slavery. Scintilla knew that she had had a hand in the enslavement of innocent people. But what troubled her more these days was the death she had caused, the fratricide she had ordered to be committed. Somehow, some way, she had to absolve herself from that guilt.

Scintus was not decapitated in her nightmares. He appeared to Scintilla intact. Only recently, she had visited a soothsayer who had assured her that her nightly visions augured only good fortune and happiness. The soothsayer had deciphered her phantoms of a dead relative to mean the continuation of their line. The words had momentarily relieved Scintilla but, the following night, her brother appeared to her again, his voice plaintively calling out to her from a void.

This morning, Scintilla had instructed her litter-bearers to take her to the Imperial Palace. And when the Empress Plotina received her in the Garden of Water, she remarked that Scintilla looked under strain. She asked if she was vexed about her husband's safety at the Games.

The young protégé, Hadrian, was also present in the garden. Scintilla had heard the court gossip that Empress Plotina was trying to find a bride for young Hadrian before Trajan returned from Dacia. The gossip-mongers said that the Empress knew that Hadrian was Trajan's lover and was trying to marry him to her niece.

In any other circumstance, Scintilla would have paid more attention to Hadrian. He was striking-looking, very athletic, but her mind was consumed with her nightmares.

Scintilla tried to sound light-hearted when she asked the Empress Plotina for the name of her soothsayer, confiding that she felt that hers was telling her flattery only for gold.

In one of her famous moods of self-righteousness, Plotina held her portly body erect on her couch, saying, 'Daughter, you spend too much time with the mystics. You must turn towards good deeds. Charitable acts.'

Cursing Plotina as both a hypocrite and a panderer to catamites, Scintilla rode back to The Palace of the Dolphins with the curtains of her litter closed for the entire ride.

Now, reclining beside a reflection pool in her private chambers, she realized that, perhaps, there might be some truth in the Empress's advice about good deeds. Charitable acts.

Immediately, Scintilla's mind went to the one person whom

she had abused the most. The old woman, Cornelia Macrinus. The mother of . . . of course!

Vesuvio! He would be eternally grateful to Scintilla. They would meet in secret. She could see him again. Perhaps even before the races. They would make love!

Her mind suddenly raced with a million plans and ideas on how she could be united with the rugged young blond, imagining herself kissing the soles of his sandals, presenting him with a whip to repay her for her past wrongs.

Rising quickly from her couch, Scintilla reached for the cloth-headed hammer and beat the brass plate which she used only to summon the slave, Kirnus, the major-domo at The Palace of the Dolphins.

When he did not appear in a few moments, Scintilla banged the plate louder, then threw the hammer across the tessellated marble floor in a fury.

Finally, one of the tall bronze doors opened and Kirnus entered Scintilla's curtained chambers.

Pacing the room, she said, 'I want you to send for a scribe. Immediately. I want to buy the old dove-mistress from you. I want the sale witnessed. I want her freed at once. And the news sent to her son.'

Kirnus stood looking at her, smiling.

'Don't just stand there! Go!'

He began slowly, 'I am afraid that I cannot obey the noble lady's orders.'

'You *will* obey my orders! Who gave the old hag to you in the first place? Me!' She screamed, thumbing her breasts. '*Me!*'

Bowing obsequiously, Kirnus said, 'As your husband, Gaius Lucretius, is the *pater familias* of this house, Lady Scintilla, all gifts are officially his bounty. Also—' He held both hands clasped to his slim waist. '—my Lord wishes that the dove-mistress remains in my bondage.'

Scintilla's painted eyes widened. This slave was defying her. He was in collusion with her husband.

Stepping back, Kirnus closed the brass door and, moving closer to Scintilla, he said, 'My noble Lord also has confided in me that Lady Scintilla is not feeling her usual self lately. He has anticipated your poor condition—'

Slowly reaching into his pocket, Kirnus produced a pair of thinly wrought iron manacles. He walked towards Scintilla, saying, 'My noble Lord also suggests that you might recover more quickly if you are confined to your chambers. At least until after the Games. He has heard you talking wildly at night. He fears for your mind.'

'Do not come closer,' Scintilla warned, looking around her for something to hurl at him. 'If you come closer, I will have you flogged! Slave!'

Moving quickly now, Kirnus seized Scintilla by one wrist. When she began to struggle, he slapped her sharply across the face.

Falling to the floor, Scintilla screamed, 'There are laws! I am a noble lady! I will tell the Empress! A slave cannot . . .'

By now, Kirnus had snapped one of the manacles around Scintilla's wrist, dragging her towards the brass couch. He snapped the other link to the bowed neck of a swan on the ornately wrought headboard. He said. 'You will tell nobody a word. Not until you have come to your senses.'

Scintilla now lay quivering on the floor next to the couch, one arm stretched to the headboard. She shrilled, 'My husband will see what you have done to me. You do not have this much power. Slave!'

Smiling thinly, Kirnus said, 'My noble Lord does not care what any man does to his wife. Nor do . . . you!'

Watching him part the folds of his white robe, Scintilla began to shake her head, to twist her hand in the manacle, warning him not to come any closer to her, calling him a slave.

' "Slave" ', he repeated, laughing.

Then, holding his phallus over Scintilla's face, he said, 'If your teeth were not so sharp, my slave mistress, I would have you service me with your painted lips. But I do not trust you. So—'

The first trickle of urine began to fall on Scintilla's forehead, washing the cosmetic of white lead from the skin. Then, as

Kirnus let his water gush like a fountain, the antimony began to run in black rivulets from Scintilla's eyes, streaking the lead-coating on her cheeks, smearing the red stains of her lips until, soon, her entire face was a flood of streaming colours, flowing down her neck and staining her *stolae*.

Before leaving, Kirnus warned Scintilla that he would return to debase her the next time in a more sexual manner – that she must wait in her shackles for him.

35

The Games drew nearer and Vesuvio had less time to spend with his mother at the *columbaria*. He had now begun driving the Arabian horses with their eyeblinds and was worried about the behaviour of the horse galloping on the inside of the track – the *funalis* – because he pulled against the team connected to the chariot by the shaft and also threw off the cadence of the outside animal. The *funalis* was the strongest of the *quadrigae* and demanded the most discipline from Vesuvio.

Also, at this time, Termico was recruiting trustworthy men to assist Vesuvio in the stables below the arches of the Flavian Amphitheatre. He needed stableboys, saddlers, grooms, a veterinarian, the dressers who would help lead the team to the starting point. These men had to become as familiar with the animals as Vesuvio.

It was often evening when Vesuvio left Termico's track, galloping towards the dingy warehouses along Via Ostiensis. He always found his mother waiting for him at the threshold of the *columbaria*. He would spread his cape on the ground and they would sit together as he produced whatever present he had brought for her. The gifts were small but always things which Vesuvio knew that his mother loved – almond cakes, Falernian grapes, a white cotton square to tie around her head, a small phial of rosewater.

Vesuvio had noticed that his mother was tiring easily, shivering in the night air. He brought woollen blankets to wrap around her. Sometimes Vesuvio and his mother would not talk, merely enjoying the presence of one another's company. But, often, Cornelia would scold him, saying that he spoiled her too much with his thoughtful presents.

Although Vesuvio tried to avoid the subject of his father, Titus, and Julia Cordonis, in the hope of not increasing his mother's misery, they often spoke about slavery itself, intelligently discussing the phenomenon and the part it played both in their own private lives and the general life of the Roman Empire.

Vesuvio had stopped pressing his mother to take him down to see her subterranean living-quarters but she now talked quite freely of how slaves brought the ashes of their relatives and loved ones to her in variously shaped jars and urns after the bodies had been burned at the slave's funeral society. She explained how the mourners always lingered in the *columbaria* until they saw that she put the funereal urn safely into one of the many niches, occassionally offering to bribe her with a sweet cake or sausage to scratch the deceased's name at the base of the stone shelf. Cornelia said that she tried to oblige them as often as she could but never accepted a bribe for scratching a name in stone. But she did, she laughingly admitted, allow a younger slave to climb up the rickety ladder when he – or she – offered. They did not want an old woman to risk the climb when the only vacant place for an urn was high in the vaulted room. Cornelia confessed that the only kindness shown to her in recent years – apart from that of her brother, Milo – had been from slaves . . . slaves showing generosity even at a sad moment in their own lives.

Vesuvio listened with admiration as his mother – with iron bracelets on her wrists – explained how Rome would collapse without slave power. It was a cruel fact to admit, she said, but they must face it. She even reminded Vesuvio of his father when she said that the Emperor was not helping the slave situation by offering public wheat to the free population. No one wanted to work. Cornelia Macrinus told Vesuvio how they had tried to run their own estate with tenant farmers but had found too few free men who would come regularly to work the soil. Slavery was an inescapable fact of life, a misfortune that would probably stay with mankind forever, Cornelia feared.

It was during one of these calm discussions at dusk outside the *columbaria* that Vesuvio told his mother about the Essenes, the Jewish sect which did not believe in slavery. Cornelia said that she had heard of them and their communities but said that she felt they were too few in number to have an impact on the world. She mentioned the other religious cult, the Christians, who believed a Nazarene was the son of a god. She told Vesuvio that there were now more than ten thousand Christians in Rome, saying that only such a fast-growing cult as that could help obliterate slavery. She added, though, that the Christians believed in human bondage, too. If they were ever to change their views, Cornelia Macrinus confessed, she might even be tempted to forsake her Roman gods and convert to a religion which upheld the common rights of all mankind.

Vesuvio still had not told his mother how he was spending his days. Nor did she ask. He suspected that his Uncle Milo frequently visited the *columbaria* during the afternoon – although Milo never mentioned any visits to Vesuvio – and informed her about Vesuvio's activities, what he was doing for his *gens*.

The evening before the Games, Cornelia asked Vesuvio if he would forgo his visit to her tomorrow. She asked him to go instead to Via Appia. She told him his father was interred there in the family tomb.

Cornelia had never mentioned this fact to Vesuvio before. Obediently, he quickly assured her that not only would he pay respects to his father tomorrow but that he would also return here to the *columbaria* tomorrow evening. He had already planned to come here directly from the Amphitheatre, to put the victor's myrtle wreath on his mother's head. His determination to win had increased with each visit to the *columbaria*.

But Cornelia Macrinus was adamant, asking Vesuvio to waive his visit to her tomorrow, going at dawn instead to visit his father's tomb. She said that, although she was a lowly dove-mistress, she was proud that her husband had been nobly interred and she wanted Vesuvio to pay homage there.

This request convinced Vesuvio that his Uncle Milo had informed her about tomorrow's Games. This was her honourable way of releasing Vesuvio from his regular visit to the *columbaria.*

Although it was dark when Vesuvio rode towards the centre of the city, he did not race towards his uncle's house on the Esquiline Hill. He trotted his horse at a leisurely pace whilst he looked at the cloud-streaked sky, deliberating on his mother's request for him to visit his father's tomb on Via Appia. Vesuvio suspected that she had not wanted him to grieve over his father's remains up to now but tomorrow would be a vigil before the Games.

The more that Vesuvio pondered the idea, the more he believed that his mother knew about the chariot race with Gaius Lucretius. She had not shown any unusually strong emotions at his departure tonight but, then, that also was her nature. She was even noble in her bondage.

The Esquiline Hill lay behind the Flavian Amphitheatre. The streets were teaming now with trade wagons and carts; crowds were beginning to form lines at the Amphitheatre, waiting to secure free seats for tomorrow's event.

Torches and lamps were now dotted across the apron of the Amphitheatre. Jugglers performed for the crowds. Beggars passed though them, holding out their hands or wooden bowls for alms. Brightly dressed prostitutes posed and sauntered, whilst the less attractive ones lurked in the shadow of the Amphitheatre, smacking their lips to attract the attention of a likely client.

Intending to pass quickly around the crowd, Vesuvio suddenly heard loud jeers rising from a group of men. Looking in their direction, he saw they were shouting at a young man leading a chain of five slaves towards the Amphitheatre.

Judging from the firmness of the slaves' bodies, Vesuvio guessed that they were potential gladiators, that the young man was a *lanista,* a travelling slave-dealer who specialized in selling fighters to the Director of the Games. The Romans scorned a *lanista* worse than a whore's pimp.

The young man moved arrogantly through the raucous men, leading his slaves by a chain and flicking a small quirt in front of him as if he were hacking a path through foliage.

Vesuvio was intrigued by the young *lanista's* haughtiness. His dark hair was elaborately curled around his forehead. He wore a fastidiously folded toga in the *Africanum* style.

Looking towards the leather quirt which the *lanista* deftly wielded, Vesuvio suddenly saw a bracelet around the young man's wrist. It was a leather thong and *bulla*. Very few men wore a *bulla* past childhood.

Reining his horse, Vesuvio blurted, 'Titus!'

The call was lost in the jeers of the crowd. So, jumping to the ground, Vesuvio anxiously led the horse by its reins, calling his brother's name even louder. He was certain now that the young *lanista* was Titus. He would be about this age now, too.

Soon, the crowd parted for Vesuvio. Men gibed for him to be cautious, that the blood-thirsty dandy might clamp him into shackles, too, and sell him to be murdered in the arena.

Oblivious to their remarks, Vesuvio reached out to put his hand on the young man's shoulder. He shouted, 'Titus!'

Stopping, the young man turned with the small whip in his hand, ready to strike.

Smiling, Vesuvio said, 'You wouldn't whip your own brother!'

'Vesuvio!' Titus gasped.

Forgetting about the crowd, Vesuvio warmly embraced him.

Pulling back, Titus soon began to stammer, 'It's been so long since I've been called "Titus" . . . I didn't think anybody was shouting for *me*!'

Vesuvio did not know whether Titus was embarrassed by being a *lanista*, shocked at seeing him, or if he had greatly changed in the last five years. But there was something wrong with this reunion.

Not able to contain his own excitement, though, Vesuvio blurted, 'Where have you been? What's been happening to you? Where did you go from Carthage? Are you a free man? Come,

Titus—' He grabbed him by the arm, leading him through the dispersing crowd towards the Amphitheatre.

Hesitating, Titus said, 'I cannot waste much time now, Vesuvio.' He nodded towards the five slaves. 'I must really try to get rid of these dogs tonight.'

Vesuvio glanced at the string of shackled men. He looked back to his brother.

Titus said, 'I've been seeing nothing but posters announcing the chariot race between Gaius Lucretius and Aurelius Macrinus. I wondered if the driver was you.' Laughing, he said, 'I knew it certainly wasn't me!'

Then hesitating again, he said, 'I suppose I am "Titus" now. If I want to be.'

Vesuvio clapped him on the shoulder, saying, 'You're alive. That's the important thing! You're alive. And you're not a slave!'

'A slave?' Titus scoffed, 'I was never a slave! Oh, for a short period, yes. But not for long. The man who bought me at Carthage owned the best gladiatorial college in the city. The best in *Africanus*. Much better than the animal farms here.'

'A *lanista* bought you?'

'Yes. But not to fight! I was his . . .'

Vesuvio waited.

Seeing the grim expression on Vesuvio's face, Titus laughed. 'No. Not what you're thinking. No, Drusus is a bull! A veritable bull with women! I even have three concubines myself at home.'

'"Home"?'

'Carthage!'

'You call Carthage "home"?'

'Why not? I became a man there. That's where my future lies. Drusus found out for me what had happened in Campania. That the estate was gone.' Titus's eyes brightened as he bragged, 'Drusus has even offered to adopt me. To make me his heir. I'm already known as "Young Drusus".'

Looking at the amulet cinched around Titus's wrist, Vesuvio soberly said, 'That means I can have back the *bulla*.'

Gripping to untie the leather thong immediately from his

wrist, Titus offered, 'Of course you can have this old thing back. I only wore it to Rome as protection. You know what happened once!'

Looking at the small curl of leather now cupped in his hand, Vesuvio asked, 'So you will go back to Carthage? Return as soon as you do your business here?' He was finding it difficult to speak to Titus, unable to look at him.

Titus also avoided Vesuvio's eyes. He answered, 'Not immediately. Drusus and his wife might join me in Italy. They stayed behind in Carthage to find a buyer for the college. And if they do . . .' He added flippantly. 'Who knows?'

'Why are they selling? I thought this Drusus prospered?'

'Oh, we prosper. But . . .'

Looking closely at Titus now, Vesuvio saw that the edges of his robe were frayed. That his fastidiously curled hair was held into position with oil, not marcelled properly by curling-irons as wealthy dandies ordered their barbers to do. Also, Titus's fingernails were lined with dirt, his body reeking of cheap scent.

Vesuvio began, 'You must remember where Uncle Milo lives. I am staying with him. When you finish your business tonight, why don't you come there. You must have many questions to ask.'

'Uncle Milo?' Titus said. 'Is that old donkey still alive? He's the last person in Rome I want to see. And as for meeting later tonight to talk—'

Titus nervously chewed his lips, stammering, 'I am staying with some friends across the river in Transtiberina. They're having a party tonight. I suppose I could invite you. There are a few Danubian girls promised. Not that many of them, though. But if you bring your own wineskin, maybe—'

Vesuvio assured Titus that the last thing he wanted to do on the night before the Games was to attend a drunken orgy in Transtiberina. But he felt at odds parting with his brother in such an uncomfortable manner.

Looking fleetingly at the silent chain of male slaves, then back to Titus, he said, 'You look to be in good health.'

'Oh, I'm in fine health. I sniff and smell nothing but attar of roses!' Looking nervously towards the Amphitheatre, he added,

'But if I don't find the Games Master tonight, I'll have trouble getting a place to bed down these brutes. I don't want to trouble my friends. Slaves are such a nuisance sometimes. I wish they would all kill each other and leave me in peace.'

Vesuvio forced himself to keep silent.

Toying nervously with the quirt, Titus finally said, 'If I can't sell them tonight, Vesuvio, I might have to put them in lodgings. That will cost money. You don't happen to have any extra with you? I can pay you back tomorrow.'

Then laughing, Titus said, 'You'll be so rich after the Games tomorrow you won't need repayment.'

Slowly producing a few coins from his leather pouch, Vesuvio said, 'Titus, I think you should seriously consider joining me at Uncle Milo's house. You say you don't like him. But we cannot meet on an off-chance like this. Then both disappear.'

Stuffing the money into his own pouch, Titus said, 'You're just as I remember you, Vesuvio. Always the protective big brother! Well, I'm a man now, too. I have my own mind. And as for Uncle Milo, I still think he's a donkey!'

Jerking on the slaves' chain now, cursing them to move along, Titus wished Vesuvio good luck tomorrow at the Games, yelling, 'And if you don't win—' Titus laughed nervously. 'There's nothing to lose. We lost it all five years ago. So long!'

Vesuvio stood watching his brother disappear towards the shadow of the Amphitheatre. He did not know whether to pity the boy or to be angry with him.

But, no. Vesuvio corrected himself. Titus was no longer a boy. He was a man. Although he looked and acted like a fool, he was undeniably a man. He might be smitten by the dubious generosity of the Carthaginian who had taken him into his business and given him his name, yet Titus was still a man.

It was not the fact that his brother had accepted another man's name, though, that truly angered Vesuvio. Titus had not once asked about the fate or welfare of his parents. Not once had he asked if they lived or died. Could Vesuvio ever forgive that callousness? He doubted it.

36

The blast of trumpets acknowledged the entrance of Empress Plotina and Hadrian onto the Imperial podium of the Flavian Amphitheatre. The dignitaries rose from their marble seats placed beyond the royal divans. The crowd of fifty thousand spectators shouted from the benches curved in the oval-shaped arena. A thin canvas awning – *hectares* of fabric stretched across the top of the Amphitheatre – flapped in the breeze as protection from the glare of the Roman sun.

Now, standing on the edge of the podium, the Empress Plotina reviewed the stately procession of white-robed priests and incense-bearers which moved slowly from The Gate of Life. They were followed by the Patron of the Games – Gaius Lucretius – driving four black stallions from an ebony-and-silver chariot. His opponent – Aurelius Macrinus – rumbled behind him in an ivory-and-gold chariot pulled by four tawny Arabian stallions. Next, trooped the hordes of solemn-faced contestants for the hand combats. Plotina held out her arms in a maternal gesture as the contestants chanted in unison, 'We who are about to die, salute thee!' The crowd roared.

The priests turned towards the middle of the Amphitheatre to offer sacrificial rites to Venus. Plotina sank down to her divan on the podium, knowing that the opening sacrifice was no more than a symbolic gesture, that the bull's intestines no longer determined the progress of the athletic contests.

Turning to Hadrian on the divan beside her, she said, 'Although the Games today are privately sponsored, the people receive me very well.'

Positioning himself on the divan, Hadrian assured Plotina that the populace loved her. He added. 'And wait until Trajan returns. Listen to the crowd roar then when their Imperial Majesty stands beside her husband.'

Reaching to pat his brawny forearm, Plotina said, 'And my niece, Sabina, stands beside you, handsome Hadrian.'

Hadrian remained silent, picturing the sour young woman whom the Empress was arranging for him to marry. Although Plotina never alluded to his sexual relationship with her husband, she constantly reminded Hadrian how happy he would be married to Sabina.

Looking back towards the arena, Plotina pretended to show interest in the crowd of surly contestants clad in leather tunics, animal skins, and metal armour gathered around the altar. She said, 'I must admit that it is clever of Gaius Lucretius to provide both hand-combat and chariot racing on the same programme.'

'It is costing him two hundred and fifty thousand *sestertii*,' Hadrian said, looking around the podium at the nobility and high-ranking government officials. 'But I do not see his wife, Lady Scintilla, here today. See, her place is vacant. That is very unusual.'

'Lady Scintilla has been ill lately,' Plotina began, but stopped as the priests moved away from the altar, returning amidst more trumpet blares to bring news to the Empress that favourable auspices had been read from the intestines – that the Games could proceed.

Nodding towards the priests, Plotina raised her arm to the crowd as they applauded her acceptance of the auspices.

After the priests, the incense-bearers, the contestants, the Patron of the Games returned through The Gate of Life, the first clowns raced out onto the sand to amuse the crowd before the actual games commenced.

Having no taste for such vulgar displays, Plotina turned back to Hadrian, saying, 'We were talking about the absence of Lady Scintilla. I would guess that she is waiting to see only the race. The contest between her husband and this Aurelius Macrinus.'

'Do you know him?' Hadrian cautiously asked. 'Have you heard anything about Marcus Aurelius at all?' He had only caught a quick glimpse of the man driving the four Arabian horses. Although Hadrian had seen that he was athletic, the silver-and-gold helmet had protected the charioteer's face. From gossip which Hadrian had heard, though, the young man was virile and had a unique mop of blond hair, exactly the kind of male who would appeal to Trajan. Hadrian had also heard that 'Aurelius Macrinus' held a Centurionship. He considered how pleased Trajan would be to have a dashing new man to meet on his return to Rome. Far from being protective of the Emperor's affections, Hadrian was constantly searching for other men to pleasure the insatiable Emperor – military men like Hadrian himself who could wrestle naked with burly Trajan, culminating the bout by vigorous sexual acts.

Raising one hand to the tall mound of curls piled at the front of her head, Plotina said, 'I have been told that the Macrinus family is old. Totally entrenched in Republican ways. The charioteer today is the Macrinus heir. I have also been told there is some contention between him and Gaius Lucretius. Something to do with the ownership of an estate in Campania.'

'Some contention!' Hadrian laughed. 'I've been told that this race is a blood challenge. That's why there will only be two chariots. Not the usual four colours.'

Shaking her head disapprovingly, Plotina said, 'That *does* sound like the Old Republic! Settling debts in some crude, bloody manner. I see now why my councillors advised me to leave after the second event.'

'But Your Imperial Highness might be amused,' Hadrian said, knowing that if Plotina left, he, too, would have to return with her to the Golden House. He wanted to stay and see more of Aurelius Macrinus.

Looking back to the arena, Plotina saw a clown with a large red phallus strapped between his legs. He was beginning to prod a rag-likeness of a swan. It was a burlesque of a Greek legend and Plotina thought that it was in extremely bad taste.

Turning back to Hadrian, she said, 'I have no power to settle legal matters between land-owners. If this chariot race is a personal vendetta, as you say, it is best that we are not present. It would be embarrassing for me, possibly injurious to my husband's standing among the rich Republicans, and could even have unsavoury implications for you as my husband's adopted son and heir.'

Holding herself erect on the divan, keeping her eyes away from the lascivious pantomime in the arena, Plotina continued, 'I have been spared the judgement of life cr death so far. I do not intend to start today. Not in any manner.'

Hadrian diplomatically agreed. 'There is no reason for Your Imperial Highness to become involved in a personal conflict. You show good judgement as always. The Macrinus business could be embarrassing. The estate in Campania was a grant from Emperor Titus. For five years there has been no proof of a male heir. I've heard that Gaius Lucretius meant to buy the land at a greatly reduced price but—'

'Stop! Do not tell me more. I do not want to hear about it! I cannot take sides in quarrels among the nobility. As a distinguished Mother of Rome, I must keep my hands pure from blood feuds. The Republicans complain enough about the taxes without the Imperial House becoming embroiled with their conflicts. That's why we have a Senate!'

Seeing a flock of ostriches running out into the arena from six gates, Hadrian said, 'Look, Your Imperial Highness! Here come your favourites!'

Raising herself excitedly on the divan, Plotina said gaily, 'Ostriches! How wonderful! I always adore watching ostriches kick! They do not kick backwards like a horse or a donkey. But straight ahead! Like a man!'

Suddenly grabbing the purple edge of Hadrian's toga, she gasped, 'Oh, no! Tigers! They're setting wild cats loose on the poor birds—'

Seeing the ostriches now running frantically in circles, beginning to kick at the tigers stalking them, Plotina excitedly said, 'Look! Look, Hadrian! See what I mean! See how they kick! Isn't it the most wonderful thing. Oooh! Poor bird. That's the last time he'll ever kick.'

Laying back on the divan, she said, 'Tell me about the handcombats. Will they be paired? Or will it be a mass confrontation today?'

'There will be two forms. The first is a fight among "Tridents" and "Fishmen". The Games Director has assured me that these fights are all fixed so that Her Imperial Highness will not have to give a life-or-death vote.'

Hadrian stopped to listen to the fifty thousand spectators

laugh at the slaughter of the ostriches by tigers, looking now as archers on elephants began to ride out of the gates to destroy the tigers with a storm of arrows.

He continued, 'As for the gladiators, they are all condemned criminals. This will be their execution. None will be allowed to leave the arena alive.'

Motioning to a slave to begin dipping a plumed fan to circulate the air around her, Plotina said dryly, 'Personally, I do not enjoy any of the sword amusements. Fixed or otherwise. But I am glad to hear that I am spared making the decision of life-or-death. I see it beneath the dignity of a Mother of Rome to be appointed executioner.'

Assuring Plotina that she would not be called upon to give either a 'thumbs-up' or 'thumbs-down' order, Hadrian promised that they would leave after the 'Fishmen' fought. He regretted more than ever that he would miss the chariot race, to gauge the abilities of 'Aurelius Macrinus'.

Suddenly pointing to the *spina* of the Amphitheatre, he said, 'The fountains are spraying now.'

Sniffing for the first hint of the perfumed spray from the centre of the Amphitheatre, large scented jets to disguise the stench of animal flesh, Plotina gasped, 'Why, it is myrrh! I don't even use myrrh to perfume my own gardens.' Again patting her tall mound of curls, she said, 'The critics of the games *do* have a point in their favour.'

'And that is, Your Imperial Highness?'

'They are ruinously expensive!' Plotina whispered. 'I'm certainly glad I'm not paying for this!'

The Flavian Amphitheatre stood four storeys tall, the first three tiers made of travertine stone and the fourth built from wood. The giant canvas awning was stretched across the top tier and the seats up there were rough benches, far above the activity in the arena.

But Titus thought that he had been fortunate even to get his hands on a pass to the wooden benches. It was better than having to stand or squat in the steep aisles and be jostled by wine-pedlars. He only hoped that he never saw the young man he had stolen the pass from last night at the party in Transtiberina. The red-faced youth had been so drunk, though, that he had not even known that Titus had filched it.

Titus was still angry, though, that he had not been able to sell his five slaves to the Games Master. The official had said that they did not need any more men. He had told Titus that the bulk of today's slaughter was being done by criminals.

The gladiatorial combat was still to come. The contest between the 'Tridents' and 'Fishmen' was being performed now. It was the sixth team.

Titus noticed that the men fought too showily, that these were all obviously fixed matches. Even the people around him were beginning to shout for more authenticity, all of the previous matches having been rushed through by the Games Master, with no final confrontation of life or death. The spectators had only seen animal blood up to this point. They were beginning to cry out around the Amphitheatre for human blood . . . or for Gaius Lucretius to forget about them voting for him to become *aedile* of the Imperial buildings in Rome.

Wait! There it was! The sharp thrust from the Fishman's dagger suddenly sliced the arm of the Trident. A stain spread on the white sand. He fell back. The Fishman stood over him, holding a blade to his throat, looking towards the Imperial box, waiting for the command to let the man go free or to kill him.

The audience became aroused for the first time today. They rose to their feet, shouting to the Empress to demand death. But from where Titus was sitting, he could see that the Empress was not responding.

Titus kept his eyes on the Imperial podium, watching a young man in a purple-trimmed toga rise from beside the Empress's divan. He turned to the crowd. He beckoned for them to name the sentence more loudly. And when the populace shouted for death, death, death, he turned towards the arena, pointed his thumb down, and the steel blade sank into the man's throat.

'Good', Titus thought, as he watched the Fishman next slice

off his opponent's head and hold it up to the crowd by the hair. He sniffed the remnants of the perfume spraying again from the fountains far below him in the middle of the Amphitheatre.

There was still a three-hour wait until the main event. But since accidentally meeting his brother last night, Titus realized that he really did not care what happened in the chariot race today. Whether Vesuvio won or lost, was killed, had his blood smeared in the sand along with his honour, or what.

Titus had changed a great deal in the last five years. He knew it. He had been accepted by Drusus, had seen an easy way of life in Carthage. He no longer had any feeling for his family. Nor could he ever remember having felt any as a child.

Family? What was a family, anyway? Titus believed that friends were the important thing in his life. He firmly believed that his future lay with the man who had coached him in the ways of buying and selling slaves, and also had taught him how to enjoy life to the hilt. To try to take more out of life than you put into it. Why do otherwise? Why choose the fool's way? He suspected that Vesuvio was one of those fools.

But Titus had no time today to be fretting about families and philosophies of life. He still had the money in his pouch which Vesuvio had loaned him last night. Also, he was equipped with the necessary documents to buy slaves. He had to start looking now for likely dupes in the crowd around him. He had to pick out the heavy betters, the plebians who became so hysterical about a charioteer that they sold themselves into slavery to have more money to place on their favourite.

Titus convinced himself that he was lucky to be sitting up here in the cheap benches of the arena. The few *denarii* he would offer a frenzied man or woman would be a fortune to such a beggar. They would literally sell themselves to the nearest slave dealer in a fever.

And who knew? Titus might leave here this afternoon with more slaves to add to his string. He was also equipped with his own dagger, prepared to prod the wretches when they were sobered by their losses, reminding them that they had signed a contract to sell themselves into slavery in a fit of sportsmanship.

Wits. That was how a man had to live, Titus told himself. A

man could only survive in the world today by using his wits. His first and only loyalty was to nobody but himself.

The sand floor of the Flavian Amphitheatre was encompassed by a wide moat, a stream of water kept in constant motion to cool the air during the Games. Also, the moat kept the animals and contestants from trying to scale the marble walls. A further protection of metal grating surrounded the first tier of stone benches, this protection only being absent from the tall podium – a lofty monolith of marble – which held the Imperial divans and the curule chairs alloted to Rome's nobility.

Milo Popiliano sat among the distinguished spectators on the marble podium. He had prepared himself for a blood spectacle and, finally, two hours into the show, he had seen enough to realize why he had avoided the Games for so many years.

The Games had started out tamely enough today – the lewd dwarfs, the ostriches, the archers on elephants, followed by the 'Fishmen' and 'The Tridents'.

Milo had noticed that the Empress and Trajan's protégé, Hadrian, had left inconspicuously after the last contest. He still chuckled to himself when he thought of how Plotina had almost been caught into having to decide whether to let a young man live or die. But Hadrian had come to her rescue. And, if Milo was right, Hadrian would provide many more solutions in Rome's future, even after Emperor Trajan was dead and deified.

The Empress Plotina's exit had spared her the sight of a sea of men swinging swords at one another, criminals prodded by attendants with hot irons into fighting if they showed any signs of reluctance.

The smell of burning flesh, the stench of human carnage could no longer be covered by the fountains of perfume spraying profusely from the *spina*.

As the criminals dropped dead or fell maimed to the sand, the crowd's excitement increased. Now only nine men stood in the arena. Guards moved through the sprawled bodies. Some carried swords to kill the wounded prisoners. Others bore hot pokers to see if a man feigned death. If a body flinched at the touch of a hot poker, a sword was quickly driven through his chest. Then, the horsemen dragged the corpses from the arena with hooks. Spadesmen heaped severed limbs into carts, leaving the sand deeply blotched with blood, taking the human remains out through the Gate of Death.

Six of the remaining nine gladiators now surrounded three other men like a unified army. To Milo's disgust, this excited the crowd further. As first, one, then a second of the defenceless prisoners fell to the ground, or lost an arm, the cheers grew louder. The Games in no way resembled the ancient spirit of the original Roman *muni*.

Sickened by the brash display, Milo thought of the other things he could be doing today. For one thing, he wished that he had not come to the Amphitheatre so soon in the day, that he had waited only to see the chariot race. But Milo had been excited by the good news he had received this morning. The politician and man of letters, Pliny, had sent him word that the stones which Vesuvio had given him were of the rarest value, that even the Empress Plotina only had four diamonds and wore them on the most special occasions. In Pliny's words, the stones were 'the most valuable gems, known only to kings'. He called a diamond '*adamas*'.

So, Vesuvio was rich! He had a fortune in Eastern gems.

Nevertheless, Milo knew that riches meant little to his nephew. He was in fact worried about the young man's dejection. Vesuvio had left the house at dawn this morning to pay a vigil to his father's tomb on Via Appia. And last night, Milo had noticed that Vesuvio had returned home more morose than usual.

Suspecting that Vesuvio was troubled by something other than the Games, Milo hoped that he did not know that Cornelia Macrinus had only a short time to live. Milo's physician had examined her, saying that even if she were immediately released from the *columbaria*, she would last no longer than a month. Cornelia herself already knew this fact. But did Vesuvio?

Hearing a piercing wail rise from the arena, Milo lifted his head and saw that only two men remained standing. They faced one another, their weapons lowered to the sand. They did not want to fight. As both men were goaded with hot irons, they still refused to kill one another.

Boos and hisses filled the Amphitheatre. The crowd called the men cowards.

Shaking his head, Milo looked at the noble people seated around him on the podium and saw that they, too, screamed for the men to kill one another, reminding them of their oath to the Empress – that they would die for her!

It was at that moment that Milo noticed a purple-draped chair. The colour, purple, was only allowed outside the Imperial box at the Games for its Patron . . . and the Patron's wife. Milo knew that Gaius Lucretius was in the stables below preparing for the chariot race. But where was his wife? Scintilla should be here on the podium. Especially for the next event, Milo thought. A whore like Scintilla should enjoy seeing the bull performing for the crowd.

Leaning back in his chair, Milo closed his eyes as the guards executed the two reluctant gladiators. He next heard wooden catapults dragged out into the sand and small presents shot towards the upper benches of the arena, gifts to placate the audience – ivory lottery tickets, Egyptian baubles, ornamental phalli, a lion's tooth, the dew-claw of a tiger.

The crowds pushed at one another, still scrambling for the gifts when two slaves led a bull out into the sand whilst four other men pulled a bed with a young woman tied to it, her arms and legs spread wide apart – her groin glistening with thick, bright smears of goose fat to allow the bull's pizzle to penetrate her vagina before ripping into her stomach.

The arched colonnade under the Flavian Amphitheatre often filled with a crowd of people between acts, men and women who wanted to get away from the heat of the stands and amuse themselves walking through the fruit and wine vendors, the soothsayers, the trinket hawkers, the claques who extolled the virtues of Gaius Lucretius for the office of *aedile*, and the prostitutes who kept to this shaded area for the entirety of the Games.

All commerce in the colonnade was strictly controlled by the Games Director, the pedlars, the musicians, the tamborine dancers, the prostitutes all paying a large commission to work this lucrative area. The female prostitute, Iucunda, had only been able to afford the necessary bribe to solicit herself in the Flavian Amphitheatre during the last year.

Iucunda had come to Rome after she had been sold in Carthage to a man who owned bordellos in Subura. He had purchased her at Byrsa for the novelty of owning a woman without a tongue. But as Iucunda grew older, her demand among the customers began to wane and her master sold her as a servant to a poor family living in one of Rome's new *insulae*.

Even the poorest free man in Rome tried to own at least one slave but Iucunda's new master did not have enough money to feed his six children. Not wanting to share the free wheat from the Emperor's *Annona* with an outsider, he eventually set Iucunda out onto the street like an unwanted dog.

Rome also had a large population of abandoned slaves, unclaimed people who had no right to public food rations, no way to earn a living. One of them was a cripple, Polycarp, who soon teamed up with Iucunda and pandered for her in dark alleyways.

But Polycarp never joined Iucunda at the Amphitheatre. They did not have enough money to buy space for two people in the colonnade. Iucunda had to try to secure customers by gestures and motions.

At today's Games, the bull had been led from the arena now, the young girl's body dragged to the cart which carried the dead gladiators to a pit outside the city serving as a common grave. The perfume fountains were spraying again from the *spina* whilst the political claques now marched around the arena, shouting their praises for the next contestant, the Sponsor of the Games, Gaius Lucretius.

The highlight of the day was approaching but Iucunda knew that she still had time to pleasure one more customer. And, hurriedly, she went behind a pillar with a fat Sicilian. Kneeling in front of him, she anxiously worked on his phallus with her mouth as she listened to the *tubae* now announcing the charioteers.

Next, she squeezed on the phallus with her hands, trying to rush him towards an explosion. She was in a great hurry. She had to see the mysterious charioteer. But the Sicilian was more interested in slaking his sexual desires and, slapping away

Iucunda's hand, he pushed her head back down to his crotch.

Iucunda had only caught a glimpse of the charioteer, the man billed as 'Aurelius Macrinus' when he had driven his horses past the arches at the commencement of the Games. She was certain that it was the same man she had seen a few weeks ago in Subura, the one who had gone to the bordello called 'Palmyra's'. She had recognized him then as the yellow-haired slave, Vesuvio, whom she had sailed with to Carthage aboard the Arab galley, the *Ka'ba*. But in Subura, he had not wanted to go with Polycarp . . . and Iucunda could not blame him.

Vesuvio was even more handsome than she had remembered him. Inwardly, she was pleased he had not followed Polycarp's spiel. She did not want Vesuvio to see how poorly she had fared in the world. She just wanted to catch one more glimpse of him.

Finally, after catching the Sicilian's seed in her mouth, Iucunda clutched the coins of payment in her hands and pushed her way through the crowd packed tightly between the archway on the edge of the arena.

Although she had only been coming to the Amphitheatre for a short while, Iucunda knew the regulations of the races. She could tell by the marble eggs placed on a cross-bar at this end of the *spina* how many laps of the race had passed.

Four eggs were turned now. The race was more than half-finished. The crowd cheered for their patron – Gaius Lucretius – and the two chariots were still abreast. A white cloud of dust filled the air from the trample of hooves.

Watching the way that 'Aurelius Macrinus' reined his horses, Iucunda marvelled at how he handled the disadvantage of running next to the *spina*. She could tell – even through the brass-and-silver protection of his helmet, the thickness of the dust, and the speed of the chariots – that he was the man she remembered as 'Vesuvio'. She had employed the fantasy of that body too often to forget him, using the memory of Vesuvio as she plyed her trade, kneeling in front of far inferior men and thinking that she was back on the *Ka'ba* giving oral pleasure to the magnificent golden slave.

Iucunda longed to cheer for him as the chariots rumbled out of view again. They were approaching the fifth lap. It was then that she saw slaves hurriedly dragging four wide archways out into the arena, placing them side by side across the width of the track. Next, she watched as they set a torch to each of the great arches. Soon, the constructions began to crackle with fire, becoming arched furnaces through which the charioteers had to pass.

She heard the horses galloping closer towards the burning arches from the far end. The sight of the flames excited the crowd. They cheered at the innovation which Gaius Lucretius had provided for them. Iucunda heard men around her agreeing that, yes, if, Gaius Lucretius had courage to race through fire, he would get their vote for *aedile*.

Vesuvio had first thought that the request for horse-blinds was a ploy to test his skill with a team. He now finally understood the reason for them. He knew that the animals would stop racing if they saw the fire of the burning arches. But Gaius Lucretius had dismissed the damage that flames might do to the animal's flesh, their manes and tails.

Having only used a whip on the stallions when he turned the far corner of the *spina*, Vesuvio feared that the Arabians could feel the heat as they approached the burning arches. He forced himself to whip them on the long stretch, to drive them harder as they approached the fire.

Again, he and Lucretius were side by side. And, again, Lucretius was edging him towards the *spina*, snapping his own whip at Vesuvio's team, trying to cause further panic for the animals.

The four arches were spread across their course. As they approached them, Lucretius suddenly veered his team of blacks through the fourth arch, the one on the outside. Vesuvio passed through the second arch at the same moment, feeling the heat surround him as if he were driving through the sun. He beat the blinded animals, holding the reins tightly for the next bend.

Five marble eggs were turned now. Five laps. He skidded around the corner with Lucretius alongside him, leaving only one lap left until the race was decided.

Vesuvio felt the animal's panic through the reins, as if the leather straps were nerves to their bodies. The two outside horses were the most unruly, the *funales* straying towards the inside pair. And, then, as they charged towards the far end of the *spina*, Lucretius again tried to crush Vesuvio against the inside wall, skidding his chariot on one wheel to push Vesuvio closer to the threat of the stone banking.

Surging forward on the last straight stretch of the sand, Vesuvio looked ahead of him and saw that the two inside arches had collapsed with flames, that the third was beginning to crumble. But the one on the outside still stood – although blazing – and provided clear passage-way.

That was the secret of Lucretius's plot, he realized, the reason why Lucretius wanted to keep his own team on the outside and Vesuvio hemmed on the inside.

The fourth – the outside arch – was made of stone. It only blazed with the pitch smeared on it. The other three arches were wooden constructions. Lucretius was trying to manoeuvre Vesuvio to drive his team through one of the the three timber arches, through a collapsing wall of fire.

Thundering closer to the arches, Vesuvio saw from the corner of his eyes that Lucretius was moving towards him again, attempting to edge Vesuvio's chariot towards the *spina*. He saw that Lucretius was using a longer whip, too, seeing its snaking black tail lash at the golden necks of his horses as he rumbled closer alongside him.

Recognizing that he had only one choice, Vesuvio let his own whip fly at Gaius Lucretius. He held his reins with his left hand and snapped the whip a second time at Lucretius. Then, as the tip caught Lucretius's waist, Vesuvio quickly jerked it as if he were pinning a fish.

Lucretius jolted. He lost his balance on the narrow footing of his chariot. His black horses were slackened. They momentarily veered towards the outside wall.

Seizing the brief second, Vesuvio pulled his horses to the right, driving them towards Lucretius's team, forcing them to continue galloping towards the moat which lay between the sand and the marble wall below the stands.

He had no ears for the crowd. He could not think of anything except to gain control again over his four Arabians and drive them through the one arch that would not collapse into flames.

He felt the approaching heat. Behind him came a splash of water. He heard the scream of horses. He drove his team harder. He concentrated on the thunder of his animals, centring them on the one arch which was not criss-crossed with burning timbers.

His body felt the fire as he passed through the construction smeared with burning pitch. He heard a wooden arch crashing to his left. He next felt a coolness, a safe passageway. But the two outside horses were uncontrollable now. They were no longer a unified team. He braced his feet, pulling the reins, skidding them to a halt in the cloud of dust.

It was not until Vesuvio had finally reined in the animals in front of the Imperial podium, jumping quickly from the chariot to grab the horses' jerking heads, to steady them, to keep them from ripping from their harnessing, that he caught the first glimpse of the debris of the other chariot behind him – spread across the moat, smashed against the arena wall . . . wood, metal, blood, flesh. He flinched as he heard the painful scream of a horse that had not been killed in the smash. One wheel of Lucretius's chariot still spun in the air. Bits of armour lay on the sand. The flesh of the black horses was heaped with the smashed pieces of Lucretius's body. But all around Vesuvio, he heard the crowd cheering, 'Macrinus! Macrinus! Macrinus!'

Book Six
Roman Master

37

Vesuvio did not know who owned this sumptuous villa on the Aventine Hill where he had been invited after the games, nor the identity of any of the richly dressed guests milling from the *atrium* to the *triclinium* here tonight. He had hastily accepted the invitation to this party delivered at his Uncle Milo's house after they had returned home from the Flavian Amphitheatre that afternoon. The messenger bearing the invitation had come only shortly after the old woman from the slave society brought word to them that Cornelia Macrinus had been found dead in the *columbaria.*

Grabbing for every wine goblet he could see at the party, Vesuvio stumbled half-drunk through the guests, talking to anyone rather than to think of his mother expiring last night in her sleep. His mind was jumbled with losses and victories, with a pitiful recollection of how he had last seen his mother – she had waved goodbye to him from the portal of the *columbaria*, reminding him to visit his father's tomb the next morning on Via Appia – and the grisly image of Gaius Lucretius's death chariot this afternoon lying smashed against the marble wall of the Amphitheatre. Vesuvio's ears still echoed hours later with the name which the crowd had chanted in unison – Macrinus! Macrinus! Macrinus!

His life, his goals now seemed worthless. Gaius Lucretius was dead . . . But, then, so was his mother, his father, Julia Cordonis. His brother was a wastrel. The only blood relative he treasured was Milo Popiliano. But Vesuvio had not even been able to stay with him when he had heard the news from the old woman from the slave society.

Milo had been telling Vesuvio the good news about the mysterious white gems when the woman had come into the courtyard and said that Cornelia Macrinus had died of consumption. Vesuvio had been learning at that moment how he was not only a sudden hero to Rome but also a rich man, that he could afford to settle the legality of his ownership of the

Macrinus Estate and still have a fortune to begin restoring it.

Riches and ugliness. Gold and despondency. A fortune in gems whilst his mother died in slavery. Vesuvio had to quiet his mind, to escape from the unbearable destiny he had reached. He was reminded of the contrasts of those days on Platea and wondered if he had been better living as an oarsman on a pirate's galley. A slave to a eunuch in Mesopotamia. Even a prisoner at Byrsa eating scorpions in a cell.

Half-listening to the praises from the revellers at the villa, he heard them castigate Gaius Lucretius for being greedy and gutless, turning their fickle admiration to Vesuvio now, showering him with invitations to their homes, toasting him with still more wine, saying that he was Rome's man of the hour, the *dominus* of the Flavian Theatre.

Vesuvio held his arm around the slim waist of a young girl with brown marcelled hair, another girl nibbled his ear as a young dandy stood talking in front of him, inviting him to his hunting villa in Etruria next week.

Small lamps flickered behind gauze curtains which hung in the alcoves lining the *triclinium.* Half-naked bodies sprawled on divans like figures in a voluptuous dream. Vesuvio had never seen so many licentious women as he was seeing now at this party, young ladies laughing as men licked *muslum* from their breasts, couples locked in feverish embraces, a man holding each hand up the *himation* of a girl reclining on either side of him.

Praetorians. Tribunes. Senators. Noble young women. Ravishing concubines. Rich wives from the Imperial Court. Every one in Rome now knew Vesuvio and beckoned him to come join them in an alcove, to recline on a couch by the blue tiled pool, to take their place on a marble throne of winged sphinxes.

A lute player sang a poem about a charioteer with golden hair who made love to the goddess, Diana, in the clouds. A team of acrobats with gold-painted skin formed a jumble of naked bodies on the black marble floor, long white ribbons tied around their necks which were held by a statuesque blonde woman who was whipping them with a length of plaited flowers as if she were a charioteer and they were her gilt horses.

The hand of a girl reached under Vesuvio's tunic as he talked now to a burly charioteer from the Red Team, the girl soon falling to her knees in front of Vesuvio to take his phallus from the cincture and hold it in her mouth as the sportsman told Vesuvio that girls used to do that to him at banquets – the last time being only last night.

An old woman with curls ringing her forehead tapped Vesuvio on the arm with an ivory fan, saying that he must come to her villa on Capri for a month. A black girl with gold chains swagging her naked breasts asked him if he would swim with her in a pool on the next terrace. A male midget wearing a woman's tall blond wig begged to arm-wrestle with Vesuvio. A slave reported that the host wanted Vesuvio to bathe in milk and then serve the drink to the guests. And, then, a buxom girl with fair skin and long red hair whispered into Vesuvio's ear that she had found a hammock nearby which she was certain that he would enjoy.

Not waiting for him to accept or decline her offer, the red-haired girl led Vesuvio by one arm towards two Corinthian columns flanking the entrance to a walled garden.

At first, Vesuvio thought that the tall walls were steeped with an array of blinking eyes. Looking more closely at the garden walls through his drunken stupor, he realized that thousands of tallow candles flickered here in the night, covering every space of the walls with small yellow flames. Then he saw the hammock, a sling of loosely woven silk cords, stretched between two lemon trees.

He did not see the red-haired girl drop her clothes to the closely clipped grass but when he looked at her now she was lying spread-legged on the hammock, holding her arms out to him to join her.

Quickly shedding his own clothes, he heard the sound of hands beginning to clap behind him. The myriad of candle flames flickered around the hammock and the stars twinkled overhead in the night sky. He heard laughter as he moved to fall naked onto the girl but slipped when the hammock moved against his sudden weight. He was drunk. But he was also determined to lie with the girl – the red hair caping her thin shoulders, her large breasts gently moving with the swing of the hammock, one curvacious leg now lowered to the lawn to steady the hammock, showing the patch of hair between her legs.

Grabbing a goblet of wine from a man standing next to him, Vesuvio downed the contents with a gulp and, then, turned again to mount the waiting girl.

Victory! She accepted him with open arms, the sides of the silk hammock wrapping around their naked bodies as the girl's legs enclosed him to the applause of the increasing crowd of onlookers.

Vesuvio tasted the sweetness of her mouth, feeling the warmth of her naked body underneath him as the night air cooled his bare back. He momentarily forgot about the walls of flickering candles surrounding them, the guests drawing closer around the hammock, a few people even falling to the grass to lay on their backs and look up at the mating couple through the loosely plaited hammock.

He performed sexually not only for the girl but for the men and women now clustered around them, making certain that his phallus pulled out far from the lips of her vagina so that it could be seen, then slicked back into her as she groaned with pleasure.

Next, he lay sideways with her so that the people lying on the ground could look up and see his plunges, the raise of her thick mound enveloping his manhood as he drove into her again and again.

He did not at first recognize the additional sensations on his body. But he soon felt lips beginning to kiss the back of his thighs, his calves, his feet, then someone tonguing his buttocks, driving their tongue deeper into him as he pulled back his phallus from the girl. Another mouth tried to secure one side of his scrotum, and yet one more mouth struggled to find room to hold his other testicle in their mouth. Women called him beautiful. Men whispered '*Domine*'. The girl under him soon became only a receptacle for his masculinity, the guests now all staring only at Vesuvio. Those admirers who could not get close enough to touch, lick, kiss or fondle his athletic body, threw rose petals which floated down to his naked skin.

Rose petals. A million flickering votive candles. A silken plaited hammock. An adoring crowd of men and women. The awning of twinkling stars. A phallus that sank deep inside – and then withdrew, only driving deeper into a female who smothered him with adulation as his physical excitement crested, subsided, worked to a pitch again.

A lull suddenly spread over the garden worshippers. The hammock still creaked on its silk ropes but Vesuvio's body lay motionless. He had seen himself. The ugly sight had sobered him. He saw what a pathetic figure he made trying to lose himself in this debauchery.

First, polite complaints spread through the crowd as Vesuvio steadied the hammock with one leg. Next, the people were silent as he stood up from the girl. They stared as he pushed his way through them.

Vesuvio moved solemnly. This was not the victory he wanted. Not what he had waited for all these years. He grabbed the first tunic and sandals he saw lying abandoned on the black marble floor inside the villa and left the Aventine Hill, taking the first horse which the groom brought him.

Vesuvio rode first to his Uncle Milo's home on the Esquiline Hill. The old man came into Vesuvio's bedchamber as he was throwing a few bits of clothing into a saddle bag. He told his uncle that he would be back to Rome for his mother's official burial but, tonight, he had to leave Rome. He offered no explanation. Milo Popiliano asked for none.

Vesuvio rode all night, leaving the first mount at a road stop and reached Campania as morning was beginning to set its first golden glow on the fields. He had travelled the last few *milae* at a slow pace, his mind clearer now than it had been for many days, even months. He knew that his anger had at last gone, his revenge sated – that there was only one place for him to be. It was not in Rome. Not basking in idolatry and rose petals. Not being a glorified master to the debauchery of a sensuous crowd. That was the fashionable Rome which his family had despised, the orgiastic decadence of pleasure-women and *homines belli* who composed the vile world his parents – and he himself – had ignored for years in preference to the gentle life of Campania.

No. He did not want to be that kind of a Roman master. But neither must he be a slave to hatred and vengeance as he had been up to now.

'Hatred only destroys the spirit,' his mother had said that to him. Vesuvio and his mother had also talked of other things – the estate, crops, slaves, the people called the Essenes who did not believe in slavery, tenant farmers, men willing or unwilling to work.

She also had told him at the *columbaria* that their family were no longer masters now but – holding up her iron bracelets – she had said they were the slaves.

Well, fortune had turned yet again, Vesuvio thought. He was once more a master. That was another paradox of what he now saw as the curse of mankind – slavery.

Galloping again, he continued towards his family's land, anxious to see the house again, wondering if the peasant boy, Primo, had become friends with the young dog yet. He thought how he could hire the boy's father to help him make part of the house immediately habitable. The fields were still fertile. There were good wells for water. The stables and barns needed little repair. There was already a town there for people to live in if he found any who wanted to work.

Vesuvio thought as he rode that, even if he had to buy slaves, he would allow them to purchase their freedom – and over a period of time more reasonable than Lucco had laid down with his men.

Vesuvio again had reason to feel optimistic. And, as the wind blew the hair back from his forehead, he raced faster towards . . . Yes, he would change the name of Villa Macrinus. His family was gone. He knew no decent woman to take for his bride. The labour system on the estate might be drastically changed if he got his way. There was no reason to cling onto old memories or to harbour stale hatreds, no sense in trying to reassemble the past. He would start entirely fresh. He would call the home of this new life 'Villa Vesuvio', using the money from his new fortune to build a world which many people could share with him. He would see if he could help other slaves become their own master, too.

Glossary

Annona	free wheat distribution from the Imperial warehouses to the City of Rome's poor.
atrium	the central courtyard of a Roman house, around which were built a series of rooms; the *atrium* was often used as main reception area.
caelum	thin strips of leather wrapped around a man's fists for boxing, occasionally reinforced with lead.
columbaria	subterranean burial spots for the ashes of slaves, known as *columbaria* – or 'dovecotes' – because of the small wall niches; predecessors of the more cavernous 'catacombs'.
domine	form of address for the head of a Roman household or superior male personage – as 'master'.
fibulae	brooches or clasps most worn by females to fasten their long outer garments.
Flavian Amphitheatre	the Roman amphitheatre completed by Emperor Titus in AD 80 and not known as 'The Colosseum' until the Middle Ages.
gens	a Roman family, inclusive of their progenitors; a tribal conception of blood and honour.
insulae	blocks of flats in ancient Rome; housing for the lower classes equivalent to modern day tenement buildings.
lares	domestic and, occasionally, wayside shrines dedicated to Roman household gods, a religious symbol often located in the *atrium*.
lanista	a school devoted to the training of gladiators; also, the head of such a school or migrant pedlar of fighting slaves.

lapis specularis	a thick opaque glass used for windows in wealthy Roman households, not dissimilar from semi-translucent panes of alabaster.
peristylium	the arched colonnade surrounding or leading from a courtyard; see *atrium*.
portus	the formal entrance to a Roman home; hence, a haven or ' port '.
popinae	eating houses or taverns; the females who served there, often prostitutes.
stolae	long garment worn by distinguished Roman ladies, usually made from bleached linen.
triclinium	dining-room in a Roman house.
quadrigae	a team of four horses for charioteering.

Kyle Onstott and Lance Horner

Falconhurst Fancy 95p

Colt was a slave called a 'fancy' – bred for his massive strength and muscular loins. And Dovie, the plantation owner's lovely daughter, finds she cannot be content with white lovers . . .

'This Deep South saga . . . has lots of love, hate and violence to recommend it' DAILY TELEGRAPH

Child in the Sun 95p

Varius Avitus Bassianus, later the Emperor Antoninus – degenerate, effeminate, licentious, cruel . . . As his passions became more and more depraved even the voluptuaries of ancient Rome recoiled in horror, and the very swords of the legions that had raised him to power turned against Varius . . .

'A study of immorality and its effects on a civilization' OLDHAM EVENING CHRONICLE

The Black Sun £1.50

Armes Holbrook, a young, virile American from Boston, arrives to take over his Caribbean plantation. Soon a mutual liking between himself and Henry Christophe, the savagely handsome slave destined for greatness, leads to Armes playing a stirring role in the bloody revolution of the Negroes against their French masters.

The Tattooed Rood 95p

A ragamuffin pimp became a man sated with the treachery and debauchery of slave-trading Havana . . . Suddenly he was Count of San Mateo – bound for Spain to be the lover of a passionate and degenerate queen . . . Then he met Zaydah, destined for the harem of the Prince of Morocco, and blood-sworn loyalties were swept away in a vortex of love and passion.

Robert Perrin
Jewels 80p

The night they stole the Irish Crown Jewels – Summer 1907, the eve of Edward VII's visit to Ireland. Two men, both enmeshed in the most dissolute of circles, plan and execute the perfect crime: the theft of the priceless insignia of the Order of St Patrick from the Bedford Tower of Dublin Castle. Captain Richard Gorges: hero of Spion Kop, soldier of fortune, rampant homosexual; Frank Shackleton: Dublin Herald to the Ulster King of Arms, incorrigible con-man and total degenerate . . .

'Fascinating reconstruction, packed with intrigue and shameful secrets' SUNDAY TIMES

Rebecca West
The Birds Fall Down £1.25

An engrossing recreation of the momentous events that led up to the Russian Revolution . . . seen through the eyes of Laura, eighteen-year-old daughter of an English MP and grandchild of an exiled Russian royalist – a vivid canvas, shot through with intrigue, conspiracy and murder, bringing to life the days of tumult that changed the world.

'One of the most fascinating true sto ries ever to have been used as a basis for fiction' BERNARD LEVIN

'An outstanding achievement' SUNDAY TELEGRAPH